MEDLOCKS

The Peractio

Blackout

MEDLOCKS

The Peractio
Blackout

DAVE BERENATO

iUniverse, Inc.
Bloomington

Medlocks
The Peractio Blackout

iUniverse books may be ordered through booksellers or by contacting:

iUniverse
1663 Liberty Drive
Bloomington, IN 47403
www.iuniverse.com
1-800-Authors (1-800-288-4677)

ISBN: 978-1-4620-5217-2 (sc)
ISBN: 978-1-4620-5219-6 (hc)
ISBN: 978-1-4620-5218-9 (ebk)

Printed in the United States of America

iUniverse rev. date: 09/28/2011

To everyone from Archmere, I feel so blessed to have all of the support of the school in reaching for my dreams. And to all of my family from Sea Isle, the memories that we have created together inspired me more than any of you can imagine.

CHAPTER 1:
A HEAD ABOVE THE REST

KAMILLE

"Wake up, wake up!" a voice shouted. Someone was violently jumping up and down on my bed. I rubbed my eyes and saw Selene planting herself on my bed then flying into the air and falling back down again. "Kamille, we're gonna be late, and Dr. Dryden's almost out of pancake mix!"

"I'll be down in a minute," I lied, trying to fall back asleep. The first glimpses of sunrise fell across my room and I groaned. Selene walked out, realizing that she had failed. I thought about everything that had happened in the last year, it all seemed like a dream that I had just woken up from. Daven and I were fine on our own until we found the comet in the park that gave us unbelievable powers. Before we knew it, we were on a rocket to a secret space academy for super powered kids. There we met eight kids that we were apparently related to, and later inducted a reformed villain into our group. We went through the rest of the year trying to protect our classmates from a trophy that kidnapped them and took them to a super villain that our parents accidentally created named Glacthia. Finally in the end of the year, we saved our friends, and Daven and I decided to stay with our eight siblings for the summer in Wisconsin. We were leaving for our parents' house today and spending the rest of the summer there.

I eventually decided to get out of bed; it would save me from the agony of having my older sister trying to wake me up again. The smell of breakfast greeted me as I walked into the kitchen. Dr. Dryden, the adopted father that my eight siblings had lived with before they got their powers, used to be a dormant inventor who never showed his face to the kids after the oldest got to the age of five. It was illegal for kids to live in space to with their parents until after they graduated from our super power school, Medlocks Academy. A person on Earth must adopt the kids and never tell them the secret of their heritage. Daven and I were separated because I'm an Otiom, a supernatural peacemaker. Glacthia moved Daven into my space pod when we were babies as an evil plot to change Daven's powers. The two of us were adopted by a hotel manager, and grew up having a penthouse all to ourselves.

"Good morning, Kamille. How are you today?" Dr. Dryden asked politely, while two robots next to him flipped and served pancakes.

"Good, I guess," I answered, sitting down as a robot handed me a plate. Dr. Dryden's inventions had always been unrealistic compared to Earth's technology, probably because he was exposed to advanced space technology. When the kids were younger, he would give his best inventions to them to test. But even at that time, he had not confronted them directly.

"So do you think we'll get to see Mr. Schny-eeek when we get back?" Aura wondered. Aura was the oldest of my triplets, along with Selene. She has the power of air and time, and Selene's powers are gravity and temperature.

"You have a teacher named Mr. Schny . . . eeek?" Dr. Dryden tried not to laugh.

"Well, we don't know; that's what he makes us call him since we don't have time to say his full last name before he gives us a detention. And he's not our teacher; he just watched over us between classes, he was our caretaker," Selene added.

"I don't know, we haven't seen him since Glacthia burnt his face. I bet he died," Wyatt smiled, the fifth oldest of the fifteen year old sextuplets. No one bothered to make him apologize because each of us had received an excessive number of detentions last year. Wyatt can control water, lift or teleport matter, read minds, and make forcefields.

"Maybe we can keep the pieces of the Metronome so Glacthia can't get it," Cobalt thought aloud. Cobalt has metal and matter for his powers. He also has four older brothers that were villains, but Ion, the youngest in our family who was his age, brought him to our side. But as soon as he said it, Aura started coughing hysterically. I threw her a harsh glare and she stopped immediately. Aura had told Selene and me that she was having visions about the Metronome being fixed, the device that Glacthia had used last year to take our powers. Since one of Aura's powers is time, her dreams are usually prophecies. Everyone turned to Aura and she acted as if she hadn't heard anything.

"Sorry, I . . . pictured what Mr. Schny-eeek had looked like after Glacthia burnt him, do you think they can heal that?" Aura saved herself, but Selene and I eyed her; she couldn't keep this from them forever.

"I don't know . . . I hope they can. If we thought he was scary looking before then, we're really in for it," Ion explained for us. Ion's powers are electricity and size.

"Anyway, I think we should leave now if we're gonna make it to Detroit," Wyatt said. Wyatt grabbed a small box of shrunken suitcases and put them in his pocket.

We all stepped onto the front lawn and waved goodbye to Dr. Dryden as we took off. Wyatt, Cobalt, Ion, Aura, Selene, and I were all going to the secret airport that transported people to other planets. While we make our trip, the rest of our family is picking up three people we invited to stay with us at our parents' house: Neva's girlfriend Becca Slomowitz, Forrest's girlfriend Alaina Bradley, and another friend, Scott Tung.

"Do you want me to make a flying, metal scooter for you?" Cobalt offered. He knew I hated my way of flying; I used balance to jump from tree to tree without falling through. I smiled as a way to thank him, but he turned all red and I looked away. At twelve he only followed my age by one year, but I wasn't interested in him. Besides, I had a boyfriend already, Dave Anderson.

"Guys, I'm just going to make us all able to run at the speed of light," Ion said this as if it were so obvious, but then he noticed all of our uncontrolled looks of anger. He added, "I couldn't do it last year if you were wondering."

We all prepped ourselves for an uncontrollable burst of energy, not really remembering how it felt to run at the speed of light, or how to control it at all for that matter. Two seconds later, I stopped myself forcefully. Looking around, I had no idea where I was. Would it have killed me to ask Ion how to use his power? And would I have died if I asked Wyatt how to get to Detroit? Okay, I can handle this, it's not like it will take years to travel all the way back to wherever they were. Taking inventory of my surroundings, I saw thin, blocky streets, water almost everywhere I looked, and pigeons eating out of children's hands.

I've seen pictures of this . . . I stopped in Venice, Italy . . . did I even pass Michigan?

"Please say I'm not the only one who's completely lost," I spoke into my communication watch to the others in our group.

"No one's even left yet." The reply Ion gave made me feel like I had done something only Aura was capable of. Well, then again, Rhochelle and I are the only blondes in the family.

"Okay Kamille you've got to travel about 4,600 miles Northwest for about two hundredths of a second," Wyatt calculated so generously for me.

"Wyatt... you can teleport me back now." A pause, and then I suddenly appeared on our front lawn.

"Now let's *actually* start our journey," Aura rolled her eyes at me. Ion briefly went over how to use the power to stop in places you want even if you were running completely around the Earth multiple times. It basically sounded like teleporting but with limitations, like how it would take Ion years to get to other solar systems and Wyatt under a second. Still Ion could use his power to get to places he had never been before and Wyatt couldn't.

After we all landed in Detroit, Wyatt turned us invisible so we could fly around the streets looking for a restaurant called The Hidden Dragon. It seemed a little obvious for a place to find out secrets about super powered people, but to the unsuspecting human, it was just a meaningless Chinese restaurant name.

"I found it!" Ion yelled into his watch, he obviously ran at the speed of light to find it. He described to us where he was and soon enough we all walked into the restaurant. A darkly lit room with soft music, small, crowded tables, and people talking much louder than the music welcomed us. We sat in the nearest booth and a waiter asked for our drink order.

"We're not ready," Wyatt quickly interrupted and the waiter walked away. All of us gave him a weird look and he motioned for us to lean in, afraid that random people would eavesdrop on our conversation about intergalactic traveling secrets. "We must order a specific combination of foods and drinks for the restaurant owner to know what information we seek. If we mess up by one refill then we could be seen as either imposters or just ordinary humans." Wyatt slowly explained to each of us what we had to order, and the waiter returned.

4

"Now are you ready?" he asked rudely to Wyatt, who rolled his eyes. We each gave our orders, and the waiter, who had no idea why we were so nervous, walked away.

"Who have you guys picked up so far?" Selene remembered the rest of our family and spoke into her watch. Silence followed, and then all of our watches burst with voices.

"We haven't even left yet! Are you already at the airport?" Neva replied. They didn't have Ion, so they had to fly halfway around the country and we got to run at the speed of light. Before anyone could answer, I got all of their attention. People at the table next to us were staring with their mouths half dropped. Right, our superhuman technology is a little beyond Earth's everyday cell phone or wristwatch. We turned off our watches and our drinks arrived just moments later.

"Aw man! I hate iced tea," I made a gross face at the drink the waiter brought out then gasped because I said it so loudly.

"Oh . . . well that's what you ordered, do you want something else?" the waiter said reluctantly, praying that I didn't make him go get me another drink.

"No. I ordered the iced tea, you got this soda," Cobalt shyly switched with me, and then blushed again when I winked at him. Wyatt crossed off "have one male and one female switch drinks upon first moment of receiving them" while the waiter walked away confused.

The meal went by pretty slowly; barely anyone talked until everyone finished eating. Wyatt asked the waiter for seven fortune cookies, and we all ate ours carefully. Finally, one fortune cookie sat in the middle of the table and Wyatt picked it up. Seeing as he was the only sextuplet in our group he pretty much called all the shots I guess.

"Your answer lies in the number of heads." Silently our eyes went from the fortune cookie to Wyatt's face. "We have fourteen passengers, but why would it say heads instead of passengers?" He flipped it over. "Moai is the word . . . I don't think that's Chinese."

"Oh and since when do you know Chinese?" Ion shot back and grabbed the slip of paper. "It translates to 'Ahu.' That's not an English word." Suddenly Wyatt's whole face lit up and he grabbed the fortune back and put it in his pocket. We hurriedly left the restaurant; sadly we had to pay for our food even though we just had breakfast half an hour ago.

"We have to go to Easter Island; that's what it meant by heads," Wyatt waited for Ion to give him the jolt, and suddenly he disappeared.

My triplet sisters and I took deep breaths. Ion and Cobalt were used to this but we certainly were not. I stopped and looked around, have I made it? This island is so strange; it looks like the carnage of two civilizations of people made of stone and being monstrously tall and heavy. Now only their heads remained because all of their bodies sunk into the ground.

"Who built these and why?" Aura shouted but Wyatt grabbed her head and pulled her down behind a wall that we luckily all stopped at. I shot down as tourists walked just ten feet in front of us. As soon as we were behind them I stood back up and looked around. Yeah, this tourist filled island is the perfect spot to launch off an alien rocket ship.

"What is your problem? Don't touch me!" Aura shouted and slapped Wyatt's arm. Aura, as flamboyant and outgoing as she was, hated anyone touching her. "We don't have tentacles coming out of our heads or sixteen eyes. We can walk around with the rest of the people without drawing attention!" I had to admit Aura had a point—until we find the airport, we look just like everyone else.

"It doesn't matter if we find it in the next ten seconds anyway. We have to wait for nightfall if we want to use our powers, and the door or gate or secret passageway probably requires us to use them," Selene threw in, which surprised me. She's always so shy I never would pick her as the one to point out a flaw in a plan. I smiled at her as a way to show my appreciation for her insights, and she returned with one of the most beautiful smiles I had ever seen. Its radiance matched her bright red hair; she was the only one in our family to have it, not even our parents have the slightest bit of red hair.

"Selene's right. We can walk around all we want, but we can't use our powers until the tourists leave," Wyatt replied, and we got up to walk towards the beach. Realizing we all picked this destination subconsciously we all started to laugh. "What's your location?" Wyatt suddenly asked into his watch in a serious voice. I guess he hadn't been one to laugh at our similarities in thought; then again, he had always been really serious when something involved Medlocks. His sense of humor had deteriorated with the ongoing battle against Glacthia. Now he just sulks and reads books.

We followed a group of tourists and finally caught sight of a reasonable destination to begin our search. A huge platform with . . . fifteen heads that towered over us like buildings rested just before the end of the island. The heads faced some cliff side or volcano, the most probable place for the rocket to shoot out of. Wyatt pulled the paper out of his pocket and read it again carefully.

"These are moai, and we are at Ahu Tongariki," Wyatt read some random sign and eavesdropped on the tourists in front of us. "Do you think when the message said 'in' the heads that we have to get inside those?"

"I can't get over how weird this planet is. Why did some ancient civilization randomly attempt to stack . . . hundreds of heads around that mountain, all of them facing towards it? What was the significance of it, and what is with the strange faces? People don't look like that!" Cobalt reminded all of us that he had never been to Earth before this summer. Compared to his life in space and around Medlocks, Earth was a cosmic freak show. But even with the negative remarks about how our plans will never work, Cobalt still has more emotional strength than anyone I know. His parents were killed by Glacthia, his older brothers formed a group of four villains, and he left them all behind to join us and get revenge on Glacthia. This makes him shy and often depressed. He's like a mini version of Wyatt, they even look somewhat alike. They have longish dark brown hair, are tall for their age, and are pretty solitary unless they have their friends to constantly cheer them up.

"Well it's possible that the Ancestors came to this planet when the first humans arrived from Polynesia and became their gods. So the people built these monuments in honor of the Ancestors and stacked them facing their landing place, which was probably where the airport is located," Wyatt recited as if this came from a Medlockian history textbook. "Then a tsunami came and wiped out a lot of these ones." He pointed to the line of fifteen stacked in front of us. "Now it almost matches the exact number of our group . . . except there is one too many." Wyatt noticed and we all stared at the line.

"Let's walk up to the mountain and see if we can find some clues there," Ion suggested and started walking. Always so energetic, Ion acts a lot like his power would make him. The rest of us sort of groaned and followed a few feet behind. Ion was shorter than Cobalt even though he was older, and as the youngest Barker, he acted innocent on the outside and devious on the inside. It took a lot longer than we thought to get up there, and since there were always tourists in sight, we couldn't just turn invisible to use our powers. By the time we got to the top, the other group could have picked up everybody and come here, and they're thousands of miles away.

"It's full of water!" Aura gaped at the huge pond, or maybe lake, of water that filled the crater that took so long to get to. How could a space rocket blast out of a pond? Then again, who am I to doubt technologically advanced super-powered aliens' work?

"Calm down; I'm sure it's here. This mountain weighs much less than it should, so it's actually very hollow. But how do we get in there?" Wyatt looked around for a secret portal of some kind, which obviously would stand out in the middle of a volcano on a popular tourist destination.

"Hey look, there's a group of heads just like the one we saw, but that one doesn't have as many heads," Aura pointed out and Wyatt looked up from the fortune to see it. He then looked back and forth between the first one we visited and this new one. Once more he stared at the fortune, and smiled.

"The number of passengers has to match the number of heads in a grouping. There must be a ton of those around the island. Let's split up and find the one with a group of fourteen heads." Wyatt walked in a random direction and we decided that he wanted to be alone. Cobalt and Ion went together and my sisters and I knew we were already a group.

"It must be around this crater somewhere, because all of the groups face the airport. Do you think it could be a group of fallen ones?" Selene spoke as soon as Cobalt and Ion were out of earshot. She doesn't need to be shy when with her triplet sisters. I scanned the landscape for a group of fourteen fallen heads, but they all seemed too scattered to be an attempt at exposing a secret airport. I suddenly thought I saw the grouping, but thought it was maybe just a rock formation. In order to check it out without wasting time, I asked Ion to give me a quick use at the speed of light.

"I'll be right back, I just want to check this out," I told my sisters and ran off. Half a second later, I gasped for air, but none was available. I immediately switched powers with my brother Daven when I realized where I had to be. Opening my eyes, I saw darkness with a few points of light, and then a giant blue and green sphere next to me. Because I took Daven's power of space travel, I can travel through space and breathe without a space suit or air. I don't feel the freezing temperature or lack of pressure and air, but sadly my watch did. It shattered and disappeared, I was going to have to fly toward the planet and wait until I could breathe safely before switching my space travel power with a flying one.

"*Kamille,*" a voice suddenly spoke in my head. I automatically assumed Glacthia and prepared for a battle. But then four figures, or at least they were somewhat figures, appeared in front of me. I fixed my hair but realized that it lacked the gravity it needed to look at all in order.

"*Kamille, you must be warned of an upcoming peril that the universe will face. As Otiom of the Medlocks solar system, you need to know that the Metronome has again been stolen. It will be used for evil once again this year. You have been warned.*" The soft voices horrified me, but before I could answer back I appeared next to Aura and Selene. Sweating and shaking, I opened my mouth to retell the encounter I had just had with the Ancestors.

"Guys I figured it out, come down to the set of fifteen," Wyatt interrupted me, and we had to walk down the cliff. I started to tell my story, and watched the sunset that began.

"You mean the Ancestors just appeared to you in space and told you that someone had stolen the Metronome and wants to use it for evil?" Selene stared from me to Aura, feeling left out for being the only one not warned.

"I guess they wanted to tell me because I'm the Otiom," I still couldn't shake the strange feeling I received from hearing their voices.

"What did they sound like?" Aura wondered, and I found it hard to describe.

"Well, it was soft, but powerful, and scary, all at the same time," I found myself describing something much like Glacthia's voice. The three of us fell silent as night arrived, and the rest of our journey was made by superpowers. When we reached Wyatt and the rest of the group, we realized he had teleported everyone in our family along with the friends we were bringing.

"There are actually fifteen of us because Alaina is bringing her sister Caroline, this is so spooky that our number matches the most famous alignment of heads on the island, it's like hundreds of years ago the Ancestors planned for our journey to Medlocks." Wyatt mentioned the Ancestors and I shuddered. The idea of being spoken to by aliens that didn't look like humans was almost too freaky. But I shook it off and tuned in to Wyatt's talking.

"We have to line up in age order, standing on top of the head with the number that matches our number in the order." Wyatt was floating over the tallest head, because it had the Roman numeral V over it, which is extremely ominous because Wyatt is the tallest. The Ancestors originally visited the Romans first, which is why they used Roman numerals here. I counted the people here, with the four people not in our family older than me I had to go to XIII. When all fifteen of us stood on the ancient heads, suddenly the top of the heads turned into a platform that began lowering us down through the heads and underground. I closed my eyes because it was too dark to bother looking for anything.

CHAPTER TWO:
THE CAVE IN

NEVA

The platforms stopped in a huge room that was inside the mountain and I looked around in amazement. There were different types of rockets, planes, jets, and helicopters that I had never seen before.

"Welcome to Easter Island, one of the many secret airports where space humans can travel away from Earth. My name is—"

"Sir Jacob Reese," Cobalt finished the man's sentence.

"You're the guy who invented that machine that can take people to a planet made of any object you want?" I asked in shock.

"That's me, someone must have learned their space history," he smiled. He looked just as I had pictured him, overweight, balding, lonely, and scraggly.

"Why do you live here, of all the places in the universe?" Forrest wondered. Forrest, my only older brother and the third oldest sextuplet, had control over all living things and could make illusions. He had long brown hair and was the shortest of all the sextuplets. Forrest was quick thinking and pretty cocky about being smart.

"I design space crafts, and I also picked this location as the secret airport. Come on, I'd like to give you a tour," he walked around each spacecraft and started explaining its purpose and design. I wasn't listening at all; I was trying to catch Becca's eyes so I could see her smile. We'd been dating since the beginning of our first year at Medlocks, and I'm still crazy about her. Eventually Mr. Reese realized that his monologue bored us out of our minds, so he showed us our rooms.

"Why would we need to stay here? Can't we leave now?" Aura asked him.

"Callidus is at least a six day trip with its rotation right now, do you want to spend five nights in one of these rockets?" Mr. Reese questioned us, and we realized that even if the rockets could hold all of us, they were way too cramped to sit in for six days.

"I guess you're right . . . so what are we going to do?" Wyatt thought.

"I'm going to call for a rocket to come pick you up, it should be here by about tomorrow if I call from the closest airport. I think it's on one of Saturn's moons, since humans haven't looked at it that much." Mr. Reese opened a cell phone immediately. I was surprised that he didn't use some walkie-talkie device, but just a regular cell phone. It also surprised me that he got service on this island.

Everyone went to go check out the cots that were in the room we were staying in. They seemed fine, at least for one night, but now we were going to have to unshrink all of our clothes so we had something to wear tomorrow. A few minutes later, Mr. Reese told us that there would be a rocket here for us tomorrow. If only Wyatt had gone to our parents' house, he could have teleported us there. Maybe when we're older and we've been to almost every planet, we'd never have to use taxis or rockets again.

We spent the whole day playing hide and seek, and the rockets made great hiding spots because all of them had closets and control rooms. There was also a game we played called sardines, which is played in the dark. One or two people would hide, and everyone would split up to look for them, pretty much like hide and seek in reverse. When a person found them, they would hide with them. The last person to find them would be "it" in the next round. Since it was late at night and Mr. Reese was done working, we got him to play, and even made him "it." He walked away as we counted to fifty, and Becca and I decided to look for him together. After about ten minutes of looking through control rooms, we figured that we were the only people still looking, and we were going to be it anyway.

I led Becca into the room with the cots, there was only one closet, and if they weren't in there then we were going to give up. But just before we checked the closet Becca turned to me and smiled.

"Neva, do we have to look for them, can't we just . . ." she stopped and gave me a kiss.

"No, if they're in that closet then they might be looking," I told her. Before I could look away she started using her powers. Her eyes became shinier, her hair became long and silky, and her lips turned bright red. Becca can make herself more beautiful based on the other person's standards.

"Come on that's not fair," I said softly and put my hand to her face. She pushed me back against a stone pillar that was holding up the ceiling. I had no intention of stopping her, but suddenly I felt something hot on my back. Trying to continue kissing her, I opened my eyes and turned around. There was lava in the spot where my back had been against the pillar. I can create either lava or ice with my mind, sadly this time it was lava.

"Uh oh," I shook my head, wishing that I hadn't forgotten that my powers can be triggered by a change in my emotions. The lava ate through the pillar; I could not freeze it in time. The ground started to shake, and everyone who was hiding came into the room. I ran back to them and rocks fell out of the ceiling. Dust flew up everywhere and Wyatt put a forcefield around everyone standing with him. I grabbed Becca's hand and we ducked and dodged boulders. Running to the forcefield, I knew Wyatt could not make it any bigger than he had it now. I slid along the ground with Becca just behind me.

"Neva hurry!" Wyatt yelled and moved Becca quickly out of the way of a rock. We ran, and dust filled our lungs. Finally we dove into a door that Wyatt had created in the forcefield and gasped for clean air. Huge boulders hit the forcefield and Wyatt looked drained of energy. Just when he couldn't stand it anymore the cave-in stopped. Aura blew away the dust and we stared in speechlessness at the pile of rocks.

"We're stuck in here," Mr. Reese told us in horror.

"That's silly, we could totally get out of this," Rhochelle stretched out her arms and got in her stance. But when she tried to lift the rocks, nothing happened.

"I'll do it," Wyatt bent his knees and tried to lift one of the boulders, although it turned up the same results.

"Psh, I'll do it," I knew I would be able to drop magma onto the rocks and melt it away. When I used my mind to drop the magma, we received the same outcome once again. Everyone tried their powers, and came to the conclusion that only Becca, Alaina, Caroline, and

Scott's powers were working. But none of them had the ability to move or destroy the rocks.

"We *are* stuck here," Aura sat down on the cot and put her head into her hands.

"The kitchen is downstairs, so maybe if we can break through the floor, then we could get out a different way," Mr. Reese hypothesized. All of us stared at him and shook our heads.

"We can't break through the floor, it's made of stone," Forrest reminded us.

"Yeah there's no way," Scott calculated.

"I know, I'm just trying to be positive. But let's face it, we're doomed," Mr. Reese conceded. No one wanted to believe our position. I looked at Becca; she seemed as if she were in shock or something. Just before I walked toward her, I decided that I needed some time to think.

"What about the rocket that's supposed to arrive tomorrow?" I wondered.

"It'll be here in about twenty four hours," Mr. Reese sighed.

"Well, then they can save us," I smiled and everyone looked up.

"Sure, if they bother checking for us behind a giant pile of rocks. Besides, can you guys last for twenty four hours? I was just about to make dinner when you asked me to play sardines," Mr. Reese made us all feel bad.

"We only had breakfast today," Forrest sighed.

"Maybe we should try to get some sleep," Mr. Reese sat down against the wall and closed his eyes while the rest of us got into our cots.

The next few hours went by; almost everyone slept but Becca and me. I knew she was awake, but I just didn't want to say anything to her. I felt as if she hadn't been herself, and she could even be Glacthia for all I knew. Complete darkness filled in the cave for the next four or five hours. Eventually some sunlight started to fade through and I could see. But still no one awoke, so I decided to shut my eyes for a while.

When I woke up, enough light from outside illuminated the cave, and some people walked around as if trying to think of something to do. The rocks keeping us in stood at least six feet in diameter, so moving them was out of the question. And since our powers apparently still failed us we had to try to occupy our time with something else.

"We could make up a game," Scott told us. His power was video games, so he probably had a couple in mind.

"So what do you got?" I sat up from my cot.

"I thought we could have . . ." he paused for a minute. "Well we don't have enough room to play a running game, and mind games bore me so . . . I've got nothing."

"'Kay that's not gonna help," Daven sighed. Daven, the youngest of the sextuplets, grew up with Kamille in a hotel. He's determined and funny, and he can copy anyone's power that he sees or travel through space. No one could think of a single thing that we could do, so a few hours went by where all that could be heard were stomachs growling and groans of boredom.

"Why did you decide to work here?" Selene asked again.

"I like designing space crafts, and I thought that I could help the youth pass from planet to planet. I actually specialized in self driving space crafts, but they need a remote to get them to work, which I left in the kitchen," Mr. Reese explained. The irony in this whole situation was unbearable. If Mr. Reese hadn't been playing sardines with us, then he would've been making us dinner when the cave-in happened. Then he could've gotten one of his spacecrafts to get us out.

"I think you're wasting your time here, there are tons of other places that could use your mind. Maybe you could invent cold fusion or something," Wyatt suggested. There was silence for a while, until Caroline stood up. She walked over to Forrest and stared at his watch. My mouth dropped and I wanted to hit myself in the head.

"That's a cool watch," she smiled, as if she knew what it was capable of.

"Mom, Dad, are you guys there?" I instantly said into the watch.

"Yeah we're here. Do you guys know when you're going to arrive?" Mom asked, having no clue that we were stuck.

"Actually, we're kind of in a situation," Kamille said in an understatement.

"What kind of situation?" Dad wondered nervously.

"The kind of situation where you're stuck inside a cave, and you haven't eaten for twenty four hours, and have almost no chance of being saved," Daven summed it up.

"Oh my gosh, are you guys okay?" Mom went into her worrying stage.

"Yeah, we're just so hungry," Aura classified our feelings.

"Well, did you have any ideas of what we could do?" Dad questioned us.

"Um . . . actually we don't," Cobalt looked around at our faces and we realized that he was right. "Do you?"

"We can't use our powers to get you out, and it would take too long to come to you," Dad thought.

"Just get back to us if you have any ideas," Ion sighed.

A couple more hours went by, we just talked about the things we would do if we got out, pretty melodramatic if you ask me.

"If I got out, I would tell Dave that I really like him," Kamille moaned. It had been a day and a half since the last time we'd eaten. Luckily we had a drink when we first got here, but it wasn't much. I was about to say something when I looked at Becca. She just stared at the ground, she felt so guilty for starting the cave-in that she couldn't stand it. When I was about to tell her that it wasn't her fault, I saw something in the top corner of the pile of rocks.

"If I got out, I would become an inventor of things other than spacecrafts. I would invent things that would make life easier; I would live in a huge house—one that had phones in every room." By the time Mr. Reese finished, everyone but him was staring at the pile of rocks.

"Well then you better get to a drawing board," Forrest smiled, realizing what was happening. Huge amounts of dust flew off of the rocks. Finally we saw a pair of hands break through, and one of the boulders toppled down, leaving a hole in the pile of rocks.

The rest of the rocks fell through in the next couple minutes as the man did his work. When it was all done he walked into the room and smiled, knowing he had just saved our lives.

"The name's Matt Cozza, my power's sliding, and I drive the space craft that is going to take you to Callidus?" he confirmed that he was at the right place. We nodded and he walked us to the space taxi. When I saw it I almost gasped, it was the size of the entire room that we were just stuck in.

"Wow, it's huge!" I said to him, and he nodded.

"One of the biggest traveling spacecrafts in this solar system," he seemed proud that he was driving it.

"Well I'll see you guys, I'm gonna call for a taxi myself so I can get out of here," Mr. Reese grabbed the phone just as we were walking into the rocket. In minutes, the top of the mountain opened up, and another few minutes later, we said goodbye to Earth for another school year.

"So what happened that caused the cave-in anyway?" Ion asked when we were all settled in the circle of couches after eating enormous dinners just minutes ago. I glanced once more at Becca then turned back to the group.

"My powers caused me to melt the pillar with lava; I guess I had no control over them," I explained, but they could tell I was lying.

"Why were your powers working then but not now?" Ember wondered. Ember, the oldest in our family, had the power of fire and flexibility. She always knew what to say, even if was overly sarcastic or harsh, because she was also really negative.

"Actually they are working now," Cobalt made a metal fork and held it up to us. Everyone used their powers and made confused faces.

"Then why weren't they working before?" Forrest jumped up when he made a hologram of himself.

"I don't know, but do you think if our powers weren't working then other people's powers could be . . . malfunctioning?" Ion asked randomly and we all turned to face him.

"Maybe, we don't have a class on how our powers work," Wyatt brought up once again that our curriculum wasn't really the best. We have a class based off of each family's power, so they're not the most useful classes.

"I think we should try and get some sleep; it's pretty late," Rhochelle walked away from the couch circle and got into a bed. Each bed had a nightstand and a small dresser next to it. Then in the back of the large room we had a bar with a refrigerator and a pantry, which we had already gotten snacks from. Just as everyone began to doze off, I walked over to Becca and we started talking.

When I first opened my eyes, I expected to see sunlight, but it was just as dark as last night. Technically there was no time because we were traveling through space, but we just followed how long we had been awake to determine the length of our days. A few lights had been turned on, but still no light came from outside the rocket. I saw Ion walk over to the couch area, where Cobalt, Selene, Kamille, and Aura were sitting. They kept looking over at me but I pretended not to be watching, until finally they got up and walked over.

"Neva, we know you were lying when you told us what happened, so fess up," Kamille got right to the point.

"I just accidentally burnt the pillar with lava and it collapsed," I tried to convince them.

"Okay thanks, we just wanted to know," Selene forced them to walk away then rolled her eyes. "I seriously doubt that; he's a terrible liar," she whispered to them.

Finally I got up the courage to go over to Becca, while the five youngest kids stared from across the room.

"Can we talk about the cave-in?" I shyly asked and she looked up at us nervously.

"Neva, I remember kissing you just once, then everything after that is blank," she seemed as if she was telling the truth, but I had no way of being sure.

"I'm going to get Wyatt to search your mind for traces of Glacthia, one moment," I ran over to Wyatt and begged him to help us for a minute. Wyatt searched her mind and came back.

"There is no proof of Glacthia in her mind, maybe he's either learning to not leave behind evidence, or she really meant to trap us in the cave by herself," Wyatt told us and walked away.

"I don't think it was him, I just . . . wasn't myself for a moment," she felt so guilty that I couldn't stand it.

"We need to see this for real," Aura interrupted her from across the room and suddenly we were spinning through a long portal. When we landed we were back in the room where the cave-in happened. Everyone watched from behind one of the larger pillars that held the room up. I saw Becca kiss me, and I whispered the message about my family in the closet. Then she became really pretty and we kissed again. But I noticed a small detail that I couldn't pass up.

"Aura go back to where she first kissed me," I told her and then we saw everything backwards. Then Aura stopped time and we watched it again. Just before Becca used her powers I noticed something and grabbed Aura.

"Play the last few seconds back in slow motion," I ordered her around as if she were a remote. Aura listened, but was on the verge of yelling at me.

"Stop!" I suddenly whispered and time froze. "Look, just before she uses her powers, she twitches a little. But how could that not be Glacthia?" I wondered and everyone noticed it.

"Yeah, I see it, let's go back now," Cobalt seemed scared, as if he thought he were in the presence of Glacthia. Soon enough Aura spun her hand through the air and landed back on the rocket.

"She definitely wasn't herself, but I'm sure that Glacthia wouldn't kiss me. And if he did . . ." I shuddered. "If her powers weren't working right, then maybe she could accidentally have her beauty take over her," I tried to cover for my girlfriend, but they weren't buying it. The younger kids found it hard to continue their little "investigation," so they just dropped it.

Just when we were about to find something to do, a rumbling sound came from the control room that Matt was in. I looked around at confused faces and got very nervous.

"Matt?" I called, but no one answered. Everyone walked over to the door and Forrest slid it open, which he regretted immediately. Forrest's feet lifted off the ground and the lack of air started sucking him out of the rocket. Somehow the door had opened up and it was sucking all the air into space. It took all of us to pull Forrest back in and close the door. Aura replenished our air since we could barely breathe.

"We have to drive the rocket! We have to find Matt!" Daven shouted. Aura and Wyatt instantly ran back into the control room, and a few seconds later, they opened the door for us to come in.

"Who knows how to drive this thing?" Alaina looked at each of us and we turned to Forrest. Just last year he drove the rocket that took us to Glacthia's lair, but of course it got us arrested.

"It's on manual, I have to find the autopilot and put in the coordinates," he explained. "Everyone look for a map of the Medlocks solar system." All of us started filing through the drawers until finally I pulled out a map that had "Medlocks Solar System" at the top.

"Here it is! I got it," I rolled it out across the floor and looked for Callidus while Forrest pulled up the autopilot on the computer.

"Okay, I need the galaxy number, planet number, and location of destination, so we also need a map of Callidus. Ion what are the numbers?" Forrest asked.

"Medlocks solar system is number 48629, and Callidus is planet A43051," Cobalt read the numbers off of the map.

"What about the coordinates of Mom and Dad's house?" Ember asked to Wyatt, who was holding the map.

"37.62 N and uh . . . 24.81 E, that's their town," Wyatt answered. The rush of the whole scene finally calmed down and I sat down all tired out.

"Now the coordinates are set and we can just relax until we get there," Forrest smiled and we walked back into the room we were originally in.

"What about Matt?" Rhochelle wanted to know.

"Don't worry, I teleported him to Earth," Wyatt seemed proud of himself. He really had advanced in his powers, just last year he could barely teleport himself.

"I want to know how the sliding doors opened," Daven thought.

"Matt's power is sliding . . . *sliding doors?*" Selene pointed out.

"Do you think it was on purpose or connected to our power failures?" Kamille wondered.

"Maybe . . . I don't know. Let's worry about that later," I told everyone and we went back to our separate groups.

"I bet it also has a connection to Becca's power failure," Aura stated, and all of us agreed. Each of us took the next couple of days to mull everything over, but still no answers.

On the morning of the last day, the autopilot told us that we should arrive that night. I was busy playing a video game that Scott had lent me. Suddenly, a red light flashed over the door of the control room. Everyone slowly stopped what they were doing to look up at the light.

"What is it?" Caroline questioned us as most of the older kids ran into the control room. Forrest came out of the control room with a face of shock and panic.

"We're out of fuel," he told us and no one seemed to care.

"That stinks, now we have to find a planet to stop at and get fuel," Scott seemed annoyed, but definitely not as annoyed as he was about to be. I remember looking at the map, and I decided to be the one to break it to him.

"You don't understand, the Ancestors probably wanted Earth to never find out about the other planets until they were very technologically advanced. The Medlocks solar system was the first one to be made, so it was put next to Earth's solar system. But it was made far enough away so that no human could see it. There aren't any planets between the solar system and the Medlocks solar system, and there's a huge space between the two. We're probably in between the two solar systems right now, so the closest planet to us is probably Callidus. If we don't have enough fuel to get to that, then we have no chance of getting to . . . any planet," I finished and caught my breath while everyone's face turned to panic.

"Then what do we do?" Cobalt sounded scared.

"I don't know, Forrest is there anything we can do?" I asked him, since he seemed to know a lot about driving rockets.

"I think there is . . ." Forrest led us to the control room and pulled out a driving manual.

"Yeah here it is, 'Autopilot is a good way to get around if you don't have directions to a place, but it uses more gas then just plain driving. It is suggested that manual driving is used if fuel is low.'" Forrest pulled up the autopilot on the computer and turned it off. Suddenly we started to slow down and Forrest grabbed the wheel.

"Mom, Dad, do you know what Callidus looks like from space, how could we tell it apart from the other planets?" I asked them on the watch. It took a moment for them to think, but they realized it wasn't a time to ask questions.

"Callidus is the least green or blue because it's very industrialized and it's the flattest planet in the solar system," Dad answered as quickly as he could.

"That's not really gonna help, if we make the slightest wrong turn we'll run out of fuel before we get back on track. We have about exactly enough fuel if we go in the shortest possible path to Callidus," Forrest said, and I held down the button on the watch so Mom and Dad could hear it.

"Try opening up a direction file on the computer, it can locate you in space and show you a map of one tenth of a light year in radius around you," Mom explained, and Rhochelle pulled it up on the computer. It was basically a GPS location of us, but in space. We could see Callidus, Medlocks, and all the other planets that share its orbit, along with the sun.

"That's good, now we just have to keep going straight and we should get to Callidus. Now there's the problem of which part of the planet you're on," Ember reminded us.

"That's no problem; we're coming toward Callidus from the part of it that's facing directly opposite the sun. We should end up in the timezone that will be at midnight at our arrival time?" Wyatt questioned them.

"It's a few minutes after seven p.m.," Mom replied.

"That's good, so if we get there in five hours then all we have to do is go perfectly straight and we'll reach your time zone at twelve o'clock," Wyatt told us, and no one bothered to try checking his math or logic.

"Hope you have a good trip," Dad said in a nervous voice.

"Thanks . . . see you guys tonight," Rhochelle told them.

"Okay, now we just have to get there in five hours, if I find out how many miles it is I can figure out how fast we have to go," Wyatt tried to be technical.

"Then figure out how far we are from—"

"About 246 million miles and rapidly decreasing, wow we're going 41 million miles per hour! But why doesn't it feel like it?" I wondered.

"So if we want to get there in five hours, we have to go about 50 million miles per hour, that's way more than what we're going now," Wyatt did the math in his head.

"Then let's speed it up!" Forrest yelled and pressed his foot on the gas. Everyone held onto the walls as we saw stars in the distance becoming stretched lines of light. "Okay. This should be good. Now we just have a smooth ride of five hours, and then we'll have to figure out how to land this thing." Everyone walked out and left Forrest to drive.

"So now that our lives aren't in peril, what do you want to do?" I asked the group.

"'Member that game we played on the plane last year?" Daven smiled, and I explained it to Cobalt. There were two adjacent square boxes and one person would stand in each. When someone crossed any line and touched the ground outside their square they lost. I asked Cobalt to draw the lines in metal and we moved the couches so we could play.

The game went by quickly with only 14 people, so only three games were played. By the second round the people left were Cobalt, Rhochelle, Ember, Wyatt, Ion, Aura, and me. In that round I was against Aura, I brought her over by making her shirt covered in ice and pulling her over to my side. Cobalt, Ember, and Wyatt played a three person game in which we made the course a circle cut into three pieces like a pie. After the second round it was Cobalt, Ion, and me, so we played another three person game. We only had about ten minutes until we got to our parents house by the start of the round.

"On your mark, get set . . . go!" Kamille shouted and I covered Ion's shirt in ice. Cobalt used a giant metal hand to lift him up, but he shocked us lightly and fell to the ground. Then he used static electricity to pull me closer and closer to the line. Just before I went over it Cobalt used a metal wall to pull Ion over his line, he was out just before I crossed his line.

"Ion get out of the match, Cobalt draw the line so that you each have half the arena," Rhochelle ordered, and I saw the metal line move around so that it only cut the rectangle into two equal squares. Cobalt suddenly shot something at me and I couldn't dodge it. When it went through me I felt like my insides had stopped moving, and my body was heavier and denser. I looked at myself to see if I had changed, but all I saw were two metal pieces on each side of my waist, one on each of my wrists, and one on each of my ankles.

"That's it; you put some metal pieces on me?" I laughed, and Cobalt didn't even smirk.

"Those aren't metal pieces, they're magnets," he smiled, and my face dropped. I looked down at the metal line, and before I knew it I was on the ground, being pulled toward the line. I froze Cobalt to the ground. It had no effect on him, neither would freezing the magnets.

"Wait this isn't fair, you can't move the lines!" I shouted when I was inches away.

"Cobalt, he's right. You can't use those," Ion sided with me and I thanked him.

"Fine," Cobalt removed the magnets and I got up. I instantly shot ice at his shirt and he grew a metal bar out of the floor. Then he grabbed onto it while I pulled him closer to the line. I gave him a brain freeze and he yelled, letting go of it. He flew over the line and just before he hit the ground, he made a metal slide that slid him back onto his side.

"My turn," he smiled, and grew a metal wall next to him. I realized he was trying the magnets out again. They were much larger this time, and in a gas form so they would be harder to dodge. Just before they hit me I ducked, and they flew past me and even passed through the wall of the rocket. They hit a comet that we were passing and my mouth dropped. Even though we were going thousands of miles per second I saw the magnets hit the comet and start to work. The comet turned direction slowly, but soon it picked up speed and started following the rocket.

"Uh oh," Cobalt sighed and every one of us ran into the control room.

"Forrest, we have a problem," I chuckled when I heard what I had said, but then became serious again. Forrest checked the rearview mirror outside the rocket and looked at it sideways, as if confused that a thousand ton comet was following us at the same speed that we were going.

"That is a problem," he understood that one of us had done something to cause the comet to follow us and didn't ask any questions. He pressed on the gas pedal as hard as he could and we all fell back onto the floor. I watched the comet in the mirror and it gained speed just as we did. Callidus came into sight and we reached its atmosphere within seconds.

"We have to slow down!" Ember shouted as the ground came closer. Forrest slowed down to about one thousandth of our original speed. The atmosphere slowed the comet down but not enough. We turned to stop heading towards the ground. Forrest kept driving a while until we got to the island that our parents lived on. It looked about 30 miles away, and we were going about 250 miles per hour. The comet chased us continuously until I suddenly got an idea.

"If the comet is going too fast to turn, maybe we could get it to go into the water if we make a sharp turn!" Wyatt hollered. Forrest took his chance and dove straight for the water. As he had hoped the comet followed us, picking up speed as it dropped. When we were a few hundred feet from the water Forrest made a turn so sharp that the bottom of the rocket skimmed the water. The comet couldn't turn in time and went straight into the water and I sighed in relief. But before I had time to celebrate I saw the huge comet rise out of the water and continue to follow us.

"Forrest look out!" Aura screamed and pointed in front of us. The land was coming toward us so quickly that we would never have time to stop. In a rush of panic I saw Cobalt run to the door that Matt had fallen out of. He pressed the emergency open button and dove out.

"Cobalt no!" I shouted at the top of my lungs as rushing air filled the room. Neva closed the door to save us from falling out. Even if we had landed in the water we would die for sure from hitting it at the speed that we were going. But in the mirror I saw Cobalt make a metal box about as big as a football field and throw it into the water. The comet finally stopped chasing us and turned to chase the metal box as if fell into the water. There was a huge splash and Cobalt flew out of sight. Just as Ion dropped his mouth to say something Forrest pressed the breaks as hard as he could and everyone flew forward. But it wasn't enough, the rocket crashed into the land and everything blacked out.

CHAPTER THREE: AN UNKNOWN LANGUAGE

AURA

The sun beat down on my eyes and I forced myself to get up. When I opened my eyes, I realized that I had no idea where I was. I looked around the room in a circle, and studied the objects in it. Basically it had a dresser, a cool closet with mirrors as doors, and a bed. But when I turned to the last wall, I jumped. The entire wall was a window, and then suddenly I learned how high I was. I looked out the window and saw a grass area that seemed to go on forever, but as I looked longer I found a huge glass dome about fifty feet high. Then I saw that I was about four stories off the ground, and the whole side of this building was glass.

My first instinct was to run outside and get a good look at the building. But someone stopped me halfway down the extremely long staircase.

"Aura, good you're awake, your parents made breakfast and they're eating it in the dining room," said a complete stranger wearing a uniform and carrying a laundry basket.

"Okay, thanks," I smiled back at her and continued my trip downstairs. On the first floor I got lost—I found the ballroom, the kitchen, and the indoor pool. Finally when I reached the dining room, my parents greeted me and I sat down. Only Selene and Cobalt were there.

"Cobalt, how'd you make it?" I laughed in joy and just stopped myself before hugging him. That would be awkward because I think Kamille has a crush on him.

"I didn't hit the water; I caught myself on a metal slide and slowed down. Then I just rode into your parents' house and told them what had happened," Cobalt took a plate and filled it with French toast, then covered it in syrup.

"How did we . . ." I cut myself off before I even started the conversation of death and life.

"Since space rockets must be able to travel millions of miles a second, there have to be really good airbags in them as well. When the rocket slows down too quickly the rocket has a setting that gets rid of all the inertia inside the rocket, which is what keeps you moving after the vehicle stops. The only person awake when we found you was Wyatt, he had thought ahead and slowed himself down by teleporting into the sky," Mom explained and I turned red because I hadn't thought of that. As each person came down, Mom and Dad would take turns explaining to them how we survived.

After that we ate, almost in complete silence, too. The only words were "hey, pass that," or "this is so good." When all of us finished we begged to get a look of the house from the outside. Eventually they gave in and let us run outside to get a quick look. When I ran out my mouth dropped even before I turned to look at the house. There was a huge garden extending all the way to the beach where we crashed the rocket. There goes the biggest vehicle in the solar system . . . I hope Matt forgives us.

The house had four walls, only one of them was glass, and went about five stories up. But the walls didn't make right angles when they met. The roof of the building was a parallelogram and tilted upward, as if one of the walls were higher than its opposite. Next to the thin building another huge building connected to it, but only two stories high. On the other side of the thin building was the glass dome, which was also attached to the rest of it. Seeing such unique beauty reminded me of the time I first saw Medlocks Academy.

"This is amazing, but what is the bubble for?" Neva asked them.

"That is the solar system's largest power practice simulator; we used it to train Glacthia," Mom's voice got quieter toward the end of the sentence.

"That's awesome, can we try it?" I asked, exciting but also scared out of my mind.

"First, we have another surprise for you," Dad led us back to the house, into the entrance hall, and then stopped.

"You know how you guys have been pretty curious about your family? Well, my sister said that it would be okay if her kids stay here before they go to Medlocks this year," Mom smiled and we made confused faces.

"Do they go to Medlocks Prep?" Kamille wondered.

"Nope," Dad gave us a look and we smiled.

"Can they do that, have a new family just come to Medlocks for the first time in our second year?" Forrest questioned them.

"It has happened in the past. The age difference between the oldest and youngest in her family was larger than most. The youngest is only ten and the oldest is sixteen. Last year, the youngest wasn't old enough to go to Medlocks, but they decided that it wasn't fair for them to be denied an education just because of their age range. So they're only going to go to Medlocks for the next five years, one year less than you," Mom explained for us and pushed the doors open to the dining hall.

"These are your cousins, the Venturas," Mom introduced us to each of them individually. There were four of them, a set of triplets made up of two girls and boy, and then a single born boy. "This is Gabby, Lianna, and Sam, they are sixteen year old triplets, and this is Craig, he's ten." Gabby and Sam both had freckles and brown hair, while Lianna and Craig were both blond. Eventually our parents left us on our own and we actually got to talk.

"So what are your powers?" I decided to ask, my curiosity was getting the best of me.

"Lianna has infinite knowledge, but just for facts, she can't read minds and she can't tell the future. I can create small stars, and even some pretty big ones. Sam can change the weather. And Craig can imitate any voice he wants," Gabby took a deep breath when she was done and we told her our powers.

"That's cool! So what do you want to do?" Lianna asked us.

Scott had a ton of things in mind; it kept us busy for days. It was either exploring the building, playing hide and seek, or a power practicing game. Our parents even taught us how to use the power practice simulator, and we fought evil beings until it was so dark we were starting to hit ourselves with our own powers.

One morning at breakfast, we were all talking happily until everyone quieted down to listen to the news on TV.

"This year's 12-9 is going to be a hard one for space kind, it is the twentieth 12-9 in history. I'm just wondering how the Barkers are taking it. We all forgive them and all, but could you just live with the guilt? If it were me I—" our parents shut the TV off and continued eating quietly.

"Guys, you have to tell us what happened on 12-9," Selene looked at her plate and not at our parents. The put down their forks and finished chewing the eggs they were having.

"12-9 was the day that Glacthia went bad," Dad said as quietly as he could.

"We know that . . . what *really* happened on 12-9?" Daven begged to know. The whole room was quiet. With nineteen kids in the room and two parents, not even one of them talked for a whole minute.

"An accident in the lab; we made a mistake when we designed him. He has an undying curiosity. Something happened then that made him hate himself. He got so mad he took out his rage on anyone he saw. We happened to be on the other side of the house when it happened, so he couldn't find us. He flew away and we have never seen him since," Mom explained it more peacefully than we thought anyone could.

"You haven't seen him since he went bad? We've seen him like six times in one year. What test are we on now?" Wyatt joked around, but realized what the mood of the room was and quieted very quickly.

"Speaking of Glacthia, I really want to know what his name means," Ion thought out loud, and our parents hesitated for a minute.

"You know that language that the Ancestors spoke, the one that all the planets and the Barathrum Evado Trophy are in? Well, it's called Glacthian, there's a Glacthian alphabet and a Glacthian language. It's basically Latin but with a little dialect, you may learn why later. When we made Glacthia we put a translator of Glacthian in him, then eventually the language died off and now he's the only one who knows it," Mom told us and we were amazingly interested.

"Luckily, there was a young girl who just received the power of language translation, one of the rarest powers next to metal and psychic. You can use it if you want," Dad pulled a small remote out of his pocket. Forrest took it and we wandered off in the next couple of minutes.

"Okay, let's check the planets. Callidus means . . ." Forrest typed it in and looked at the screen. "Intelligence. Cool, we were all born on the intelligent planet," he smiled and then looked at Caroline and Alaina, who were not born on this planet. Forrest was pretty big-headed sometimes and really good at creating awkward moments.

"Let me try," Alaina grabbed it and typed in Voliturus. "It means athletic, sweet!"

"I want to try one," Rhochelle typed in Praeclarus and waited. "It means beauty."

"Last one . . ." Sam typed in Eximius. "It means not alike, uncommon, and extraordinary."

"All of these are the ones that Miss Monohan told us, try the moons," Ember typed in each of the moons and they all came up as "moon."

"That's boring, try Barathrum Evado," Wyatt ordered.

"Bar . . . a . . . thru . . . m," Kamille typed it in and gasped. "Darkness, why would it be darkness?" She typed in evado and we all stood for a minute in horror. "Darkness escapes . . ." Selene was as silent as us for a few seconds then we all sprinted to our parents.

"Barathrum Evado means darkness escapes!" Cobalt yelled and they looked completely unsurprised.

"We know . . . we had it translated a couple days ago. The Barathrum Evado Trophy is a fairly new thing. Someone just thought it would be cool to put a party in a trophy. It turns out that Glacthia had possessed the person whose idea it was. He had been planning to capture your classmates since you were born," Dad said calmly while our mouths dropped.

"That's insane and creepy at the same time," I told them and we walked off again.

"Let's go to the power practice simulator," Sam suggested and we ran there as fast as we could. We hadn't been there without our parents yet, but we had a good idea of how it worked. All of us wandered around for a while to get our first good look at it, and suddenly someone yelped in happiness.

"Guys, look at this," Lianna showed us a bunch of scratch marks on the wall.

"What is it?" Scott asked.

"The Glacthian alphabet," she pointed out. Immediately Neva pointed the remote at it and pressed "scan". A blue light shot out and scanned the code. It came up on the screen "Dissimulo Recordatio" and we typed it in. After a short wait the screen read "Secret Memory".

"Secret memory," Lianna read aloud and we heard a rumbling sound. Suddenly the room was spinning and we were falling through time. The room continued to spin for a while until we hit the ground with a hard crash. We stood up slowly; everything looked the same except for that the symbols were gone.

"What time is it?" Becca asked.

"Same time, same date," everyone but me murmured after looking at their watches.

"Mine has the time that I'm in, since I travel through time a lot," I checked my watch and gasped. "December 9th, 3:25 p.m. Oh my gosh the portal sent us back to where Glacthia went bad. We have to find our parents." All of us ran through the house looking for them until we saw five people sitting at the dining table watching TV, just as we were. Mom, Dad, a man who we had to assume was Glacthia, and two strangers were eating lunch. Scott began breathing quickly and his eyes filled up.

"That's my aunt and uncle, I've seen pictures of them," Scott couldn't take it anymore and looked away.

"Come on, Glacthia, this will be your last practice and then you'll be completely done with all your training. Although this one will be the hardest, this villain's power is pretty complicated," Scott's uncle said, and he, Scott's aunt, and Glacthia left our parents. Scott finally started to yell.

"No! Don't go . . . please!" he was crying hysterically. His aunt and uncle didn't even hear him. They walked off and we knew we couldn't leave with Scott if we truly wanted to know what happened. All I knew was the Glacthia killed Scott's aunt and uncle, but now Scott had to see something no kid should ever see: what really happened.

Glacthia and my mom and dad's greatest helpers with making Glacthia were in the power practice simulator. They started setting up the difficulty level, number of villains, and all the other settings. We stood behind Glacthia, (unable to be seen of course,) and watched what he did. He was amazingly good looking, very handsome and tall, with muffled brown hair that was just messed up perfectly. I hate saying these things about Glacthia but that's just how my parents wanted him to be. He looked . . . human.

Suddenly Glacthia looked around and curiously pressed two buttons on a control panel.

"What's he doing?" Craig asked, not understanding what was going on.

"He's pressing those two buttons that your Mom and Dad told us never to press. One of them . . . makes it so that you lose your powers. The other one makes it so that you can actually feel pain if something hurts you," Lianna only had to look at the buttons and automatically knew what each one did.

"Then we have to get out of here, I have a feeling I know what's going to happen," Wyatt tried to pull us out of the room until everyone felt an emptiness in their stomachs.

"We lost our powers, too," Sam cried out and all of us began heading out of the room.

"Wait we can still save him, Glacthia doesn't have to be evil!" I screamed and tried to open the door to press the buttons and turn it off. I fought all I could but didn't get in, for some reason the door was locked.

"Curiosity definitely got the best of him," Neva said sorrowfully. Scott's aunt and uncle walked into a room and closed the door behind them.

"Look, they're leaving the room; something must have caused the future to change," Forrest smiled at Scott. Suddenly a villain appeared in the simulator. He looked like a completely normal villain, desperate, wanting, and alone. As soon as he noticed Glacthia he threw a small, baseball sized glass ball at him. He dodged it without his powers and it hit the floor, causing it to explode. Back and forth the villains, or at least the villain and Glacthia, fought as Glacthia began to realize that he could feel the heat coming from the explosions. He ducked and dove around each bomb that the villain threw, but we could see who was going to win.

Then the horrible tragedy happened, just as we had always pictured it. The bomb-thrower threw a huge bomb at Glacthia. He did dodge it, but it didn't matter. A huge explosion filled the whole bubble with fire, Glacthia was covered in it. The door covering Scott's aunt and uncle blew up and we heard their final screams. There's nothing worse than watching someone die, but this was probably in the top five ways no one would want to watch a person die.

"No!" Scott cried out as loud as he could and we held him back from entering the fiery dome.

"There's nothing we can do Scott, it's over," Daven told him between small cries.

"Guys, look," Selene pointed to Glacthia and everyone looked up. He was covered in blood and his robotic bones even showed. Glacthia yelled in rage and ran out of the power practice simulator in anger. We had to walk slowly when we tried to catch up to him. We were practically carrying Scott down the halls. Finally he pulled himself together; obviously his aunt and uncle had passed away before he was born, so he never got to meet them. It's easier to miss something that you never knew, so Scott was a little bit stronger than most people after something like this.

We found Glacthia in a room that was most likely his. His skin was so permanently burnt that no one could bear to look at him. He was cutting a black cloth into a square shape. Then he tied it around his neck and we saw the hood that went with it. When he walked out of the room it got stuck on a nail on the floor and ripped. Glacthia pulled on it and it ripped even more. Now he looked exactly as he did when we met him, and he teleported out of sight.

"That was fast; the minute he got burnt he decides to become evil?" Wyatt could tell we had missed a lot of built-up anger that Glacthia had towards being good.

"Come on, we should get back to the present," I slowly put my hand forward and everyone else joined in a chain. I closed my eyes and concentrated, and everyone braced themselves for time travel.

"Our powers must still not be working," I confirmed. Ember shot fire out of her hand and stared at me. Everyone was able to use their powers except me, so I tried shooting air. On the first try a small gust of wind took over the room.

"It must just be your time travel that's not working," Forrest agreed.

"Let's find the scratch marks," Wyatt teleported us to the spot where we first fell through time. Glacthia was sitting on the floor with a knife, chipping pieces off of the wall.

"Secret memory," he said slowly, as if trying to speak clear enough for the wall to understand him. It flickered with dust and sparks, then he teleported away again.

"Secret memory," Daven spoke to the wall when Glacthia was gone. The room spun for a while and I held my head so that I wouldn't get dizzy. This was much weirder than my usual time travel. Eventually we landed back on the ground and everyone checked their watches and sighed.

"It worked; let's go tell Mom and Dad," Ion ran out of the room at light speed and we followed a normal pace.

We explained everything to Mom and Dad—from when we wandered off to find things to translate all the way to when we just came back from the past. Mom stood still for a minute, then decided that we deserved a real answer.

"My power is memory, and Glacthia has it too, so we can both make something called a memory jogger. It helps people remember things by revisiting their past. All you have to do is write something down somewhere, say the password and use your power to turn it into a memory jogger. Whenever someone says the password they fall into the memory and get to relive it. That must have been horrible for you to see it all," she finished telling us and we nodded.

That day ended just as any other sorrowful day did. Scott wouldn't talk to anyone, and no one did anything but sit around and mope. When I went to bed, the only thing I wanted to change from the past was us going to watch that memory.

The summer ended in no time, we had a lot of fun playing games and practicing in the nice, outdoor air. Just like the memory jogger itself, everything that happened that day was just part of the past, and had to eventually be forgotten. When we were finally ready to leave for Medlocks, we actually didn't want to. There were so many fun things that we had done at our parents' house.

One of our most memorable adventures was when Cobalt suggested that Rhochelle build a giant arch over the ocean and we bungee jump off of it. The arch broke when Neva bungee jumped off of it and he fell into the water.

Another important one was when we went to the roof of the taller part of the house and Neva pushed Wyatt off. He had to catch himself by surrounding himself in water and lowering it to the ground.

There was even one time when Selene and I had an argument over what destroyed the dinosaurs. I knew it was a comet but Selene said there was a really long drought and they ran out of water. We had a pool and everyone made a guess on how they died out. Then I took everyone to the time when dinosaurs were dying off and we saw a very strange sight. There were comets landing everywhere, but none of them were blowing up. Each one gave dinosaurs a different power, and they were using them to kill each other. When all the dinosaurs were gone we each paid Forrest the money that we owed him.

Finally the day came when it was time to leave, and my mom was getting hysterical about it. She was packing our bags and reminiscing on all the adventures that we had.

"Aw, remember yesterday when you went back in time to see the dinosaurs?" she asked and I rolled my eyes.

On the morning we left, she kissed us all goodbye. It was extremely embarrassing to have my mom kiss our friends and newly met cousins. All of us grabbed hands and Wyatt concentrated—this was his first time teleporting from one planet to another.

"Medlocks Academy on Medlocks Island on planet Medlocks," he almost chuckled when he recited that and the ground started to leave our feet. Then I realized that instead our feet had actually left the ground, but by that time we were almost hundreds of thousands of miles away.

CHAPTER FOUR: THE STRUGGLE FOR A DATE

DAVEN

Medlocks seemed the same as it was last year when we left it. We went straight to Miss Monohan's office when we arrived on the front steps. I held the door open for everyone and she looked up from her desk. Her hair was longer, but still she looked the same.

"Hey Miss Monohan, how was your summer?" Rhochelle asked her politely.

"Mine was nice, I met a nice man and . . . now we're dating," she seemed so happy that she didn't even notice the Venturas, and she definitely hesitated before revealing her personal life to us. We kept moving our eyes from her to the new students, and finally she stared at them.

"Oh right. I have the paperwork for you right here. You will be staying on the twenty ninth floor, and we have it decorated according to your general power, you can go there now and meet your new caretaker, Mr. Schnyder." Miss Monohan continued with her paperwork and we left her to run to their new room. The name sounded familiar, but I ignored it. The stair climb exhausted us and by the time we were at their floor we almost dropped sleeping.

"Are you guys ready? You are so lucky that you're on the same floor as Mr. Williams—he's the coolest teacher ever. I wonder if you'll have a class based off of your powers . . . probably not since you came a year late, and since there are no more classrooms. That would be cool, but I wonder what class we would have based off of your—"

"Ion!" Ember yelled and he snapped back into reality. He slowly opened the door and we all gasped.

Their room kind of looked like our secret base. It had an entrance hall, but with rugs and couches and paintings. Then along the walls, there were doors to other rooms, left open so we could see into them. Craig's was closest, going around the room to Lianna's. We walked over to Craig's and it looked completely boring. No one said anything and there was a long silence as we listened to the random voices echoing in his room.

"This is so cool," Ember said to Craig sarcastically trying to make him feel better. But Lianna recognized the sarcasm and explained the strangeness of Craig's room.

"Craig can imitate voices, it's part of his power, but he can only imitate ones that he's heard before in his life. When he hears this he'll be able to copy more people's voices, it's a really good disguising technique," she explained, and we all nodded, happy that the room served a purpose to Craig even though it made no sense to the rest of us.

Sam's was next; it was just a regular room but the weather was out of control, there was a small tornado with rain flying everywhere, yet nothing got wet. Sam walked into it and smiled, but it actually looked like it would be more a hassle than it would be cool.

Gabby came next, her room was really phenomenal. When we walked up to the room it felt like we were standing in a glass box in the middle of space, but when we stood in the doorway and looked down we saw a small sun, with a diameter the same as the width of the room.

"At least one person doesn't already have a bed and everything," Wyatt smiled, last year we had to all make our own rooms and beds in the forest that we lived in. Gabby, still in the doorway, stared at it for a minute, and then jumped into her room. Unexpectedly she fell straight down into the sun, but popped out a few seconds later.

"This is my room," she laughed. I was about to jump down and see it for myself, by Lianna stopped me.

"It's a sun that only she can go into, I wouldn't jump into it if I were you," she saved my life, and I thanked her. Gabby came out and we went to the last room, Lianna's. Her room was next, and it turned out to be even more unusual than Craig's. It was practically a library; her room was probably the biggest in her family. There were books on everything, except they were all nonfiction.

"A book on laws of science, a book on sand, jeez this has everything," I told her, and she blushed. We were just about to give them a tour of our room when the doorknob started to turn. Someone entered, and everyone but the Venturas gasped. The person wore a mask that covered half his face, and he would have been unfamiliar if it wasn't for his gray, knotty hair.

"My name is Mr. Schnyder and I'll be your caretaker," said Mr. Schny-eeek as if he was getting tired of saying it. He walked toward us and we stared at him.

"That's you're real name, Mr. Schnyder?" Scott asked him and he rolled his eyes.

"Yes, I've made a lot of changes to my life since I got burnt by Glacthia. I now know that detentions are given to punish people, not for enjoyment. I shouldn't have been so mean to kids just 'cause I don't like being old," he said in his usual angry voice, but it still seemed somewhat sweeter and more inviting.

"Thanks, Mr. Schny-ee . . . I mean Schnyder, that's really nice of you. So you're not going to start them all off with a detention?" Kamille inquired in her nicest voice.

"No, I'm not," he smiled back. This was way too weird for me, and I didn't even get that many detentions last year.

We left the Venturas in their room and went to ours for the first time in the school year. Becca, Alaina, Caroline, and Scott returned to their rooms and we played games in our rooms until we retired for the day.

The next morning was the last day before school started, and we played outdoor games the entire time. Each game of hide and seek dodge ball lasted about two hours, and then at night we played sardines until people started falling asleep in their hiding spots. But the next morning when class started we learned of something we could previously only imagine. We were in astronomy, and someone was passing around a note behind Mrs. Parker's back. When it came to our table I took it from Wyatt and read it.

"There's a dance this Friday, get a date before they're all gone," I whispered and Mrs. Parker turned around. I shoved the note under the table and smiled. She turned back to talking about the rotation of comets, and I passed it to the next table. Who was I going to ask? There was no one in the school that I really liked right now. For every girl that goes without a date, there's a boy that will go without a date. And that's only if there is the same amount of boys that there are girls in the school. The thought of the dance filled my mind with fear and dread. But no matter what happened, I was going to at least ask someone.

On the way out of the class, Neva was in complete denial of the dance that he started pointing fingers.

"This dance is such a lie. Who would believe that? Who wrote that note anyway? I bet it was George—what a liar. I can't believe he would do something like—"

"Neva, look at the poster," Rhochelle turned him so that he faced the wall. It was a sign for the dance this Friday. "Welcome back dance, for all students to attend, Friday from 8:00 to midnight," Rhochelle read and smiled at Neva.

"Neva, can I talk to you for a minute?" Becca came up to us and waved to Ember and Rhochelle. The two of them walked off and we rolled our eyes.

"She's probably going to ask him to the dance," Ember told us and we departed for lunch. All of us were pretty anxious to get there for reasons dance related. We could see clearly that the whole school knew about the dance already, and we were wondering if anyone would ask us.

"Hey, guys, did you hear about the dance yet?" I asked our cousins, who ended up being at the table next to us. They laughed a little, and I felt like I had asked a stupid question.

"Yeah, we did, we saw the poster on our way down," Sam told us.

"Are you going to ask anyone?" Neva asked them, and we just realized that he was with us. I checked his facial expression for any hints as to what Becca said to him, but there were none that I could identify.

"I don't know, probably not," Lianna was about to continue but realized that we weren't listening. She didn't even seem like the kind of person that would show up at a dance with someone. It wasn't that she wasn't pretty, or fun to be with, but she was too independent to need a date.

"I just hope I get to meet enough people to pick from," Gabby said in her excited voice.

"That's cool; I really want to ask someone," Rhochelle missed the days when she was crushing on Cobalt's eldest brother, Mac. He told her at the end of the last school year that she wasn't evil enough. Now she's in the phase where she doesn't want to like anyone, but still wanted a date for the dance.

The next few days were very slow ones. By Monday, Aura and Selene both had asked people. We asked Kamille why she didn't ask Dave, but she didn't answer. After Tuesday I had decided who I was going to ask. I had been walking to the lunch tray drop-off when I bumped into someone and all of my trash dropped. When I looked up to see who it was, Nicole Magerr was already picking up my trash and apologizing. She caught my eye and we had the longest interaction I've ever had with a girl. For about ten seconds, we smiled at each other before we realized we were causing a hold up. When I got back to our room, I learned that Ember and Forrest had dates, but wouldn't say who. The worst part was that both of them were currently in a relationship and yet they wouldn't tell us who they were going to the dance with. Ember dated some older guy that we met last year who worked on Medlocks Island.

Wednesday was the same, except no one turned out to have asked anyone, and I kept catching Nicole's eye in class. When I tried to ask her, I tripped down the stairs and woke up in the nurse's office with a small concussion and a huge bump on my forehead. For some strange reason, it felt as if someone had tripped me, and I hadn't fallen on my own.

"You must stay inactive for twenty-four hours, so I'll keep you hear until tomorrow afternoon," she told me, and I made a horrified face.

"But . . ." I stopped myself before going into my personal life with the school nurse.

On Thursday morning, I woke up and the bump was gone; I had to jump up out of bed and do a dance around the whole nurse's office. She ordered me to sit down and I started to think logically. Someone must've either given me a potion, or the nurse is just that good. Just before I started asking myself a million questions, Ion walked in with a proud smile on his face.

"I guess you've realized my work by now," he talked like he were a sculptor and I was his masterpiece.

"Ion, you did this? Thank you so much, if that huge bump took up my forehead for the whole dance, I would've never gotten a date," I pretended to flatter him, but I was just pleased that my forehead was normal again.

"I gotta go to class; dude, you have so much homework right now, but when you can leave just meet us in the room," Ion didn't even let me answer, he walked off and I was left alone for an incalculable amount of time. I sat there, counting the ceiling tiles, when someone walked in. I shut my eyes and rolled to one side, pretending I wasn't listening. Miss Monohan walked into the room to talk to the nurse. She started whispering to her, but I was close enough to catch some of the words.

"There has been . . . with the Metronome . . ." As soon as I caught the word Metronome I opened my eyes. We had destroyed that last year, Glacthia tried to use it to take our powers. Only if they would speak up! " . . . blackout . . . soon," Miss Monohan explained, and the nurse gasped. I noticed that Miss Monohan showed the nurse something, but Miss Monohan turned to look at me and I shut my eyes as fast as I could. I need to see what this is, I tried to start a calm rolling over but the bed creaked. There goes my chance of finding out. She stared at me for a while and then her shoes squeaked. Is she walking toward me? I calmed my breathing down and concentrated on not opening my eyes. Shoot, I think my stomach is about to growl, and I'm definitely turning red.

"We'll talk about this more later," Miss Monohan squeaked farther away and finally I heard the door open and slam shut. What had they said? What's happening with the Metronome? Does Glacthia have it again?

I didn't understand anything she talked about. There weren't enough words that I had caught to form an idea. But if it had to do with the Metronome, then I didn't like it. We had destroyed the Metronome last year, but with Glacthia anything is possible. Okay, I fell at about 4:00 yesterday, then today I can leave at 4:00. I glanced at the clock, 2:45. This will take a while.

My sentence dragged on for all eternity, I could have solved some universe changing mystery by now. Finally at 4:01 the nurse gave me the okay to leave, and I ran up the steps to our room in excitement. It didn't surprise me that I made it up the seven or so flights of steps without having to walk; my heartbeat had the combined work of keeping me thinking of what had happened and keeping me running. I burst into our room, but no one greeted me. An empty tree house too, and no one seemed to be hiding anywhere. I went around calling them, but received no answer. Dang it, they were in class. The pain of knowing this information and having no one to tell felt like I was trapped in an insane asylum.

I had to wait for another hour, but finally they started arriving. They looked exhausted, as if they had just run a marathon.

"Guys, what happened?" I begged for them to tell me, and they waited awhile to catch their breaths.

"Cobalt's brothers . . . tried to take Cobalt. They're really getting better . . . using gadgets to replace their powers . . . or lack of," Neva explained for the rest of them.

"They almost beat us; one of their gadgets made it so that whenever we used our powers we felt a ton of pain in our stomachs," Aura told me.

"That's terrible, how'd you win?" I was really interested in their battle tactics.

"We won when Cobalt and Ion took their gadgets by making an electromagnet. The gadgets flew right out of their hands and to us. After that they ran away and swore to return, as they always do," Forrest smiled at Cobalt and Ion.

"So did you end up asking Nicole to the dance yet?" Ion asked me and I sighed.

"No, I came straight here after the nurse's office." The rest of the group looked at me and then I gasped, remembering what it is that I had to tell them. Just when I started to open my mouth the phone interrupted me. Why is a phone even in our tree house?

"Yes?" Rhochelle picked it up and listened for a moment, while looking at me. Then she hung up and explained, "Mr. Williams needs to go over what you missed, go there now." But I had to tell everyone about what I heard!

"Okay, but when I get back, I need to tell you what I heard Miss Monohan talking about." I angrily stomped out, but the news about the Metronome could wait at least a few minutes.

"Good afternoon, Daven. How was your summer?" Mr. Williams asked me when I walked in. I told him it was fine. "You missed class this morning and we had an important lesson on scelums. I gave you your notes on them, but you still need to make up the practice lesson in the simulator. If you'll step into the room I'll turn it on," he gave me a small push into the room and I started to disagree with this idea.

"Mr. Williams I'm not really prepared for this, I think I should . . ." I noticed him pressing some of the buttons that he usually doesn't press. One said "pain", the other said "real", the same two buttons Glacthia pressed the day he went evil. I gasped and Mr. Williams realized that I had caught on. He started to change, and suddenly he became Glacthia.

"Have fun, Daven," he turned away.

"Why are you doing this?" I yelled. "Why just me?"

"It's part of my, 'eliminate one at a time' plan. I'll eliminate one of you, and then wait a while before I eliminate the next. For whatever reason, you work better when you're together, but separately you'll all

41

be at my mercy." He teleported away and I ran to the door out of the simulation room. Great, locked.

Suddenly, it appeared across the room from me. It had vicious claws, fangs practically past its chin, and a hunchback like a coyote with back problems. The scelum was part bear and part wolf, so it stood on two legs but looked more like a wolf. I felt as if my life had just been ripped out of me and handed to it. Just as it jumped at me, I did a back flip and landed on the wall—the coolest and most fun combination between Kamille and Selene's powers. But no time to have fun—I pulled the machine out of my pocket that tells me what powers I have copied.

"What do I have from Wyatt?" I yelled at it, but obviously it wasn't aware that I was in danger for my life.

"Teleporting, levitating, and reading minds," it spoke in Dr. Dryden's voice since he programmed it to be voice activated. I tried to teleport, but nothing happened; no teleporting out of the simulation room. Then I tried to think, what did it say on my notes about scelums? They can spit a chemical at you that turns your bones to dust, which is what they eat. Before I could continue to think, I realized what I had just thought in my head. I turned to the scelum. It was getting ready to spit at me. I walked across the ceiling on my hands and knees and then made a metal bar going across the ceiling in front of me, which I could do because of Cobalt. Letting go of the ceiling, I grabbed the bar and swung my feet, kicking the scelum in the face and causing it to fall down.

It howled like a wolf, then started swinging its claws at me. I grew a small branch out of the ground and swung it at the scelum. I hit it a couple times, but eventually it took it from me and broke it. Then I remembered I had some of Ember's powers, and shot fire at it. Since I only had a little I stopped just after I started, and the scelum stepped back and fell down. But it got right back up and ran to me. I remade the metal bar and started swinging it.

"That's right, you live in volcanoes, how could I forget?" I was starting to rethink my whole "no paying attention in class" routine. I fought it for minutes, running out of things to use and powers to copy.

"Oh my gosh, I know how to beat you!" I said as I was shooting water at it. My notes said that scelums were afraid of the sunlight, a reason for them living in caves and volcanoes. I stood back and held my hands out. A sun started to appear in front of me, and I closed my eyes. The scelum started to howl and whine, scurrying into the corner in fear. Finally it couldn't take it anymore and ran to the door, breaking it down with one swipe of its claws. I turned the sun off and ran out of the room as well. It was running toward the stairs and I turned to the controls. Pressing a couple buttons, the simulator turned off and the scelum vanished with one last howl.

I ran down the stairs all the way to Nicole's floor, and when I got there I took about a minute to catch my breath before walking in. Their room was a bunch of detailed maps of places, put together to make a mosaic of a map of the whole Earth.

"Wow, this is really cool," I said to them, and all of them turned around. "Nicole, can I ask you something?" I hinted for the others to walk away, and they obliged. Nicole automatically saw it coming, and smiled. This boosted my confidence so much that nothing could stop me from asking her.

"Nicole, will you go to the dance with me? I mean I know it's last minute, and you might have another date already. You can say no if you want, I just really thought that I should at least ask you so that I can—"

"Daven, I'll go with you," she smiled at me and my mouth dropped.

"Seriously?" I double checked, and she nodded her head. I went into a state of shock, and it took almost a minute to force myself out of it.

"Cool, should I see you there, or come get you on my way there, or—"

"I'll see you there," she interrupted me again, but I was very grateful for it.

"Okay, see ya there," I left the room with such a big smile that I had to turn my head away from them so that I wouldn't embarrass myself. The whole four floors down to our room I skipped, not caring if anyone saw me. When I reached our floor I ran into our room and started singing on my way to the tree house. But after a minute I realized that it was a mile to the tree house, and that I had just been attacked by a scelum. I also remembered that Glacthia had just tried to kill me.

"Guys, guys!" I yelled as I flew to the tree house and teleported to the study room, where we mainly hang out and avoided doing our homework.

"Guys I got a date!" I screamed when I burst the door open. Wyatt, Ion, and Cobalt all sighed, but everyone else congratulated me.

"That's awesome, with whom?" Selene asked, apparently interested. Aura and Selene were the only people that actually told us who they were going with, which was a scary fact for the people who were currently dating.

"You'll see at the dance," I smiled, and they all rolled their eyes. That excuse was so tiring, but I didn't feel like them bugging me about the person I asked. "Oh wait, and Glacthia also tried to kill me with a scelum," I added, and they stared at me with widened eyes.

"You think you'd mention that uh . . . first!" Forrest shouted at me and I stared at him the same way he was staring at me.

"No, you put the more important one first," I joked, and they all gave me a serious face, so I stopped. "It was fine; he said that he has this new plan to eliminate all of us separately and that I was first. He just locked me in the simulation room and turned on the pain button and the button that makes the villain real. I beat it easily, I remembered that it was afraid of sunlight and used one of Gabby's suns to get it to break down the door. Then I asked Nicole to the dance and she said yes. I'm also going to ace that test on scelums," I smiled. It seemed like my idea of a perfect day, except for the part with Glacthia. I knew I was extremely downplaying the fact that I just avoided a death experience but for some reason I was tired of Glacthia's pointless threats.

"That's a bad thing. If he's going to eliminate us all separately then we have to constantly be alert." Ember reminded us, and we all looked at the floor.

"But we don't need to worry about that now, he said separately, so that means the next person won't be for a while. And maybe since Daven is still alive, then he's thinking of a new plan right now," Wyatt said.

"Yeah, let's just enjoy the night and think about this later," Rhochelle pleaded, and Ember sighed.

"Fine, but we have to start trying to think of what he's planning," Ember got back to getting ready. If she was going with Chris, she would've told us. Just like all the other people that are dating, but won't tell us who they're going with. Forrest and Kamille were both already dating, yet they won't tell us who they're going with. Tonight was definitely going to be a night of shock and jealousy.

I got ready as most boys do: in a quarter the time a girl takes. When I was ready, I waited for everyone else, so we were held up another half an hour or so. Finally, we walked down to the cafeteria where the dance was being held. I opened two doors and all of us gasped. The decorations were completely unbelievable, like everything else in our lives. The streamers were flying around the ceiling like there was a small tornado only tall enough to affect the things on the ceiling. Lightning was striking the ground wherever there wasn't a person standing, so people had to look at the ceiling before they could walk around. Sparklers were coming off of the walls and flying around the room like birds on the first day of spring. Confetti wasn't raining down like gravity would normally make it, but it went in any direction; up, down, or sideways.

"This is amazing," Rhochelle smiled and walked off to find her date. I looked around for Nicole, but didn't see any sign of her through the crowd. A DJ in the front of the room was playing songs that were actually popular, unlike the ones a school dance would normally play.

"Daven," a voice cried behind me, and I turned around in slow motion to take in the moment. Nicole's outfit blew my mind away; she was wearing the most amazing dress, it looked like it was stolen from someone on the red carpet or something.

"Wow, Nicole, the most amazing dress . . . ever," I tried to compliment her, but I forgot what verbs were.

"Thanks, you too?" she took me by the hand and led me to the dance floor. When we got there, I got a look at some of the couples and gasped.

CHAPTER FIVE: RAISE THE ROOF

WYATT

I sat at a table with Ion, Lianna, Gabby, Sam, and Craig. We decided to go as a group since we all weren't going to ask anyone. Looking around the room I noticed some of the strangest couples. The only people in our family that had gone with the people that they had been originally dating were Aura and Selene. Forrest came up to us with Caroline, and my mouth dropped.

"Forrest, weren't you dating Alaina, I don't know . . . yesterday?" I asked him.

"Actually, we broke up a couple days ago. I told her that we needed to see other people," Forrest meant Caroline, his previous girlfriend's sister. The two of them walked off, and Kamille and Cobalt came up to us.

"You guys are . . . together?" Ion choked on the words.

"Yeah," Cobalt smiled at Kamille, who sort of returned it.

"That's cool," Ion lied, and Cobalt noticed it. Then Neva walked up to us by himself, and we raised our eyebrows.

"How come you're not with Becca?" Lianna wondered.

"We . . . broke up on Monday," he finally told us. We had assumed that for a couple days, but barely believed it. Ion gasped and stood up.

"Oh my gosh, Neva and Becca broke up!" he shouted, and the whole room gasped and got quiet. Even the music stopped, and Neva turned redder than a tomato.

"Ion, just shut up," Neva said in an angry voice.

"Sorry," he apologized and Neva sat down with our group.

"Oh my gosh," Neva gasped and pointed to a couple on the dance floor.

"What? Where? I don't see," Craig complained.

"Ember, Rhochelle, come here!" I yelled when I saw them with their dates. The two of them came here, red in the face and looking at the floor.

"Introduce your dates to our cousins," Ion said with his teeth gritted, as if their father.

"This is Jerod Anderson," Ember mumbled, and we sat there giving her our "have you gone completely psychotic" faces.

"This is Mac Iron," Rhochelle mumbled so softly that we could only assume that she was saying her date's name. Mac always looked to me like he was from the fifties: he had on his tough façade with jeans and a leather jacket and pretended to be cool to everyone he met.

"Some party, huh?" Mac asked, as if trying to be polite.

"Yeah, it's going to be a real scream," I laughed, and the two couples walked off. It was quiet for a while, and then someone finally broke the silence.

"This is so boring," Sam complained, and Neva and him left. After another minute Dave, Kamille's old boyfriend, came and sat at our group.

"When did you and Kamille break up?" Ion demanded to know, being a little overprotective.

"Two days ago," he said as if he was keeping count.

"Who broke up with whom?" I was curious.

"She broke up with me. She just said that she thought the chemistry between us wasn't working. I don't even get what that means," Dave put his chin in his hand and his elbow on his knee.

"It's girl-talk for she doesn't like you anymore," Gabby said to him sympathetically.

"Well that's just great. She probably just dumped me so that she could go out with Cobalt," Dave sighed.

"Going out, who said anything about going out? They're just on a date for crying out loud," Ion starting freaking out, and Lianna calmed him down.

"I don't know, maybe they'll start going out after this. That's how a lot of relationships start, with a dance or something," I pretended that I was the expert. All of us sat at the table feeling lonely. Then eventually we got up and decided to dance together. Every couple that our family was a part of came to join the group, then we started to feel more comfortable.

The dance got at least five times more fun from the time we saw each couple until now. But I could not accept the fact that Ember liked Jerod and Rhochelle liked Mac. After all the things that Cobalt's brothers had done to us? They had devised that whole fight we had earlier today just to ask Rhochelle to the dance. They weren't invited to the dance, so they shouldn't be asking anyone anyway.

And Jerod was the reason we met Glacthia last year on the plane. He provoked Ember to shoot the flame that caused it to blow up. Who's to say that he hadn't planned for that to happen, he could be working for Glacthia as we speak.

Even though I had serious feelings against Ember and Rhochelle's dates, I had to put them aside to enjoy the dance. It was so much more fun than I thought it would be—I didn't even want to come and now I'm having a great time.

"Aren't you glad you came, Wyatt?" Forrest asked as one of my favorite songs turned on.

"Yeah I guess so," I kept my cool, and our huddle of dancers came closer and closer together.

"Break it up, no dancing like that," a deep voice said and pushed us apart. We turned around to see Chris, Ember's boyfriend, well, previous boyfriend. Ember jumped behind Jerod and moved him to the back of our group.

"Hey, guys," Chris realized who we were and changed his mood completely.

"Chris, what are you doing here?" Rhochelle asked, completely surprised.

"I volunteered to chaperone the dance, they have way too many rules against certain types of dancing. But actually, I came to find Ember—have you guys seen her?" he asked, completely unaware that she was standing about ten feet in front of him but ducked down.

"Um . . . no . . . she's sick and had to stay in our room for the night," Daven answered and Chris sighed.

"That's a shame; I'll go see if she's alright," he walked off and we stopped dancing to make a plan.

"How does he plan on finding me in our room anyway?" Ember wondered.

"He probably has a tracker that can locate you," Selene laughed.

"Probably, I mean I used to like him, but now he's just so invasive. If you guys had said that I was in the bathroom, he would've come in and gotten me," Ember explained and smiled at Jerod.

"I'm on it," Forrest thought for a minute and then nodded his head. "You have a hologram that's going to tell him that you can't talk, and he'll just leave."

"You can't hide that you're not dating him anymore forever," Kamille burst Ember's bubble and she sighed.

"Really Sherlock?" Ember groaned, and we continued dancing.

"Oh my gosh, there's Alaina," Forrest jumped behind Ember, who was standing behind Jerod.

"I thought you told her that you wanted to see other people," Daven reminded him.

"I did, but she doesn't know that I meant her sister," Forrest hid his face until she had completely walked past us. "I need a better disguise." Forrest covered his entire body with a hologram that had the same face as him, except he changed the hair a little and he added a mustache and sideburns. He also made himself taller, made his shoulders grow up to his mouth and his chest out past his chin, and made himself so muscular that he couldn't put his arms down completely.

"How's this?" he posed as if he were about to throw a football and we rolled our eyes. Cocky Forrest—always pretending to be something that he's not. It looked like Caroline was on a date with a professional football player.

"Wow," she smiled, and they started to dance again. We started to dance too, but were interrupted by one of the dates.

"Would you mind if I left for the lavatories?" Mac asked Rhochelle.

"No, go ahead," she seemed as if she was still in shock that she was at a dance with him.

"I'm surprised he knew what a lavatory was," I shook my head when he was gone.

"I'm surprised he knew what mind meant," Cobalt crossed his arms. "There's no way that he just came to be on a date, he must be up to somethi—ow!" Cobalt stopped when Ember hit him in the arm. He turned to see what made her do that, and instantly realized. Rhochelle was turning red and getting angrier by the second.

"There's no way he just came here to be on a date? You mean he's using me? Is that what you think?" she demanded angrily. Everyone slowly walked behind Rhochelle and shook their heads vigorously for Cobalt to say no.

"Rhochelle, he handed me over to Glacthia last year," he answered and we all made faces behind Rhochelle telling him what a bad choice he had just made.

"Well, maybe you should be on Glacthia's side for not giving people a second chance," she threw the corsage that Mac had given her on the ground and ran out. Or at least, ran as fast as a fifteen year old girl in a dress and high heels can run.

"Good job, Cobalt," we all murmured sarcastically in different words.

"How could she be dating my brother, he's a villain?" he made as clear a possible.

"Maybe Rhochelle's right. Maybe he's changed," Ember considered the possibilities.

"I've known my brother for as long as I've been alive and he's been a villain the whole time! He had to fight you just so that he could ask her to this dance. He hates dances and I *know* he's planning something!" Cobalt started yelling now, and everyone turned to stare at us. That alone could've been about the worst thing that happened all night. Everyone noticed Forrest instantly, a couple inches over everyone in our group. People started whispering, "Who's that guy with Caroline?" and, "He doesn't go here . . . is he a teacher?"

"Forrest?" Alaina finally shouted over all of them and the whole dance stopped again, like when Ion told everyone about Neva and Becca being broken up.

"Uh oh," Forrest returned to his normal self and hid behind our group. All eyes were on us, which made things even worse.

"Ember?" Chris shouted from across the room.

"Yeah, that's not good," she hid herself also as Chris and Alaina walked toward our group. When they got here, their reactions were completely different.

"Forrest, I can't believe you dumped me for my sister!" she screamed and pushed Caroline out of the way.

"Ember, I couldn't find you in your room . . . I guess you felt better and decided to come down," he smiled and moved Jerod out of the way. He started to dance with her and she stopped.

"And you—I thought I could trust you and now you're dating my ex-boyfriend!" Alaina yelled at Caroline and pushed her again.

"Ember, what's wrong?" Chris asked when Ember stopped dancing with him.

"Chris, I don't think this is going to work. I think you're a great guy, and I had a great time dating you. But I just feel like we need to see other people," she stole Forrest's excuse, but Chris didn't take it as well as Alaina did.

"You're dating someone behind my back?" Chris asked instantly and our mouths dropped. We, being the spectators of these two fights, had a hard time jumping from fight to fight. It was like watching two tennis matches at the same time. Just when we thought things couldn't get any worse, we heard a crashing of glass. I put up a forcefield out of reflex, but the glass landed somewhere else, away from any victims. We looked up to see Reggie, Johnny, and Ashton, breaking each window.

"I thought Miss Monohan put a forcefield over the ceiling of this room?" Aura shouted over the smashing glass.

"There's a switch in Miss Monohan's office, you can turn it off with that," I explained, thinking of Mac instantly.

"I think Rhochelle might be in danger!" Cobalt turned to rush out the door.

"I don't think so, but there's something else that could be," Miss Monohan put her hand on his shoulder and looked at the falling brothers.

"Okay, don't be afraid. We're here to collect one item and that's it," Reggie said in his booming voice.

"Sorry, but you're not going to get it," Miss Monohan shouted and they raised their eyebrows.

"Excuse me, but that's not the right answer," Ashton pulled a small knife out of his pocket and held it to Miss Monohan's neck. Everyone gasped, and just when I was about to use all the force I could to throw him across the room, I heard something roaring in the hallway.

"I got it boys!" Mac yelled as he flew into the room with rocket shoes. I couldn't see it that well, but once I saw that shape I new what it was. It was the Metronome, in one piece and being stolen by the second most evil people we know.

"He's got the Metronome!" I shouted, and the whole school knew what I was talking about. At least forty powers were shot at him, and he went down in an instant. I teleported the Metronome to myself before he hit the ground and put a forcefield around him. But when I looked down to see if I had it I was holding something else.

"Guys, I don't have it," I showed them the thing I was holding, and accidentally let go of the forcefield. Mac got back up when I wasn't even looking and flew past me, taking whatever I was holding and flying out the ceiling window. Reggie carried Johnny and Ashton out and we all got into our flying positions. I lifted myself out of the room, but when I reached outside I became enveloped in darkness.

"Ember, I can't see!" each of us said in our own words. Ember and Ion led the way and Forrest sniffed for their scent. But when we got close to the roof we heard something that couldn't have been good.

"That's for taking my girlfriend," Chris said as he grabbed Jerod from off of his weight a plummeted toward the ground.

"How could you? I can't believe you're my sister!" Alaina pushed Caroline off her soccer ball and they both fell down. Ember and Forrest dove down and we were left by ourselves.

"We don't have enough light," Ion confirmed for us.

"And we lost our trail," Neva sighed.

"We have to get them," Selene told us, and someone backed her up.

"Are you kidding? Do you know what that thing was that Mac had? It was a model of the Metronome," Daven said, but we weren't following. "On the roof, there's something you can set up so that you can turn models of things into the real thing. If we don't stop them they'll have the real Metronome. Who knows? They could have more than one Metronome. They could have a hundred."

"What would they do with—" Aura was stopped for asking such a stupid question. We flew to the roof and got there just as they were typing in the settings.

"We're not going to make it," Gabby said, who, along with Sam, were the only Venturas that could fly.

"I will," I told them and teleported into the machine just as it was beginning to spin.

"Hey what's he doing here?" Reggie asked in a somewhat unintelligent voice.

"Get him," Mac ordered, but I put myself in a forcefield.

"We can't, he's in a forcefield," Ashton said to Mac, but realized that Mac already knew that.

"What should we do?" Reggie questioned their leader, almost smiling.

"Let's change the settings," Mac smiled, and started pressing new buttons.

"Wait, I could teleport you into space right now if I wanted," I threatened, but they laughed.

"We know you're just a good kid who wouldn't hurt a fly," the brothers lifted my forcefield and threw me out the door when it opened. Without even wanting to look at where I was I turned invisible and teleported back into the elevator.

"Do you think we actually killed him?" Ashton actually sounded nervous.

"Nah, we just changed what was on the roof, it's still the same dimension, he could just fly away and find his little family and tell them what happened. That is, if the giant six headed octopus monster doesn't eat him," Johnny explained as I gulped.

"Which is why we have to get the Metronome before those rotten brats," Mac explained.

"Got it," Reggie answered. The machine finally came to a halt and they opened the door. The machine looked like two top halves of an hourglass, each floating over a different table. One table was for the model of an object and the other was where the real one would appear. Instantly my siblings came out from the sky and landed on the ceiling.

"Distract them," Mac whispered and ducked down. Reggie started inflating to block all of their powers. I snuck up on Mac and grabbed the model of the Metronome right out of his hands. He reacted and punched me in the mouth, taking the Metronome back. I put my hand to my mouth and turned visible.

"You!" he shouted and punched me again. I was bleeding severely now and the machine turned on.

"What's your problem?" I shoved him as hard as I could. He flew back because I added a little of my powers to it and then he stopped with his heels on the edge of the building. Mac wobbled a little then fell back. I gasped and ran to the side, afraid that I had killed him. He had fallen onto the top step, the roof of the power practice room. When I turned back around knowing that he was okay, I gasped again. Ashton had put the model of the Metronome on the table and each table had an energy field around them.

"Oh crud," I told myself as the whole Medlocks building began to shake. Ashton was smiling to himself, and then he turned back to the fight. I lifted him up and put him where Mac was. The only way he could get back to us was by climbing a ten foot wall or jumping down twenty eight more ten foot walls and then climbing twenty nine flights of stairs.

"It's ready!" Johnny said a little too loudly. Everyone started pushing each other and moving closer to the Metronome. When the forcefield turned off, a foot came out of nowhere and kicked it. The Metronome went flying so far that the darkness covered it and we couldn't see it anymore. We looked up to see Ember using rocket shoes and behind her, a group of people fell to the ground fighting.

"Grab them!" Forrest yelled as Reggie and Johnny were flying away. We shot whatever we could at them but they moved down to pick up Mac and Ashton. None of them could fly, but when Reggie inflated himself enough, he rose. It was a slow way to fly, but we didn't stop them.

"Come on, we have to get back to the dance," I reminded them.

"What do you think will happen since we broke the Metronome?" Aura asked.

"Well it wasn't turned on and no powers were in it, so nothing I hope," Forrest tried to make us all feel better. The fifteen of us went back to the dance and tried to enjoy the rest of our night.

CHAPTER SIX: THE DISAPPEARING ACT

SELENE

The dance ended that night in silence; no one was in the mood to dance. After that, the routine went back to normal. Glacthia hadn't shown up yet, or at least, shown up physically. The Iron brothers hadn't shown up either, it usually took them a while to think of a new plan as good as trying to make their own Metronome. Classes continued to get harder and homework piled up. Projects and essays were constant—with seventeen classes and seventeen different teachers, there's no telling how much homework they could give. The schedule introduced at the beginning of last year where we only have a class once a week was helping a lot. If we did get homework, we always had about seven days to do it.

A few weeks passed, the older kids' birthday was coming up. Soon they would be able to take their driver's test. In the middle of October, the weather cooled down at a pace that we weren't enjoying. Everyone's love life changed, the people who had dates to the dance completely altered who they were going out with now. Daven continued to go out with Nicole, Aura and I kept our old boyfriends, while everyone else ended up alone.

We were on our way to power practice one afternoon. It was our last class of the day and our homework planners were running out of room to write down all our homework. So far none of the projects we've done yet had been that interesting, considering our classes were excruciatingly boring.

"I wish we could do something fun today," I said to Aura and Kamille, the only people in our family that were in my class. Craig was just old enough to be in Cobalt and Ion's classes. Sam, Gabby, and Lianna were in the same classes as my older siblings.

"We always do something fun in power practice; it's the only class we get to use our powers," Kamille laughed.

"How come you haven't asked Cobalt out yet?" Aura brought up. The two of them were acting all nervous around each other. Kamille even sometimes went outside and flew in the windows of our classes to avoid him.

"I told you! I don't like him like that. When he asked me to the dance, I didn't feel like hurting his feelings," Kamille explained.

"Sure," I laughed and nudged Aura.

"If it were me, I wouldn't be torturing myself like that. I would say 'uh . . . no you weirdo,' and that would be it," Aura said in her usual straight up way and we rolled our eyes. Pushing the door open, we saw the older kids walking out, which was probably a once in a school year thing. The probability of having a class right after the older kids was less likely than not getting homework in any of our classes for a whole day.

"The best class ever," Wyatt whispered to us, smiling.

"What'd you do?" I had to ask, knowing what answer I would get.

"You'll see," Sam left us without an answer and they walked away.

"Sit down, sit down," Mr. Williams ushered us. "Come on guys I have an important announcement." Everyone found their seats and quieted down.

"We are going to start a project," he started off, and we all groaned.

"Great, the older kids like projects now. Remind me not to grow up," Kamille told us.

"Kamille, would you let me finish?" Mr. Williams put her on the spot and she turned red. "Anyway, this isn't just some boring project that no one will want to do. Since we've been learning a lot about Immortals, I went to the Planet of Immortality and pulled a few strings." Immortals were people that had done such great deeds that they were granted immortality by the Ancestors themselves. Usually, they were people that went back in time to save history, but since most of them got seen by humans they are known on Earth as legendary figures, which is Miss Monohan's power. Most Immortals are Greek and Roman gods to Earth people, but to us, they're just citizens who saved history and were granted immortality.

"Each of you will be assigned an Immortal that matches your power to be your mentor. You and that person will create a presentation using both of your powers. It can be a dance, a reenactment of what that Immortal did to gain immortality, a talent show, or just a presentation on what you learned by having an Immortal as your mentor. I will now read you your mentor and you will meet with them tomorrow morning in the front of the school at nine a.m." Mr. Williams read off the names of the kids in our class. Finally he got down to us and we crossed our fingers.

"Aura Barker, Aeolus, Selene Barker, Houdini, Kamille Barker, Irene," Mr. Williams continued with the rest of the names and I gasped. When the class ended I jumped out of the room shouting and dancing.

"I got Houdini, he's a magician, this is gonna be awesome," I sang as Kamille and Aura rolled their eyes.

"Lucky, we both got a Greek or Roman god and goddess," Aura sighed. "I've never even heard of Aeolus, the god of all winds. I don't even know who that is."

"Yeah, and Irene is just the goddess of peace," Kamille sighed. We ran to our room and asked who got who. The Venturas were there as well and we learned who they had gotten. Wyatt got Neptune, Forrest got Mother Nature, Neva got Jack Frost, Ion got Zeus, and everyone else just got gods and goddesses that we had never heard of.

"I'm definitely doing a magic show for our presentation," I smiled and some other people glared at me.

I was restless about meeting Houdini tomorrow. I spent all night studying up on him so that I could pretend that I knew a lot about him. He was a Medlocks graduate, while at the same time going to a school on Earth. He fooled the entire Earth population by making them think that he was a real human. Houdini dedicated his whole life to one big trick: his disappearing act. He became extremely famous, did one huge show, and then faked his death with some sickness. In actuality, he really just teleported back to one of the planets. The Ancestors realized that after his show, the world became intrigued by what they called "magic." It also made humans more interested in science, which the Ancestors were proud of because they know that humans are far less technologically advanced than us. It has been a goal of the Ancestors since the beginning of humankind to have the Altrians and the humans one day living in peace. Once humans became interested in magic and the world of illusion, the Ancestors granted Houdini his immortality. The weirdest part was that he "died" on Halloween.

The next morning, the whole school stood on the front of the building and waited for the space ship to arrive. It didn't bother to land on the airport. The ship just lowered itself down until it was on the ground. About a hundred people walked out, only one third of the school didn't have a partner for their project. They all looked like they've had thousands of years of experience in their lives, while still looking like they were in their thirties or forties. Houdini stood out like a sore thumb; he was one of the latest people to become Immortals, along with Martin Luther King Junior and Neil Armstrong. Everyone else was either a legendary figure or a god or goddess from ancient times, so they were dressed like they were from that time as well. Some of the ones that people in my family had were also obvious. Jack Frost really was covered in ice, and Neptune had a huge merman tail. Mother Nature's dress looked like the dress of a conservative queen, and she had at least four birds on her shoulder. Basically everyone looked just like people had drawn them, since they were the only Altrians that humans know about. As they walked past us, looking for their students I tried to guess who each of them were with Kamille and Aura.

"I bet that's David, you know, the one who defeated goliath," I pointed to the tallest most muscular person in the field.

"I bet that's Santa Claus," Kamille pointed to Santa Claus and we looked at her. Since she had a serious face on we rolled our eyes and laughed.

"Doesn't that kinda look like Einstein," Aura pointed to a man walking past us.

"Duh, who better to make the theory of relativity than someone who's experienced it," Forrest whispered to us.

"Isn't that Neil Armstrong?" Gabby asked us and we squinted at a guy in the back.

"Yeah, I have him, his power is the same as mine, survival on the moon. I learned from the AIS that something actually went wrong with his space shuttle. If that wasn't his power, then he would've died," Kayla Centone said, just coincidentally standing behind us. The AIS was the Altrian Internet Service, it's the internet that we can use and humans can't. It has all the things that the Internet on Earth doesn't. We can learn about what really happened to the famous people, listings of

Altrians, everything you would need to learn about secrets that humans don't know about.

"None of these people saved history though," Ember pointed out.

"That's what you think. How do you know they didn't? Something terrible probably happened, and they went back in time and stopped it from happening," Aura guessed.

"People can also become Immortals by helping humans make extreme advances in science and math. Earth would be nothing like it is today if it weren't for Altrians secretly helping out. Galileo, Columbus, Newton . . . all of those people became Immortals," Mr. Williams explained from behind us.

"I should've gotten Newton, gravity fits perfectly with him," I sighed.

"He studied motion," Rhochelle pointed out. I shushed them all because I was too shy to think of a comeback. Houdini walked up to us and I introduced myself.

"I'm Selene," I held out my hand for him to shake it and he kissed it.

"Hello, I'm Ehrich Weiss," he exclaimed and we raised our eyebrows.

"I thought you were Harry Houdini?" Wyatt asked.

"That was my disguised Earth name for the humans. I made sure that no one knew anything about me, but some things slipped. If you look on the Earth Internet you'll find at least three different answers for where I was born, how I died, and the spelling of my real name," he laughed and pulled a flower out from behind my ear and gave it to me.

"Thanks," I smiled and twirled the daisy in my hand. Everyone else met up with their mentors, and we showed them to our tree house. I was curious about how the other families found places for their mentors, but decided not to ask.

"Now what should we do?" Ember wondered.

"I think we should probably get started on our projects, it's barely noon and no one has any other projects to do," Daven said. If the older kids didn't have projects, then no one did, since their classes were the hardest.

"Well if you'll excuse us, Ehrich and I have a magic show to think of," I told them as the two of us left to find a place to work.

"So what tricks do you know?" I asked Ehrich when we were standing on top of the huge rock where Rhochelle's room was.

"I was thinking about some of the tricks we should do for the show, and I think they should be top notch, since even the most amazing tricks on Earth will be worthless to you. Now that means that I'll have to think of some completely new tricks, things that even Altrians will doubt. And I've got just the perfect idea," he smiled a clever smile and we got to work.

Everyone, even people who normally procrastinate, eagerly got to work on their presentations. To work with someone who has such power and knowledge is just amazing by itself. I had so much fun working with Ehrich. I only got to participate in a couple of his tricks, the others I just stood there and smiled at our future audience. But the things he could think of were just phenomenal, even with my power and his power of reality, his tricks still seemed impossible. It was my idea to do it in a room that we would convince everyone to be powerless. That way, we can do human tricks and still get the audience amazed. His tricks were mostly escape tricks, but he had the strangest card tricks and even tricks with animals. One day while practicing, Ehrich thought of a trick that would amaze the crowd so much that their hands would get tired from clapping. We decided to make it our finale, and we practiced it so many times that I could've done it myself.

"Our show is an A plus before we even get to the second trick," I said one day at lunch.

"Neptune and I are doing a water show," Wyatt explained.

"Aeolus and I are doing something like that, but with wind," Aura told us.

"Mother Nature and I are doing a reenactment of what caused Meteor Crater in Arizona," Forrest said and we made confused faces.

"Wasn't that a meteor?" Cobalt asked.

"That's what humans say, but it has something to do with how Mother Nature saved history," Forrest smiled and we acted impressed.

"That's cool, but Jack Frost and I are going to kick all your butts with our amazing icicle drawing," Neva told us, and we rolled our eyes.

"We made a reenactment of how Irene became an Immortal as well, she ended World War I," Kamille nodded her head.

"Everything we learn about history is a lie," Ember realized.

"Yeah, you're right. A lot of things we learn are lies," Ion pointed out and everyone thought for a minute.

"But at least we're in the loop," Rhochelle smiled.

"Yeah, good thing," I laughed.

"Hey, do you guys wanna go to The Arcade?" Neva asked, and our eyes widened and all of us smiled.

Within ten minutes, we were at the door of The Arcade. It wasn't that crowded, being the day before the project was due and all. I asked Ehrich to come with us, and he happily came. Everyone played games for about an hour until Ember wanted to show us a really cool game. It was virtual reality, but not the kind that humans would think of. In this game you *actually* went inside it. The game was set on an uninhabited planet, with all types of creatures trying to colonize there. Basically, you had to start a small colony, and then fight off aliens trying to conquer your territory. But you also had to steal their territory as well, which usually took a few hours.

"Okay, are you guys ready?" Ember asked, starting the game.

"Yes," Ehrich answered.

"Here we go," she pressed a couple buttons and we fell through a portal. I landed softly on the ground since I lowered the gravity, but everyone else hit it hard.

"Okay, older guys and the older Venturas, go around and map out the area. Everyone else, let's work on the campsite," Aura started pulling tools out of her pocket. Each player started out with the regular supplies in their pocket. Aura put a small probe on the ground and activated it. Instantly a robot person unfolded and awaited its orders.

"Can you make the mining building right about there?" I handed it one of the probes in my pocket and it got to work. Within minutes it was mining the area and a small hologram on the top was showing us how much we had. It felt like a computer game, since the robot only had to dig about a foot to find gold.

"What should we do now?" Ehrich inquired.

"I'm not sure; this is my first time playing this," I told him. Right when I said that, I heard a rustle in the bushes behind us.

"Guys, I think we have invaders. Everyone get ready," I told them. It was Cobalt, Ion, Aura, Kamille, Craig, the Immortals, and me, so we had a pretty good chance. But when this creature came out we got so scared that we couldn't use our powers. It had fangs like a snake, teeth like a shark, and drool dripping like a Saint Bernard.

"Get back, it's a scelum," Kamille shouted and everyone stepped back.

"Someone kill it," Craig said nervously.

"I got it," Neptune "walked" forward and shot water at it. Immediately it lunged, flipping over the water and running toward us. No one's powers worked on it for some reason. There was something wrong about that creature. Before anyone could stop it, the scelum dove at Ehrich and the next second seemed to go by in slow motion. Ehrich swiped his arm in front of the scelum, expecting it to disappear. It worked, but just as it faded away, it bit him in the arm and he went down. He dissolved away and my eyes widened.

"Ehrich!" I shouted and pressed a button on my belt. It took everyone a while to come out. One of them must've called for the older kids to get out, making them take longer.

"I think he's really hurt," I said, standing over him. There was blood all over his arm, and his jacket was ripped through all the way to the skin.

"Let's go to the nurse," Wyatt teleported him to the nurse's office, a place we've all been too many times.

"What happened?" the nurse asked.

"We were at The Arcade and he got bit by a scelum in a virtual reality video game!" I yelled, even though it only increased the tension. She sighed, wishing we hadn't been out playing video games on a school night.

"Okay, I'll fix this. You just come back in the morning to get him," she explained and we nodded, it was the usual drill for injuries like this. As we walked out we tried to make sense of it.

"Do you think scelums can carry diseases?" Gabby wondered nervously.

"I don't know, but that one definitely seemed like it had rabies," I nodded.

"Wait a minute; you can't get hurt in a virtual reality game. They wouldn't make it like that," Forrest realized. The rest of us thought about it and agreed with him.

"You're right, no arcade would buy it," Sam thought.

"Guys, it's just a video game. He's going to be fine—so get over it," Ember ordered us and we headed for our rooms. I spent the rest of the night trying to fall asleep. If our magic show went wrong, not only would we fail, but someone could get really hurt. People need their hands to use their powers, especially Ehrich, who's a very good showman. He's used to waving his hands around his magic tricks for emphasis.

The following morning, it poured; it didn't feel like a good day. I picked Ehrich up from the nurse's office, and he seemed fine. He almost yelled at me when I brought up cancelling the magic show. I made a nervous face and decided to agree with him.

Everyone was getting out of school for the whole day since some kids who shared an Immortal weren't in the same class. The presentations were going to be held in the cafeteria, since it was the biggest room in Medlocks.

"Andrew Anderson," Miss Monohan called. Andrew stepped onto the stage that wasn't there this morning with sweat dripping down his face. His Immortal followed him and they did their act. This continued for a while until it got to our family. Aura went first, her show was really amazing. She and Aeolus flew around the stage leaving trails of colored sprinkles. They spun around each other and made shapes with the sprinkles. Then it was Daven, Ember, Forrest, Ion, Kamille, Neva, and Rhochelle. I knew I was next, and told Ehrich to get ready.

"Selene Barker," Miss Monohan said and my mouth dropped.

"Yes," I smiled as Ehrich and I headed for the stage. I had set up all the stuff backstage while they were building it with whoever had the power to make stages appear.

"Trick one, the disappearing wallet trick," Ehrich said to me as we got on our costumes. I didn't need to assist him for that; I just stood there and looked pretty. Ehrich introduced himself, explaining what he could do with his powers so the audience would know if his tricks were just a use of his power, or real magic. Then he asked everyone in the audience to check their pockets. He asked if any of them were missing anything, and all of them said no. Suddenly he pulled a wallet out of his pocket and asked who it was. A boy from the audience came up and retrieved his wallet. I had no idea how he did that trick, but I wasn't as amazed as the audience.

"For my next trick, I will use my lovely assistant," he motioned for me to step forward and I did. This trick was hard for me, the only time I had to use my powers.

"What's your power, miss?" he asked for the millionth time, like in all of our rehearsals.

"Gravity and temperature," I told him with a smile, as if this were all new to me.

"Well could you levitate this huge water tank filled with piranhas?" he wondered, and I automatically lowered its gravity significantly.

But suddenly, before it would have lifted off the ground, a bouquet of flowers appeared in my hands. My eyes widened, he hadn't told me about that in the rehearsals.

"I guess you got the wrong power. No matter," he clapped his hands and the tanks rose from under the stage. It was like a small pool, circular, about five feet off the ground, and ten feet in diameter.

"Does anyone have something in their pocket that they wouldn't mind getting rid of?" Everyone raised their hands and Ehrich called a small girl in the front row. She came up holding a pencil, and Ehrich asked her to drop it into the tank. She did as he said and the piranhas shredded it to bits.

"These piranhas are very hungry, they would eat anything. Miss," he waved for me to walk backstage and lower a box from the ceiling. It lowered down and he grabbed it, it was filled with locks and chains. He helped me lock him up and then I lowered a hook. He grabbed it and I lifted it back up. Ehrich swung a little then jumped into the pool. Everyone gasped as a small tarp fell on top of it.

"What are you guys so afraid of?" a voice said from the back of the room, and everyone turned to see Ehrich walking up the aisle. He got back to the stage and announced his next trick.

"Does anyone have the power to generate electricity, and can have electricity put on them without it hurting them?" he asked, centering on my family since he knew all their powers. Ion raised his hand and came up. I wheeled out a dangerous looking machine that had a bunch of needles on the inside of a glass sphere all pointing at one spot on the ground.

"Does anyone know what a cotton gin is?" Ehrich asked the audience, and some of them raised their hands. "The cotton plant goes in one end, it grinds it up, and seedless cotton comes out the other. He signaled for me to wheel out the cotton gin, and I followed his directions. He led Ion to the sphere with all the needles and turned it on. All of the needles shot little bolts of lightning at that one spot.

"Can you tell me if that's real lightning?" Ehrich questioned him, and Ion put his finger in it.

"Yeah, it's real," Ion told the audience and walked back to his seat.

"I bid you adieu," he stepped into the sphere and I turned it on. The lightning struck him and smoke came up everyone. Everyone got quiet and I turned it off. I walked inside it and picked up a small, white bunny. A couple people awed, but it wasn't over. I put the bunny into the cotton gin and turned it on. We saw the spinning blades do the most horrible thing to the bunny, causing the entire audience to gasp. Then out of the bottom of the cotton gin fell Ehrich. Everyone cheered and clapped, amazed by his performance.

"For my last trick, I will include my lovely assistant in more than just turning on the machines. Step forward please," he gestured for me to walk forward. He wheeled out a big box, about ten feet long, four feet wide, and two feet tall, standing on a cart the same size, but taller.

"I am going to perform a trick that you are aware to be very dangerous, but don't worry, I'm a professional." He made sure I was ready, and then I got into the box. I looked for one last time at the crowd, and noticed Connor walking toward where my siblings sat. He whispered something to them, and they shook their heads and smiled.

"Now, I am going to count to three, and my assistant will be in the exact position so that these swords won't hurt her. One, two . . ." I got into the position that we had practiced, taking notice in the holes where the swords were going to be put through. "Three!" The first sword went through, nowhere near me. A pause, and then another sword went through. My eyes widened, it didn't go through one of the holes that we had planned. Another pause and then one went through the part of my dress that was lying beside me. Instantly, I started screaming, this had to be a different Ehrich. It didn't matter who it was, if it wasn't someone I practiced the trick with, the sword would easily pierce me.

"For my final trick . . . I will . . . disappear!" I started to spin and then was teleported. The whole time I screamed. The person kidnapping me was someone I certainly did not know. He also had at least ten swords in his possession.

CHAPTER SEVEN: HOME FOR THE SHOW

COBALT

The disappearing act became a huge deal in the news. If we hadn't convinced Miss Monohan that Ehrich was possessed by Glacthia, the Ancestors would've taken away his immortality. We had no way of finding Selene.

"I've got the newspaper," Neva held it up, walking into the secret base and throwing the rubber band at Ember.

"What does it say?" I asked.

"Nothing . . . nothing . . . nothing," Neva skimmed through it and sighed.

"Let me see," Ember took it from them and flipped through the pages. Ember read silently while Rhochelle lifted the rock under her off the ground to read over her shoulder.

"There are morbus, whatever they are, missing around the universe. Scientists say they may have died out by not getting enough blood to drink." Rhochelle looked around for other interesting topics. "Reports of people losing their powers for short time periods . . . hey that happened to us! I wonder if something's wrong." There was another pause, and Ember finally found a topic worthy of saying aloud.

"'Driver's tests are available for anyone above the age of sixteen! Permit test required.' We should do that when we turn sixteen in a month," Ember smiled at Neva and Rhochelle, but they glared back at her for getting distracted from the ultimate goal. Everyone else was off searching the island. I should have gone with Ion and Kamille, but they left while I didn't know the plan. The oldest four Venturas didn't have their licenses either. The driving age on Callidus was eighteen, and they were sixteen. They decided that when the older Barkers turned sixteen, they would take it with them.

"Nothing about . . . what we are looking for?" I asked and everyone rolled their eyes.

"We're looking for . . . robberies, magic shows gone wrong . . . I don't know," Ember tried to explain it.

"There's nothing here," I sighed, and the three kids who acted like older siblings to me stared at the floor in sadness.

Four days went by, newspaper after newspaper turned out unhelpful. We missed Selene more than anything, and there was nothing we could do to find her. There was nothing harder than losing a triplet, I could tell by Kamille's eyes. The more and more time went by, the more we began to panic that something big was going to happen.

One morning, I was sitting in a room with Kamille, Aura, and Ion doing homework. This work made me sick. It was like our teachers didn't even care about Selene missing. I got up to take a break and then suddenly an idea came to mind.

"Mr. Williams has the human tracker!" I yelled and the four of us jumped up and ran to the Venturas' floor. We skipped every other step and didn't even need to catch our breaths.

"Mr. Williams! Mr. Williams!" Aura shouted as soon as we entered the classroom. He sat at his desk facing the control panel. We had never felt so anxious than we did right now.

"Can we use that power tracker to find out where Selene is?" Kamille said in her nice voice. Between her power for creating peace between people and her insanely nice attitude, no one could resist denying her what she wanted.

"I'm afraid that that's impossible. It was banned from power practice rooms because villains could use it to track people hiding from them." Mr. Williams felt bad, we could tell, but it just wasn't enough for us.

"But doesn't it kind of do more good than evil?" Ion started to raise his voice and Mr. Williams refrained from getting him in trouble because he understood our pain.

"I'm on your side, but sadly the program was already removed over the summer," Mr. Williams tried to look away; Aura and Kamille's eyes began to swell up with tears.

"But isn't there some way you can get it back, even if it isn't . . . allowed?" Aura started to beg, and Mr. Williams knew he was in an awkward position.

"Aura, I understand that you're upset, but I honestly can't help you," he looked down and away.

"Don't you realize that our sister could be out there dying right now? What kind of monster are you to deny us a chance to at least help her? And that's just to say if she's not dead already! Can't you just help us?" Kamille started bawling now, and I grabbed her hand.

"Kamille, he knows you miss her, we all do. Come on, it's okay." I've never felt so emotionally helpful in my life, and I knew Kamille would be grateful when she looked back, but right now she wasn't ready to accept anything as helpful other than us finding Selene.

"I used to look up to you—now you're worthless to me," Kamille glared at Mr. Williams and Ion and I had to pull her out. Aura followed, tears soaking the sides of her face. This was really an unexpected turn for the worst; Kamille had been so nice before. I now know that I will never underestimate the bond between triplets again.

Just as we walked out, the parrot-like delivery creature that drops off the mail used its tail to throw the newspaper in the window on the top floor of Medlocks. It instantly multiplied into about twenty newspapers, and I picked one up. I threw the rubber band off it, but Ion took it from me and flipped through it. There was nothing for a while, and we started to lose hope. But in the bottom corner of the ads we saw something that made us jump out the window, literally. I grabbed Kamille's hand and created a metal sled under us. We jumped in the window of our floor and ran to our room. Ion beat Kamille, Aura, and me by a lot, but eventually we got to the tree house.

"Guys, guys!" we screamed when I got to ground and Ion had been slowly regaining his sense of balance. He tended to lose consciousness a little when he was traveling at light speed, so it took him a second to get back.

"What?" some of them asked in a bad mood.

"We found it!" Ion held up the newspaper and they all ran over to it.

"Magic show on Callidus, Friday, October 13. It's a Friday the thirteenth, but still, it's only a week away," I added, and they all seemed as if the color had just been restored in the universe.

"That's great, now we just have to have a plan," Rhochelle smiled and looked at us.

"I have an idea," Neva started running up the stairs and we followed him.

"Wait, tell us your plan," Forrest shouted as we ran up the stairs. Neva turned on the second floor and ran into the main room. All of us followed him until he got to Miss Monohan's office and held his hands up to get us to stop. He knocked on the door lightly and waited for the answer.

"Come in," Miss Monohan called and he opened the door.

"Miss Monohan, I . . . we . . . were thinking a lot about Selene. We think that we need to spend some time with our parents. It's going to be hard for all of us. We'll probably need a whole week, if that's okay. We'll get all of our homework for the days that we miss, and be back for class next Monday," Neva looked at the ground and Miss Monohan made that face that girls always make when they feel sorry for someone.

"Aw, sure, you go visit your parents, I don't mind. And you take your time on that work, okay?" she asked and we nodded, our eyes watering. We went one floor up at a time to get all of our work. By the time we were at the Venturas' floor we had folders of homework. We were all set to go, then realized that it was almost midnight. It took us from mid-afternoon to midnight to get our homework from seventeen classes. Each teacher practically gave us the whole lesson before giving us our homework, so it took almost a while for each one. We didn't want to give Mr. and Mrs. Barker the wrong impression by barging into their house at midnight, so we decided to leave the next morning.

When I woke up on the Sunday morning I found the Barkers and got ready to go. The Venturas were ready as well, so we gathered on the front steps and left. We didn't talk at all on the plane ride, and it took a little over an hour to get there. We arrived at the airport on Callidus and just flew to Mr. and Mrs. Barker's house.

"Mom, Dad?" Wyatt said into his watch and it took a couple minutes for them to come. For some reason, he felt no desire to ring the doorbell.

"Guys, what are you doing here?" Mrs. Barker didn't have the slightest bit of worry, but then she counted us and gasped.

"Where is Selene?" Mr. Barker realized it as well.

"Why don't you sit down and we'll explain everything," Forrest warned them and we headed for the dining room.

"Selene had Ehrich for her Immortal project, so she decided to do a magic show for her presentation. Well, Ehrich got possessed by Glacthia at the show and . . ." Ember looked at Mom, who got so nervous that she grabbed Mr. Barker's arm and her eyes watered.

"And he kidnapped them," Daven finished her sentence.

"We couldn't find them for a while," Gabby stared at the floor tiles.

"We checked every newspaper for the past four days," Aura continued the chain sentence.

"Then this one ad turned up," I said that part that I had discovered.

"And there's a magic show this Friday," Ember started to pick up the mood of the story.

"So we're going to stay with you for the week," Wyatt told them.

"Then on Friday, we'll get them back. We promise," Sam finished it.

"Now hold on just a minute," Mr. Barker started. "How do you know what Glacthia's capable of while he's possessing Ehrich?" We could tell that he didn't know who Ehrich was, so we filled him in some more.

"Ehrich is Harry Houdini, so he's pretty much capable of anything," Forrest tried not to say that too loudly, hoping that maybe they wouldn't hear him.

"But if we take Selene before the show, we might be able to escape," Lianna tried to think positively, but we pretty much had no plan.

"I have the perfect idea," Mrs. Barker suggested, and led us to the power simulator. "There's something on this that lets me pick the power of the person you're fighting if I wanted to. If I set it for illusions, along with all eight of Glacthia's powers, we'll see if you can stand him." Mrs. Barker clicked on a couple things, then sighed.

"Oh, it has to download all of the things that the villain can do with those powers. It says here that it'll take at least twenty four hours. Tomorrow we'll start it up and test it."

"That's okay, we'll just hang out 'til tomorrow and wait," I decided for us.

The next morning after breakfast it was finally ready. We gathered around the power simulator until Mrs. Barker told us to go in.

"Are you guys ready?" Mr. Barker asked nervously and we nodded. He flipped a switch and someone who looked a lot like Glacthia appeared hovering over us. Everyone got into the air except Lianna and Craig.

Glacthia started to do the weirdest things—things that we didn't even know Houdini could do. It was like being in one of those nightmares where you have a villain who could defeat you in half a second, but chooses to toy with you until you can't take it anymore.

"What's our plan?" Ember wondered as he started to shoot fire at us. She led it away with one swipe of her hand, turning it around and sending it back at him. He blocked it with a forcefield and shot hypersonic blasts at us, Mrs. Barker's power.

"Ahh!" I yelled and covered my ears. Rhochelle threw a rock at him and hit him square in the face. His neck bent back in the grossest way and everyone looked away. There was a cracking noise and then it was back to normal. I shuddered and turned back to look at him. He was changing into an animal, but not just one animal. When he was done changing, we stopped and stared at him. He was made of so many different animals, like a mix of all the best. There were at least four different kinds of teeth, with a wolf snout and nose. Then it had a body sort of like a horse with legs like one as well. The front feet were horse hooves, and the back feet were cheetah's paws. It had a dolphin tail, and a scorpion tail that curled up around. The most noticeable thing about the animal was the huge wings, probably bigger than albatross wings. It looked like the wings of a flying horse. The creature flew at us and Wyatt shot water at it. With a small shriek, the animal stepped back, and then lifted its scorpion tail. All of us ducked down, and the acid started to shoot out like a water gun.

"Someone just kill the thing!" Ember shot fire at it and it was moved away by the creature.

"I'm on it," Rhochelle shot a ton of lasers at it, but a forcefield appeared in front of it. Kamille touched the floor and a dimensional portal opened up. This was part of Mr. Barker's power of dimensions. He can travel through the dimension of space by opening up portals, kind of like bending the space so that it becomes closer.

The fight continued with everyone using everything they had against him. Sam created tornadoes, Ion struck him with lighting. Somehow Glacthia could always be one step ahead of us and still fight back.

When everyone tried their best, Forrest closed his eyes and put his hands out. Everyone stopped, including the creature, staying on four legs and in a jumping position. Then it started to look sick and leaned to one side and fell over. It felt like there was less oxygen in the room, and the lights flickered a little. Wind picked up, and Forrest's hair starting to rise and the color left him. We all put our hands up to stop the wind from knocking us down. The creature started breathing heavily. Finally the lights blacked out and his heavy breathing stopped. Mr. and Mrs. Barker lifted an emergency power switch and the lights turned back on.

Forrest was on the ground unconscious, and everyone ran to the creature. I felt for a heartbeat, but couldn't feel anything. The heart might've been in a different place, but if it's a mix of all of these animals then it would be in the same spot that it is for most Earth animals.

"It's dead," I exclaimed, and all of us ran back to Forrest. The Barkers' parents turned off the power simulator and the animal disappeared.

"His heart's barely beating," Mrs. Barker said with her hand to her mouth.

"We have to get him to his room; he probably just needs some rest," Wyatt lifted him with his mind and we brought him to his room. A few minutes after the entire episode we were discussing the situation in the living room.

"Could you imagine having the power to take away people's lives?" Neva asked, sitting on one of the couches and looking at the floor.

"I couldn't," Craig said, and we all smiled for a second.

"But what if he got really good at it. What if he used it for the wrong reasons?" Wyatt thought for a second then no one talked for a while.

"I just hope he's okay," Craig said in a nice voice, the one that we had supposed to be his own. Barely any one every heard Craig talk, with Ion and me he just listened and absorbed.

"That's such a strong power, I'm glad Glacthia doesn't have it," Ember told everyone, even though they had already been thinking about that.

"Forrest is gonna be okay," Mr. Barker said, walking into the room and sitting down with Mrs. Barker on another one of the couches.

"Are we still going to the magic show on Friday?" Ion asked, and everyone had to think about it for a while.

"Well, it's only Monday, and Forrest will be fine by then. You guys have to at least give a try to save Selene. We have a lot of faith in you, but if there is a chance that you don't succeed . . ." Mrs. Barker started to cry and Mr. Barker had to take her out of the room. It left the rest of us silent for a while, and no one had anything else to say.

"What are we gonna do for the rest of the week?" Kamille questioned our group, and we sighed, realizing that we forgot about that.

"We have no choice—we have to keep practicing," Daven made our reluctant decision final.

Every day for the rest of week, we were constantly in the power simulator. We had told Forrest that he couldn't kill Glacthia even if he was beating us. Our last resource was to turn it off, since Forrest's power was still too dangerous for him to use. Mr. and Mrs. Barker said that the only reason he lived was because the creature wasn't real, just a simulation. But whenever we got better, it just used harder moves on us. Houdini could make holograms appear out of nowhere, and then turn them into real things. It was the ultimate combination of Ehrich and Forrest's power.

"Are we almost done? This is good enough for now!" Aura shouted when we were fighting the creature on Thursday night.

"Good enough for now isn't good enough. This is our last practice until we leave for the magic show tomorrow morning," Wyatt told her and she groaned. Glacthia shot fire at us and Ember reflected it. Forrest made a ton of wasps start attacking him, but he used telekinesis to turn them all towards us, so Forrest had to get rid of them. Suddenly, out of nowhere he became twenty feet tall and put us in a glass box.

"What's he doing?" Rhochelle shouted in fear. Then it started to move the box around and we were dragged with it. Wyatt shot water up at the top and it broke through. Then when we looked up we wished that Wyatt hadn't done that. Huge spikes were falling from the ceiling and coming straight for us. Rhochelle noticed that they were made of rocks, and redirected them to him. Then Gabby blasted a hole in the side and we got out.

"We have no way of beating him!" Ion told us.

"Yes we do," Neva thought back to his past. Then, he thrust his hands out toward Glacthia and started to concentrate. At first he looked like his heart had just stopped, but then we saw what was happening. He opened its mouth and ice poured out, just missing us. Then he fell down onto his knees and stopped breathing. We watched as the giant man froze from the inside.

"You did it!" Lianna cheered and the rest of us smiled.

"I knew you could," Forrest looked at him, knowing he had unleashed a unique and dangerous ability.

"Come on, let's turn it off," Wyatt walked out of the room and turned off the simulator. The rest of us followed him out and watched the giant simulation disappear.

"What do we do now?" Kamille asked and we thought.

"We could go bungee jumping off the roof; I know Wyatt wants to," Daven laughed along with the rest of us. But just as we were heading toward the door, I noticed something flying toward us. It was a strange looking creature; since I had no knowledge of the bugs on Earth, I wasn't sure if it was an alien or not.

"Guys, what is that?" I asked, and everyone turned around.

"It's a wasp," Ember said in confusion.

"How did it get here?" Ion wondered, swatting it with his hand but missing.

"I don't know, but I don't want it to sting me," Forrest twitched his hand a little and smoke covered it. When the smoke cleared Forrest turned his head to the side. It was still there.

"That's weird," Ember pointed at it and shot some fire out of her finger. It went right past it and the creature showed no signs of feeling the flames.

"Great, a supernatural bug and it finds its way to us," I said as if it were just too typical.

"Ow!" Neva shouted and swatted it. The bug fell down to the ground and Neva stepped on it. "It stung me," he said in shock.

"Come on we should ask your parents if they have anything to put on that, it could get infected," Lianna said without even looking. We went to them and got something for his arm. After that it was pretty late, so we just went to bed. I had a little bit of trouble sleeping because I was nervous about the next day. The show was tomorrow night, and we were heading to the other side of the planet in the morning. There was just so much pressure on us to get Selene back. We had no idea what Glacthia's real intentions were, which worried us even more. Even though she wasn't my sister, I felt like part of the family when I was around everyone.

In the morning, I woke up and looked around the room. Even with the vast number of rooms, there weren't enough for each person to get their own, so I was with Ion and Craig. Neither of them showed any signs of being awake, but I got up anyway and went downstairs. Just as I walked down the staircase into the main hall, I heard some voices, so I turned into a gas.

"I'm telling you Riddock, he can't go," Mrs. Barker said to Mr. Barker.

"Aubree, if Neva doesn't go there's no telling how much it could affect their fight," Mr. Barker debated with her.

"I know, but we can't just force him to go, he's been throwing up all night," she told him, and if I had a mouth it would've just dropped. I flew back upstairs and woke up my roommates.

"Neva's sick; he's not going with us," I told them and they gasped.

"How did he get sick?" Craig wondered, getting dressed and ready to run to Neva and get him to come.

"I don't know. It's hard to eavesdrop when you have no ears," I nodded my head and then we smiled.

"Well then we'll just have to go without him," Ion figured, and Craig and I sighed.

"But Neva and Forrest are the only ones that can beat him, and Forrest could die trying," Craig reminded us. Then someone burst into our room and shook her head.

"Neva and Forrest are the only ones . . . so far, that can *kill* him. All we need to do is distract him so we can take Selene," Ember explained, having eavesdropped on our entire conversation.

"So we're still going to go?" Ion made sure.

"Yeah, we have a good chance. It's . . . fifteen against one. Or fifteen against . . . however many people he's possessing." I realized how negative that sounded just after I said it. "Anyway, we should get ready now," I looked at the clock. We split up to wake everyone up, and then had breakfast. Neva was still asleep; we thought that if we woke him up, he would try to come. But Mr. and Mrs. Barker said that he definitely could not.

When we left, we called for a taxi and waited about half an hour. Once it came, Wyatt turned into a soul and jumped inside him. We all stared at the driver for a second then Wyatt returned.

"What was that for?" the man yelled and Wyatt looked a little startled.

"Sorry sir, my powers aren't working," Wyatt lied through his teeth. The man sighed and leaned back in his chair.

"Whose powers are working?" he said rhetorically, and we looked at each other with our eyes wide, thinking about all the times that are powers really hadn't been working.

"What was that for, really?" Lianna questioned as we stepped into the taxi. Those of us who attended Medlocks last year understood why, but Wyatt explained it for her.

"Well, this would be our first time ever that our taxi driver wasn't being possessed by Glacthia, or just someone that we wished it was not," Wyatt told the Venturas, and they raised their eyebrows.

"To . . . ," Ion had to stop for a second, and then I realized that I never told anyone the exact location of the magic show.

"To Oppidum," I told the driver and he started the taxi. It moved a lot faster than a jet rocket or a plane from Earth. We were planning on getting to the other side of the planet in about five hours. And since this planet is the same size as Earth, it's about six times faster than anyone on Earth can travel. It's weird that it takes longer to travel across Callidus than it takes to get from Medlocks to Callidus.

The ride was extremely boring; if we had any faster way of getting there, then we would've taken it. It wasn't that we were cramped because there was a lot of room for all of us. The room was about the size of an apartment, even though it only looked like a taxi from the outside. We just had nothing to do, which was like having a theme park all to yourself when none of the rides worked.

"Look at all these maps," Forrest pointed to a wall when we were about twenty minutes into the trip.

"Whoa, these are all the maps that the Matt's ship had," Ion remembered.

"Wait, this can't be right," Wyatt put his finger on one of the maps and looked at it closely.

"What?" Gabby asked him, and everyone huddled around the map.

"It says that the Medlocks solar system is one light-year from Earth's solar system. That's impossible; 'member when we got turned into frogs last year? Ion ran all the way to Earth at light speed, so it should've taken him a year to get there. But remember he said that he got there in the time that he could hold his breath?" Wyatt explained to us, and Gabby laughed.

"You guys got turned into frogs last year?" she smiled, and we rolled our eyes.

"Um . . . when Ion runs at light speed, he turns into energy, and therefore doesn't need to breathe," Lianna told us.

"But still, it would've taken him a year to get to Earth," Wyatt pointed out, and she nodded in agreement.

"You guys don't understand," Ion looked at me and rolled his eyes. "They think they're so smart," he whispered to me. "Don't you know that if light travels for a whole year from Medlocks to Earth, it would be a year in the future on Earth? Well, that's why the Ancestors had to do something so that people could get from Earth to Medlocks in only a week. There's a huge wormhole, undetectable by all human technology, going from Earth to Medlocks. When something travels at the speed of light from one to the other, time freezes. I did run for a whole year that night when you guys got turned into frogs. I just got to Earth at that exact second because the wormhole brought me back in time. And when we went from Earth to Medlocks last year on the rocket, the wormhole was actually moving us at light speed, then taking us a year back in time. So none of us really existed during that whole ride because we were moving at light speed, which is why we didn't grow up," Ion finished explaining and sat down on the couch to take a breath.

"Oh," Wyatt and Lianna said together. I looked around at the faces of everyone else. They were completely unaware of what he had just said. It's like people know about their powers more than anyone else just because they have to try to understand them. The same thing happened when Aura tried to explain all the time traveling stuff to us last year when we made the tree house in one night.

"Anyway," Rhochelle said loudly and we got back to being bored. Everyone sat around doing nothing for the rest of the ride. So when we arrived in Oppidum, we were not only hungry, but also about to drop dead in boredom.

"Well we made it, let's have lunch," Aura walked away and Forrest tripped her with a vine.

"We have to find where the show is going to be, and then we have to check if they're in it yet. If they are, then we just get Selene before the show. If not . . . then we'll come up with a new plan," Forrest decided.

"Sounds like a good plan," Ember said sarcastically.

"Yeah, I try," Forrest almost chuckled a little, and then remembered the situation that we were in. The group walked down the main road and I pulled the address of where the magic show was being held out of my pocket.

"Come on, this way," I jumped up in the air and made a metal disk under me. Everyone followed me down the road and through the neat little city. When we reached it there was no doubt that it was the right place. It was shaped like a dome, with the only entrance through the top. But for those who couldn't fly, there was a teleporter in the front. We just lifted the people who couldn't fly and went in the top, since the teleporter barely fit four or five people, and we weren't sure if it would split us up or not.

"Whoa, this place is huge," Aura said in amazement as we flew in through the top. From above, it looked all level—just a few seats and a stage—but the few seats ended up being the balcony, with multiple rows of seats below it that we hadn't seen from the outside.

"But there's no backstage," Sam noticed.

"It's under the stage," Lianna pulled off of the top of her head.

"Then why don't they call it an understage?" Ion laughed and everyone got silent. We landed on the stage and looked for the "backstage."

"This is just like when we were looking for Glacthia's lair on Medlocks's moon," Ember reminded us, but then we sighed.

"But we're barely a month into the school year," Kamille complained.

"Yeah we're really in for it this year," Daven nodded his head.

"I found it," Sam found a nail that just stuck out a little higher than the wood. We pressed on it and a couple boards of wood folded and slid under some of the others to make a hole.

"Is anyone in there?" Forrest wondered.

"No," Lianna answered before any of us even went in. The place looked like a basement that hadn't been remodeled since the beginning of Altrians. The walls were huge stones that barely looked like they fit.

"Okay, that's good enough. Let's go," Gabby teased, but still turned around as if she were leaving.

"No, we have to see if they're here, look there are more rooms," Forrest went up to a door and pushed it open slowly.

"Neva's so lucky," Kamille realized, and everyone stopped.

"How come, he's really sick? I hate being sick," Craig notified her.

"Yeah but he gets all our stuff when we die," Aura said in a "duh" voice.

"We're not going to die . . . right now," Wyatt sounded a little doubtful in even that statement.

"No one's here; we have no choice but to leave," Forrest turned around, a little scared himself. Everyone slowly turned around in the cramped room and eventually the person who was in the back became the person in the front. Aura now led the way as we walked out and then Wyatt stopped us.

"Come on guys, we didn't come here for nothing. We have to do something, so that when we come back we'll have a plan," he almost tripped half the line by stopping suddenly.

"Okay, what's your plan?" I asked him, and it wiped the smile off his face.

"I don't know, we should leave a note for Selene or something," he gave his best plan.

"Or a hologram," Forrest caught on and walked over to the room that had the bars on the windows and the little machine on the door that makes a room powerless, the power degenerizer.

"I have the most perfect idea in the whole wide world," Kamille pushed Forrest out of the way and closed her eyes for a second. "Give me a really sharp claw on my finger," she ordered and Forrest did as he was told. She pulled the Glacthia translator out of her pocket and started writing on the wall.

"Wow, Kamille this is big for you," Daven admitted.

"Ion whispered the whole plan into my ear, I just took the credit and have the powers that will make it work," Kamille made us all laugh for once.

"So what are you doing anyway?" Ember asked her.

"Well, this says 'Glacthian Translator' in the English alphabet, so Selene will read that. I made it so that when she says it she will fall into a memory that we're going to make right now. Then we'll give them the translator in the memory and they'll leave the memory. After that they'll use the Glacthian translator to translate this, and they'll fall into a memory that only happens a few seconds before they read it, and the memory takes place wherever we are. So then we'll just go home after that," Kamille smiled and stepped away from the wall. I got so confused trying to understand what she was saying, but finally I got caught up with the group.

"What if Glacthia reads it?" Rhochelle saw the flaw in her plan. At this time Ion pushed her out of the way and started to take credit for his plan.

"That's why Kamille switched powers with Wyatt so that whoever reads the memory will be mind scanned, it can only work for Selene," Ion smiled and we raised our eyebrows.

"That might really work! All we have to do is watch the show and then they'll teleport right next to us," Wyatt congratulated my best friend and crush on their amazing plan.

"Let's get out of here then," Forrest pushed the line until we were back through the hole and on the stage.

"Yes, we made it, now we just have to find something to do until the show," I told everyone and we left to explore the city.

The next few hours went by quickly. We visited all the coolest places in the city, like the restaurants, and an arcade. But finally it was time for the show, and we sat in the back.

"Look, he's disguised Houdini as a different magician," Sam pointed to the curtains that had a poster of him on it.

"Ehrich," Aura reminded him.

"Shh! It's starting," Rhochelle told us and we quieted. The curtains opened up and applause filled the showroom.

"Thank you, thank you. Quiet now, I need to do my job," he laughed and the audience followed his advice. "Tonight's show is definitely going to be . . . stunning. Be ready for the amazement that we magicians see every day," he laughed again and it made us sick.

"Now, for my first trick, I'm going to handcuff the entire back row to their seats," he announced to the audience and our eyes grew wide.

"But first, look at this trick," he did a small trick with a bird and a bouncy ball and Wyatt put forcefields around our arms and hands. Then vines started to grow around the forcefields, and we smiled at Wyatt in thankfulness.

"Look, they can't move their hands," he pointed to us and everyone turned. Wyatt dropped the forcefields and the vines fell loosely over our hands.

"Good call, Wyatt," I whispered to him.

"And now a trick with my assistant," he put his hand to the floor and we smiled, expecting Selene not to come out. But to our surprise, she walked out of a hole and stood next to Glacthia.

"I'm only going to do one trick with her, and it's a trick that so many magicians have thought to be too dangerous. But for us, not even a challenge," he levitated a box out of the hole and put it on the stage.

"I don't like this; she has to be possessed by Glacthia," Ember told us.

"The saw trick," he yelled, holding up a huge saw.

"Teleport her out of there," Lianna said to Wyatt in a nervous voice.

"I can't, Glacthia is stopping me, I can't until he gets out of her head," Wyatt explained to us. Glacthia put Selene in the box, and put the saw to the top of the box.

"Now?" Rhochelle almost yelled.

"Not yet," Wyatt put his hand up.

"Here I go," Glacthia started to saw through the box. We all covered our eyes in terror.

"Wyatt!" Daven shouted as quietly as I could.

"Still can't," he had his eyes closed in concentration.

"Wow what a hard box," Glacthia started to smile and we heard a scream.

"NOW!" Wyatt shot his hands out and Selene appeared next to us. They didn't realize where they were until they hit the floor. Even from the last row we saw Glacthia's eyes widen, and Wyatt teleported us all out of the audience.

CHAPTER EIGHT: SLEEP TIGHT

CRAIG

Aunt Aubree and Uncle Riddock were undyingly grateful for our return, and we asked them why they were so worried now and not before.

"Didn't you feel it? There was a massive blackout, almost 99% of the universe's population felt it. Any closer and . . ." Aunt Aubree stopped herself and we begged her to tell us.

"It would be better if you guys just left for Medlocks now. We love you," Aunt Aubree led Uncle Riddock away and we stared at each other.

"Let's go then," Wyatt teleported us to Medlocks. The familiar look of the Medlocks Island at night made us feel a bit better.

"How 'bout we ask Miss Monohan about the blackout? She'll tell us," Selene suggested, the sound of her voice was so comforting.

"Good idea," Ember told her and the rest of us walked up the stairs. We took the usual second floor turn and knocked on the door in her office.

"Come in," she said, sounding a lot more inviting than usual. We walked in and squished ourselves around her desk.

"Miss Monohan, we heard about the blackout, and we were just wondering . . . what it was?" Daven smiled a little and her jaw dropped.

"Were any of you using your powers between 7:47 and 7:49 p.m. today?" she pointed to us.

"Yeah, Wyatt was," Lianna answered and we stared at her in amazement.

"Barkers, Venturas . . . Iron," she smiled at Cobalt, "do you know what best represents a person's power?" she questioned us and there was a pause.

"An atom?" Wyatt wondered.

"No, an electron," Ion nodded, thinking he was right.

"A seed?" Aura guessed.

"A grain of sand," I told her.

"A light bulb," Lianna rolled her eyes.

"Right, and a blackout is when all the lights are out. Today at those times, 99% of people's powers were not working. Do you know what happens when it's a 100%?" she asked us, knowing we would guess until Lianna told us. "When 100% of the population loses their powers, it is called a Peractio Blackout, meaning a never-ending blackout, and no one's powers will come back," Miss Monohan decided to save us the embarrassing guesses.

"That's horrible, has it ever happened before?" Aura asked and we all hit ourselves in the forehead with our palms.

"So do blackouts just randomly happen?" Forrest wondered, and she shook her head.

"They have to be caused by a large power surge, where too many people use their powers at once, or by a Metronome," she told us, and we looked at each other. "The news said that this one was from a Metronome," she looked at her lap and we sighed.

"I bet that was the trick that he was doing while the vines were being wrapped around us," Ember realized.

"You mean the Metronome and the ball trick?" Selene wondered.

"He called it the bird and the ball trick," Rhochelle rolled her eyes.

"Yeah he turned the Metronome into a bird and he turned it during his trick," Sam explained the most we knew about Glacthia's plan for this year.

"What do you think he's planning?" Wyatt didn't even try to guess this time.

"Well, the only way that a Metronome can cause a blackout is if it tries to take away everyone's powers. There will be a large blackout, then small blackouts that follow it until the final blackout. The whole process takes about seven to eight months," Miss Monohan tried not to ruin our whole school year, but it was too late.

"Great, May or June," Gabby whimpered.

"You guys are in for a real challenge this year. I hope you're ready, this could be the end of all super powers as we know it," she turned her chair in a circle, hiding her real feelings on the situation. We left her office and took in the whole conversation.

"The end of all super powers . . ." Daven's eyes were wide.

"As we know it," I added, not even looking at anyone in particular.

The Barkers said goodnight to us on the ninth floor, and we kept going up the stairs. At the twenty-ninth floor we stopped and turned into the room. It felt empty. The lights were off and it was completely silent. I went into my room and lay on my bed for the longest time. It felt like I would never fall asleep. Finally my eyelids became too heavy for me and I dozed off.

Another couple weeks went by: class after class, weekend after weekend, project after project. Ion, Cobalt, and I had a lot of homework for just ten and eleven year olds. On Halloween morning, I woke up and decided to stay in my bed for a while. But suddenly, my room became very dark, and I couldn't see anything. Then the light turned off and the door closed. Just when I was about to get up a metal mask flew at me from the ceiling.

"Agh!" I yelled and hit it with my hand. Ion and Cobalt came in laughing, with the mask in Cobalt's hands. "Ha ha, that was so funny," I said sarcastically, pushing them jokingly.

"Come on, I heard they have the scariest things in the world for breakfast," Ion pushed us out the door and we ran down the almost thirty sets of stairs.

"Like what?" I wondered while we were about half way down.

"Someone told me that there were green waffles, attacking pancakes, and *real* deviled eggs," he said, and we looked confused.

"What do you mean real deviled eggs?" Cobalt wondered as we were sprinting down flight after flight.

"I have no idea, but it sounds cool," Ion told us and we nodded. Finally we made it to the bottom floor, completely out of breath but still full of excitement. The three of us ran into the cafeteria and sat down with our families. Once I lifted the cover over one of the plates, I realized what deviled eggs were. They had little red horns and tails, and were jumping around. One of them flew out of the dish and bit me on the hand. Ion shot it with a lightning bolt, and I watched it fall to the ground in ashes.

"Ow, it bit me," I flapped my hand and then sucked on it.

"Speaking of little things attacking people, you never told us how you got better, Neva," Ember reminded him, and he sat up to tell the story.

"Well we had to call a curer, which is a person who can cure diseases with their powers," Neva started to explain to us. "Her name was Morgan Lawless from Eximius, and she just walked in, pointed at me, and asked for Mom and Dad to pay her. It was the funniest thing ever," Neva laughed a little and then stopped when none of us did.

"Wow, people's powers can be cures, they could save a lot of lives on Earth," Gabby said, and we turned to her and realized that she was right.

"I asked Mom and Dad about that. They said that people would start to realize something was wrong when random people were being cured around the world. Then they would figure out we exist, and our whole society as we know it would be jeopardized. So we can't do it," he told us, and we nodded.

"We are finally sixteen years old," Ember breathed it in and smiled.

"You won't be 'til 11:30 tonight. I won't be 'til 11:55 tonight," Daven sighed, and everyone opened their mouths in disgust.

"Could you not talk about the speed at which Mom gave birth to us?" Wyatt begged, and Daven rolled his eyes. The whole thing about our birth grossed us out. If our parents only told us that Altrians had different ways of giving birth than humans, then we wouldn't be so disgusted that our mom used to be pregnant with six kids.

"So what are we gonna do for your birthday?" I asked, hoping they had something really fun planned.

"Nothing I guess, or we could have a party in the tree house like our end of the year party," Forrest suggested with his eyes wide.

"Last time we had a party there, it took us three days to prepare, and Glacthia tried to kill us all," Aura remembered.

"Yeah and you, Brian, and I had to do a scavenger hunt in the dark for the remote that turns off the lockdown mode," Ion turned to Cobalt and he changed to a bright red.

"Then are you going to do anything?" Gabby asked, not able to last one weekend without doing something exciting.

"I know! Can we go to the haunted house?" Cobalt laughed and we glared at him. "I was just kidding," he put his hands up in defense and we turned back to the table.

"What's with you and that haunted house? You're always talking about it." Sam pointed out, and we looked at Cobalt, wondering the same thing.

"I thought it wasn't that bad. I mean, there's no way that the same thing could happen again. Glacthia's not trying to make us use our powers, so it's probably a lot safer," Cobalt tried to convince us, but the rest of them couldn't agree.

"We could just invite a couple people, it wouldn't take that long to prepare," Gabby thought it was a pretty good idea, but they still weren't sure.

"But we're party people, and party people—"

"Ember, we know the party people theory!" Neva almost shouted.

"I'm just saying that if we forget one person, they could spread a rumor that we're horrible people and are extremely rude," Ember stared at us with a completely serious face and we just had to seize the opportunity to laugh.

"So it's agreed?" Kamille smiled, looking at each person's face. Our two combined tables of people thought for a minute, and then caved in.

"Fine, but don't tell anyone that's not invited," Ember gave in and we smiled and high fived each other.

"We should get started right away. Let's go, hut two," Forrest ordered them all to get up and we laughed. Our group ran up a small number of only nine flights of stairs and flew to the tree house. Cobalt gave me a hover scooter since voices really didn't help me fly.

"So we're having it in the super large game room, which is still super large from last year," Forrest looked at a map on the bottom of the tree trunk to find which sector the room was in. We followed him to the room and went inside. It still had all the stuff from last year's party, so we only needed food. There was even a drawer with the ingredients from all of last year's food, now we just had to make it. Cobalt, Ion, and I were sentenced to get food. Ion pointed to us and told us to start running, but we didn't get it. Finally we listened to him and everything started to blur. The three of us ran as fast as Ion could make us to the door, then ran at regular speeds down the stairs, and sped up again when we were out the door.

The whole island flew by me at light speed, but I could see small blurs of certain things. One I noticed really well was the haunted house, which we passed about halfway through the millisecond long jog. It was a small blur, but the creepiness ran through me like goosebumps. I felt the chill as if I were being locked in it, and then screaming for help when no one was there to hear me. I let it pass and we reached The Grocery Store before I could even realize we had left.

"That was intense!" I shouted in a commentator's voice and we laughed.

"Come on, we just have to get a few artificial flavors for the . . . cheese curls . . . candy . . . and snow cones," Ion read off of a list.

"You can buy all that stuff here?" I asked in shock.

"Yeah in the artificial flavors section," Cobalt said just before he pushed the doors open. Once he did my mouth dropped, and I looked up at how high the shelves were. Then I looked both ways at how many aisles there were. It was about the hundredth time I've seen the illusion where the inside is bigger than the outside.

"Come on, I remember where it is," Ion led us to the 52nd aisle and we went down it until we started to see little colored tubes.

"This one says, 'artificial flavors for snow cones,' is that the one we need?" I read off the bottle. Ion nodded and I picked it up.

"This is the cheese curl flavor," Cobalt grabbed it and Ion tried to find the last one.

"Okay, got the candy ones," Ion grabbed a couple and we walked about a quarter mile to the register.

"Is that it?" the women took our bottles and put them through the scanner.

"Yep," I smiled and she glared at me, she must've known that we were throwing a party; anyone on the island could recognize what we were up to by what we bought. I stepped back and Ion handed her our money that our entire family saved up.

"You can come to our party," I gave her an even brighter smile. She looked at me, and then her face started to light up.

"Yeah, okay, I'll come," she even smiled a little and I smiled back.

"Okay, follow us," I whispered for Ion to give her the ability to move at light speed, and the four of us ran back. Once we got there I turned to the person who worked at the store and smiled.

"What's your name?" Cobalt asked her when we found the strength to stop.

"Kirsten Keenan," she told us and we nodded, leading her into our room and running to the tree house. Then we teleported to the game room and everyone stopped working. Neva dropped the food bowls he was holding and turned red.

"Guys this is Kirsten, we invited her 'cause . . . she looked like she needed to come," I smiled and everyone stared at me.

"Okay?" Ember said, and we continued to work on the party. A couple hours later, we were finally ready to start the party, and we split up to find each of the people we invited. It was everyone on our team, which was everyone born on Callidus, the Bradleys, the Magerrs, and a couple other people that we just saw in the hallway and decided to invite. Within a couple minutes, everyone had arrived and the party started.

We put on some music and a disco ball and a strobe light. Everyone seemed like they were having a good time and I even saw a few new couples. Neva was talking to Kirsten, and Forrest was talking to some random person that I didn't even know. I enjoyed the party as well, although I didn't talk to or dance with a single girl—then again, I'm the youngest kid in the school. But just as the party was getting really good, I noticed Kirsten talking to Neva in a panicked way.

"Neva, I really have to go, I'm sorry," she started to run off, but Neva grabbed her hand.

"Fine, just let me show you something real quick, this way," Neva led her out the room and she looked up at the ceiling nervously. I continued to talk to Ion and Cobalt for a while. We were debating on whether people get older when they time travel.

"They have to. They're existing, so they're getting older," Cobalt was trying to convince Ion, but he just wouldn't believe him.

"But that means that we might not be the age we think we are. What if the older kids time traveled so much that they're not actually turning sixteen today? Maybe they turned sixteen yesterday 'cause they time traveled for a total of twenty four hours. And what about that time we froze time for three days just to build this tree house? If we grew up during that, then we'd be three days older than we actually think we are," he was telling us, but we were positive that he was wrong. Maybe we were a couple days older than we thought.

"So you're saying when we time travel we don't grow up at all?" I laughed along with Cobalt, and Ion nodded and we rolled our eyes.

"Kirsten, I'm sorry, I didn't know!" Neva shouted from about fifty feet away. The three of us forgot our disagreements and got ready for something to jump into the room. Everyone got quiet, but no one remembered to shut the music off. All of us stood in the room looking at where the shouts had come from. After a while, everyone figured that it was nothing, so they went back to their conversations. The three of us didn't step down, so when the doors burst open we were ready. A huge scelum flew into the room and ran at us. Everyone screamed and shot powers at it. It dodged everything that came its way and suddenly started running towards me.

"Craig look out, it always goes for the youngest person!" Lianna yelled and I remembered our lesson from power practice and fear went through my entire body. It stopped about ten feet in front of me, and sniffed for the youngest person. Then it turned its head toward me and the scariest thing of the year happened. It ran to me and I shouted in terror, unable to think of how to stop it. Just as it jumped into the air to bite me, a huge rock hit it from the side and sent it flying through the air. I turned to Rhochelle and thanked her for saving me.

Everyone gathered around it, but Forrest made vines come out the floor and strap it down. But right when it was all strapped down, Neva came in and looked up, the moon became covered by the clouds. The scelum started to change shape, and Forrest had to take off the vines to give it the room to grow. When it stopped changed we realized that it was Kirsten, and she got up, half crying.

"I'm so sorry," she whimpered, looking at me, and ran to the teleporter. She pressed the ground button and when Neva was about to follow her, she disappeared.

"*This* is why we don't throw parties," Ember said in an "I told you so" voice. The party tried to continue, but it never returned to its original cheerfulness. Eventually people started to leave, and we ended the most awkward birthday party ever.

"That was the most amazing night; I guess I'll see yah later," the girl that Forrest talked to said as she stepped into the teleporter. Forrest nodded and waved to her, but all of us just stared at him, thinking the same thing.

"Who was that?" Gabby smiled at him and he turned a little red.

"That was Kaitlyn . . . Bradley," he turned even redder and we rolled our eyes.

"Do Alaina and Caroline know about this?" Aura smiled and nudged Selene.

"Yes, and they're alright with it, but Kaitlyn is so amazing. Her power's swimming. She can swim through anything, even air, much cooler than making soccer balls and basketballs."

"I hope you don't like her just 'cause she has a cooler power than Alaina and Caroline," Gabby told him and gave him a stern, threatening look.

"No, she's so nice, and funny," he sighed, looking out of the window.

"Well, I'm so tired, I'm gonna just sleep in our rooms in the tree house," Daven walked off and we nodded. I decided to stay here as well instead of walking up ten floors to my room. We had copies of our room in the secret base in the upper level of the tree house, so I just teleported to it. Once I was in there, I found the copy of my room and got ready to go to sleep. It was so dark here, and I was about thirty feet away from the nearest person in my family, including Cobalt. Then I started to think that maybe I should've went to my room, but there I would've been even more alone. Thoughts of the day started to swirl in my head, and then I drifted off in fear with a strong feeling that I was in danger.

"Boo!" Cobalt yelled with his mask on and I screamed loudly. He laughed, and then put me on a metal saucer that floated out of the window.

"Come on, we're going to the haunted house, everyone's in danger there," Cobalt got on his own saucer and we hovered out of the window. We were flying about two hundred feet from the ground, and I held onto the saucer as hard as I could. Out of the eighteen people in our group, Lianna and I were the only ones that needed help flying. So if I fell right now, I would have to have someone save me. But right when Cobalt started to lower me down, the saucer flipped over and I fell out. Screaming, I prayed that someone would catch me with something. But as I fell closer and closer to the ground, my hopes started to fade. Just before hitting the ground, the saucer moved under me and pulled up like the bottom of a drop on a roller coaster.

"Sorry about that, I think we just had a blackout or something," Cobalt sounded like he was hiding something, and I felt really unsafe riding this saucer. But we were only a few feet from the ground and almost there. We ran down the stairs and then I got back on the saucer for the ride to the haunted house. Once there, we snuck in through the back since we didn't have a ticket.

"Come on, they said they're on the top floor," Cobalt ran to the front of the house and up the stairs. I walked behind him as slowly as I could, waiting for something to pop out. Just as I made it to the bottom step, it fell into the basement, bringing me with it. I couldn't see anything, so I looked up and waited for Cobalt to send something down to save me.

"Cobalt, are you there?" I called after a couple seconds, extremely scared that something was going to grab me. No one answered, so I got up and looked around. I couldn't see a thing as I walked with my hands out toward what I thought were the stairs. But when I put my hand on it, it lit up and turned out to be the furnace of the house. I sighed, knowing that this house had no heating or electricity anyway. Stepping back, I tripped over something and fell down on my back. Picking it up, I looked at it closely. Then I screamed and threw it, it was the body of a dead bat. Finally I found the stairs and walked up them, still not seeing Cobalt. Then I went up the next set of stairs to get to the second floor.

"Guys, come on, are you here?" I asked, wishing they would say something. But as I made it to the top step, my whole life flashed before my eyes.

"Yes, Craig, we're here," they all said in unison. But none of them were themselves, they were all scelums. I screamed and ran down the stairs with fourteen scelums chasing me. But just as I ran to the door, I tripped and my face went into something hard. I looked up, frantically thinking about the scelums running at me.

"Hello, Craig," Glacthia said, and put his hands on both sides of me. Like I was a basketball, he picked me up and lifted me over his head. Although I was about to die, I realized how strong Glacthia actually was. "Well, it wasn't nice knowing you," he said with me struggling to get out of his grip. But before I could kick him as hard as I could, he threw me at the scelums that were my own family. I screamed as loud as I could as my entire life flashed through my eyes. And just when I was about to expect something to happen that would save my life, I hit the floor and felt the scelums tackling each other to bite me. And if I thought that this wasn't real before, I was positive that it was now. I could feel each of them taking bites of me and shouted in pain. But no one came to my rescue, and I closed my eyes for the last time.

CHAPTER NINE: ESCAPE FROM REALITY

FORREST

Ion ran up to me, and I closed my eyes to pretend that I was still asleep.

"Forrest! Forrest! I can't find Craig anywhere, do you know where he is?" Ion climbed onto the foot of my bed and started stomping so that I would get up.

"I'm not even awake, why would I have seen him?" I wanted to have an elephant lift him up with its trunk and take him out of the room, but the floor might not hold.

"I don't know, he's not in his room in the secret base, and he's not in his room in . . . his room," Ion worded incorrectly and I rolled my eyes then closed them. "No, you have to get up and help me find him," he grabbed my sheets and ripped them off, causing me to groan and roll out of bed.

"Why me?" I moaned and started to walk like a zombie out of the room, but without my hands up. We walked out of the secret base and found the teleporter that brought us to the door.

"Well I already asked everyone else, and they . . . burned me, froze me, teleported me out, and some other things I can't describe," he said and I made a disgusted face. The two of us walked up a couple stairs and noticed the clock on the wall.

"Oh my gosh, we have class in like ten minutes," I exaggerated by about fifteen minutes and ran back to our room. It wasn't that I didn't care about where Craig was, but Ion was completely unaware of how far Craig could be by now.

"But we have a huge test first period, if he misses it . . . he'll completely fail the class," Ion started to freak out as we walked into the teleporter. When we were back at the tree house, I went to the bathroom and started to get ready.

"He can make it up," I said and closed the door in his face. I didn't see him again after that; I went to my first class, sports, and had to split up from my group to practice swimming. When the class ended, I went to geography, and I talked with my family at our conjoined table. It was Lianna, Gabby, and Sam, and my sextuplets and me. I brought up the topic of Craig as soon as we sat down, since we didn't have much time until Mrs. Pauffer told us to be quiet and get started on our work.

"Did Craig wake up this morning?" I whispered to them.

"No, but I am positive he went to bed in that room, and he wasn't there when we woke up," Sam told us.

"Guys, are you serious? I'm sure nothing bad has happened to him," Ember tried to assure them, but of course she wasn't as optimistic as she said she was.

"But Glacthia has that plan . . . to eliminate us all one by one when we least expect it . . . what if . . . I mean, he doesn't have that much to defend himself with," Daven made a nervous look and all the Venturas suddenly went into shock.

"Daven, stop trying to freak them out. I bet he's fine," Rhochelle yelled at him and Mrs. Pauffer stopped talking to a student to glare at her. She lowered herself in her seat and was silent for the rest of the class. When we walked out of the class, Miss Monohan stood by the door studying the ceiling. The rush of kids startled her, and she seemed to jump a little.

"Oh, Barkers . . . just who I was looking for," she turned to us and we pretended to look surprised. The rest of our classmates left, leaving the nine of us standing with her in the room.

"Could you come with me? I need to talk with you in my office," she looked around, thinking that this wasn't the best place to discuss whatever she wanted to talk to us about. It must've been really important. It seemed pointless for us to follow her all the way to her office just so that she could tell us something.

Once there we crowded ourselves in the cramped room and six more people joined us. Aura, Selene, Kamille, Ion, Cobalt, and Craig walked into the room and we pushed each other against the walls so that they could fit.

"Craig, where were you, what happened?" Lianna asked in a worried voice.

"I had a nightmare and woke up late," he said and we all glared at Ion.

"But I checked your room and you weren't there," Ion told us and we rolled our eyes. Craig then spoke up on Ion's behalf and proved him right.

"Yeah, I went to bed in the secret base, but I woke up in the middle of the woods. I took me forever just to walk to the door and get to my first class," Craig explained.

"About that," Miss Monohan butted in, "the test that you missed is unable to be made up, so you have to take a zero for the test. And because of that, your grade in that class has plummeted to an "F." I don't know if you know our policy with failing, but we do not tolerate it. I've been generous before about letting you come to school a year late, but now I have no choice. If you do not find a way to get back the points, you will be removed from Medlocks Academy." All of our mouths dropped, but Miss Monohan was not in the mood for an argument. She turned her seat around and we left the room.

"How could she do that? That's not a policy," I had to bring up.

"How do you know? None of us have ever read the school handbook," Ember pointed out, and everyone else but me nodded. I haven't read it, but there's no way a school can just kick someone out for failing. Maybe Miss Monohan hadn't checked the handbook recently . . . or she wasn't feeling herself.

"Wait, so you missed class because of a nightmare you had. What was the nightmare about?" Daven wondered, but the rest of us thought it was a strange question to ask.

"Well, Cobalt took me to the haunted house, and then when we got there he disappeared. I walked upstairs to see if he was there, and all of you guys were sclums, and you chased me down the stairs. When I was at the bottom of the stairs I ran into Glacthia. He picked me up, and then fed me to you. The weirdest part was that I could actually feel you guys biting me, and everything seemed so real," Craig seemed scared by his dream, even now when he was awake.

"It probably was," I said and everyone turned to me in shock.

"Well Glacthia has my power of illusions, so he can enter dreams and control them. He also gave you the illusion that it was real by telling your mind that you could really feel the pain. Then your subconscious mind probably reminded you about the test, which was the only reason you woke up just before you died. If you didn't wake up just before you died, you could've really died in there. I think we have a serious problem," I explained to all of us.

"Wait, what subject was the test in?" Daven turned back to Craig and he seemed lost in his own mind for a second before he responded.

"Human sciences," he told us and we smiled at each other.

"Well then it's perfect. Tell Mr. Blair you're going to write a report on your brain activity while you sleep. Then tonight Forrest can take us all into your dream and we'll try to stop Glacthia from . . . killing you," Ember told him, and Craig smiled for a second, and then shook his head in confusion. We rolled our eyes and then explained in terms that he could understand.

"A dream journal," Rhochelle nodded her head and talked to him like he was a baby.

"Oh, sorry, I just wasn't listening. I'll go ask him now, and then we can plan for tonight," he ran off and we continued to walk to our floor.

"Do you think we can just go into Craig's dream and fight Glacthia? He'd have the advantage, being able to control the dream," Aura reminded us.

"But we can fight back with Forrest's power, we'd be pretty evenly matched," Ion told her and she understood. When we got to our floor, we went straight to the teleporter that took us to the tree house.

"That's true, so now we just have to find out what we're going to do," I told everyone and they sat for a minute. The silence was broken when Craig teleported into the meeting room.

"I checked the study room, the homework room, and the secret base, I didn't even think to check the meeting room," Craig smiled, and then dropped it when he got back to the point. "Okay, Mr. Blair said I could do the brain activity journal for my project, but it has to have ten different dreams. How are we gonna do that if it's only one night? I can never remember my dreams except for the one I had last night," Craig told us.

"Maybe we could change the scenery of the dream every couple minutes, that way Glacthia will get confused and you'll have ten dreams to write down," Ember thought and we agreed with her plan. Then we had to go to class, lunch, another class, and finally we were back. All of us brainstormed what the ten scenes were going to be. Once finished we had nothing to do but to wait until Craig fell asleep. He agreed to play a few games outside until he got tired, so we were up for a while playing sardines in the dark.

"Guys, I'm gonna go to bed," Craig eventually told our group, and we waited for a couple minutes for him to fall asleep. When we looked in his room and his eyes were closed we tip-toed into the room as quietly as we could. I looked at them, asking if they were ready, and all thirteen heads nodded. Then I concentrated; I had never transported this many people into a dream before. Then the floor seemed to fall, and all reality collapsed in front of us.

"Did we make it?" Aura wondered when we were standing in the haunted house.

"Just don't answer," Rhochelle told everyone and we smiled at Aura, who actually seemed to have some seriousness put into the question.

"Craig!" Wyatt shouted and teleported us to the top floor of the house that we hadn't been in for about six months. When we got there, we heard the sound of Craig making small, nervous noises, but the fog was too immense to see him.

"Craig, where are you?" Sam called and there was a second's pause.

"Lookout!" he shouted and we all ducked. A huge axe swung over our heads and just missed us. When it was gone, we stood up slowly and then heard it coming back. Wyatt took the liberty of making sure that we were all ducked, by making a forcefield that lowered itself until we were crushed into the floor. No one even bothered to stand up, but this time when it came around Cobalt turned it into a liquid. The watery axe lay in a puddle on the floor and this time we stood up with confidence. Aura blew away all the fog and it revealed the horrors that were in the room.

Four axes were still swinging, each with the handle attached to a small pole that spun it around. With each swing they got closer and closer to Craig, who was tied to a larger pole in the middle of the room, and we got more and more frantic. But before anyone could do anything, I pointed at them and they evaporated into the air. When they stared at me, I decided to explain myself.

"This is all just a dream, so none of it is real, and since it isn't real, I can do whatever I want with it," I told them and they sort of understood.

The whole thing with my power was very confusing, so keeping up was pretty much mandatory. I didn't expect them to understand everything; I just wanted them to know that I had it covered.

"Okay, the next scene should be . . . a movie theater," I read off the note card and closed my eyes. We started to fall again, and when we stopped I opened my eyes. Everyone stared at me with perplexed faces. This was definitely not a movie theater. Gravestones stood in lines in front of us for as far as the eye could see.

"I think we need to investigate your perception of a movie theater," Daven decided.

"Wait a minute, where's Craig?" Lianna looked around and then we smiled.

"Don't you know?" Aura stared at her, happy that for once she didn't know something.

"Well, I know he's still at the haunted house, but I just wanted to let you know that he wasn't here," she told us and our smirks dropped.

"Come on, we have to figure out why we're—" Rhochelle started but then stopped randomly. For over a minute we stared at her as her face stayed in shock.

"Are you going to tell us or just stand there?" Selene asked finally.

"I feel movements in the ground under us, and we're at . . . a graveyard," she told us and we all moaned. The ground started to shake a little, and then hands popped out the ground.

"How predictable can this be?" Rhochelle complained and got ready for the attack.

"You were the one who just asked why we were here," Wyatt pointed out and he threw a forcefield at a skeleton coming at him.

"Well that's 'cause we're supposed to be at the movies!" Rhochelle shouted and threw a boulder at a group of skeletons that had just pulled themselves out of the ground.

"Less talking, more beating up skeletons," Daven yelled and shot fire at a skeleton running toward him. Everyone turned around to fight separate skeletons. I turned into a rhino and knocked a huge pile of them down. But no matter how much I did, they always pulled themselves back together to come at us again.

"I don't think this is working," Craig realized and we stopped fighting them off.

"Did you just get here?" Lianna would freak out at the thought of possibly being incorrect.

"No, Glacthia put me in one of the coffins next to a skeleton. It was about to start attacking me but it pushed open the coffin and I was able to get out." Craig smiled for having successfully been awarded pure luck.

"I have an idea, but I'll need Gabby's help," I told everyone and they came together to hear my plan. I whispered to Gabby and she nodded, feeling pretty positive about the plan. Then we turned back to the skeletons, which were still pulling themselves together, some even trying to stand. Gabby pointed to the horizon, trying to make contact with her power. Then, the sun started to rise, and the whole graveyard lit up with sunlight. Once it was my cue, I began pointing to random spots, and even waving my hand over large areas. Flowers stared popping up everywhere, and the skeletons instantly began freaking out. They ran around as if they were being poisoned, and eventually jumped back into their graves.

"Yes! It worked!" Ion jumped into the air in happiness and I pulled out the list.

"Okay, next thing is Mom and Dad's house. I'm positive it's going to work this time," I concentrated as hard as I could, if I could get everyone into a dream then I should be able to move them in it. But when everything around us collapsed and fell into a nothingness of space, only to be replaced by a highway, I lost all hope.

"This isn't Mom and Dad's house!" Ember yelled at me and I started to get angry.

"Well I don't think I have that much control over where we go, okay!" I shouted back at her and it got quiet. I looked around, everything around us was just all desert, with a highway going on for as far as my hawk eyes would let me see. Of course it was nighttime, but I didn't really get what could happen to us here on a highway.

"Um . . . I see our problem for this scene," Ember told us, pointing in the distance. Glacthia was flying toward us, and everything that he was flying over (including the desert) was getting sucked into a dimensional portal that we could only identify as darkness. Without even a warning, we all started using our powers to fly down the highway. I tried to run as fast as I could as a cheetah, but that would be dumb if

I wanted to go a long distance. Glacthia was gaining, and people were starting to fall behind.

"Aura!" Kamille screamed when she started to be pulled back. Just a few seconds after that, Kamille was lifted off the ground, then Selene. I didn't even have to think about what I was going to do. Just a few days ago I discovered that I could do things that certain animals could do without even turning into the animal. I shot a spider web out of my hand, catching each of them in it. But I had to stop running to do that, which brought Glacthia right up to me. I flew into the air, and just before the four of us flew into the vortex, Ion stopped and shot a ray of light at us. Once it hit me, I felt the ability to run all the way around whatever planet we were on in less than a few seconds.

"Guys, run!" Ion hollered and all of us listened. Everything started to blur and I saw Ion shoot the rays of light at everyone else. After that all of us were running at light speed down the extremely long highway. After running a couple thousand miles we stopped, and before I could even pull out the list we fell through space and time.

"Great, where are we now?" Neva wondered, but sat down when the raft started to sway.

"We're on a raft in the ocean," Aura told him in a serious voice and we rolled our eyes. All of us sat down since the raft started to turn a little.

"How is this sca—" Ember was about to ask when I covered her mouth.

"Don't say it, then something will—" I stopped when we all felt a movement under the boat. Just when someone was about to ask what it was, our raft went flying several feet through the air and us even higher. But Aura started spinning air under us in the middle of our back flips and we slowed down and were lowered until we were just a few feet above the water.

"Whoa how are you doing this?" Wyatt asked her in amazement.

"The air is spinning under us so fast that it forms sort of a solid-gas surface that we can stand on," Aura explained and we all said "ooh" in admiration.

"Can we get back to the huge thing that knocked us off our—" I tried to stay, but my mouth stopped moving when a huge octopus leapt out of the water. It was about a hundred feet long and had at least thirty tentacles that made up almost its entire length.

"The Kraken," I told everyone in astonishment and they all moaned.

"Isn't that the giant mythical creature that captures ships and lives at the bottom of the sea?" Daven asked and I nodded, still staring at the huge ripples coming toward us.

"This is bad," Neva didn't even try to think positively. I gulped and nodded once more. Our hearts pounded, like drummers in a war just hoping that maybe the first shot wouldn't come. But the silence came to an end when the huge predator jumped up from right under us. Aura didn't expect the attack, and was so jolted by it that she dropped her air platform, sending all of us into the water. Most of us flew back up, escaping the Kraken's vicious tentacles, but not all of us were so lucky. Craig, Lianna, and Kamille were taken by the beast and pulled underwater. Wyatt, Rhochelle, and I dove after them in hopes of thinking of something we could do to save them. Rhochelle had a bubble of clear diamond around her, which she could move around as easily as Wyatt or I could swim.

Once under we followed the creature, which swam faster than jets or planes could fly. But suddenly it hit me, my light bulb moment. If the Kraken was a living animal, then I had all powers over it. Just when I was going to turn it into a seahorse, Rhochelle used her powers on the Kraken. I had been thinking about my idea too long to notice that the beast brought my cousins and sister closer to its mouth.

When Rhochelle used her powers the Kraken's eyes widened, as if something had just happened that it never would've expected. Then Rhochelle put her hands toward it again, and the entire thing turned to cement. Sinking to the ground, I turned the captured people into fish, since they were almost unconscious from the lack of air. They swam up with us and I turned them back into themselves.

"That was a close one," Lianna thanked us as the scenery began to change again.

"Great, where are we this—" Sam stopped breathing for half a second when he saw the next dream. It was the top of a skyscraper. But this was not just a skyscraper; it was the mother of all skyscrapers. The Empire State Building looked a bit more dangerous when you weren't standing in the confinements of the safe walls of metal and glass. We sat on the very top, next to where the cell phone tower stood. It was barely a dozen or so feet on each side. The first thing I pictured coming when I saw the landscape was King Kong, but that theory was disproved a second later.

As if a massive hand had just pushed us off, we were suddenly falling off the immensely high building. We were far out enough not to hit anything, but the shock really alarmed us.

"Our powers aren't working!" Wyatt had to yell into his watch because of the distance between us. I tried turning into a bird, but I had no success. Everyone started to scream at that time, having no way of saving themselves.

"Guys, concentrate, it's just a dream. Our powers aren't really gone. If you try hard enough they'll come back!" I shouted into my own watch and the screaming ceased as all their attentions went to their minds. I myself tried it, forgetting everything around me to create peace in my mind. There was a short pause, and then feathers sprouted up all over my body. Using the fall as a dive, I swooped up and stopped falling. Everyone continued until eventually they were all randomly stopping.

Suddenly I remembered the people who couldn't fly, and dove down to save them. I was very far back, but there was a chance I could save them with the diving skills of my falcon form. Cutting through the air with my beak, I felt my speed go way past the speed of a person falling. It didn't matter if I didn't make it. I just needed them in eyesight, which I was close to already. Once that hit me I realized the most obvious thing that I hated myself for overlooking. Without even trying I used the falcon's impeccable eyesight to track them down. Finally they were visible to me and I turned each of them into birds like me. They realized what they had become and swooped up just like I had.

"Thanks," they told me again and we instantly fell into a new landscape. I turned them back into themselves and looked around. We were in an underground hallway, about forty feet high and twenty feet wide, disappearing into the darkness lengthways.

"What's this, a volcano? What do we have to do?" Neva asked, getting ready to freeze whatever he had to. But Rhochelle got that dazed look in her eye and shook her head.

"Nope, we're definitely in a cave, but I hope you can dodge," she looked at the wall, unmoving. Her eyes wouldn't leave the same spot, and we stared at it, looking for what she was gazing at. There was nothing there, so we knew that she was unquestionably waiting. Then we felt it, the vibration in the ground that was always a bad noise to hear in a cave. The earthquake only lasted a few seconds, but the boulders that followed it were disastrous.

They came mostly from the ceiling, as the entire thing came from over our heads. Rhochelle and Wyatt put their hands up, along with Aura, Cobalt, and Selene. They had to catch each boulder separately, since they involved a split concentration, falling at different speeds.

"How are we going to stop this?" Ember wondered.

"You could help!" Selene yelled, reversing gravity for all the rocks above our heads. Every single rock stopped, and then floated back up away from us. Selene realized what she did, and then smiled, feeling proud and content. "Oh, well then I guess you don't need to help," she went on about how cool that was while the dream changed once more. Knowing Glacthia's advanced knowledge of trickery, there were four more dreams left. This one was clear as soon as we fell into it. All of us were underwater, with chains attached to our feet, holding us to the ground. We were in a circle, so we could see each of our dying faces. Everyone turned to Wyatt and Aura, who looked like they were trying to open an invisible lighter. They looked at us and shrugged, out of ideas. Instantly, everyone's cheeks puffed out, as if trying to conserve their air. Cobalt was studying the chains, which looked like they were made of some type of material that was neither crystal nor metal.

Rhochelle was moving around the sand with her hands, trying to find the bottom of the chains so that she could unbury them. No one had any luck, until Wyatt started speaking into our minds. I didn't expect it at first, since his other powers weren't working.

"How come I can do this and not breathe underwater?" Wyatt wanted to know as much as the rest of us, but we had no time for that. I noticed something in the distance, which is something I usually don't do underwater since I like to keep my eyes closed. But I saw a small thing moving toward me at a speed way too fast for something underwater. I looked at it with hawk eyes, which hurt even more underwater, but could still see farther than mine. It was a shell, coming at me at over fifty miles per hour. My eyes widened as I looked at everyone else and Wyatt saw it as well. He threw his hands out just as it came to the center of our group. The force hit it and caused it to move position, but continue moving. It swished past me, just piercing the skin. I howled in pain and clutched my arm to stop the bleeding. But once the blood had touched the water I saw Glacthia's plan.

Not only did sharks come from every direction, but piranhas as well. They swarmed us, but each person was able to defend themselves. The only person I saw getting bitten was Craig. But Sam took the responsibility of saving all of us. He started to spin around, even attached to the chain.

"Good idea," Wyatt told him as we started to spin in a whirlpool away from the swarming creatures. When we began to raise the chains stopped us, but Rhochelle finally blasted the sand away until nothing but the anchor keeping the chains in the ground were visible. After the chains rose off the ground we fell straight into the next dream. It came up pretty fast; we just fell into what seemed to be a jungle.

"Stay calm, there's a giant tiger on the other side of this wall," I said instantly between huge gasps of air. Everyone turned slowly to the wall as quietly as possible. But the tiger, freakishly bigger than a regular tiger, leapt over the wall and landed in front of us.

"Run!" I shouted and turned into a cheetah, sprinting for my life. I looked around for Ion; he must've accidentally run too far and couldn't find his way back.

"Wait, why are you doing this?" I shouted to the tiger.

"We must eat to live, and kill to eat. I'm just keeping the order," he growled out loud, but I knew that everyone else just heard the roaring of his huge mouth. It must've been at least fifteen feet tall, with teeth about six inches long.

"But you out perform and outrun us," I told it, everyone staring at me, wondering what it was saying to me.

"And you don't think you do that with your guns and your hunters and your moving vehicles?" it asked. Way to go, Earthlings.

"That's not my fault, here, eat this," I piled gazelle after gazelle in front of him, and stopped running. Everyone else stopped reluctantly, while the tiger fed on the food I gave.

"Thank you . . . maybe I will *change my perspective on your species,"* it lowered its head and I returned the bow.

"Too bad this is a dream," I saluted it and fell into the next dream. There were only two more left, but once I saw this next one I wished that it was the last one. We were in the power simulator, with Glacthia standing right in front of us. He was his old self, as he was before the explosion, which told me that we were in the memory jogger.

"For the first time in this dream we meet, although I have been following you for the past eight. You've managed to elude all eight of the treacherous perils that I set upon you, so I have to congratulate you for that. But now, I will not allow you to pass to the last one," he got in a firm stance, ready to fight at any time. Out of nowhere we all sprung at him using whatever we could, and he only deflected about half of it. It seems as if every time we fought him our advantage in numbers showed itself. His strength was no match for our abundant number of powers. But still he managed to stay in fighting condition until finally he threw us all. It still felt weird to see how strong he was really when he always relied on his powers to do whatever he needed for him.

"We can't hold him off; he's going to win," Ember told us while lying on the floor of the tiled room. Using all of her strength to get up, I watched her shoot fire at him, causing him to take steps back until he finally felt the need to block it with a forcefield.

"I have an idea, Rhochelle, Cobalt, come here," I motioned for them to lean in so that I could whisper to them my plan. They made faces as if they understood and I stepped back. In less than a second they put their hands together and formed a bomb between us. Without even telling her anything they gave it to Ember and expected that she knew what to do. She nodded to us and chucked it at Glacthia. Wyatt saw our plan unfold and covered us all with a forcefield. The explosion, although we saw it coming, still surprised us with its noise. The forcefield became shattered with pieces of metal and fire. Wyatt lifted it off after a few seconds and we waited for the smoke to clear.

"Is he still here?" Kamille wondered, but we started to fall into the next dream. It came up fast, since there was not really anything to materialize. There was nothing but darkness, which made the regular night sky feel like staring at a light bulb.

"What are we supposed to—" Daven tried to ask when Selene forced us to the ground by increasing gravity. A blade swung over our heads and everyone held their breaths, as if whatever was swinging the blade would miss if it couldn't hear us. Ion made a small light appear in his hand, along with Gabby and Ember. They stood up since the blade was no longer swinging, but even in the faint light we could see their eyes widen in amazement. As far as we could see in this diminutive radius was scythes, parallel to the ground so that they could swing straight in a circle. Each person found a spot where they could stand freely without a blade hitting them even if it was swinging. But once everyone thought that we were standing too far apart, the scythes began to spin on their own.

"You cannot win," Glacthia voice echoed through the seemingly infinite darkness. "I'm going to destroy your minds from the inside until your only hope for freedom will be to surrender to my will. You won't get a wink of sleep until each and every one of you has failed your way out of Medlocks." It hit me, at that exact moment, how this nightmare was going to end. I had to use the exact same principles of trickery that he had used to get us into this mess, and it all went back to one little rule.

Without even trying, a small book landed in my hand. It said "Medlocks Academy Rules and Regulations," and I waved my hands in the air to get Glacthia to notice.

"Hey, Glacthia, can I read something to you?" He turned to me and I opened the book to the contents page. Going down the line I finally found "failing" and flipped to the page. "Page 62, Section 8-B: Failing. All students must keep a passing grade in Medlocks. Anyone failing will have an automatic detention once a week until they pull it up. Only in extreme cases—when a student fails every class for a whole year—then the student is expelled from Medlocks Academy." I didn't bother to continue, everyone stared at Glacthia with a gaping mouth.

"You were Miss Monohan when you told Craig about failing and you were Mr. Blair when he suggested that he do a dream packet. This whole thing is a lie!" Ember smiled, as if she had just solved the mystery herself. Glacthia yelled into the air and faded away. The entire dimension fell apart and I took everyone but Craig out of the nightmare.

CHAPTER TEN: A CRASH COURSE IN DRIVING

EMBER

Only a couple days passed since Craig's nightmare. He ended up being able to make up the test, and never even had to do the project. Each of us signed up for the driver's test, but we had to take a written test first. It was this Saturday at noon, which only gave us three days to study. We were given a handbook of all the information to study. There definitely wasn't as much information as people on Earth had, which was better for me. It basically wanted you to understand wormholes, light speed, and escape velocity. Although the planets were exactly like Earth, but their escape velocity—the speed you had to go to leave their atmosphere—was much less. You only had to be going thirty miles an hour to leave the atmosphere of all the manmade planets, which is how it was possible for us to leave them.

"How long is that handbook?" Aura wondered while trying to read over our shoulder.

"Barely forty pages," I said, flipping through it like a cartoon.

"Who's taking it again?" Kamille wondered as our group looked at each other.

"Me, Forrest, Wyatt, Neva, Rhochelle, Daven, Lianna, Gabby, and Sam?" I checked with everyone else and they nodded. Forrest gave me the annoying "you're supposed to put yourself last look." I glared back and got back to reading.

"Are you guys all ready?" Kamille smiled.

"Yeah, as long as we pass this part, then we get to take the actual driving test in one week." Forrest informed us.

"But they have so many accidents, with all the traffic they have. So they want you to have a lot of practice before they let you do it legally," Neva told us and we agreed that it made some sense. Then we got back to studying for a while until it was too late to read and take in the information, although actually for me that happened a while ago. We went to bed and fell asleep in an instant.

By the time we were ready to take the test I had read the handbook so many times that I couldn't count it on my fingers. I could recite the entire thing if that were part of the test. I knew everything from what you should do if you see another vehicle in space to how to park on Earth without letting anyone see you.

"Are you ready?" Miss Monohan asked while we sat down in the elements room. She didn't give us time to answer since she passed out packets to each of us. The test was very long for such a small handbook. Then she passed out the answer sheet; there were fifty questions then an essay. Miss Monohan waited for everyone to get situated, then bowed her head and stepped back.

"You may begin," she told us and we lifted our pencils. I filled in the bubbles for my name, age, birthday, class number, date of test, and time started. Then I opened it and began the first question. It was easy, the escape velocity of a Medlocks, 30 mph. But as soon as I finished filling the bubble some rude jerk invaded my personal space.

"Did you guys get number one?" Wyatt asked, and everyone looked up to see if Miss Monohan had noticed. Of course she didn't, so I turned my attention away from the test and to my mind.

"Wyatt, this isn't right. If you don't know this stuff then you shouldn't be able to drive," I told him and he projected it into everyone else's head so they could stay in the conversation.

"She's right, we need to work on this test alone," Daven vouched for me and I nodded.

"But Lianna's cheating; she didn't even study and she's going to get a hundred," Wyatt pointed out and I looked at Lianna next to me, she was rolling her eyes.

"It's A. Now be quiet," she shushed him and I turned back to my test. But he didn't stay quiet; he bugged us for more answers, as if each question was to be debated with the whole group. I tried to ignore it, but some I did get stuck on and relied on my siblings to help me in return for the help I gave them. The last essay was the only thing that

we split up for. It asked to explain a wormhole and how to go through one.

Eventually, feeling horrible, I stood up after waiting a couple minutes so that we didn't hand them all in at the same time. I left the room and waited for the rest of the people. When Wyatt came out I glared at him.

"How could you do that? I hope you fail," I gave him a disappointed look and he shrugged.

"If it wasn't meant to be cheated on, then they would've made it a powerless room," Wyatt tried to explain but I ignored him.

"Ember, look on the bright side. Soon, we'll all be driving, maybe we can even get space cars," Forrest gazed into the future and smiled.

"Fine, but you are never going to do that again during a test," I pointed at him and he promised. Liar.

"What are we gonna do now? We have one week until we take the actual test, then we can drive whenever we want," Gabby shook herself in happiness.

"Let's . . . I have no idea," Forrest ran out of ideas. We all searched for an idea until we had made it back to the tree house. Everyone was arguing whether we should work on our astronomy projects or play hide and seek dodgeball freezetag.

"We're back!" Lianna called out to our family. Everyone in the tree house flew in from either the window, the balcony, or just through the teleporter.

"How'd you do?" Aura wondered. I could tell that she couldn't wait to turn sixteen.

"Let's just say we all got pretty close to the same score," Wyatt didn't want to seem like a bad person by admitting to cheating, so he didn't tell them at all.

"Told you they cheated. You owe me five bucks," Selene told Kamille without even looking at her. We rolled our eyes and decided to go with working on the projects. Obviously Kamille bet on us having morals and being good, saintly individuals. She should have learned by now.

The week took absolutely forever. After a painfully long wait, it was the night before the test and we were all freaking about, not having studied at all.

"How do you turn on the windshield wipers?" Neva shouted at us and all the rush stopped so that everyone got a chance to laugh.

"You're in space, what do you use windshield wipers for?" I had to ask him.

"I don't know, alien blood, comets," Neva tried to keep a straight face but he ruined it.

"Yeah, anyway, how do you activate a hyperspace portal?" Wyatt wanted to know since he didn't learn anything from the test.

"Put the drive on five and press the hyperspace pedal," Daven remembered and I nodded to show that I agreed with him.

"We're all going to fail," Lianna said and our eyes widened as we turned to her.

"Are you serious, we're all going to fail?" Forrest stared at her with a more horrified face than when we saw Glacthia for the first time.

"I can't predict the future, 'member? That wasn't my power talking," she reassured us and we all sighed in relief.

"Psht, most of you aren't going to take it anyway," Aura murmured and everyone stopped again. No one could think of what to say just yet, but the silence was starting to become irritating.

"How are most of us not going to take it?" Gabby said in the calmest and sweetest voice she could muster to get Aura to tell us.

"I can't tell you that, it might destroy the face of time itself. But trust me; I'm saving your lives by not telling you. I saw it in a dream, and although it was pretty blurry, I'm positive that I'm doing the right thing," she started out yelling then calmed down as her explanation went on.

"Aura, you two timing, double crossing little . . ." Neva began.

"Neva, she said she was saving your life!" Selene yelled in defense for her triplet and Neva stopped talking for a while. It was obvious that practically the whole family knew but us, and it was going to drive us downright insane.

"But how are we not going to be able to take the test, what's going to happen?" Rhochelle burst out a rush of questions and the younger kids rolled their eyes.

"We can't tell you, it would alter the course of time and change the future significantly," Ion tried to explain, but we just wouldn't accept that answer.

"Guys, let's just try to get some rest. It's clear that we're not going to find out from these guys," I led the older kids into a huddle in the next room.

"Okay, Wyatt, spill. What do their minds say?" Forrest asked him in a forceful tone.

"I can't, somehow they're blocking themselves from me. I've never had this happen before, can you guys do it too?" he asked and we nodded, staring at him.

"Yes, Mr. Williams taught it to us last week," I nodded, talking to him like he was a younger kid. He thought back and then nodded.

"But then what are we gonna do, who knows what could happen that could stop us from taking that test tomorrow?" Daven told us in a nervous voice and we didn't even try to comprehend it. With all we've experienced since the day the comet landed in our backyard, nothing was impossible anymore.

"I say we don't go to sleep, maybe we have nightmares and don't wake up," Neva proposed. We looked around the group, thinking it was a safe way to miss the test.

"I'm looking into the future, but Glacthia's blocking it again. That means he has something to do with it," Wyatt told us and we groaned.

"Yeah, I think we should all stay up," Forrest thought Neva's plan was a good one, but I had perfectly good reasons to disagree.

"But what if you're too tired to take the test anyway, then you'd regret staying up," I explained to the people who were siding with them. They ignored my comment and went on listing why it would be a good idea.

"Wait, so who's with me?" Neva wondered, in shock of how many people actually thought that his idea was good. Gabby, Sam, Forrest, and Neva stood on one side of the room with the rest of us on the other.

"Fine, we'll just go to study room with as much soda as possible and stay up all night, while you guys are the ones who don't get to take the test," Gabby tried to convince her sister by mocking us with lies. Obviously, I felt on the right side with Lianna here.

"Come on guys, we're going to get a good night's sleep," I led them out the room and to our bedrooms. We fell asleep slowly, worried about the rest of our family. The younger kids possessed a secret strong enough to change the course of the future, while our siblings were dooming themselves by staying up all night.

When I woke up, I ran straight to the study room to see if they actually made it through the whole night. Once I got there I stopped when I saw that all of the four people were snoring on the beanbag chairs with Lianna studying one of the many empty soda bottles lying around.

"A very, very powerful sleeping potion, they'll sleep for another twelve hours at least," she explained to me and I sighed.

"It had to be the last soda they drank," I looked around, not seeing a single bottle with soda in it. Lianna sighed as well, and the rest of the group eventually found their way here, along with the younger kids. We explained the story to them, and Aura nodded.

"Just how I saw it," she snapped her fingers and my eyes widened.

"You knew this was going to happen, and you didn't stop it from happening?" I had to yell to get her attention and she rolled her eyes, tired of explaining this.

"What if they didn't fall asleep and miss the test? What if they took the test and something horrible happened while taking the test just because they were there? What if they got hurt, or even got a mere scratch while taking the test? It would lead to something bigger, which would lead to something bigger, which would eventually change your futures. What if they passed the test? What if they had their licenses and it caused something horrible to happen? I'll tell you—"

"No, don't tell me . . . I get it," I put my hand up then sighed in relief when she stopped. "I'm sorry I questioned your . . . judgement," I murmured the word so quietly that only Aura heard it. "But these are the only people that will be missing the test, right?" I asked nicely, hoping she would tell us. The younger kids went into a huddle, speaking in whispers that were just slightly too quiet for us to understand. Then they turned back and nodded.

"Yes, this is all," Kamille smiled and I glared at them.

"Okay if you're telling the truth then why'd you have to huddle?" Lianna pointed out and their smiles dropped. They sighed and rolled their eyes, either snapping their fingers or saying something. I looked around nervously at our group, not knowing who would take the test and who wouldn't. It was a terrible fate, knowing hints of the future but no details.

"Who wants to play hide and seek dodgeball freezetag?" Craig wondered and we glared at him. Everyone shook their heads and caught on.

"No way, you're just saying that so the future comes true. See all of us right here? We're going to take this test," Ember smiled at them and Craig took it offensively.

"They didn't even tell me, I feel so left out!" he shouted in a deep and cracky voice at the entire room and the people who were sleeping didn't even move. He blew out a big scene and we couldn't help feeling sorry for the kids, so we decided to play.

The game started out slow, until I became it. I chased around for anyone I could find in our entire room. One round usually lasts about an hour since you have to find someone and freeze them three times. I was using my rocket shoes to fly through the woods, dodging each tree and rock I could. Then suddenly I heard a shout and a thump just a couple feet away. Moving around a couple of plants to make a "u," I swerved until I found the rock formation that was Rhochelle's room. Lying at the foot of it was Rhochelle, Daven, and Lianna.

"Guys!" I shouted and flew over to them while trying to turn off the rocket shoes. I spoke into the watch and got everyone to come, which they did in about a minute. The three people, all of them taking the test today, were moaning and holding their arms.

"Where's Wyatt?" I asked when I noticed that he was missing.

"Ask for him on the watch," Cobalt suggested.

"Wyatt, are you there?" I said onto the watch a couple times but there was no answer.

"Come on, we have to take these guys to the nurse's office," Aura lifted all three of them with air vents and we walked to the nurse's office. I was the only person left—other than Wyatt—who could still take the test. All three of them had broken arms, and had to stay in the nurse's office for the day while the nurse made the antidote.

"That's it? Doesn't someone in the human science family have the power of bones?" I asked. The thought of taking the test before just made me a little nervous, but now it was a huge lump in my throat that I just couldn't swallow.

"I'm sorry, but there's not. I'll have them mended in one night, no problem, though," the nurse tried to make us feel better but didn't understand our situation.

"Okay, thanks," Aura told her and pushed me out of the room before I could argue anymore. I was still in a state of shock, amazed by how eight people could be handicapped, poisoned, or missing in one morning.

"Ember, do you still wanna go take your test?" Selene asked me in an almost sweet voice.

"I guess, I'll be back later," I waved to them and walked off. This was such a dumb idea.

"No way, Ember. You can't go when all of this has happened—it's a sign," Cobalt tried to warn me, but I wasn't in the mood to listen. I walked off, leaving them standing in the doorway of the second floor. The test was to be held at the airport, where all the crafts were kept. Once I made it outside, I got ready to use my rocket shoes. But I noticed that the sun was setting, and my shadow started to get longer and longer by the second. When it was about three times as tall as me, it did something I was totally not expecting. It pulled itself off the ground, and when it was standing straight up it was about my height. Before I could say something or do anything, it leapt at me with terrorizing fangs. I dove off the front stairs and turned on my rocket shoes in midair.

"Well that's great, now I'm going to have a fear of shadows after this," I yelled to my own shadow as it chased me to the airport. Trying to think of an idea, I had to drain practically all my power to keep matching its gaining speed. Eventually it came to me, and I smiled at the shadow, unaware if it noticed my smile or not.

"Let's see if you can stop as fast as I can." I immediately stretched until my molecules were far apart enough to not be seen, and I fell to the ground. The shadow slowed down, and when it could no longer see me, faded away.

"Wow that was a close one . . . why do I keep talking to myself?" I yelled when I remembered that I was alone. For someone with nine brothers and sisters, a villain who became part of the family, and four newly met cousins, company is constantly needed.

Finally I arrived at the airport to see a sign in the distance for people taking their driver's test. I ran to it and when I got there, a man with such unexpected enthusiasm greeted me.

"Hey, the name's Andrew Davis," he shook my hand with such a firm grip that I felt my hand being crushed a little. "Is this it? I was told there was going to be more."

"They . . . couldn't make it," I told him the truth . . . technically.

"Well, that's okay. I have to go tell the boss I'm headin' out; then I'll be right with yah," he told me and I nodded, wondering what he had just said. He walked off and I got into the space car. There was a newspaper in my seat, so I picked it up to look at it for a while. The headline read, "Giveaway Powers, A Good Idea or Not?" and it talked about how powers were now being sold to people who did not get them from the comet.

"That's crazy, who would buy those?" I said to myself again, then sighed in boredom. I decided to keep reading, since the topic interested me.

MEDLOCKS VONUS

Giveaway Powers, A Good Idea or Not?

By: Richard Tecco

"These powers tap into your brain cells and figure out which power would be best for you," says operator and president of the 'Powers with a Pricetag' corporation, Bob Della Polla. But what if a person with a destructive mind were to go in and get powers? Then they could walk out with a power capable of mass destruction. "This is an extremely bad idea; it should be stopped as soon as possible," says Meldocks Solar System President, William Johnson. Bob replies to this remark by saying that people will only be able to get one power and it will not be a power that could be used for evil. "We have just defied science and figured out how the Ancestors have given us our powers. I have been living without powers for over 30 years and was the first person that the Power Enhancer was

tested on. I believe that it's a perfectly safe way to give power to people who were unlucky enough to get the quadruple recessive alleles." Bob tries to explain this to President Johnson, who refuses to agree with the idea until it has been used for a useful purpose. If the Power Enhancer does not prove to be extremely useful in the next month, the program will be shut down for good. Bob has a plan for the Power Enhancer to do great things, but if he cannot get the okay from President Johnson, then his efforts would go to waste.

"Hey are you ready?" Andrew asked while I buckled my seatbelt and nodded.

"Yeah," I told him quickly and threw the newspaper into the backseat.

"Right so all you have to do is take off, leave the atmosphere, circle the planet, and land here," he told me and I tried to keep it in my head. I slowly turned the vehicle on, and then pulled into the runway. All space cars were either called runway cars or liftoff cars. Liftoff cars could hover off the ground, but runway cars need a runway to take off. Runway cars are usually used for beginners and are rarer, since liftoff cars are easier and don't need to be taught how to drive since they are all self-piloted.

"There will be flags to mark where to go, but also obstacles to try to stop you. If something goes wrong and we have to stop or teleport back here, just press this button," Andrew pointed to a red button behind the steering wheel. I activated everything that I needed to and took off as carefully as I could. When we were in the air I veered upward so that we were moving straight up. This was why runway cars were replaced by liftoff cars, because they could leave the atmosphere without having the passengers sitting facing the sky. About a minute later, we reached space and I slowed down to a safe speed.

"Very good," he nodded to me and checked off something on his clipboard. I noticed a red flag just hovering randomly a couple yards away. Just when I was about to drive to it, an arbitrary meteor shower started. I pressed a couple buttons and then a metal casing went around the entire space car except for the window. I sped up for a while, checking for each red flag every couple hundred miles. It was a boring ride; there weren't many obstacles except for when the power went out because of a solar flare from the solar system's sun, Crinis. I had to switch to solar power, which is barely as strong as the power from the radiowaves that we were using before. After a while it passed and then I kept going. Then later, just before we were done, another space car was coming from a different direction right at me. I had to press a bunch of switches just to make the atoms of the car, Andrew, and me pass through the other car. There wasn't really anything else to driving a space car than that, so I just had to land and then I would've passed.

"Good, now you're coming close to the runway. You probably want to wait a while to land, if you land on the grass it would be a bumpy landing," he told me as Medlocks Island came into view.

"Okay, how am I doing so far?" I just felt like asking, since any more silence would've destroyed me.

"Let's just say that a student has never failed in two years and right now it probably won't change," he told me with a nice smile and I nodded, understanding what he was trying to say. We came close to the runway and I pulled down, making an almost perfect landing. Everything would've gone perfectly if the speed had dropped when I landed. I touched the ground, but I was still going the same speed that I was going when I came back into the atmosphere. About a mile ahead of us was The Movie Theater, and I wasn't planning on crashing into it.

"Ember, slow down! You're not going to stop in time!" he shouted as the end of the runway came closer and closer. I lifted my foot off the pedal and even put it on the breaks a little, but nothing happened.

"It's not working; I can't get it to stop!" I yelled back at him, trying to stay as calm as possible. I threw my hand at the emergency button, but again nothing happened. I wasn't worried about crashing as much as other things. Space cars were resistant to inertia, so if the car suddenly stopped, the passengers would suddenly stop without feeling anything or being thrown forward. It was the explosion the car would have when it hit the movie theater, even though space cars don't blow up when they crash. The part that we were headed for was the basement, where they had the heating system and all the other electrical things. I also worried about the people in the theater, whether they would be affected by it or not. Just when I was about to try to think of a way to get Andrew out of the car without dying, the wall came right up to us.

The whole thing seemed to happen in slow motion after that. We crashed right through the cement walls, proving the strength of a space car. I looked around the room quickly before anything happened to it. Electrical wires were everywhere, with spare projectors, a generator, a furnice, and a kitchen area. Then I remember putting my hands up as the fire started. It felt like I was generating a forcefield, the fire just seemed to pass around Andrew and me. Then the car finally stopped and I gaped at Andrew for a second. The power had gone out in the movie theater, and I could hear complaints upstairs, but we were completely unharmed. But Andrew had a different face then my relieved one.

"Because of the construction damage and the cost it will be to fix all this . . . I'm sorry, but you fail your test," he told me and my mouth dropped.

"I saved your life! You should be thankful," I muttered as I stepped out of the car and walked upstairs to the main lobby of the movie theater. Once I was out of it, I flew back and slammed every door I opened. When I got to our room, I stopped to stare at the mountains in the distance. There was a small, smoky fire at the peak of the closest mountain. I put my watch to my face and called for the family.

"Guys, did you find Wyatt yet?" I wondered, in a curious tone.

"No, we're sorry Ember, we looked everywhere and begged Mr. Williams to let us use the tracking thing, but he said it was illegal," Forrest answered for the group and I continued to gaze at the mountains.

"Well I think I just did."

An hour later we were all ready for our trip to the peak of the mountain. The "let's stay up all night" kids had woken up, and the other kids had their casts on already. Miss Monohan had given us a map of our room, which only helped when we were trying to figure out how much farther, not how to get there. Forrest and Lianna worked on food, Lianna provided the recipes and Forrest supplied the food. There were also sleeping bags from the sleepover room that we brought. Ion shrunk everything down so that it could fit in a pouch that he put in his pocket.

"Everyone ready?" Neva called to everyone as we were standing at the trunk of our tree house. There was no answer, but the sound of boots on the dirt getting ready to take off was good enough. Everyone jumped into the air, and I got ready to create my rocket shoes. A second later I heard everyone hit the ground with a thump.

"Oh great, another blackout. What are the odds?" Forrest shouted and we stared at the ground in frustration.

"Greater than you think, actually," Lianna tried to explain but it only made our situation more gloomy. "People with more than one power are more likely to be struck by a blackout when all the powers in the universe are being taken by the Metronome. So it'll happen to you guys more than it will happen to us. But on this occasion, it's happened to both of us at the same time."

"Plus, Glacthia can target who the Metronome blacks out at certain times," Cobalt added, and we glared at him for bringing Glacthia into the conversation.

"I guess we're walking then," Neva smiled sarcastically at the group and their faces dropped in agony. Everyone groaned but Forrest, Rhochelle, and Sam. Rhochelle and Sam are just optimists, but Forrest refrained from groaning because he was too busy with something else.

"This blackout is going to do much worse things than make us walk," he said in sort of a trance, staring at a bush a couple feet in front of us. Two yellow eyes with a thick black curve going down the middle were staring at us from the other side.

"I suggest running," I told the group before Forrest got the chance to.

"Go, I'll try to hold it off," Forrest waved his hand at us, causing the whole group to stop walking backwards slowly.

"Are you kidding? Our powers aren't working, you idiot," I reminded him. Does he have to be so stupid?

"I know, but I know their weaknesses," he glared at me, his loss I guess. Our group turned to leave, but Aura turned back.

"Come on Forrest, what weaknesses could a mountain lion have?" she begged to know, but he stared at her and rolled his eyes.

"Considering the fact that I know it's a cheetah and not a mountain lion, I know its weaknesses," he ended the conversation. Before any of us could argue, it leapt out from the bush and tackled Forrest. He wrestled it for a while and we all gasped. "GO!" he hollered at the top of his lungs and we ran for the tree house. We ran straight to the teleporters and teleported to the meeting room. All of us sat for a while, nervous . . . waiting. About ten minutes later, a blood-stained Forrest appeared in the teleporter.

"Forrest, are you okay?" Rhochelle asked in a sympathetic voice.

"I'm fine, well . . . I will be," he held his arm as if it were in a cast like Rhochelle, Lianna, and Daven's. I suddenly remembered something Neva had told me that Wyatt kept in his stump in the meeting room. Going to empty stump, I stared at the lock and motioned for Cobalt to come over and open it. Inside the stump I found a long post-it note, almost like a receipt, with a list of letters and codes.

"It's a list of all the things that we can teleport to," I smiled at the group and looked for anything that had to do with the mountains.

"Right there, it says 'foot of closest mountain—mp'," Cobalt pointed to it and I walked over to the teleporter. Sliding out the keyboard, I typed in the code and pressed the green button. The teleporter spun a little and I fell against the rocky wall of the mountain. Since there was no other teleporter to go back and tell them that it worked, I contacted them by my watch.

"Guys, it worked, just type in 'mp' on the keyboard," I said and waited for about a minute. When everyone arrived we took a look at the mountain, which was not very tall but very wide. The part of the ground that was directly under the peak must've been about a mile away, but going on an angle and trying to get around the spots that were too hard to climb would make it much harder.

"Are you guys ready again?" Neva wondered and no one made a noise. But we started walking, there was sort of a cut path for us, but it went zigzagged up the mountain, so we decided to climb some of the parts. For hours we trudged through the dirt, mud, ice, and snow.

When we got to the ice it got extremely difficult. We encountered an ice bridge, which absolutely no one wanted to cross.

"Come on guys, we could use the spurs that we brought so you just have to crawl across, digging them into the ice with every step . . . crawl," Rhochelle explained, unaware of the unit that crawling was measured in. One by one, we started going across the bridge over the deep crevice in the mountain. I made it; I was the third one to go. Everything seemed fine until Lianna, the last person, began to cross the bridge. She dug each spur into the ice with a cast on one arm, crawling across it slowly and carefully. But three quarters of the way across the fifteen foot bridge we heard a crack in the bridge. She stared at us for only a moment, her eyes filled with sorrow and sadness beyond compare. We looked back at her, not even hit by the impact enough to cry yet.

The bridge fell right after that, and Gabby did something implausibly considerate without even thinking. She dove after her sister, catching her by the feet. Sam was next, he dove after Gabby who was sliding off the edge and grabbed her feet. One at a time we all started grabbing each other's feet as each new person slid toward the end a little. With five people over the edge and ten on the ice, we managed to pull them up and save their lives. Once Lianna was up, we all fell back and took a deep breath of relief.

"That was such a close one, thank you so much," Lianna thanked us all and we nodded. But the journey still continued with all of us hiking through the snow now.

"Um . . . how are we going to get past that?" I wondered when we got to a giant wall of ice about thirty feet high. It gave the people in the back a chance to catch up, but they stopped and stared as much as the people in the front did. For a whole minute, there was complete silence as the entire group just gaped at the obstacle in front of us.

"I suggest . . . tying the spurs to our hands and feet so we can climb up it," Forrest tried to think; just brainstorming random plans out loud.

"How would we do that, there's no way we'd all make it?" I told him, but no one was in the mood to listen to an argument. We also used the string to throw up to the top of the wall and lasso around a small ice block at the top. Each person tied the spurs to their gloves and boots, getting ready to take on a mission too dangerous for even professional climbers. When it was the younger girls' turn to go, we had to get some of us to climb down so that we could force them to go up. They came after a long fight, saying that we had to get Wyatt in case he was in danger.

"But that's just it, how do we know he's in danger? For all we know this could be a trap," Aura said, but no one listened. The fire on the top of the mountain surely meant that he needed us, or else he never would've made it so big.

"Glacthia probably put him there so that he couldn't take the test, didn't you see it coming?" I smiled at her and she glared at me.

"Guys, we can make it up, it's fine," Rhochelle told us optimistically and the argument stopped. I dug my blade into the ice along with the one attached to my boot. Stepping off the ground, I swayed for a minute, and then continued. Everyone watched me for a minute then followed me.

"Don't put the spur in the same spot that I did, new ice would hold stronger than ice with a hole already in it," I told them, although I didn't have to worry about that. The rope that was tied around the spike at the top of the ice wall really helped me climb, since I could use it to pull myself up when my blades couldn't find a good spot.

Finally, Aura climbed up the wall last. I was almost at the top by this time. But about ten feet from the top I stuck my spur into the ice and heard a gushing sound coming from the ice. This wasn't just a wall of ice . . . it was a frozen waterfall. The ice around me suddenly turned from ice to slush, and I realized what was going to happen next. I waved my hands in the air to get the group's attention and started shouting.

"Guys, climb down, climb down!" I yelled and everyone stared at me. Then they started to realize what the wall really was and repeated my commands. Aura was down in a few seconds, but there was no way that I was going to make it. About halfway up I heard the burst, and grabbed onto the rope along with the other people that were still climbing. The rope when through a loop on our belt, in case we fell at any time. But the power of the water pushed and I spun like a windmill. Eventually the water slowed down and we were far enough away from the wall to not get hit by the water anymore.

"Oh my God it's so cold!" I screamed and shivered.

"We have to get to the top, and then we can come back down," Sam told everyone and continued climbing. I made it to the top a lot slower, being forced to just climb the rope with my gloves. The rope was so thick that I could dig the spurs into it and use it to help a little, but it was still not the same without the ice wall. When I got to the top, I immediately started pulling up the rope until everyone was up.

Each person shivered and fell to the ground once they got up. They moaned and got up slowly. I waved my hand for them to keep going, but no one wanted to follow.

"No, we're not going to go any further, we're going to freeze and die up here!" Cobalt screamed at me.

"Guys, come on, we have to save Wyatt. Here, I brought this battery powered hairdryer, use that," Aura threw a hairdryer out of her bag and into the air. The whole group stared at her as I caught it and used it until I was dry and warm. She passed it to each person and Aura tried to explain.

"Well, I can use it to strengthen my power, and sometimes I can use it like a gun and shoot a line of air that could cut through skin," she smiled at us but the entire group continued to stare at her until everyone was dry.

"Okay, is everyone ready now?" Neva asked as he finished warming himself with the hairdryer. We turned around and walked toward the peak, which now seemed a lot closer since we were over the wall.

Barely two minutes after climbing up the wall, we came to the positively last obstacle of the hike. All of us could see the top of the mountain, about a hundred yards away, and at first, it seemed like nothing was standing in our way. But when I walked a few feet in front of everyone, I slipped and fell on my stomach. If I wasn't wearing about ten pounds of snow gear it would've hurt much more than it did.

"Wow, all this ice up to the top of the mountain is way too slippery to walk on," Neva pointed out, and then walked on it anyway. He slipped and fell as well, making all the Venturas stare at his absurdity.

"Wait, I thought walking on ice was one of your mind powers. Like it was something you could do even if your powers weren't working," Forrest wondered and Neva stood up angrily.

"So did I," he growled and I stared at him.

"What's a mind power?" Sam asked him and all of us Barkers stared at them this time.

"It's a power that you could do when your powers aren't working. We don't know why, but last year when we lost our powers we could still use our mind powers. But this time, for some reason, I guess we can't," he explained to us and we nodded, adding it to their vocabulary. Quickly thinking, Lianna put the spur on the bottom of her boot instead at the toe, where it had been from climbing up the ice wall, and stepped on the ice.

"It's too hard for the spurs to go through," she told the group and we groaned in exhaustion. We all stood there for a minute trying to think, but no one had any ideas.

"What if we use the hairdryer to cool it off?" Aura smiled, holding up the hairdryer as if it were an infomercial.

"Because that would take days," Forrest tried to explain, but he was outnumbered. No one liked the idea because it was so time consuming, but we had no choice. Aura held the hairdryer against the ice and turned it on. About a minute later she stepped on the snow that was under the ice and nodded.

"It worked, but Forrest is right, in about five hours we'll be . . . right there," Aura pointed to about thirty yards in front of her.

"But what other ideas do we have?" Neva demanded to know, and the group was silent. After a minute of no talking Selene smiled and threw her backpack in front of her. We stared at her until she pulled out a pair of ordinary shoes and nodded to us.

"I made these shoes last year when Aura told me that we were going to lose our powers. They push off the ground for you, so you can just walk about a foot off the ground without having to touch it at all." She took off her boots and put the shoes on, tying them to the rope. Then she jumped up and turned them on in midair. They worked just as she said they would, she only came down a little bit then went back up as if she had just taken a leap into the air. In seconds she was on the other side of the ice and took the shoes off, putting her boots back on. I was holding the rope, so I just pulled the shoes back across and put them on, giving the rope to Neva.

"Whoa, this is so weird," I said as I hopped across the ice field. All of us went across one by one, and then we found ourselves waiting for Cobalt to get across. Cobalt laughed as he was jumping over the ice, as most of us did because of its weird feeling.

But something terrible happened when he was running along the ice. A huge pile of snow fell from the top of the mountain and landed in front of him. It was so tall that the gravity shoes didn't have time to react. He hit the snow and fell to the ground. Without even realizing it he was sliding down to the where the ice waterfall was.

"Cobalt!" we all yelled and chased after him. Then we slipped and started sliding down as well. Cobalt slipped out of our sight at the end of the cliff, and we all shouted in agony, knowing we were next.

"Use the blades!" Neva yelled and dug his into the snow that we were now sliding over since we had passed the ice already. I grabbed mine out and shoved it into the snow, thank you sharp metal. Ion stopped just at the edge, his feet dangling in front of the waterfall.

"Where'd he go? I don't see him!" Ion shouted then noticed a loop of rope attached to the iceberg that we had used to climb up.

"He lassoed the spike; his shoes are tied to that rope!" Selene squealed with hope and we all ran to the edge.

"But he should either be dangling halfway up or on the bottom, which he's not," Kamille pointed out, and we all checked. There was nothing on the bottom, so I looked around. There were two chunks of ice hanging off the edge of the cliff. One was a perfectly flat piece that stuck out like a deck. Then the other one was the spike that looked like the bottom half of an anchor that had been stuck in the snow sideways. We had used it to climb up, and now Cobalt had used it to catch the rope with. Forrest stepped back in amazement, realizing where he was.

"I think he slid off the side, then the rope got caught on the spike and he swung back into the waterfall. Then I guess his spurs got caught to the bottom of this ice block right here and he's stuck under it right now," Forrest used his finger to show his path.

"How do we get him out?" I shouted, wanting to know how to save him.

"The only way is to cut off this big piece of ice. Then it'll fall down, and when the rope won't let Cobalt fall anymore he'll stop falling and the ice will break off his spurs.

"Hurry up he's underwater right now and stuck to the bottom of all this ice!" Ion shouted and grabbed both of his spurs, digging into where the flat piece of ice was connected to the edge of the cliff.

"Get back it's going to break now," Neva realized and pushed Ion back so that he was safe from the soon-to-be falling ice. We watched in amazement as the ice broke off, swung in almost a complete semicircle, and then broke off from Cobalt. He was hanging by his boot, swinging back and forth. When he finally stopped we pulled him up and Aura handed him the hairdryer. Fifteen minutes later he was ready to cross the ice field and we did it all over again.

Finally everyone was across, and we climbed the last dozen or so feet to the top. It was a short hike, no one had any problems. Eventually we were at the top, and we practically dropped dead. It was a flat mountain top, about twenty feet in diameter and almost a perfect circle. Then I remembered that it was manmade and looked up at the person standing in the center of the peak.

"Go back," Wyatt told us. His hair was rugged and dirty, and he sat on the ground as if he had been dreading our arrival. For about half a second, I thought about turning around, but then remembered how hard it was to get up here.

"Wyatt, it's okay, we've come to save you!" Forrest told him and waved for him to follow us back down the mountain. Wyatt just stood there, with darkened eyes and an emotionless face.

"*Go back!*" he screamed at us and we got a little nervous. Neva walked forward to get him, but that was the biggest mistake of the day without a doubt. "*No!*" Wyatt shouted and Neva continued to walk. Then Neva stopped and looked at the ground. He removed his foot, and a little red button was revealed. He stared at us in shock, as if trying to apologize for whatever was about to happen. And before anyone could do anything, the part of the peak that most of us were standing on collapsed.

CHAPTER ELEVEN:
THE DESCENT

LIANNA

I rose from the freezing snow and stared at my surroundings. Thirty feet six inches from the top of the peak, an enormous pile of snow blocked us from getting back up. I thought about the people that had fallen off the peak with me. The names rung in my head like a bell, our powers were definitely working right now. Ember, Sam, Kamille, Forrest, Craig, and I were the only ones that had fallen off, nine people not with us. It seemed as if the making of two separate groups by the avalanche was not an accident. Although it was clearly night, I still dug around the snow to find my two brothers. Before I could dig them out of the snow, I saw that most of the group was starting to wake up. Then I counted each person and realized who was missing. Hitting them to get them to stay awake I told them who wasn't here.

"Guys we have to find Kamille and Craig!" I ordered and used my powers to find them. Digging in the snow I eventually found a glove sticking out. Unburying it I found Craig, frozen and frostbitten worse than I've ever seen. Kamille was the same, but the whole group was still staring at me.

"Oh my God, we have to get a fire next to them, quickly," I said in a nervous voice and looked around for sticks.

"How did you know where they were?" Ember wondered and I looked at her. She should've realized that her powers were back by now.

"Aren't your powers working?" I questioned her and she snapped her fingers. No fire came, so she shook her head.

"Mine are," I told the group and they stared at me.

"So are mine," Sam said while making it start to snow. Only Sam and my powers were, it's just our family.

"Oh, I guess just ours are, sorry," I said to them and grabbed a couple sticks lying around and put them together.

"How do you plan on making a fire?" Ember stared at me and I shrugged.

"The old fashion way," I told her and rubbed the two sticks together. About half an hour later, we had a fire the size of a water droplet, and I was ready to explode in anger. But we managed; it kept us warm enough to melt the snow off of our outfits.

I remembered that Forrest was in our group, and dug through his bag for food. He had mostly foods that didn't need to be cooked, so I opened a granola bar and ate it, happy that I didn't have to make a new fire.

"Guys wake up, we have to have some breakfast so we can get going," I told them and everyone moaned. Getting up, I waited for each person to eat a small portion of our rations. Then within minutes we were ready to leave for the bottom.

"Hey, I have an idea," Sam walked over to a long piece of ice shaped like a rectangle. Then grabbing some sticks and rope from his bag, he motioned for us to tie them around to form a toboggan.

"Thank you so much, Sam," I said and got in the front, and Forrest and Ember got behind me. Kamille and Craig were barely conscious, so we carried them into it and tied them down so that they could lie down.

"Okay . . . let's go," Ember pushed off of the ground and we started to slide.

"No, we're not ready yet! We're going to fall off the waterfall!" I screamed and put my hand out to stop it. The only thing that it did was spin us, not slow us down. Everyone dragged their hands on the ice as we spun in circles toward the waterfall. Then each person started to scream, aware of how close death was. But just as we went off the waterfall, Sam saved the day again. He turned our spinning into a tornado, and we flew off the cliff but then slowly spun to a stop. Just at the bottom, we hit the snow and slowed down. When we came to a stop, each person got out and caught their breaths.

"That was a close one, thanks again, Sam," Forrest smiled to my triplet brother, while breathing as if he had just run a mile.

"No problem, I feel like the only one with powers that can save us. No offense, but Lianna doesn't really have a . . . physical power, and Craig's incapacitated right now," Sam told us and I glared at him, but didn't have the will to do anything about it. I thought about the trail ahead to the bottom of the mountain.

"Sam, do you think you could rebuild the bridge over the crevice in the mountain?" I asked him, remembering the three obstacles we faced coming up the mountain, two of which we had just passed.

"Sure, I'll do it when we get there, I can't do it unless I see where it's about to snow. Come on, let's get back in," he got in the front this time, and I pushed off the snow so that we would start moving. We were at the top of a hill, and even with the thick snow slowing us down we were able to move down the hill. Sam was constantly turning cliffs and bumps into snow so we had a smooth slope and we didn't fall or tip.

The riding went on for about two minutes, going down was definitely easier than going up. But then we came to a field of trees that were right before the bridge.

"Uh oh, this is not good," I ducked as each branch came near us. It was like watching the inside of a piano during an elaborate song. Everyone was going down at different times and coming up only if they chose to.

But right when we almost came out, a branch hit Sam right in the head. He fell back, only knocked out, but now we were coming toward the bridge. Everyone screamed and grabbed onto the sides of the toboggan. For the fifth time in two days my life was in mortal danger.

"Hold on!" I screamed to our group just as we neared the drop. Just before falling in, we slowed down a little, and then fell nose first. If it wasn't for the grass that was starting to appear in patches, we would've had so much speed that we might've shattered the toboggan on the other side of the crevice. But just about ten feet down we stopped where the crack got too thin for us to fall into. The toboggan was sitting straight from one side to the other, since the back had caught up with the nose and it got caught where a rock stuck out of each side of the walls. Craig and Kamille flipped out of the toboggan but the ropes caught them, leaving them hanging like puppets.

"We're alive!" Forrest yelled and tried to stand up. But the toboggan shook and he sat down. We were stuck; even standing up could've caused it to tip and send us to the bottom of what I now realized to be a fault.

"We can't get up, so we just stay here?" Ember wondered, and half the group turned to Sam while most of us tried to lift Cobalt and Kamille up, who were just moaning and hanging by their hands and feet.

"Forrest tell me my power is failing me and we still have food?" I asked Forrest and he looked around the toboggan. Then he looked over the edge and sighed.

"Not unless you can get it," he pointed to a bag of food sitting on a boulder about six feet under us. We all made glum faces and sat back in the toboggan. Sam had to wake up eventually, he could just make a twister and make it rain until the crevice is filled and we could walk right out of here. But until then, we had to remain calm.

"Guys, I don't think Craig and Kamille can last much longer," I realized, studying the severity of their frostbite.

"Aura has the hairdryer, why couldn't she be in our group?" Ember complained. Right now, it was just Ember, Forrest, and I, everyone else was unconscious or too cold to speak.

"That's it, the other group, we can call for them and maybe they could come get us!" Forrest told us and we all gasped.

"Guys? Are you there?" I hollered at the top of my lungs, but it was covered up by everyone else just making noise.

"Let's say it all at the same time," Forrest suggested and we nodded. He counted to three silently with his hands and then we screamed it.

"*Guys!*" the three of us screamed at the same time and there was an echo for about a whole minute. We looked at each other and nodded, thinking that it was a pretty good call. Then about a minute later, when nothing happened, we gave up.

"They must've heard it—Miss Monohan could've heard that," Ember said and we nodded. But for a while we sat, wishing that we had never fallen for the trap at the top of the cliff. We weren't even sure if the other group was hiking down the mountain with us, Glacthia could've taken them somewhere.

"I have an idea!" I stood on my knees as if it made me sound more in charge. Then I turned to Craig and prayed that he was able to understand me. "Craig I really need to you make a noise loud enough to cause an avalanche to fill up this crevice." I spoke to Craig and he only groaned.

"He can target his voice so that it will cause an avalanche just big enough to fill in this hole?" Forrest stared from me to Craig in amazement.

"Yes, the right vibration and tone will cause any amount of snow you want to fall, and in any direction," I told them and they made faces showing that they understood.

"Craig please just a yell and then we'll get you to safety," I assured him and slowly covered my ears. He barely had to open his mouth; he knew his powers pretty well. A deafening shout shot through our ears and almost shattered our ear drums. Then I smiled, starting to hear another noise coming from far away.

"Here it comes," I grinned as if an evil plan of mine had just unfolded. The entire crevice shook as 40,853 pounds of snow poured into it. It felt like we were having an earthquake. Ember leaned out of the front of the toboggan and held onto the rocks around her while I did the same to the back.

"Come on guys; it stopped," I told them, jumping out of the toboggan. Although it was a jump that would've killed me a minute ago, I now fell two feet and landed in soft snow. Everyone jumped out, and then we untied Craig and Kamille and took them and Sam out of the toboggan. Then, we began our long hike down the grassy part of the mountain. It took a few hours since we were carrying three people, but eventually Sam woke up just as we were getting to the bottom of the mountain.

"What happened?" he wondered and we explained the entire ordeal to him, from the time he got hit to now. Then he felt his head and touched the bloody mark on his forehead, and looked sick again.

"Come on, we're almost down," Ember told him then stopped. She looked around, as if she had just smelt or heard something unordinary. Then she stared down at her hands and gasped, jumping into the air. Her hand was on fire, and she started screaming and running around. But then she stopped, and held her hand up to her face, still covered in flames.

"Your powers are back . . . my powers are back!" Forrest yelled when he saw his bear hand. "I'm beginning to think that these blackouts aren't as unpredictable as everyone thinks."

"Let's fly back—come on," Ember smiled, as if she hadn't said that in a long while. Forrest turned Sam into a bird while Ember gave me rocket shoes. Ember and I were stuck carrying our younger siblings since we had available arms. It took two minutes to fly to the tree house, and then we burst into the meeting room to find the other group sitting there.

"Guys, you made it, we thought something terrible had happened to you!" Rhochelle blurted out when we entered the room and we stared at them in suspicion.

"Are you kidding? We thought something had happened you," I pointed at the group and they shook their heads.

"Yeah, Wyatt. That was Glacthia's plan anyway; did he talk to you?" Sam asked him and he recollected his thoughts for a few seconds, as if he hadn't told this to the other group yet. Then he started the story of how he was just sitting in a tree during our game of hide and seek dodgeball freezetag.

"Well, then Glacthia just teleported me to the top of the mountain," Wyatt continued. Then I realized that we were all wearing hiking clothes and he was just wearing a shirt and jeans. "He was trying to kill you with the avalanche generator, but you were very lucky to survive. Then our group just hiked down and when we got our powers back I teleported everyone here."

"Well, we barely survived; look at Craig and Kamille! We need to get them to the nurse," Forrest said and we ran straight to the teleporter. Wyatt had added a nurse's office to the keypad and I just pressed the bottom, holding Craig over my shoulder. It was a lot easier to carry someone when you were flying, but still I carried him all the way to the bed nearest to where the teleporter had placed me.

"Oh dear, what planet were you just on, Niveus from the solar system over?" the nurse asked us and we pretended to know what she was talking about.

"No, we were at the top of a mountain, and we got trapped in an avalanche," I told the nurse and Ember put Kamille on the bed next to Craig.

"Are they going to be . . . okay?" Cobalt wondered, not really aware of the harshness of the frostbite.

"Sure, they'll be fine in the morning, come pick them up then. What about you boy, you could use a couple stitches?" she turned to

Sam and he agreed, sitting on one of the beds, but in no mood to lie down.

"Come back in the morning and I'll have them as good as new," she shooed us away and we walked out of the room.

"How come it always takes everyone one night to heal? She could heal Sam in twenty minutes," Forrest pointed out and we nodded. When we got to the stairs my group from the mountain stopped then turned back around. The other group ran in front of us, as if about to tell us that we lived on the ninth floor and not the second.

"Where are you guys going?" Neva wondered, stopping us from going any further. Then we reminded them how Neva's mind powers hadn't worked on the top of the mountain, and then they agreed to follow us to Miss Monohan's room.

"Wouldn't you want to know why your mind powers weren't working even when they did last year when we lost our powers?" Ember asked them and then we knocked on the door, nervous that she wouldn't answer.

"Come in," the familiar voice called and we entered, cramming ourselves into the room that seemed to be shrinking every time we came. "Oh, children, I haven't seen you in a while. You haven't gotten into another situation with Glacthia have you?" she questioned, as if she were a little used to it.

"Yes, he set a trap at the top of the mountain that caused us to hike all the way up there and risk our lives several times," I said for the group and they agreed with my synopsis of the last couple days.

"Oh my, are you alright?" Miss Monohan asked in a sort of caring voice, but since we were standing here she already knew the answer.

"Yeah, but we came to ask you a question about the blackouts," Rhochelle told her and she sat back in her chair.

"We were at the top of the mountain, and I tried to walk across a field of really slippery ice. Well normally, I can walk across ice even when my powers aren't working, because it's one of my mind powers. But this time, I slipped and fell, so does that mean that we're going to lose our mind powers, too?" Neva was curious to know, and she sat up again, as if about to tell us something that was going to be hard for us to hear.

"Last year, you never officially lost your powers, because Aura always kept them with you. What you saw in the Metronome was just pieces of your powers. Last year, I made Mr. Williams make up the story about mind powers. I'm sorry for that, but I just didn't think I'd ever need to explain to you that you only lost most of your powers, not the entire thing. But now with the Metronome causing blackouts, whenever you lose your powers during power flickering, they are truly gone. Power flickering is the word for small blackouts that happen when the Metronome is taking everyone's powers. The Metronome wasn't as powerful last year, but Glacthia has found a way to amplify its powers so that it can take everyone's powers and leave no trace of them at all. When you lose your powers in a blackout . . . you lose them for real."

November ended in the blink of an eye, and we were left with December's frosty afternoons and short days. Not much happened as it ended, things went back to normal as they did after each of Glacthia's attempts to destroy us. Ember started to go out with Chris again. He seemed to forgive her for going to the dance with Jerod. No one wanted to retake the driver's test.

One Friday we were on our way to geography block, our most dreaded day of the whole semester, and a voice echoed through the rooms of the school. There was no loudspeaker system, so it must've been a machine or someone's power causing the voice to be heard in every room. Then I looked around and realized that Miss Monohan must've called Craig down to do it.

"Will all students and faculty please report to the cafeteria for a mandatory meeting at this time please," Miss Monohan's voice called out to us and we instantly reared ourselves down to the first floor. It was just luck that we got out of geography today, we had forgotten about an essay on the reason for plate tectonics that was due today. When all of us got to the cafeteria we met up with our siblings and pushed our tables together as we usually did. The people who cleaned the cafeteria seemed to always move them apart, and we have no way of stopping them because no one's ever seen the cafeteria cleaners.

"I wonder what this is about," I questioned our group to see if they had heard any rumors lately. No one jumped right ahead and said anything, so I assumed that they were all just guessing.

"Maybe another dance," Neva smiled to Sam and Forrest, they've become sort of a trio lately. I rolled my eyes and looked to see if anyone else had a guess.

"I don't know. We're probably in trouble. 'Member last year's assembly when the first family disappeared? They thought it was a prank," Daven reminded us.

"Most likely," Ember said, finishing the conversation when all the teachers started to shush us. Miss Monohan stood up from the teachers table and waited for the noise to cease, then began her speech.

"As some of you may know, next Friday is Ancestor Day, one of the most important holidays in our culture. Now this happens once every five years, and it is the thousandth one in history. So five thousand years ago from next Friday, the Ancestors took people from Earth to the first human inhabited space planet, Medlocks.

"Although Medlocks is the planet that Ancestor Day is associated with, the parade is to be held on Praeclarus, because it has more land than us and can hold more people. Now most of you probably don't understand the importance of this holiday because it is your first one, but it is a family holiday. For this reason, you will be given the next week of school off to visit your parents and go to the parade with them." She didn't even bother continuing, the applause that followed her statement was deafening enough to be heard on Medlocks Plains.

"Now, I have only one piece of advice for you. Stay with you parents, even if you think you are old enough. The crowds at this parade can range from two million to two hundred million. The skies are filled with people trying to get a good look, and the crowd on the ground goes on for miles. People stand dozens of miles away from the parade just to be there. If you are lost, your chances of seeing your family for the rest of the day are slim.

"Lastly, there is a rumor about the parade going around that I'm probably not allowed to tell you. If you repeat this to any other soul except for a schoolmate or a parent, the consequences will be grave. It is considered confidential on some planets, so I especially advise you not to tell anyone from other school boards. The Ancestors are supposed to make an appearance at every hundredth parade, so only one every five hundred years. But because of the treacheries going on in the universe people are assuming that they won't come. Yes, they are going to come to the parade next Friday, and that is all I'm going to tell you." For a minute it seemed as if her speech wasn't over, but then she sat down and we all started talking again.

"Oh, wait I forgot!" Her voice was more powerful than a megaphone's, but she looked like she wasn't even trying. We instantly got silent and then continued. "There will be four space buses on Sunday that will go to each of the four planets, in case you want to visit your family before going to Praeclarus. That is all," she ended and then the rise of voices overpowered the silence.

"Cool! Our first time going to a planet other than Medlocks and Callidus," I told the group and they nodded.

"Yeah and I hear that Praeclarus is beautiful," Rhochelle smiled, thinking about the snowcapped mountains, long beaches, and blue oceans.

"Wow, this is gonna be the best week off ever, there's only one thing bad about it," Forrest said, specifically to the other kids.

"What?" almost all of us asked in one way or another.

"We have to go back to geography," he stood up and all the older kids groaned in annoyance. We walked back to our class, just in time to get yelled at for not having our reports.

No one hesitated for the upcoming adventure. Each person had packed enough stuff for a week in a suitcase that Ion made the size of a calculator. Then we spent the entire Saturday lying around wishing that we were on the bus.

Finally Sunday arrived and at 8:17 in the morning all of us stood on the sunrise lit grass waiting to get on the buses. Although the airport sat just minutes from the school, technically vehicles were allowed to land anywhere they wanted. Airports just marked civilization on desolate planets that were uninhabited.

"Come on, come on, I wanna get on the bus. I packed a bookbag of stuff to do so that we don't get bored," I overheard Selene saying to Kamille and Aura. I rolled my eyes and stepped onto the bus that was just now opening its doors, I just had a few books that I wanted to read. We all rushed to the back seats and got either seats by ourselves or with someone else in our family. After that came the Tungs, then the Slomowitzes, and then the Andersons. Once all four families were on the bus, it waited for the other buses to make the signal, and then took off.

"Yes, we're on our way to Callidus, then . . . Praeclarus! We're gonna get to see the Ancestors in a parade!" Aura squeaked with delight and everyone else gave her confused faces.

135

"Weren't you there when we saw them last year? You know, right after we saved the whole school," Neva reminded her and then she squinted, looking off into the distance and thinking.

"I don't remember," Aura finally decided and everyone hit themselves in the foreheads, some rolling their eyes.

"Remember, eight people came to Caelum when Miss Monohan threw the Barathrum Evado Trophy at Glacthia. Mom, Dad, Mr. Williams, Miss Monohan, and all four of the Ancestors were those eight people. They left just before we went into the lair to get the keys and unlock all the doors." Wyatt stared at her with a confused but still not surprised face.

"Oh, I remember now. Well, they barely talked to us anyway. Once everyone walked into the lair where the cells were, they were gone," Aura realized and then everyone went back to their own conversations.

"So, Lianna, what do you wanna do for four hours?" Gabby bothered me, she knew I wanted to get to understand the new method that scientists believed the Egyptians to have used to build the pyramids. Then she stared at me, confused for a minute.

"Don't you know what's going to happen?" Gabby asked me and I closed the book, glaring at her for stopping me from reading.

"I read it anyway," I said quickly then went back to the book.

"But that ruins it!" she yelled and the bus got quiet. Then I turned red and shrunk down in my seat.

"I know, but I try not to think about the ending. Sometimes I can tune out of my powers to just read a book," I explained in a kind voice, then jerked back to her book.

"La la la, singing, I am singing," she sang. "This is my song that I am singing, la la la la, la la! I am singing!" Gabby shouted to me and I closed my book again.

"You're not going to let me read are you?" I asked and she smiled an evil smile at me. Then I switched to the seat next to Wyatt, he was asleep. Gabby suddenly felt alone and jumped into Rhochelle and Ember's seat. They were taking pictures of themselves, and she jumped into one of them with Rhochelle. My eldest cousin took it and then the three of them laughed at the strange faces that they had made.

"What do you guys wanna do?" Gabby asked them, bored out of her mind. She needs to be quiet, or I'm not going to get any of this reading done! My eyes slowed down until I wasn't reading at all, just staring at one word. I tuned into the conversation going on behind me.

"We have no idea, we're just going to take pictures and laugh at how weird they are," Rhochelle explained, and then they rushed a few seats back to the small area in the back where they had room to walk around and stand. I put the book down and looked up.

"Let's make a video," Ember suggested and she ran over to Rhochelle. Immediately Ember started filming and Gabby had nothing to do. With a flick of Gabby's wrist, two small suns appeared on each side of her hand, like a sparkling baton with an invisible handle. She moved her hand and the two suns, making it look like she was twirling the baton. Pretending to make it really fancy, she did a little dance with the sparkler. Then she made it disappear and fell onto my knees.

"Thank you universe, I'll be on Callidus 'til Friday," Gabby quoted a rock star and then walked off the stage. Ember finished the video and then we watched it, laughing the entire time. Then Rhochelle jumped up and down and pointed at the camera.

"I have the greatest idea in the history of great ideas," she yelped and then took the camera. Fine, if I can't eliminate them, I might as well join them. I walked over to her to see what she was doing.

"Wait, who are you sending it to?" I asked her, pushing Gabby out of the way to get a better look.

"Nicole," she said as if it were so obvious. We smiled as she typed in the name for Nicole's camera. Digital cameras made by Altrians had the ability to send pictures or videos to other people's cameras just by typing in the name that a person selects for their camera when they first get it, called the digital code.

"Message sent," Rhochelle read and then took the camera back.

"What are you guys doing?" Ember wondered and looked at the camera, she had been staring out the window at the sun that we were whipping around at 58,245,386 miles per hour.

"Sending a video to Nicole," Rhochelle explained. The four of us laughed and kept making new weird videos, all the way to Callidus.

The rocket landed just a couple miles from my Aunt Aubree and Uncle Riddock's house. It was the center point of the four family's houses that were on the plane.

"We made it, no problems," Daven smiled as we were walking off the plane.

"Is that a first or what?" Neva pointed out and each of us nodded.

"Are you guys ready to find your house?" I asked and everyone stared at me.

"Why find it? We're already there." Wyatt forced our eyes shut for just a second, and when they opened, we were standing on the doorstep of our house. Smiling at Wyatt, I knocked on the door and no one inside the house hesitated. Aunt Aubree, Uncle Riddock, and another person who was cleaning the floors all pushed each other out of the way to answer the door. When it opened there was just a mess of people standing there trying to talk. We walked in and sat down at the dinner table, starved, and my aunt and uncle finally came to us.

"How can you afford all of these people cleaning your house?" Sam wondered, watching a woman walk into the room and put a sandwich on each of our plates. We stared at the two adults for an answer, and they looked as if they had already expected us to know it.

"Well not all of our inventions turned out to be catastrophic disasters. There are some robots and machines we invented that did a lot of good for the world, which is why people don't hold a grudge against us for inventing Glacthia," Aunt Aubree explained, and Uncle Riddock finished her explanation.

"You know the machine on the top of your school that can change the scenery of the roof to make it whatever you want?" he asked, and we nodded. "We invented that using parallel dimension vortexes, it just goes to Earth and clones the things that you want on the roof of the building."

"That thing almost gave the Metronome right to Cobalt's brothers. In fact . . . that's probably how Glacthia got it," Forrest realized, and we stared at each other's shocked faces. If Cobalt's brothers were working for Glacthia, maybe they could've snuck back to the school and recreated the Metronome to give it to Glacthia.

"He must've promised them a couple powers in return for giving it to him. If Glacthia has all the powers in the universe, he could spare a couple useless ones to give to your brothers," I told Cobalt, and he lowered his head in shame.

"It's okay, Cobalt, don't feel bad," Ion told him and he nodded.

"It's not that. I'm just wondering why my brother's would give it to Glacthia. If they were aware of what the Metronome could do, they would've kept it for themselves and stole all of our powers with it,"

Cobalt explained, adding another mystery to our own lives. We stared at each other nervously and waited for someone to break the silence.

"So what do you guys wanna do?" Aura finished her sandwich and waited for an answer. Instantly, all of us ran outside to start a game of capture the flag.

When it got dark we began to play manhunt. One team hunts for the other in the dark, and if they tag someone they can bring them back to jail. You get out of jail the same way, by having a teammate tag you. And once the hunting team gets everyone on the hiding team in jail, the teams switch places.

Finally by the end of the night when everyone was gamed out, we retired for the day in our soft, comfortable beds.

The next morning I awoke to the sound of a knock on the door. Running downstairs in my pajamas, I stopped and my mouth dropped as I saw the people at the door.

"Mr. President! What a surprise! How can we help you?" Uncle Riddock spoke to him as if he was expecting bad news. Next to the President of the Medlocks solar system stood two girls, about my age, and a short, stubby man with a couple long red hairs wrapped around his bald head in a spiral. The president was tall, with short brown hair that stuck up only seven eighths of a centimeter.

"The name's Luke Pelliccio, CEO of the Ancestor Day Parade Committee," the stubby man stuck out his hand and my aunt and uncle shook it. Then he did something that almost made me gasp and fall down the stairs. At that moment almost half our group walked down the staircase to where I was. The man pulled a digital camera out of his pocket and showed a video to my aunt and uncle.

"We were sent this video yesterday and were amazed to find out that it was the cousin of the Barkers. I was about to ask all of the kids to be on a float in the parade, because of their . . . importance, to the people of the universe. But after I saw this I just realized, why not make them sparkler twirlers? I ask this of you because Mr. President's two daughters, Tory and Alissa Johnson, are also sparkler twirlers. It would be a great experience and I think that—"

"How could you send it to the president instead of Nicole, what is wrong with you?" Gabby yelled to Ember and shoved her. Instead of just stumbling a little, she fell back into poor Aura, who rolled the down the rest of the stairs. I gasped and chased after her, along with the rest of our group. The sight must've been really strange for the four people at the door to watch. At the bottom of the stairs I asked if Aura was okay. She had only fallen a couple stairs onto a rug, so she said that she was fine.

"Well, I . . . uh . . . had no idea that . . . I for one am . . ." Mr. Pelliccio ran out of things to say so Uncle Riddock just interrupted him.

"I'm terribly sorry for that, I don't think the video was meant to be sent to you. But they are grateful that you ask them to do this, although that wasn't a sparkler, it was just her powers," he explained, and Gabby walked up behind him and nodded.

"Hey, I'm Tory," said the first daughter, looking a little older than Alissa. She had curvy red brown hair that sort of was clumped on the top of her head.

"Hey, Tory, I'm Gabby, hey Alissa," Gabby waved to her and then waved to Alissa. She just had long brown hair that went down to about where her elbows were when she had her hands at her sides.

"You want us to be sparkler twirlers?" Neva asked in a "no way" voice and Mr. Pelliccio nodded. Then the rest of our group stared at me to make the decision.

"I think that the float idea is better," I told him then noticed Alissa and Tory, who were pointing to themselves mouthing things that looked like "us too." "And the president's daughters definitely shouldn't be walking in a parade, they should have something to sit on so they can wave to their nation." They made small "thank you" faces and I exchanged it with a "you're welcome."

"Is that okay with you, girls?" Mr. President asked them and they pretended to think for a minute, just to make it look good. Then they nodded, and he turned back to us. "So it's settled, we're not going to have them as sparkler twirlers, they'll sit on a float to wave to everyone," he decided and we all agreed.

"That's perfect, I love it, we'll start on the float right now," Mr. Pelliccio decided just to make the president happy.

"Come on girls, we have to go now," Mr. President led away Alissa and Tory and they waved to us. The door was closed and my aunt and uncle turned to me.

"Thank you universe, I'll be on Callidus 'til Friday?" Uncle Riddock asked Gabby and the group started laughing.

The entire week went by before we knew it, and soon enough we were landing the rocket after a six hour ride. Before we were going from Medlocks to Callidus, which are right next to each other on their orbit. But Callidus and Praeclarus are on completely opposite sides of the orbit.

"We made it!" I jumped out of the plane and lay on the ground. I hated flying because it disturbed my reading. The ride was pretty boring. We had agreed not to send any videos in case we had the wrong digital code.

"Come on, we're late for the meeting with all the people in the parade," Ember jumped into the air and turned on her rocket shoes. The rest of us followed her through the town of Moenia and looked for the amphitheater. When we found it we turned to the Barkers' parents, who turned to leave.

"We're going to be watching the parade from a friend of ours' house, which is pretty far away but has fantastic binoculars. You kids have fun, and don't get into any danger," Aunt Aubree hugged all of us and we stepped into the theater.

"And that is all," Mr. Pelliccio told the crowd of people wearing strange costumes and holding what seemed to be instruments, and they started to head out. I noticed Alissa and Tory and met up with them.

"What'd he say?" I wondered, trying to figure out if it was anything important.

"Uh . . . don't mess up?" Tory recalled.

"And don't ask for the Ancestors' autograph," Alissa remembered, and we laughed.

Everyone headed out and I told the group that the speech was nothing important. Practically at the exit of the amphitheater was the beginning of Adeo Calceata, the longest road in Medlocks solar system. The parade didn't walk across the entire thing, for it was 6,483 of miles long, but the road was just important because it was the first road built on one of the five planets other than Medlocks.

We walked onto our float inspecting it and nodded, accepting it. It had a giant statue of Medlocks Academy and there were glowing stars that were spiraling around it, leaving sparkling, glowing trails behind them.

"This is so cool, when's the parade going to—" Daven was about to ask when loud music was heard. We looked ahead to see where it was coming from. The marching band was playing instruments that definitely were not invented on Earth. Instantaneously, all the floats and marchers started moving and we all fell back into our chairs. Alissa and Tory's chairs were on a platform behind us, so they got a better view of the audience. Then, a man standing on one of the floats threw his hands out. Every couple feet a metal pole with a hole near the top rose out of the ground. Then a growing, yellow rope as thick as a pipe started threading itself through all the holes. Looking around, I noticed the only float that was empty, and had four chairs sitting on a platform. Behind it was a ninety-foot four-inch wide projection screen, showing the four empty chairs. I had a feeling in the pit of my stomach that the Ancestors weren't going to come after all, and that it was all a big lie waiting to let everyone down.

The parade went on for a while, with the people in the audience literally lined up for miles to see it. But then, just when the crowd seemed to stop growing, a roaring applause started as loud as if the entire universe started playing the drums at the same time on the same planet. We turned to see the projection screen, with a dark figure sitting in each chair. All of us cheered along with the crowd, and I even jumped out of my chair to clap.

Hours went by as we smiled to all the people we were passing. The sun was close the horizon and the shadow of the Ancestors went about two miles behind the parade. They were the last float, so it didn't cover anyone. We were right in front of them, so the screams for them were loudest near us. Whenever someone behind us stopped screaming for them, someone in front of us would start.

For a while I thought that they would eventually change the song, because for us it got really boring very quickly. But then I remembered that each person only sees the parade for about ten minutes, and the people far enough away to see the whole thing don't hear the music anyway.

Later that night, the parade came to an end, and all of us seemed to be in a good mood after a whole day of people cheering for us and the Ancestors. Just when we thought that the parade had come to an end, I noticed something happening to the road.

"Guys, what's going on?" I questioned the group with its two new members and they stared at it. The road seemed to be rising, like an empty balloon being put under a piece of paper and then being blown up. When the front of the parade rammed the giant bump in the road, all the floats kept going until they hit the float in front of it.

"The Ancestors!" Forrest pointed up, and we saw the projection screen showing four empty chairs. Then I noticed four small figures falling off the platform. Just when they were about to save themselves, a dimensional portal opened up in front of them and they fell into it. Rhochelle jumped off of the float to pull a rock out of the ground that could lift her up to the portal, but she only fell to ground.

"Our powers aren't working, we have to use the stairs," Forrest leapt off of the float and onto the Ancestors' one. He opened a door at the bottom of the stage, and the rest of us ran inside it and started up the long staircase.

"Can we come with you?" Tory asked and stopped me from leaving. It wouldn't be right putting the president's daughters in danger, but they deserved the choice to help or not. I nodded, and Alissa, her, and I ran up to the rest of the group and up the stairs. Once Forrest opened the door to the top of the platform he jumped off, falling straight into the portal. It looked like it was about to close, so no one hesitated to jump off in fear that waiting would cause them to jump just when the portal had closed, and they would be falling four stories without powers. We fell in and then pounded into a pile of sand.

"Where are the . . ." Neva didn't bother to finish when he saw that Glacthia was standing in front to us.

"Well, well, well, what a surprise to see the people that should have been dead on several occasions," he told us, and we were just about to run to him. But bars started to come out of the sand and wrap around each other, putting us in a cage.

"Where are the Ancestors?" Selene asked in a serious voice, actually thinking that he would answer. For a second everyone stared at him, deep down hoping that maybe he might answer the question. Then after a long silence, when I had given up hope on getting an answer from him, he spoke up.

"Oh don't worry, they're alive. At least, they will be, until 5:30 p.m. next Saturday," he told us. For a minute we were all relieved that they were still alive, but then all of us gave him confused faces.

"Why are you telling us your plan?" Ember wondered, staring at him right where his eyes should be, as if she knew that something was wrong.

"Yeah, isn't that against villain rules?" Daven questioned him bravely, even though he was aware that villains obviously didn't have rules.

"Well, the answer to that is very simple," he told us, savoring our moment of curiosity, and wanting to hold it as long as possible. For almost a whole minute his answer remained a mystery, and I was about to say something to him asking him to think faster.

"Because I know that you won't remember any of my plan," he answered in a slight whisper, and a white mist started to rise out of the sand that we were standing on.

"What's happening?" Sam demanded to know, but then he got a dazed look on his face. I started to feel tired all of the sudden, and my eyelids were getting heavier by the second. I looked at Alissa and Tory, who were standing next to me, stepping back and forcing Rhochelle into the corner of the cage.

"I'm sorry," Tory said to me, she and Alissa looked tired, but Rhochelle didn't. But then she started to look drowsy as well. Before I could say anything asking her what she was talking about, I fell to the sand in a deep sleep.

CHAPTER TWELVE: AMNESIA'S EFFECT

RHOCHELLE

I woke up to find that I was sleeping in the tree house, in the sleepover room. Getting up, I walked over to Ember and shook her awake.

"Ember, wake up, wake up, do you know what happened?" I asked her, and she didn't even open her eyes, as if she didn't care. But then she jumped up so that she was sitting on the side of her bed, facing me. For about a minute she stared at me, turning her head every couple seconds as if she were looking at something new each time.

"Who's Ember?" she questioned, and my mouth dropped open.

"You're Ember," I told her in a kind voice, all of my fears exploding in my face.

"Are you kidding? Don't you think I'd know my own name? I'm probably fifteen years old or something. My name is . . . well I mean . . . I know that it's . . ." she looked around, trying to remember her own name. This was very bad, Ember had no memory about anything at all. I ran to Lianna, she must know what was going on, it's her power.

"Lianna, wake up, come on, wake up," I shoved her until she fell out of her bed. Once she hit the floor she jumped up, only half awake.

"Lianna?" she asked, blinking over and over again until she could see me.

"What's your name?" I asked her in a nervous voice, begging that she knew it.

"Well it's . . . a name that . . . I don't know," Lianna realized and then it hit me. They had lost their memories; they didn't even know that they had powers. I ran to the meeting room and pressed the loudspeaker button and picked up the microphone.

"Could everyone immediately go to the meeting room please? That would be the one with the satellites and cell phone towers coming out of the top," I told the tree house, hoping that my plan would work. According to the reactions of Ember and Lianna, they didn't know that they lost their memory until I asked them a question about themselves. So if I didn't ask them a question about themselves, maybe they might not know that they lost their memory and come to the tree house. Otherwise they wouldn't trust me enough to come here. One by one each person arrived, it took almost ten minutes for everyone to get here. They sat down on the stumps, staring around at each other and thinking back to see if they knew what was going on.

"We're going to go around in a circle, and each person is going to say their name when I point to them," I started, skipping Lianna and Ember and going to Gabby.

"I . . . have no idea," she told me, and then the same thing happened for every single person in the room.

"Okay, raise your hand if you believe me that you lost your memory," I tested them, but no one in the room raised their hands.

"Just because we don't know our names doesn't mean we lost our memory," Forrest spoke up for the group. They seemed to have a bond with each other that only proved that they were still siblings and cousins.

"Then what do you think it means?" I asked the group, and they were silent. "Exactly. You guys just have to believe me; you lost your memory. It must've been that white mist that hit us. I'll take you to . . . the doctor's house . . . and she can get your memory back. If you want to know your name again, then come with me!" I cheered and pretended to march out of the room. I didn't want to say "Mom" because then it would leave them to believe that all fifteen of us were siblings, which would freak them out.

"Oh my gosh, I just realized," my eyes grew so wide that they suddenly looked interested. "Don't you guys know what today is?" I asked them, and they all shook their heads. "You don't know?" I wondered in a shocked voice. "Today is the day where you go to all the teachers, and they give you a piece of candy for visiting them!" I shouted and they stood up. We walked out and went down the stairs out of the tree house that I had made in case the teleporters weren't working and our powers weren't working. I didn't want them to have to use the teleporters because they weren't aware that we were on a planet where everyone had superpowers. For all I knew, they might even think that they're still on Earth. The Venturas didn't because they grew up on Callidus, where their parents found a way to hide them from the government, just as Cobalt's parents had done with him. Each person was terrified of steps, as if every one of them was afraid of heights all of the sudden.

We walked the entire distance from the tree house to the door. Everyone looked around the forest, and at the animals staring at them. Forrest went up to a fox and pet it, definitely proving that he still was in touch with his powers. But once we walked out in the main room of our floor, everyone stopped and turned back to the forest.

"That's not possible, there are no greenhouse walls," Ember pointed at the forest. Suddenly the whole group glared at me, as if I had lied to them.

"Guys, what's the matter? I didn't lie to you. You're . . . actors . . . and this is the set for the movie," I pointed all around me and then into the forest. The group started to smile again, for as long as I remember everyone had wanted to be famous. And so far they've proved that they remembered basically their whole lives until the comet came to us from Praeclarus. We kept walking, and eventually I turned into the second floor. Walking in, I knocked on Miss Monohan's door. We waited about a minute, and then I figured that she wasn't in there.

"She's outside talking with the president. Did you hear that his daughters' memories are gone?" Mrs. Reichert asked us, and my eyes grew to the size of kiwis. I shook my head, then thought of something to say.

"We need to see her—it's really important," I told her, and she nodded in approval, thinking that it had to be important enough to interrupt the president.

"Be careful, it's about to pour," she warned us and I turned to leave. But the group stayed, smiling at her, expecting something.

"Can we have our candy?" Wyatt finally asked and she stared at them in confusion. I made hand signals to Mrs. Reichert behind the group for her to say "no."

"Sorry . . . I'm all out?" she asked me and I nodded. The group sighed and followed me out.

"That's okay, Miss Monohan is the principal, and she has the most candy out of all the teachers," I told them and walked down the stairs and out the door. It was drizzling a little, but not enough to be considered pouring. We walked out to Miss Monohan, and for a second I waited for her to watch the president leave. But once he was gone, I turned to my siblings, cousins, and Cobalt, and twisted my hand. All of them twisted into the ground until the dirt was up to their knees. They fell back and I raised a stone chair out of the ground so that they could sit.

"Rhochelle, what are you doing?" Miss Monohan asked me and I looked at their astonished faces. This was going to be fun to explain. How do I tell the principal of my school that the president of the entire solar system's daughters' memories are missing because we let them come with us to face Glacthia?

"Alissa and Tory came with us to find the Ancestors, and Glacthia wiped everyone's memory. I think I still have mine because Tory's power is blocking things, and she blocked the white mist from wiping my memory. But now I have to take them to our parent's house so that our Mom can give them their memory back. The problem is that they don't trust me, and won't come with me. Can you help me convince them to come?" I asked Miss Monohan and she stood in front of them.

"Well what do you want me to say?" she asked me and I thought for a minute.

"Just try to make them believe that they lost their memory, so they can come to Callidus with me and I can help them get their memory back," I told her and she tried to think of a way to put that in words.

"Students, try to think about where we are? Do you know where we are?" she questioned them for a minute and no one answered. "Exactly, you don't know, and why is that? You lost your memory in an accident yesterday, which I will learn more details about," she turned to me and I frowned. "But there is a way for you to remember your lives, and everything that you once knew. If you go with Rhochelle, you can get your memory back. Your mom has the power to give people their memories back. So what do you say?" Miss Monohan asked them and it was quiet for a minute. I was sure they were going to say yes, it was clear that they wanted their memories back. I let them go, and they stumbled a little bit when they had no dirt holding them up.

"Are you guys going to come with me?" I questioned them and waited for their answer. All of the sudden it started to pour, and I noticed that all of my siblings were glaring at me with anger.

"How could you lie to us?" Aura wanted to know, and everyone seemed to be on her side. They suddenly ran off, all in different directions. I couldn't catch any of them, for the rain wasn't allowing me to see more than five feet in front of me. Miss Monohan looked at me and shrugged, out of ideas.

"Give them some time, they'll come around," she started heading back toward the school. I watched her leave, and then I followed her inside. I walked slowly to my floor, the feeling of failure like a weight on my shoulders, dragging me down. When I walked inside, I saw everyone sitting on the stumps in the meeting room that we had made outside of the tree house. They looked up at me, as if they had just been talking about me.

"We've decided . . . that we want to go with you," Ember told me, and I smiled, laughing to myself a little.

In minutes we had called for a taxi and were waiting inside the school, watching the rain. When it pulled up we all went inside, and I felt like I was part of the family again. The ride to Eximius was more boring than I had hoped. I had to explain to everyone everything they wanted to know. They asked about more things than I could possibly imagine, if Alissa and Tory hadn't gotten their memories wiped then we wouldn't even have to visit our parents. The capital of the Medlocks solar system was on a very secluded town on Eximius. It was a huge building with tons and tons of grassland around it. When the taxi landed there, we gave the driver his money and he drove away.

"Wow, another time when we made it through a taxi ride without being kidnapped," I laughed by myself and the group stared at me. I walked around the perimeter of the building, trying to find the window of Alissa and Tory's room. Finally I looked into a window and saw two girls sitting on a couch, discussing something. I knocked on the window and Tory came to open it.

"Who are you?" she asked in a rude voice and I rolled my eyes.

"I'm Rhochelle, come with me," I ordered her and she stepped back.

"Okay, just because we have no idea who we are, doesn't mean we're dumb enough to follow some stranger out of the window," Alissa told me and my mouth dropped. But then I remembered that I just had to keep calm and keep my patience.

"What if I told you that I could help you get your memory back?" I bribed them, but they made no expression showing that they were intrigued.

"We wouldn't believe you," Tory explained to me and I lost it. Not wanting to destroy the president's house, I lifted eight rocks out of the ground and moved them into the window. They hit Tory and Alissa's hands and feet and melted around them, forcing them to be under my control. I moved the rocks around, making them feel like puppets. Then I carried them out of the room and walked back to where the taxi had left us.

"Ugh, that's right . . . he left," I remembered and looked at my siblings and cousins for an idea. They didn't say anything so I thought now would be a good time to tell them about their powers. But then I lifted rocks out of the ground under each person, and they staggered for a second then regained their balance. I also put a clean rock over Tory and Alissa's mouths so that they could not shout for help.

"Are you sure that we should bring them? They seem like they don't want to come . . ." Ion pointed out and I shook my head.

"They have to; we're the only ones that can get their memory back," I answered him and then he seemed to agree. We got to the president's private airport. There was the same taxi driver there, so he was willing to give us a ride to Callidus.

The flight went by quickly, no one talked as they watched Tory and Alissa scream for help. Three times the driver asked him if there was something wrong with them. We told him that they had a fear of flying, but we were going to visit our parents. But when two girls scream for six hours, a driver can get pretty annoyed.

"I'm going to land if you don't calm them down!" he shouted over their screams and I wished that I had kept the rocks that kept their mouths shut. For another couple minutes they started to lose their voices, but then their cracking voices became even more annoying. Finally the vehicle stopped and the driver turned to look at us.

"I will turn you into the police soon for kidnapping the president's daughters if you don't tell me why they're really screaming," he ordered me to tell, and my mouth dropped. I stared at him for a minute, trying to figure out if I could recognize him, but then I gave up and started to explain.

"Glacthia made them lose their memories, and our mom has memory for a power, so she can cure them. But as you can see, they don't know who we are, and they don't trust me. They didn't want to come, but I made them because I want them to get their memory back," I said in a very sad voice, and suddenly wished that I had Craig's power to add more of an effect.

"I see, but I still think that you'll be in a lot of trouble for kidnapping them," he turned the car back on and continued to drive. I already am in so much trouble. I turned back to watching the sisters scream. When we landed I lifted their legs by maneuvering the rocks attached to them so that they would walk. They screamed and tried to kick, but I had too much power over them.

I rang the doorbell at our parents' house and they answered quickly to try to stop the girls from screaming. But as soon as they answered the door their mouths dropped and they looked at me.

"Are those the president's daughters?" Dad asked, knowing that something was wrong from the start.

"Yes, can we come in?" I begged and walked in before they could answer. Everyone followed me and I forced Tory and Alissa in after them. Everyone but Tory and Alissa stared at the house in amazement, thinking that they were seeing it for the first time. We sat down on the couches in the living room and I waited for one of my parents to ask what was going on.

"What's the matter? We haven't seen you since before the parade. Did you hear that Glacthia kidnapped the Ancestors? What a horrible thing to do, I can't believe he would do that. One day all this guilt is just going to build up and it's going to destroy me," Mom explained to us, almost crying a little but not her usual amount.

"Yeah, we jumped into the portal that he captured them in, and Glacthia wiped everyone's memory. Lianna let Tory and Alissa come with us, and I think that Tory might've blocked the white mist that wiped everyone's memory from getting to me. I don't know why they picked me, but now I'm the only one that could remember stuff, and I kidnapped everyone to get them here so that you could give them their memory back," I told my parents and Mom looked at them, trying to figure out their condition. Then she flung her hands out and everyone got that same dazed look in their eyes, and then fell asleep.

I waited for a couple hours, explaining what happened at the parade in detail to my parents. Finally when they woke up, I asked Tory and Alissa to give us a full scale report on what had happened to them.

"It all started when we were sitting on our float, and the road started rising. Glacthia jumped into our minds, and made us ask to go with you to save the Ancestors. He said that he wanted our memories wiped as well because we were so close to the president. Then just before the white mist came, he jumped out of Alissa and me. Then I knew that if we got one person to remember everything, then they could save us. My power is blocking, so I blocked the white mist from the first person I saw, Rhochelle. I knew that if we all were protected from it, then Glacthia would know right away that his plan didn't work," Tory remembered, as if it was the last thing that had happened to her.

"And my power is sleeping. I thought that if Rhochelle didn't fall asleep, then Glacthia would know that the mist didn't affect her. Then I put her to sleep and Glacthia teleported all of you guys to the tree house and us to Eximius," Alissa recalled the moment and suddenly it all fit together.

"Why couldn't you block it from all of us then put all of us to sleep?" Neva wondered, jealous that I was the one who got to remember everything.

"Then the mist wouldn't be there at all. I blocked it from Rhochelle because she was in the corner, and it was subtler. If I blocked it from everyone it would just push it away from us and Glacthia would know that it wasn't even getting to us," Tory told him and he nodded to show that he understood.

"Well, thanks for giving us our memory back, but we have classes tomorrow," I said to our parents and everyone groaned, having not known that the flight from Medlocks to Eximius and Eximius to Callidus had taken all night.

"Okay, have fun with that," Dad said sarcastically and hugged all of us goodbye and Mom called for two taxis. One would take Tory and Alissa back to Eximius and the other would take us to Medlocks. When they got there, we waved to our parents and watched them get smaller and smaller until they were gone.

"So what are we gonna do now?" Forrest wondered, bored from all the road trips.

"When we get back it'll probably be about noon, and I'm really tired," Lianna told us and everyone in the car agreed.

"Do you think what that guy said was true?" I asked the group, knowing they had no idea what I was talking about.

"What guy, what was true?" Cobalt questioned me for detail and I hushed my voice so that the driver could barely hear me.

"When our taxi driver from Eximius to Callidus got mad at me for not quieting the president's daughters, he said that we were gonna be in trouble for kidnapping them," I told them, and they looked at the floor. It was quiet for a while, since no one really knew what to say.

"Maybe no one even knew that they left, and they needed their memories back. I'll be surprised if we're not heroes," Wyatt said, and lay back to enjoy the ride.

When Medlocks was in sight I felt better because I was at home again, where I belonged. At the airport I ran off of the rocket, happy to be back. But I bumped into a very tall, extremely strong man, who grabbed me and turned me around. While he was putting handcuffs on me the rest of the group was bombarded by guards who handcuffed them as well.

"What are you doing?" I asked him, and was shocked that he actually answered.

"Taking you to jail, you've committed a crime according to the laws of the Medlocks solar system," he told me, and everyone in our group gasped.

"What crime would that be?" Kamille asked in an innocent voice.

"Kidnapping the president's daughters," one of the other guards answered and led us to a long black car that could barely hold us all.

The jail cell smelt like chili and dirty laundry, and I sat on one of the chairs staring fixed at the wall. I looked around to see if I could find someone to talk to, everyone was either half asleep, or in their own world.

"We're going to die in here," Aura said negatively with her eyes closed.

"Of old age or boredom?" I asked her, still staring at the wall.

"Probably old age, dying of boredom is really hard," Selene told us while sitting on the floor.

"Wait a minute, is that Dad?" Kamille asked, leaning against the bars and looking down the hallway at a person walking toward our cell.

"Dad, you won't believe what happened, we got back from—"

"I know what happened, it was the least confidential piece of information of the week," Dad interrupted me, and we made faces as if we understood, but then stared at each other in confusion.

"So are we really stuck here for a month?" Ion begged him for the right answer, and he got it in return.

"No you've been summoned for court tonight and I'm going to be your lawyer," he explained, and then everyone stood up to listen to him.

"Thanks so much, Dad!" Ember yelled, and about ten guys in other cells stared at us. Dad gave us as much of a hug as he could and then left.

We waited all day until finally it was time for the court session. The court was crowded with news reporters and the president's secret service. Then the president walked in with Alissa and Tory behind him. They sat down at one table and we sat down at the other extremely long table. The judge did all the starting things and then Tory was called to the stand.

"Tory, what happened on that beach after you fell into the portal?" Dad asked, knowing that there was no way we could lose this case.

"Glacthia sprayed us with this white mist and I blocked it from getting to Rhochelle. Then everyone lost their memory but her. Then the rest is sort of like a dream that I was just watching from the outside. I remember waking up in our room, and then Rhochelle taking us to Callidus and getting Mrs. Barker to return our memory. They really are innocent, they kidnapped us to get our memories back," Tory said honestly and the whole courtroom was quiet.

"So your memory was wiped, but they went to jail because they took you to their house to get your memories back?" the judge asked in confusion and Tory nodded. "Then what are we doing here? I hereby decree that all the Barkers and Iron are innocent," the man knocked the gavel against his desk and the court was adjourned. Everyone stood up and we went over to Alissa and Tory, shaking our heads and rolling our eyes.

"Adults," we all sighed and watched as the police apologized to our parents. Then they gave us a ride back to the school, and we were left to go to bed. It was the most pointless day of our lives and it made us sick just thinking about it.

For a couple days the memory of the court erased itself from our minds and we concentrated more on the upcoming holiday. One morning, we took a break from making ornaments for the mile high Christmas tree to work on our geography project. Mrs. Pauffer had been extremely hard on us. We had to map an entire city on any planet we wanted, house by house. It was a tireless job, each of us had to take turns on the computer to find out how many houses were on each street and which way the streets curved. Mrs. Pauffer said that she was going to check that the town was perfectly proportional with the real thing. I was doing Garnet Valley, a small town in Pennsylvania, just on the border near Delaware. Just as I was drawing the countless curved roads, the teleporter lit up and we saw George standing where the blank space was just a moment ago.

"You guys have to come quick," he told us and everyone stood up, quick to put down the project and do something to procrastinate.

"I'll stay behind, I'm never going to get this done by tomorrow unless I work on it all day," I smiled to everyone and they shrugged.

"Suit yourself," Lianna sighed and walked into the line behind the teleporter. I sat by the computer, counting the number of houses on a street called "Hunt Meet Lane." It was boring, there was no one to talk to, and I knew that I really should be working on this when I didn't want to.

"Rhochelle, can you hear us?" a voice suddenly echoed in my mind. I paused for a minute, and then smiled, knowing who it was.

"Wyatt?" I said out loud, knowing that I only needed to think it.

"No, Rhochelle, come save us," the voice called again and I suddenly got freaked out. There was a voice in my head, and it wasn't Wyatt, and Glacthia is the only other person I know that can speak telepathically.

"Who is this?" I questioned the mysterious voices.

"Rhochelle, save us!" a number of voices yelled and I tried to shut them out.

"Where are you?" I wondered, thinking that maybe I should save them.

"*Save us, Rhochelle, save us,*" one of the voices said and I got so angry that I ran into the teleporter and placed myself at the exit of our room. A minute later I was on the main floor and I saw all of my siblings gathered around a creature that I have seen so many times but never knew its name.

"His name is Hilay, and he's a lockmed, I need to calm him down so that we could take him back to the zoo. Someone opened his cage and started shooting him with paintballs, the idiot," Forrest explained, taking cautious steps toward the creature. It was the same creature as the one that the man turned into from the power simulator at my parents' house.

"What are you going to do to calm him down?" George asked, looking around at the empty school and then gulping.

"Feed him," Forrest laughed and walked outside to use his powers, and then came back a few seconds later. He was holding foods for about every animal that the lockmed was made up of and dropped it in front of the creature that suddenly looked interested.

"Lockmeds only eat the vine of the eruca plant," Lianna pointed out, and Forrest sighed, taking the food away and coming back empty handed.

"But I don't know what that looks like. How am I going to give it to him?" Forrest realized, and thought for a minute.

"We're going to learn about it in chemicals next week. Mrs. Morse has some in her room," Lianna spoke as if it were her powers talking, then Forrest ran up the stairs. A minute later he came back with the vines of the plant in a tangled mess in his arms.

"You stole it?" Neva asked, wondering if our brother was a thief.

"No, I copied it, she has the same amount that she had before," Forrest smiled, proud that he was one step ahead of us. He held it out to the lockmed, who almost tackled him to get to it. "Good job, Hilay, now let's get you to the zoo," Forrest smiled, and walked outside with Wyatt, who teleported him to the zoo.

We all went back upstairs, and I finally ended up finishing my project halfway through the night. I went to my bedroom in the dark, scared out of my mind that something would pop out of nowhere. When I walked into my room I heard a voice and almost dropped dead.

"Rhochelle, save us, Rhochelle, save us," the voice called like a moaning ghost, and I tried to block it out of my head.

"Save us, Rhochelle, you have to save us," it rang in my head and I wanted to knock myself out just to make it stop. Why was it talking to only me? Craig's power is voices, but Wyatt can speak telepathically.

"Go away, I'm tired," I told it and rolled over in my bed. The voices went on all night, practically nonstop. I kept my eyes closed the whole night, but never fell asleep. Over and over again I tried to ask who they were and where they were, but all I got in return was a cry for help.

The next morning we were outside during study hall sitting under one of the huge oak trees that populated the space from behind Medlocks to the nearby beach.

"You guys grew up on Earth right?" Cobalt was curious to ask the Venturas. We all looked at him for a minute, trying to see if he had any reason at all for asking. Then I saw that my cousins were waiting for Gabby to answer.

"No, we've lived on Callidus our whole lives with our parents," Gabby told him, and she noticed him flinch when they mentioned their parents.

"What are your parents' names? We've never met them," Wyatt wanted to know, for some reason the conversation had turned to my aunt and uncle, but they were obliged to answer. This time they all stared at Lianna, who rolled her eyes and answered.

"To us they're Mom and Dad, but to you guys they're Aunt Jody and Uncle Steve," Lianna explained.

"We should stay with you guys this summer!" Aura asked randomly. Most of us had spent every summer at our house in Wisconsin since we were born and half of a summer at our parents' house. Kamille and Daven spent every summer except for one at the hotel. I wasn't sure about Cobalt, but last summer he stayed with the rest of us.

"No, we're staying at the hotel this summer," Daven smiled to Kamille, and we all nodded with smiles on our faces as well.

"Yeah that'd be the best; we would have an entire floor to ourselves where the owner, Daven, and I used to stay. There's so much to do there, and with powers we could do a lot more," Kamille thought of everything that we could do.

"The summer after that we'll be with the Venturas," Ion told us, and we all stared at him, holding in laughs.

"No let's go to Australia," Forrest asserted his opinion. I stared at him with the most confused face. Australia?

"That was so unbelievably random," I pointed out. He smiled and explained.

"I know, but we should stay in Australia anyway," Forrest told the group, and we thought about the trip. But just as we were thinking about it four people walked up from behind us.

"Well, well, well, if it isn't the . . . wait a minute . . . who are they?" Mac asked and pointed to the Venturas.

"They're our cousins, now we have fifteen instead of eleven," Ember told him and he shook his head.

"Fourteen, Cobalt can hang out with you but you can't count him as part of your group," Mac told us, and then I noticed that Reggie was walking away. I was just about to say something, but then the pounding voices came back. This was the first time that they had talked to me when I wasn't alone, so it caught me by surprise.

"Rhochelle, come save us, we need you to save us," all the different voices rang, and I put my head down on the ground to try to stop the headache.

"Rhochelle, are you okay?" Gabby asked and the whole group moved their attention to me. I had no time to answer the question. I saw Reggie inflating himself to push himself off the ground and go up the giant stairs that made up the classrooms.

"He's getting—"

"Rhochelle, come save us, save us!" they yelled, and my headache got worse, I lay on the ground and wished that it would go away, but there was no stopping it. Get out of my head! Nothing I thought or said worked, so I turned my attention to the Irons.

"Get him, he's—" I yelled at them, but the voices wouldn't let me. Everything started to spin and then I blacked out, unable to stop Cobalt's brothers from whatever they were doing.

When I woke up I was in the nurse's office, and the nurse told me that I just had a small headache. She also said that I could leave whenever I wanted. Just as I was about to get up the group came in to visit me.

"What happened? We're so confused—Cobalt's brothers fought us, and we were too distracted to notice that they took Cobalt," Craig told me in a sad voice, and I realized that they still didn't know. I groaned and watched Miss Monohan come in.

"It wasn't anything . . . I was just hot," I told them. Then I sat up so fast that I might've broken a world record. "I can't believe you let them get away, how could you not see Reggie going to the top of the school? He probably stole something. What if they stole their own Metronome, they could've—"

"They didn't steal the Metronome," Miss Monohan interrupted my rampage.

"Then what did they steal?" I asked, being the only one who was caught up with this. Miss Monohan looked at the ground, almost not wanting to tell us.

"Cobalt," Ion mentioned angrily, and as much as we cared, we ignored him.

"They stole a large quantity of money from the same machine that they tried to create the Metronome from," Miss Monohan explained, and I groaned and put the pillow over my head and lied back down.

"Are you serious? That's big for them," Forrest told us, and the group was silent.

"We're going to have to make it against the rules to go onto the roof, the things that people could do with that machine are infinite," Miss Monohan told us, and we sighed and got quiet again. No one talked, and then Miss Monohan finally left us alone.

"We're going to go . . . do you have to stay here?" Ember asked me and I thought hard about my answer.

"Yeah, just a couple more hours," I lied to them, and they nodded and walked out.

"Is there a reason you have to stay?" the nurse asked me, and I explained the entire thing about the voices to her. She got out a small machine, like Daven's machine that told him which powers he had copied. It went into my ear and then scanned my brain. She watched the small screen then shook her head when a few words came up.

"I don't see anything wrong with you, not even the voices," she told me, and I stared at her with a confused face.

"Then what are they?" I asked her, ready to do anything to make it stop.

"It's probably just the work load . . . or your imagination," she said while packing up the machine.

159

"Okay, thanks," I told her even though I didn't mean it, and ran out of the room. I went straight to the other side of the room and opened the door to Mr. Williams' office. He was sitting in a chair reading, and then he turned to me and smiled.

"Rhochelle, what can I do for you?" he asked me kindly and motioned for me to sit. I explained the same thing to him as I did to the nurse, and then told him what the nurse had told me and what I thought about it. He started nodding and pointing his finger at me while he dug through a drawer on his desk. Then he pulled out a small earplug and handed it to me. I inspected it and waited for him to tell me what it did.

"This device can contact your brain and decipher what's going on in it. As soon as they start talking to you again, I have it set to tell me who, or what, the voice came from on this computer screen. Once they contact you, run down to me and I'll tell you who they were," he told me and I thanked him, walking out.

A couple days went by, and the voices stopped talking to me. At first I was sort of glad that I had some peace and quiet, but then I was angry that I would never figure out who they were. One Saturday we all decided to spend the day swimming, but I was the first one dressed for the pool. I sat by the side of the pool, waiting for everyone else, when I was suddenly contacted by an outside source.

"Rhochelle, come save us!" one of the voices yelled, and within two seconds I was in the teleporter. Then another minute later I was catching my breath at Mr. Williams' door. Then I burst in to find him sitting at his desk watching something load. I walked up behind him and then got too confused to understand what the computer was saying, so I waited for him to finish reading it. When he was done he shook his head, turning to me with a disappointed sigh. Then suddenly he gave me a weird stare, I forgot to change out of my swimsuit. My pink and purple bikini did sort of ruin the seriousness of the situation. Immediately he got back on track.

"Rhochelle, I don't really know how to tell you this, but those voices that you hear . . . this says that they aren't any living person known by man," he told me, looking at the ground. I nodded, standing up, and turned to walk away. But then I turned back to say one last thing that I had on my mind.

"Then why do they want me to save them so badly?" I asked him a rhetorical question and walked out. Descending the stairs to our floor, I thought about what dead person could be contacting me. Then I went into the teleporter and teleported to the pool room.

"Guys?" I called when I saw no one there. I ran around the entire tree house, and then came back to the same room. My hypothesis turned out to be correct. I was completely alone in the tree house.

CHAPTER THIRTEEN: DEATH ROW

SAM

The dark room was filled with my sleeping siblings and cousins. I looked at the molded bread, wondering how all of them survived in here last time. For me this was my first time, but some of them have been here three or four times.

"You guys awake?" Wyatt asked, lying on the floor.

"No," everyone moaned. This place was a nightmare. All we did was sit in the room for hours with nothing to do and nothing to eat except toxic bread. I sat against the wall trying to fall asleep, but the dust all over me was preventing me from closing me eyes. Just when I was about to start a conversation, the door opened and a dark figure floated in the doorway.

"Rise!" he called and we rose off the ground by our hair. We shouted in pain and came with him, down a very dark hallway that we couldn't recognize at all. Then he pushed open a door and we walked in, all walking in a line of chained, invisible handcuffs. Then the door closed behind us with Glacthia on the outside, and we stared at the giant contraptions on the enormous conveyor belt that we were standing on. Everything around the belt was darkness, so we assumed that if we fell there would be no coming back. The first contraption in front of us was a huge lead cube about ten feet wide. It rose a dozen or so feet off the ground then smashed back down into the belt.

"This is my latest invention!" Glacthia's voice echoed through the darkness and then we saw him hovering on the other side of the belt. "I call it . . . death row! Unless you haven't figured out, the Barkers' powers

162

are gone, so it's up to the Venturas to save them. There are five obstacles, and if you get to the end . . . you fall into the endless pit anyway," he laughed, and we gave each other nervous looks. Suddenly the conveyor belt started moving, and the dropping box started coming closer.

"I got it!" I yelled and ran to the box. It came down directly on top of my head, and I put my hands up. The box instantly turned to rusted metal and fell apart around me. The whole group walked through without trouble, but I made a tornado take away the scraps just in case. The next obstacle coming up was made up of blades that spun from both sides of the belt, each about a foot higher than the other with no space at all to cross.

"I'll get this one," Gabby smiled, and pointed at each of the two bars that held up all the blades so they could spin. Two stars came out of her hand and they flew straight into the bars. In an instant all the blades started spinning out of control and they fell into the endless pit that we were doomed to fall into after we finished this anyway.

The one after that was made up of giant hammers that smashed down on the conveyor belt like someone karate chopping cookie dough. Just when Gabby was about to shoot another star, Lianna put her hand in front of her.

"Wait, if you hit them with stars they'll start moving out of control and probably hit us. I know what to do for these ones. If you go in at the right time and at the right speed you'll make it through. I'll tell you when to go and then just go as fast as you can." Lianna waited for it to come closer then said, "Someone go!" Ion ran through and then smiled when he was in one piece. He started walking back toward the hammers so that he didn't get to the next contraption. Lianna told each person to go through at the right time, and before we knew it we were all on the other side, thanking Lianna for saving us.

Right after that came the next machine, which kind of looked like something you might see in a factory. It was a metal cylinder, laying on the belt and rolling so that it stayed in place. But the cylinder was covered in spikes, each about three feet long. I made them rust again and they started to get thinner and sharper, like needles. Finally they got so sharp that the weight of the metal cylinder was pushing them into the conveyor belt. It dropped through until the spikes were stuck, and then it broke off of the bars holding it up and moved along with us on the belt.

"That's going to be bad . . . duck!" Wyatt yelled when the cylinder got to the next part of death row. There were sheets of metal being lifted then dropped back down, just like at the beginning with the box. The sheets chopped up the cylinder like it was a carrot, and then it fell off the edge of the conveyor belt in scraps. Before anyone could call it Gabby shot stars at the sheets. Huge gaping wholes appeared in the metal, which made it seem like giant doorways. Smiling at Gabby I hardly noticed that the metal grew back into its original shape.

"Shoot a star again!" I yelled because I was first in line to get chopped. Gabby shot without aiming, and sadly shot just where the belt was. I fell into the gaping whole along with everyone else who didn't have time to react. All of us screamed in agony, and waited for us to hit a bottom and end our lives. But it seemed to never come, and minute after minute passed until we got used to the constant falling.

"This is taking forever!" Ember yelled from behind me, and I looked to see if I could see her, but she wasn't there.

"We're going to fall until we die of thirst!" I told everyone and they groaned, angry with the realization.

"But then where are—" I started but we felt a very strange sensation. It was as if we were falling into a pool of jelly, and we were heavy enough to sink through it. Then we hit a soft couch and kept our eyes closed, afraid to see where we were. Eventually I opened my eyes and saw that we were sitting in my aunt and uncle's living room.

"What happened to you guys?" Rhochelle asked, and all of us stared at her, wondering why she was here.

"We got kidnapped by Glacthia; what happened to you?" Ember asked her, and she sighed, as if tired of explaining this.

"Well, you know that the reason that Cobalt was kidnapped, and the money was stolen, was because I was distracting you guys with my headache? It wasn't a headache; I was hearing voices in my head. Then I went to Mr. Williams and he gave me an earpiece that could tell me who was contacting me. The next time I heard the voices was while I was waiting for you guys at the pool, so I went straight to Mr. Williams. Then he told me that the voices weren't from any living person. Then I got really nervous, and decided to come back to tell you guys. But then you were gone, so I came here to tell Dad to get you by a dimensional portal," Rhochelle explained, then took a break, as if she hadn't breathed the entire time she was telling us.

"I was so worried about you guys when Rhochelle came and told me. Did anything happen when you were with Glacthia?" Aunt Aubree asked and we stared at each other, wondering who would tell the story.

"Glacthia made this giant conveyor belt, and put us on it. It had all these obstacles that we had to get past. Then at the end we fell into this endless pit, which is where we fell into the dimensional portal. Dad, that's so amazing! You can just summon people with a dimensional portal all the way from here?" Neva changed the subject and we looked at Uncle Riddock, who was smiling with pride.

"Years of practice, son, years of practice," was his answer, and then we stood up.

"Well, we should get going now, we have a lot of things to do," Wyatt told them, and we stared at him. We didn't have anything at all to do, so there was no reason for us to go on such short notice.

"No, no, no, why don't you guys stay, just for the rest of the weekend. One night . . . what do you say?" Aunt Aubree asked and we decided to agree. Wyatt didn't seem too excited about it, but he didn't want to speak up about his feelings. He teleported us our projects so that we could work on them, but we never really got to them because of all the things that we did. We went to the beach, since it was only about a mile away, and stayed there with the Barkers' parents. It was a beautiful day; we even went in the water because it was warm enough.

That night I was working on my project when I remembered that I needed a compass that I had left at the tree house. I walked down the hallway to Wyatt's room to ask him to teleport it to me. It was a long walk; we were pretty much the entire floor apart. Tiptoeing through the hallway, I opened his door and looked inside. At first I thought that he might be in the bathroom, since his room was empty. So I crossed the hall and knocked on the bathroom door quietly. There was no answer, and I remembered that the power simulator had a tracking device that could track anyone in our group.

I snuck downstairs and walked into the dome where it was. Then I found a computer and turned it on. When the light turned on I had to close my eyes for a minute before I could get used to it.

"Okay, let's figure out how to work this thing," I whispered to myself and started opening programs, trying to figure out where it was. After fifteen or so tries I found a program called "family search line" and clicked on it. It opened up a list of all of our names and I clicked on

Wyatt. The computer pulled up a file that started asking me questions about him. I answered nine out of ten of them correctly; I didn't know his middle name. Then it pulled up a map of the galaxy and started searching for him. I waited for over five minutes, and then a bar finally came up that said "person out of solar system." I stared at it for a while, in shock, and then turned to leave. That night I couldn't sleep, I was too busy thinking about what Wyatt would be doing out of the solar system. Isn't the only place out of the solar system that he can teleport to Earth? Where else would he be, or why would he be on Earth?

The following morning I went down to breakfast to tell everyone that Wyatt was gone. Walking into the dining room I grabbed their attention and started to talk.

"Guys there's something I have to tell you about—" I began to say when I saw Wyatt sitting at one of the chairs finishing a glass of orange juice.

"About who?" Ember asked me to finish, but I ignored her. Forrest and Lianna glared at her for her incorrect grammar, but the face Ember made at them told them to back off, so they did.

"I went to the power simulator and used the tracker to find you. It said that you weren't in the solar system at all. Where were you?" I asked Wyatt and everyone stared at him, wanting an answer.

"You left the solar system last night? Wyatt Michael Barker, how could you?" Aunt Aubree accused him and he put his hands up like he was being taken prisoner. Michael! Now next time I'll get a perfect score.

"I didn't leave the solar system last night; I went back to the beach to get my sunglasses. They fell out of my bag when we were leaving and I realized it just before I fell asleep. You must've went into my room while I was there looking for them," he told everyone and they turned back to me, waiting for a response.

"Then why did the tracker say that you weren't in the solar system?" I questioned him, and he shrugged.

"The tracker isn't working that well, I've been trying to fix it," Uncle Riddock covered for him and I sighed. Wyatt looked at him for a minute but he ignored the look.

"Oh, well I wish I knew that last night," I told everyone and sat down to have breakfast. The meal was a quiet one—no one talked except to ask someone to pass something. Ion mentioned once how we needed to start planning how to get Cobalt back. We laughed, saying he was completely safe and able to free himself whenever he was with his brothers, and dismissed the subject. When the meal ended, we packed our stuff and got ready to leave for Medlocks. We only had two more days of classes and then we started Christmas break. We were going to come back after our classes ended to spend Christmas here, but until then we had to go back and take all of our end of term tests.

I was walking toward the door to leave for the taxi that our parents had called, but I heard something off in the distance. It sounded a little like yelling, and when I got closer I proved that hypothesis. Uncle Riddock was shouting at someone in the privacy of the study, but I peeked open the door to see who it was.

"Wyatt, I don't know what you were doing out of the solar system, but next time they find out, I won't cover for you. This path you're going down . . . it's not a good one. I don't want you to be the one who turns into an evil villain. With this many people in our group it's unlikely that one of you won't, but I just don't want it to be you. The stories that surround your destiny go on forever, and there's talk about them all the time. Prophecies, fortunes that are read, everything, and they all surround you. I'm only go to say this once . . . don't make the mistake that the whole universe will regret. Okay, go, you have a taxi to catch," he pushed him off and I ran around the corner so that they would not think that I was eavesdropping. A minute later I was standing with the group by the door and Wyatt and Uncle Riddock came walking down the hallway.

"Okay, good luck with your midterms guys," Mom hugged all of us goodbye and we walked outside. We stepped into the taxi and sat down, getting comfortable for the long ride back. The doors got locked and the taxi lifted off the ground into the air. Then blinds went over the windows so we could not see outside.

"Um . . . excuse me, could you move these blinds up so that we could see where we are?" Forrest asked, and there was no answer.

"Hey, mister, we want to see outside!" Ember yelled at him and grabbed his arm to pull him into the back. Then she let go with a horrified face and the window separating us and him started to close.

"Mac, let us go!" we all yelled as the taxi pulled out of the atmosphere and into the unknown space.

CHAPTER FOURTEEN: THE PLAN OF THE LITTLE PEOPLE

COBALT

It was just a couple days after I was kidnapped by my brothers, and I was ready to pull my hair out. They were scheming something, something so out of their league that it seemed like a plan Glacthia himself would make up. I was stuck in this stupid jail cell that they built because they stupidly didn't trust me, and it made it even stupid harder to figure out their stupid plan from here. So far they had just stolen the money from Medlocks, but after that, I hadn't seen anything that they'd done. They often leave "to-do" things involving their plan, but I'm stuck in here the entire time so I don't know where they keep going.

The following morning, Saturday morning, I was eating breakfast with them for the first time since they had captured me. It was quiet, since they weren't quite ready to tell me anything about the plan yet. I had to do something evil, something to prove that I was on their side. This was the longest undercover mission I had ever been on—although it was probably the only one. I had to leave as soon as I figured out their plan and not a minute before. But until then, I was to be evil and harsh. Nothing would stand in my way of figuring out their plan. Not even the Barkers could stop me now, wherever they were.

"So, what have you guys been up to lately?" I asked casually and they stopped eating. Reggie, Johnny, and Ashton stared at me and Mac for a minute, and then he put down his fork.

"You think you can just come in here and ask us our plan like you've never even met those snot heads?" Mac returned the question and I sat quiet for a while.

"I don't want to be with them anymore, and I could prove it. But since they're not here you guys will just have to trust me," I told them and they shook their heads.

"Not so fast, bro. You'll have to prove yourself alright, but until then, you're not learning a thing," Reggie explained to me and I sat back in my seat in failure.

"But for now . . . we've decided that we trust you enough to stay out of your cell for the day. You can wander around wherever you want, but we're going to take your watch from you so you can't contact those brats," Mac gave me the privilege and I took it without a word. After breakfast they took my watch from me and I walked outside where they couldn't see me.

Once I had found a good spot I stopped to take a look around the planet. There was grass as far as I could see. That eliminated snowy and desert planets, but there were still hundreds of planets that I could be on. Then I laughed to myself and pulled my spare watch out of my pocket that I had been carrying with me since before the day they captured me. Putting it on, I pressed the button and talked into it.

"Guys, are you there? It's Cobalt," I called for them, then waited for the reply. It was silent for a while and then I gave up on it. They were either too busy to talk or they were in trouble, or it could be both.

"Come on—guys, it's Cobalt. I really need you to help me," I repeated and again there was no answer. I put the watch back in my pocket and walked around the building. It was a huge house, with three floors, at least six or seven bedrooms, and a pool in the back with a poolhouse next to it. If I didn't know my brothers any better, I'd say that we were on Earth.

I went inside to look around the house. My brothers must've hidden everything if they trusted me enough to wander around by myself. Walking around on the first floor, I found one bedroom, a kitchen, and a room that was half a living room and half a study. All the floors were stone, as if it were built a long time ago. Then on the deck, which was built on a hill so that one side of the deck was at ground level and the other side was one story up. Walking down the stairs, I found the garage connected to a long driveway that eventually attached to a dirt road. I made a metal disk under me and flew up over the house. There was a wall of mountains going around the huge, three mile wide bowl that my brothers had all to themselves. The house, along with another house about ten yards from it and a pool in the back, was close to edge, so everything else was grassland. The road swerved up the mountain like a zigzag and then eventually went straight all the way to a small town with nothing but a gas station, a grocery store, and a few other shops.

"Wow, if the flight was any longer, then I would be sure that we were in Italy," I told myself. I had seen pictures of Italy, and this definitely looked like it. But I landed and went to the small house next to the main one that looked at first like a guest house. Then I realized that it was more of a greenhouse, just with furniture and rooms and everything. There were plants lined up everywhere, in jars, pots, and baskets. They weren't normal plants, definitely not from Earth. I stared around at the strange variety of the plants. One had a huge black head like a Venus flytrap, but it hung down and was more curved. There was another one with thorns on the petals instead of the stem.

In the jars on the tables were just liquids, all different colors and densities. There was one that just looked like dye, and another that could be the stuff used in lava lamps. Then I saw a jar, in the back corner, that I stared at for a while just to make sure I knew what it was. It was a wasp, just a small one buzzing around inside the jar. There wasn't anything important about it, just a small bug in a jar. Now one thing made sense, this was the creature that had bitten Neva back at their parents' house. Was it my brothers that placed the wasp in the room and got it to bite one of us? Then what in the *universe* were my brothers planning? What was with the plants, the hideout, the random wasp, and even stealing money from Medlocks? This plan of theirs was becoming so hard to comprehend that I was beginning to think that it couldn't have been theirs.

Just as I was about to open the jar with the wasp in it, I felt a firm grip reach my shoulder. Jumping, I turned around, knowing who it was already.

"Sneaking around the project area, were you? Sorry bro, but we just can't have that, can we? You'll be fine back in your cell for a while," Reggie pushed me as I walked all the way back to the main house and into the cell. When I got there he pushed me in and closed the bar door as I turned around.

"See ya later, bro," he walked off and I was left to just sit and think. It had to be something big, and something really important. I stared at the metal bars, and thought of an idea I should've realized a long time ago. Flicking my hands to the bars, I expected it to disintegrate, but nothing happened. My brothers were actually smart enough to make a power proof cell. Without anything to do, I sat down and waited for the next day.

When I woke up the door to the cell was left open. They must've decided that I had come close to gaining their trust. I stood up and walked out slowly, careful not to make them notice me just in case they didn't actually want me out. As I neared the breakfast table, I noticed three of them sitting on each side, all three sides of the table taken up with an empty plate on one side. Without even wondering where Mac was, I stepped into the room to let them know of my entrance. Although my brothers wanted to be villains, they always sat down together for each meal.

"Cobalt, there's pancake mix next to the griddle," Johnny pointed at the counter and I went over to make some.

"So you guys trust me now?" I asked nicely and turned to look at them.

"Not as much; but if you're good, you don't have to stay in that cell," Reggie told me. For once in my life I felt like I belonged with my brothers, and I poured the pancake mix onto the griddle.

"Enough to tell me your plan?" I sort of muttered, and it got quiet. I twisted to face them and then they laughed for a minute. I turned back to the pancakes and waited for them to say something, but they thought that the laughs were enough.

"If you prove yourself, in time we will," Reggie finally answered and I sighed in relief, hoping that my words wouldn't cause them to decide not to ever tell me. After breakfast I roamed around the fields and house again. I even went to the store and bought a bathing suit with some of the money that I had in my pocket. Then I went in the pool, figuring that I might as well stay out of the house with the plants in it. The pool was a square, with a stone moat around the edge so that water couldn't spill out onto the patio. When I faced the house, there was nothing behind me but grass for miles. To my left was a line of trees that blocked the dirt road from my sight. On my right I saw a small fence going around an area right before a hill. Getting out, I walked down to the bottom of the hill and saw that it was actually a stone wall with a door. Inside I realized that there was an entire underground pool house. There was a main tiled room, then two doors on the wall in front of me and one door to my right. The doors in front of me turned out to be a bathroom and a closet, while the one on my right was actually a small steam room. Then I walked outside and noticed something in the sky.

A small spaceship landed down in the grass behind the fence above the pool and me. Mac stepped out, and then opened the door where the passengers were. Out walked fourteen handcuffed kids that were chained together. They looked around, and then looked down at me. I ran up to the top of the hill, and they stared at me in shock for a while. For a minute I thought they would be happy to see me, and then I realized that I was soaking wet in my bathing suit and I understood their impression.

"I found these guys on Callidus, now you'll be able to prove yourself," Mac smiled at me and grabbed Aura's hair, she was in the front. He walked them all off and I stared at them in amazement. For over a minute I stood there staring at my brother for what he had done. But when he was gone I chased after my friends faster than I even knew I could.

As soon as I reached the doorway I curved around the couch and into the room where my cell was. All of the Barkers were crammed into it, only a few of them could sit down at a time. But then I hit something hard and bounced back and landed on the floor. My entire body suddenly felt numb, and I closed my eyes.

I woke up in a bed, in my favorite room of the whole house, the only bedroom on the first floor. There was an icepack under my head, and I pushed it away because it was so cold. Slowly getting up, I tried to remember what had happened. I must've bumped into Reggie, a wall wouldn't be as elastic. Holding my head, I walked out of the room into the study room, connected to the sitting area. Then I could see the cage, with all fourteen of them in it wishing they could be asleep. Just when I was about to get their attention, something got in the way. Looking up, I smiled brightly, then sighed. Mac shook his head and turned me around.

"You're not allowed to see them just yet, we have some important business to attend to," he led me outside where I noticed the same spacecraft on the driveway instead of where it had landed on the other side of the house. I walked inside of it and sat down so that I was in between two empty seats. It was just a regular taxi, just smaller and meant for shorter trips that didn't involve sleeping. Basically it was a circle of seats, then a bar in the middle with a small fridge on it.

"Where are we going anyway?" I wondered, hoping that they would be dumb enough to tell me the plan.

"You'll see. Don't you have any patience?" Mac asked angrily and sat back, putting his arms behind his head and placing his feet on the low bar. Reggie, Johnny, and Ashton leaned forward to look at the bar, and Reggie pressed a button on the bottom. I watched in amazement as the bar flipped upside down into the taxi. On the newly showing side there was one of the things that I had never hoped for my brothers to possess. It was a Worlds, the invention by Sir Jacob Reese that could alter dimensions and allow you to visit any planet made of any object you want. Johnny started pressing buttons, and I watched to see what it was. He went to animals, then insects, flying, yellow, and then clicked on the word "morbus." Suddenly gravity was altered as entire dimensions changed, and then a beam of light flew out of the Worlds and illuminated the entire taxi. I closed my eyes and held onto the door handle, only to have the entire door fly off. Then, just as I was about to yell for help, I was ripped out of my seat just as the destination planet came into view.

As soon as I hit the ground, I was happy that I wasn't stuck in some random dimension and had no way of getting out. Then I realized that out of all the planets I could've landed on, I wouldn't have survived on any others. But I looked down at the ground, it had a softer touch, like it had fur. Just at that moment, I realized that it was moving. And not all at once, each fuzzy stone moved in separate directions. The entire planet was made of the insect that I saw in the jar back at the base. For a second I wanted to study the wasps, but then I felt a little prick on my leg and looked back. There was a wasp pulling its butt out of me, and I noticed a sharp point on the end of it. Without a millisecond to waste, I jumped into the air and created a metal scooter that allowed me to ride away from the angry wasps.

For hours I rode on the blank planet, with the wasps just covering the ground so that the planet looked yellow and black. But eventually I saw something huge in the distance. Riding for a couple more minutes it eventually became clear that it was a giant machine operated butterfly net. There were tons of flowers at the bottom of the net, so the wasps flew up and into the net. Then two metal doors from either side of the rim would come together. After that the metal wall would move back into the net until the wasps couldn't fly anymore. It gave them enough room to live but left enough room to catch more. When I first saw the net my brothers had made three catches, but were working on their fourth. As soon as I got to them they noticed me, and smiled as if they actually thought I was on their side.

"What are you doing?" I wondered, maybe thinking I would get a piece of this puzzle that dated all the way back to the dance in the first week of school when they attempted to steal the Metronome.

"Catching morbus," Ashton answered and I sighed.

"For what?" I smiled at all of them and they stopped what they were doing to stare at me. Mac walked up to me, and I looked up at him, wishing that he would just give up and tell me. But he stared at me for a while, and then I gave up on that fantasy.

"Cobalt, don't you get it? We're not going to tell you the plan until you prove yourself," he patted my shoulder so hard that I had to bend my knees to keep my balance.

"Okay, we got enough, let's go," Johnny told the group and he pressed a couple buttons on the control panel. The net started to glow, and then disappeared altogether, leaving sparks falling to the ground where it just stood. I gazed at the lights for a while and then got back into the spaceship to leave this place.

"I don't get what you're using the wasps for, or whatever you call them, morbus, this all makes no sense," I reminded them that they still needed to clue me in. But no one said a word as Mac put his hand on the Worlds to turn it on. He started pressing buttons, and just when the planet was about to open up, Reggie tackled me and inflated himself. I was being crushed against the seat by his chest, and I wasn't able to breathe until he lifted himself off of me.

"What was that for!" I shouted at my idiot brother and he turned to Mac and glared at him.

"How could you be stupid enough to open up to the planet name right in front of him?" Reggie bickered with Mac for a while. But the Worlds started to work and they didn't want to be fighting while we traveled millions of lightyears in a minute.

"How'd you fix the door?" I wondered as I noticed the new door in the spot where the old one had flew off its hinges. No one answered, and this time I held onto the bar on the ceiling that holds the dry-cleaning.

This time I survived, and we landed on the planet that I did not know the name or location of.

"Get out," Ashton yelled at me, since I was sitting next to the only door that he could get out of. I stepped out, and then waited for the group of villains to get out behind me. We walked back to the house through the deck, entering in the kitchen.

"Come on, we have to feed the brats," Mac told me as everyone else walked off to do whatever. I could see the bars of the cage, but didn't look into the eyes of the any of the prisoners that lie within them. When we had made all fourteen sandwiches I walked into the room to give them to the prisoners. They all looked up at me and I tried not to notice them. I handed all of them a sandwich, but kept one for myself. Forrest stared at me, waited for me to hand it to him. Then after a minute he stood up.

"Cobalt, come on, you know we need one more," he told me and put his hand through the bar. I stood there, transfixed on the floor, holding back tears. Then I looked up at him and stuck the sandwich in my mouth, and mustered the most of a voice I had left in me.

"What can I say? I'm hungry," I ate the rest of the sandwich and walked off, leaving to go into the TV room.

"Nice job Cobalt, I'd say that you just proved yourself to be one of us," Mac patted me on the back and called for Ashton, Johnny, and Reggie to meet us on the deck. When they had gathered we sat down at the table with Mac at one head and me at the other. Then he folded his hands and stared at me for a minute, while I looked around. Suddenly I noticed a small dot in the sky above us, and coming closer. Trying not to let my brothers notice it, I turned back to them to let them talk.

"Cobalt, we think that we're ready to tell you the plan," Mac started and my three other brothers gasped and turned to see my expression. I was shocked, and if there wasn't a cloaked spaceship landing next to the pool right now then I would be thankful. There was another silence, and I waited for him to continue, hoping that maybe I could hear the plan before I was rescued by whomever the Barkers had called to save us.

"Well, it started back in September when Glacthia paid us to steal a copy of the Metronome. We had come back the next day and succeeded if you were thinking of our failure during the dance. But we had all this money, and we understood the properties of the machine on the roof. We spent weeks trying to think of a plan, and finally we came up with one." Mac didn't start the next sentence because a loud crash came from the kitchen. Without hesitation everyone got up from the table but me, this was exactly what I hoped wouldn't happen. Before I could do anything, I was lifted off of the chair by an unidentified force, and I flew through the doorway and past the kitchen. I went out the back door and suddenly flew into the spaceship that Chris had driven here.

"Cobalt we're not going to let you explain, we're just going to trust that you're still on our side," Ion said as he tied a blindfold around my mouth. No matter if I felt like part of their family or not before now, I definitely didn't because of the blindfold around my mouth, am I their prisoner? But if this was their way of trusting that I was still on their side, then I would be worried what would happen if they didn't trust me.

"Come on, Chris, here they come," Ember yelled as my brothers were running to the car, but it was already taking off. A few minutes later we left the atmosphere of whichever planet we were on. But they didn't bother to figure out, since they had no idea which way Medlocks was anyway.

"Wyatt, just teleport us to Medlocks," Daven ordered and we landed just outside the atmosphere of the planet that we were able to call home. As we landed, Ion was untying my blindfold, but it wasn't fully off until we had gotten out of the taxi. Once I stood on firm ground I ripped off the rest of the blindfold and shouted in rage.

"You guys, I was there to figure out their plan! How could you just take me away from there, why do you think I was being mean to you?" I screamed as they looked at the ground in shame. I felt bad for a minute, but then made my decision. Standing firmly on the ground with my back straight, I said, "I'm going to go back." There was a silence, as if they were waiting for someone to knock some sense into me, but then Ion stepped forward, away from the crowd.

"I'm coming with you," he told the group and Wyatt nodded, flicking his hands at us so that we disappeared from their sight.

Wyatt teleported us to the second worst possible place that he could. We hit the water and started coughing since it was the last thing we would've expected. I swam to the edge of the pool and climbed out, wishing that between the two of us we had a way to dry off.

"Come on, let's pretend I caught you and everyone else got away," I told him and we walked toward the house, handcuffing him to me with my mind.

"Guys, I got one!" I called through the house and just as my brothers were walking in, I felt like someone had just dropped something into my pocket. Wyatt and everyone probably got us some gadgets from Mr. Williams' office.

"Wow, I thought they had taken you, I can't believe you actually fought back, and captured one!" Reggie seemed impressed, but I shrugged and lied my heart out.

"It was easy; I could've gotten them all if Wyatt hadn't teleported them off," I murmured angrily to myself, and they all felt sympathy for me.

"It's okay, we'll get them next time, so which one is this?" Ashton stared at Ion like he was a piece a meat, and I immediately regretted this plan.

"I don't know . . . Pyon, Lyon, Ion," I listed some names and then wished that I had just gone with Ion.

"Ha, Ion, like the electro charged atom," Mac laughed and pushed Ion like a punching bag, who fell down. All five of us gaped at him, but the look he gave was enough to stop anyone from saying anything. "Take him to the cell," he waved his hand and I grabbed Ion's arm to take him away. When we got to the cell I opened the door for him then pretended to push him in and then knelt down to talk to him.

"If they try to do anything bad to you, just yell and I'll come," I told him and walked outside to sit by the pool for a while.

A few hours later my name was called to appear on the deck. I walked around the house to avoid Ion, so that they didn't think I was visiting him. Then I walked up from the garage to the stone steps on to the deck.

"Yeah?" I asked why they had called me, knowing that they were about to tell me the plan anyway, and I noticed that Reggie wasn't there.

"Well, we were thinking that since nothing else could distract us, that we would tell you the plan now," Mac explained and I sat down at the other side of the table.

"It's a pretty simple plan really, but we just had to make sure that none of those brats figured it out by planting all those tricks to hide what we were really doing," Ashton told me, and I was impressed. For a while I thought that Ashton wasn't smart enough to figure out their own plan, but then I realized that he really did know all along.

"So back to the roof of Medlocks, that's where we got all the money we needed to buy this place and the net. We had been searching, for a special ingredient, we had checked plants, bugs, everything. Finally we found it in wasps. They're not real wasps, they're actually called morbus. Their skin has a special poison in them that causes—" Mac didn't get to finish the sentence because a scream echoed through the entire fields area and forced me to cover my ears. Everyone ran into the cell room and I saw something that made me wish I had never come back at all.

"What are you doing?" I shouted, but then remembered that I was undercover as an evil villain. They stared at me, but then turned back to Ion who was being tortured by Reggie. He was holding a long metal pole, with a symbol attached to the end that was red hot. It was one of those things that people used on horses or donkeys to mark them. This one read, "IB MARJ", which clearly stood for "I be Mac, Ashton, Reggie, and Johnny".

"That's disgusting, you can't do that to him," I shouted, but then they really thought I had turned good again.

"Cobalt, are you on our side or not?" Reggie smiled at his brothers and they stared at me, waiting for an answer. I looked at the ground, giving up, and Ion's mouth dropped.

"Wait, Cobalt, you're not really going to let them do this to me, are you?" Ion asked me, begging for a straight answer. I waited for a couple seconds, and then answered with such a small voice that I barely heard myself.

"You need to do it," I murmured, and turned away. Ion started screaming, and Reggie came closer to him with the piercing hot metal. I noticed Johnny closing his eyes, and then Ion shouted louder than I ever thought a person could. The screaming went on for a while, and then stopped abruptly. I turned back when he was beginning to moan in pain. I noticed something peculiar about his moaning though . . . it didn't seem real. I know that it's impossible, but it looked as if he had just acted the entire thing, and wasn't really in pain. Leaving the subject, I walked away from Ion and sat back down on the table, ready to hear the plan so that I could get out of here. The nurse could heal Ion from the wound, I hoped. Eventually they all walked over to me and sat down. Finally they were about to tell me the plan and nothing could go wrong.

"Okay, so in the wasps we found a special ingredient, a disease actually. This disease was special, it could only be put in someone if they were stung by the wasps. The first person we tested it on was one of those brats, we don't know which one." Mac paused for a minute, giving me the opportunity to answer.

"Neva," I muttered under my breath and they all looked at Mac for his reaction. He just looked away, knowing that it would take some time for me to completely leave behind everything I knew there. But just as he was about to pick up, my pocket started vibrating. I reached into my pocket, and pulled out a cell phone. Shock exploded on my face, they had gotten me a cell phone?

"Oh my gosh, they're trying to call me, hold on one sec," I put my finger up and they stared at me as if I was kidding. But I flipped open the phone and put it to my ear. "What, no I don't want to change my mind about being evil. Stop calling me I've changed sides!" I shouted so loud that even Ion could hear me. Then I closed the phone and looked back at my brothers. The Barkers understood, they probably figured out that I was in the presence of my brothers right now. I smiled at my brothers and motioned for them to continue, but they shook their heads.

"Nah, it's getting late, I'm going to bed," Mac said out loud for the first time in his life. He walked off and I groaned, wanting them to stay. After a few minutes of sitting there in the dark I figured that I might as well go to bed.

"Cobalt, are you there?" Ion asked me while I was walking past the cell toward the stairs that were in the TV room. I turned around, knowing that I had no chance of sneaking past the cell.

"Did you figure it out yet?" he asked me, and I noticed tears streaking down his face. I looked away from him, and he groaned, taking off his shirt.

"I'm really sorry about that," I told him, and his mouth dropped in agony.

"You seriously can just stand there and apologize, that thing was melting hot. I'm surprised I lived through it. I don't think this is worth it, we have other ways of finding out their plan," Ion started to yell at me and I shushed him so that my brothers would not wake up. But it was too late, and someone was heading down the stairs now. I ran outside and down the hill into the garage. I noticed Reggie walking down the stairs and as soon as he left the last step I came back up. I tiptoed up the stairs and slid into my bed, which just had to be the farthest one from the stairs.

The next morning I awoke and went downstairs for breakfast. There were a couple eggs on a large plate sitting on the table, so I helped myself. When I was finished I walked into the room with Ion in it, he was sound asleep. I stared at the cell for a minute then walked away, thinking that maybe there's someone watching over me that doesn't want me to hear the plan.

"Where are you going?" Johnny asked me as I was walking out the door to the pool. I sighed, and turned around to save myself from being yelled at.

"I don't know," I answered honestly, then swerved back to leave.

"Wait, Cobalt, come with me," Johnny begged me, and I heard the kindness in his words so I followed him. We walked into the second house, where all the plants were kept and the caught wasps were placed.

"What?" I questioned him when we had arrived, and he took me upstairs to a small empty room.

"You need to get out of here, do your friends have a way of taking you back?" he asked me and my mouth dropped. I must've been a worse liar than I thought. But I tried one last time to make him believe that I was evil.

"Those brats, please, those aren't my friends," I lied and he stared at me, raising his eyebrows. Then he shook his head, stopping himself from saying something stupid.

"Come on, you may be smart enough to trick Reggie, Ashton, and even Mac, but I'm not that thick," he told me, and I laughed. Johnny never really was evil, I knew it all along and now I had just been assured that I was right.

"So you want me just to leave, but I don't even know the plan," I reminded him, and he led me downstairs.

"So those wasps, all shrunken down and in that jar. There's a special poison in their sting. When it goes into someone's body, it causes a special disease. First, the victim will start bleeding, in random places, at least once a day. It won't kill them, but it will make them very weak from blood loss. After that they start to cry, not really cry, but their eyes start pouring out tears. That's all the symptoms of this disease, so it can't kill anyone unless they've had it for years."

"So you don't plan on killing anyone, right?" I asked just to make sure, and Johnny nodded. I stared at the wasps, all buzzing around the jar like they wanted to sting someone. Johnny walked me over to another jar, but this one looked more advanced. It had one jar on top of the other, like an hourglass. There were two nozzles at the top that looked like they were used to spray something into the top jar.

"This machine sprays an orange liquid that causes the wasps to sweat out all of their poison, which will fall into this jar. Then we will grow the poison so that we have an unlimited amount. Do you know where tap water and bottled water comes from?" he asked me randomly and I shook my head. Now that I thought about it, there was no way to have a plumbing or sewage system unless each planet had their own one.

"Well it's teleported from a planet completely covered in freshwater. If you've ever seen the bottom of a sink or toilet then you'd know that there are no pipes, just a small box that teleports the water as soon as you turn the knob or whatever you use to start it," Johnny explained, then got back to the plan. "So Mac wants us to go to that planet and dump all the poison into the water so that whenever someone has a drink they get the disease. It'll take a while, but people won't be able to figure it out fast enough before the entire universe . . . except for Earth, has had the water. Then we found the cure, in this plant," he pointed to a plant that I didn't notice when I first found this place. It had green petals like hands; it could even walk on its petals while it sat in the pot. The center was so minute that at first I thought it was a black seed. But then it opened its mouth and revealed a tongue that was about a foot long and a millimeter wide.

"What's it called?" I asked my brother, as it shook my hand then tried numerous handshakes on me.

"It's a rememdium," he explained, and I nodded, even though I knew that I wouldn't remember that name. "We're going to tell the president that if he wants the cure then he'll have to do something for us. I'm not sure yet, but I know that it's going to be bad," he finally finished, but I still didn't get something. When Neva got bitten we just called a curer and they healed him.

"Won't people be able to call curers if they get sick?" I asked, finding a flaw in his plan, but he rolled his eyes.

"You think we didn't think about that, come here," he led me over to a file, and opened it to pull out the sheet of paper on top. "This list shows everyone in the solar system that has the powers of cures, we're going to kidnap all of them," I noticed the list of about thirty people, and my eyes widened.

"There's a very simple way to stop this plan from working, protect a curer, and when the disease spreads, help her cure everyone," Johnny finally ended his tour and stared me straight in the eye.

"Okay, I understand," I said, glancing at the list. Morgan Lawless, the one who cured Neva, lives on Eximius.

"Get Ion out of here, and then tell your friends to help stop us," he pushed me toward the door but I fought back and turned around.

"Wait, if you don't want this plan to work, or even this life, why don't you come with us? The Barkers and the Venturas are really nice. You could have a better life than this if you just come with Ion and me," I told him, and I remembered how early it still was by looking out the window. He stared at me, with a face so wanting that I just wished I could've taken him with us. But then he looked at the floor, and shook his head as if he were being threatened to stay.

"I can't, my place is here, where I can secretly stop their plans from succeeding and keep you guys safe," he took such a big responsibility that I thought he was in over his head. But then I understood why all the times that my brothers tried to take over the world before some small detail would change and the whole thing would be ruined. One time even Mac accused me of being the one who ruined the plan. I stared at him for another minute then ran outside and to the cell. As soon as I opened the door to the kitchen I saw Mac and Ashton eating breakfast. My feet froze, causing me to fall flat on my face on the stone floor. If I didn't put my hands out I could've broken my nose.

"Cobalt, what are you doing?" Mac interrogated me and I drew a blank.

"I'm . . . um, I have to go the bathroom, be right back," I ran off and went upstairs to make it look like I was actually going to bathroom. A minute later I came back down and saw that they were both gone. Walking over to Ion, I threw a small suitcase out of my pocket and in front of him.

"Can you make it big again, I don't know what else to use," I asked, looking around for a key so that he could get out of the power proof cell. Then I heard someone walking up behind me, and I froze in place. Slowly turning around I sighed in relief when I saw Johnny holding his arm out to me. I put my hand out, and he handed me the key to the cell. I unlocked the cell and Ion got out, immediately growing the suitcase so that we could open it.

"Who was that?" Reggie yelled and I gasped, grabbing the suitcase and leading Ion into the study down the hall.

"Come on, we gotta find some type of teleporter," I ran into the pool house with him behind me and we opened the suitcase.

"This looks like some type of laser," Ion held up what looked like a toy gun, and then put it back down. We rummaged through the suitcase until we found a small machine that just looked like a screen with no buttons. Then we turned it on it became a touch screen device. I pressed Medlocks Galaxy, then Medlocks, then Medlocks Island. Directions appeared on the screen and I read them out loud.

"This machine is only able to teleport one person at a time. If multiple teleportations are needed, the first user must teleport this device to the second person to get it back to the them," I read, then handed it to Ion. "Here, you go first, just teleport it back to me when you get there." I made him promise and he nodded, pressing 'teleport.' It started to load and then he waved goodbye. Just as he disappeared the door slammed open and I saw Reggie standing in the doorway with a tired face, he must've ran here when he heard the cell door open.

"Cobalt, we trusted you!" he yelled as he started to charge at me. I ran around the room as he chased me. When I began to get tired, I jumped into the air and landed down on a metal glider. Reggie eventually stopped, and I had to stop so that I didn't go around the room and knock him over from behind.

"Wait, Reggie, think about what you're doing. How can you live with yourself knowing that you got an entire universe of people sick?" I asked him, but I noticed something appearing in the center of the room. "Sorry gotta go," I smiled and dove for the teleporter. When I got there I grabbed it and closed my eyes, for Reggie was running toward it as well. He tripped over my side, which hurt more than I thought it would, but then I shot a metal probe into the air and broke a hole in the ceiling. Then I flew up into the air, and when I was safe I set the coordinates for Medlocks Island. Just as Mac looked out the window to yell at me, I shot through space and time.

CHAPTER FIFTEEN: THE BIG SAVE

EMBER

Cobalt fell to the grass and looked at our feet. Without counting, he knew there were fourteen pairs of shoes in front of him.

"Oh, jeez, Cobalt, we thought you weren't going to make it, Ion told us about Reggie," I told him, and he got up, handing Wyatt the teleporter.

"Well, then how are we going to figure out the plan now, we're back here and now Cobalt's already blown his cover," Ion complained and started to depart. Then Cobalt smiled and Ion stopped walking when he realized that no one was following him.

"Who says I didn't figure out the plan?" Cobalt grinned as widely as his mouth would let him, and we all laughed for a minute together.

"Come on, we'll sit under this tree and you can tell us," Sam suggested and no one followed him either.

"Are you crazy? It's January," I told him and set fire to my hands, while walking away. People actually followed me, so I went to our floor and teleported to the meeting room. When everyone had arrived, Cobalt stepped to the front of the room and explained the entire plan, from what they were doing on the roof of Medlocks in September to what they're doing after they dump the poison into the water.

"Oh my gosh, that's horrible," Lianna covered her mouth with both hands and Cobalt nodded, then sat down so that he joined the circle of chairs.

"But then I found out that Johnny was actually a good guy, he wants to stop their plan from succeeding. He told me that he's going to stay there undercover and he told me what to do. We have to go to Eximius and protect Morgan Lawless, since she's a curer. If they don't capture all the curers, their plan will fail and they'll give up," he explained while we listened intently.

"Then what are we waiting for? They could be attempting to capture her right now," Forrest stood up and walked out of the room. No one followed him, they did not feel like wasting their time stopping a plot that would more than likely fail anyway, so a couple seconds later he came back.

"Come on guys, let's go!" Wyatt yelled and people agreed reluctantly. We decided that only a few of us would go. Daven and Gabby volunteered to watch after the younger kids, and after that the rest of the older kids left the room. We went downstairs and found the nearest taxi driver, telling him that we'll pay him extra to just borrow the taxi. No one was in the mood to trust a taxi driver right now, even if this one was good. Then we realized that we didn't know which way Eximius was, so we had to find a map that showed the entire solar system. When we found a three-dimensional one showing the rotation of each planet at the exact moment, we were quick to leave since it was summer on the part of Eximius we were headed for.

"Are we close yet?" Wyatt walked up behind me in the space car.

"Yes," I told them, I had decided to drive since I *almost* passed my driver's test. There are no space police anyway so there is no way for me to get caught. When the planet was in view, I swooped down to get out of view of the president's house.

"Wait, we don't even know where she lives," Neva remembered, and all of our mouths dropped in anger.

"This taxi must have some type of address book," Forrest started opening drawers and digging through papers. When he found a big red book he looked at the cover, but it said, "Addresses and Locations of Voliturus Residents."

"I found it," Rhochelle picked up a green book and handed it to Lianna. She looked at the cover, then nodded to us and opened it to the exact page. Then her mouth dropped when she found the last name, and I looked over her shoulder to see it.

"There's like fifty of them," I rounded and everyone else agreed with my assumption. There must've been over five "Morgan Lawlesses," so we abandoned all hope and sat down on the chair.

"But it doesn't matter, look," Forrest noticed the addresses of all the people. "They all live in the same town." We realized that he was right and wrote down the town on a piece of paper. Then we did all of their street names and numbers so that we didn't end up at the wrong house in the right town.

"Okay, let's land in . . . Boothwyn" I read off the paper. We rode around the planet until we were on the spot where the sun was just setting, and landed in an area where no one could see us. Eximius really was a fantastic planet. It was pretty much all beautifully lit cities with skyscrapers and bridges that were unimaginably tall. There were no short buildings spread out in large cities, only tall buildings lined up together in small cities.

"Wow, it's like New York, Tokyo, and Las Vegas having their own planet," Rhochelle noted, but no one knew what she meant other than our siblings. The taxi was lowered into a park and we got out. Looking around, we realized that this would be much harder than we thought. But Lianna walked off and we found her a minute later standing in a phone booth looking into a town directory. Then she walked out and pointed to all the people with the last name "Lawless." It showed where all of them lived, the number of kids they had, and even their names.

"Would Morgan count as a kid or an adult?" Sam questioned us, and we shrugged. But then Wyatt put on his thinking face and figured out something resourceful.

"It depends if she lives with her parents or not," he added, and everyone slowly turned to Neva. If he was the only one who'd seen her, he could tell us if she looked young or like an adult living by herself.

"She told me that she graduated four years ago, so there's no way she lives with her parents still," he tried to clear up, and we looked for adults with probably one or no kids.

"How is that possible? The last session from Medlocks ended eight years ago," Wyatt calculated and we waited for the first person to explain.

"There are schools other than Medlocks that start on different years, just in case the family doesn't want to go one year to Medlocks, they can wait a year and go to a different school," Lianna told him and we got back to the phone book.

"This one . . . it says 'single woman, class of session 35 from Ludus, curer.' That must be her, we're class of session 36, so that means she graduated last session from her school, unless they're a couple sessions off," Neva figured, and we nodded.

"Okay it says . . . 48 Lawless Lane, cool the street is named after her," I jumped into the air and took off, so they followed me down the street until we got to the house. It was a nice house, with pillars on the front porch holding up part of the roof. We walked toward it, and then paused before knocking on the door. But after we did, there was a brief moment of silence, and soon after we heard footsteps coming toward us.

"Can I help you? Oh, Neva, hi! How are you?" Morgan smiled at us, then invited us in. We stepped into her house, then stood by the stairs until she told us to sit down in her living room. "So what brings you guys here?" she finally asked, and it was quiet for a while. No one answered until everyone was sure that we were ready to tell her.

"The truth is . . . you're in danger," Forrest started, but waited for somebody else to pick up to the story.

"We know for a fact that someone is out to kidnap you," Wyatt told the woman, and she immediately turned white as a ghost. She has straight blonde hair and blue eyes. She was short in stature but normally proportioned for her height.

"Are you sure? I mean I know a lot of other people with the name Morgan Lawless," she reminded us of the phone book, and we shook our heads.

"These villains plan to spread a disease through the entire universe, and unless they kidnap every curer in the universe, their plan will fail. We could've picked any curer to protect, but you're the only one that we know that lives in this solar system," Sam explained the plan of Cobalt's brothers. She gasped, and covered her mouth with her hand in a slightly dorky but admirably honest fashion.

"I know a curer, she lives not too far from here actually. I can give you her address if you want," she suggested, and we raised our eyebrows.

"So you'd rather have four villains kidnap you and hold you hostage for weeks than just have us protect you until we know their plan has failed?" I asked her sternly and she thought for a minute. Then she sat back down and sighed.

"No, I just wish this wasn't happening to me," she told us, and we nodded understandingly.

"We know, but the universe depends on it," Neva informed her like it was nothing important. My gosh we need to stop being so dramatic. Morgan stared at us for a minute, and then smiled, making all of us feel a whole lot better about this.

"Fine, but you have to tell me more about these villains. Maybe I can help somehow," she inquired, but we shook our heads. Was she serious? If I were her, I would be thankful that we picked her in the first place.

"Staying out of danger would be enough help, no offense," Forrest laughed and stood up, hoping Morgan would have a couple extra beds in this house or even a few sleeping bags. We soon learned that she had three bedrooms in this house other than her own. She also had a ton of blankets, pillows, and sleeping bags. We stayed in the three bedrooms, but spent the whole day playing the power battle game in the backyard to see who would get the beds. Neva, Forrest, and I won, but Wyatt came close in fourth. When we finished the last round of Neva and me, Morgan congratulated Neva who beat me by making me slide on a special kind of ice that pulled me toward his side.

"You know, most schools have a sport sort of like that. I was never on the team because of my power, but it was fun to watch," she mentioned, and everyone was interested to hear about it.

"What was it called, and how come Medlocks doesn't have it?" Wyatt instantly questioned, and she smiled, knowing we would be attracted to the idea of having a sport to play at school.

"It's called Venatus, and some schools don't start it until their second or third year of school. But there's a huge tournament on Voliturus for all the schools the year they start it, called the Venatus Tournament. I know for a fact that Medlocks starts it on their third year, so that'll be next year for you guys. Each school starts out with four teams, then they pick the top ten people to move on to the tournament, where hundreds of teams compete. It's a huge deal," she added in the end, and we were speechless. The idea of having ten of us go to Voliturus for a tournament playing our favorite game was astonishing. There was a silence, and then we realized how dark it was.

"Okay, we're gonna go to bed now, see ya in the morning," Rhochelle waved to her and we walked inside to find the stairs.

"Thanks so much for letting us stay. And don't worry—with us here their plan is sure to fail," Forrest added then walked into his room and turned off the light, so Wyatt had to create a teleportation field of light going from the hallway to the book he was reading. I got into the bed that was rightfully mine, and waited for Lianna and Rhochelle to walk in before I turned the light off. They had their sleeping bags and blankets all ready, so from there it was just a few minutes until I did not hear a sound. It didn't take me long to fall asleep, the bed was so comfortable compared to the bed that Forrest had built last year.

"Ember, Forrest heard something," Lianna pushed my shoulder so that I would wake up, why couldn't I for once just sleep?

"Ugh, tell him to come in here and tell me exactly what he heard, then maybe I'll get up," I told her and she walked out of the room. I closed my eyes until my little brother stepped into the room and turned the light on.

"Ember, I know what I heard, there's someone trying to sneak into this house," he told me, and I just had to laugh. Everything about him was normal, but he had two floppy dog ears coming out of his head and a dog's nose where his should be.

"Where?" I groaned and threw the sheets off of me so that I could get up.

"In the backyard somewhere—you know how there's that basin behind her backyard? Well, I think they're hiding in it; come on, help me wake everyone up," Forrest left the room but I chased after him to make him repeat it.

"Wait, you want me to wake up Morgan, why?" I questioned his plan, but he waited a second before letting me in on the secret.

"If she's about to get kidnapped, she can scream for help, and we'll come to save her," he explained in a low voice, and I rolled my eyes. But I woke her up still, and she turned instantaneously alert and nervous. We told her to stay here with half of us, while the other half went to check out what was there. I was in the group that left the house, so I went out the backdoor and down the deck stairs.

"This is a bad idea. Who else thinks this is a bad idea? I think we should go back inside to protect Morgan," Lianna shivered as we walked toward the basin about fifty feet away from the house. It was pretty deep, about twenty feet under us. As we neared it, we noticed a shadowed figure lying against the ground as if it would make him look invisible in the dark. We stared at the person for a while. Didn't he know we could see him? He just lied there and stared at the ground in front of him.

"Reggie, come on it's over, we caught you," Sam finally said and walked up to him. But as soon as Sam and Neva were standing over him he inflated like an airbag and hit them, who had not seen it coming at all. The two boys went flying through the air, hit the ground ten feet away, and did not show any sign of still having consciousness. We were about to run over to them, but Reggie was standing up.

"Let's settle this here," he clenched his fists and turned his head to each side to crack his neck. I looked away, disgusted, but kept him in my eyesight. When he attempted to attack I stuck my hand out. Although I was sent hurtling through the air, I did about two back flips before slowing myself down and landing on the ground.

"I'm on fire, you freak! How could you do that?" Reggie yelled at me as he put out the flames on his shirt.

"It wasn't easy, I might've broken my arm trying to do that," I told him, then noticed a light turn on in the house. After that followed a bloodcurdling scream, so I forgot Reggie and ran for the house. My breath sounded so heavy; I had no idea what to think, but thoughts were racing through my mind anyway. Everyone was sprinting after me, but we weren't fast enough. When we got there the whole house looked as if a tornado just went through it. I continued running until I got to Morgan's room, I had already planned out the worst in my mind, but I still wasn't ready for it. She wasn't there. We had failed, and now we had lost all hope in defeating the Iron brothers' plan.

"Where are Sam and Neva?" Forrest suddenly asked, and my eyes widened with the realization of what we had left them to. I ran back to the basin, praying that maybe they had left them there. But that was not a reality; the two boys were gone, along with the four brothers and the last hope of saving the universe.

As soon as Wyatt teleported Forrest, Rhochelle, Lianna, and me back to Medlocks the following morning, we ran to Mr. Williams, thinking that he had a way of tracking Morgan, Sam, and Neva.

"Come on, we know that you know that there is a way to get them back. All we want to know is how," I begged him, but he downright refused.

"Ember, if I had a way I would share it with you, but truly and honestly, there is no way that I have access to a machine that can track a person down," he informed me sternly, and I stared at my family, wanting them to help me find an answer.

"Can't you search like . . . wasps, or rememdium, orange spray, something that can help us track down where they are?" Rhochelle interrogated him, but the man just whipped away from our glances, avoiding all eye contact.

"Please, Mr. Williams . . . they're family," Lianna looked at the ground, giving him a puppy face. He stopped what he was doing, and slowly turned around.

"Guys, I really wish I could. If there was something I could do to find them, I would do it in a heartbeat. But there just . . ." he sighed and turned away again, "isn't." We stared at each other for a long time, not wanting to say anything else.

"Fine, we'll leave, come on, guys," Forrest waved and we walked out the door to go back to our room. The rest of the day was quiet compared to the night before. We sat in the meeting room for hours trying to figure out a plan. No one in our family could understand how we got Neva and Sam kidnapped, and the worst part of it was that the staff at Medlocks barely seemed to care.

The next morning we were in chemistry, listening to the most interesting class of the year. We were learning about caligas, which were different colored sprays that each contained different temporary powers. There were ten colors in the group, and they were all elements only known to Altrians. We knew three of them already. Pink gives people their destined powers, orange makes people hot and sweaty, and white makes them lose their memory. But there were seven others that we had know idea existed.

"This one is a blue, can anyone tell me what it does?" Mrs. Morse asked, and no one raised their hand because this was all new to us.

"This one is the second rarest of them all, it's a truth potion. This one is also the only one that can be used in a drink, which people do all the time for interrogations. All the others work only if they touch your skin. Now red is the absolute rarest, it's like gold and diamonds combined for Earthlings," she told us, and I couldn't help but smile at Rhochelle. Mrs. Morse held up a small test tube filled with a red liquid, and everyone waited for her to explain.

"Red, the most valuable of any caliga, can track a person down, no matter how far away they are. All you have to do is pour it onto a picture of them and then in your mind, you will just know their location," Mrs. Morse explained, and we all sat up straight and looked at each other, eyes wide and minds set. "It only tells the person who poured it, so you can't get a group of people to know. Today we're going to have a contest, and the winner will win this caliga to use however they please. The contest rules, you have to make a green caliga, the one that changes your appearance. You only have the ingredients on your table, and you get to work with your entire table. On your marks, get set, go!" Mrs. Morse watched as everyone frantically ran around trying to figure out what to do.

I opened my chemistry book and found caliga. The directions were pretty clear, puffrat fur, lockmed horn, crayhorn claw, and a couple other ingredients. The hard part was figuring out which ingredient was which, and how to add them. We worked the rest of the class, and when it was over Mrs. Morse came to each table and tested the ingredients. She tested them on a clone of herself, which was able to change its appearance for each one, except for the one that Becca made with her two triplets. Mrs. Morse tried to change her hair color to blue and make her nose longer, but she ended up catching her hair on fire and sneezing out blue gunk on the floor. Last one was ours, and when Mrs. Morse tried it she made no distinction that she liked it the best. Then she went to the front of the room to announce the winner.

"And the person who will take home this caliga is . . . the Andersons!" Mrs. Morse cheered while the rest of the class was silent. The three boys laughed and took the test tube from Mrs. Morse, who didn't even realize that she was probably doing something that could change the course of the future. We left the room with disappointed faces, and glared at Jerod the entire way out.

"That was our only chance of finding Sam, Neva, or Morgan. We need that caliga," Wyatt told us, and we all nodded in agreement.

"Come on, I have an idea," I walked over to Jerod and stared fiercely at him with a face that almost made him give it to me anyway. "Jerod, I bet you that caliga that I could beat you in Venatus, outside, right now," I challenged him in front of his brothers, knowing that he felt really insecure right now.

"You're on, but what do I get if I win?" he asked curiously, and I thought of something so important that he couldn't refuse.

"If I win I get the caliga," I repeated, and then looked at my siblings and cousins, "if you win you get the . . ." but I blanked out and couldn't think of anything.

"You get the power enhancing ring that Neva got last year on the plane," Wyatt butted in, and we remembered that Neva came in third place in the tournament on the plane ride here last year. Jerod and I never got our prizes because I blew up the plane, but I guess Kim, or Glacthia, did give him his prize when he won. I looked at Wyatt's hand, he had borrowed it from Neva last night when he was protecting Morgan. Jerod stared at his brothers for a minute then put his hand out.

"Deal," he replied, and I shook it. He attempted to crush my hand while he shook it, but I smiled at him and pretended I didn't feel it.

"Outside, Rhochelle can draw the lines and Lianna can make sure they're equal squares," I told him, and we walked outside. It felt weird walking next to him, like we weren't about to attempt to destroy each other. It was pretty much like the time we faced Cobalt's brothers for the first time, we all flew away from The Theme Park with a truce, even though none of them kept it.

"Okay, I'll draw it here," Rhochelle drew the lines, and then Wyatt moved them so that they were perfectly equal. I stood on one side, and Jerod stood on the other.

"Let's have a clean fight here, no dying," Forrest joked, but Jerod started to feel that he was in danger. Wyatt put the ring on the ground next to the caliga, and everyone stepped away from the prizes.

"The first person to touch the ground on the other side loses, on your marks, get set, go!" Daven yelled and I threw fire at the boy who asked me to the dance in the beginning of the year. He blocked it by spinning a weight in front of him like a propeller, then stretched it out so that it wrapped around my ankle. It started to pull me toward the line, but I became super flexible and slipped through its grip.

"Ooh, Ember's second power just saved her there, will she over power Jerod's weights?" Rhochelle asked the crowd with a booming, deep voice. I stretched my arm out and grabbed Jerod by the back of his shirt, then started to pull him toward the line. He made a weight appear in front of him and dropped it. To avoid a weight crushing my arm, I let go and pulled my arm back. Jerod started throwing weights at me; I was starting to feel like I was in danger.

"Jerod, stop, I can't dodge them all!" I yelled, and didn't notice one coming right at my face. In the flash of an eye I stretched my hand out and stuck my finger into Neva's ring sitting on the ground. Once it was on I put both my hands out and shot white, hot fire at the weight a foot from my face. It completely dematerialized in front of my eyes. There was a small pile of ashes in front of me and nothing else.

"That's cheating, I win!" Jerod shouted and his brothers high fived each other. "Now hand over the ring." He put his hand out and I seized my chance.

"No, there were no rules against using the prizes to help you," Forrest smiled at them. I threw both of my hands at Jerod and wrapped them around his waist. Then I lifted him into the air while pulling my hands back. He flew through the air spinning and then landed a couple feet next to me on my side.

"Ember wins!" everyone in my family shouted, but Josh Anderson ran over to the caliga and kicked it, sending it twenty feet through the air and into the school wall. It exploded open and a small cloud of red smoke covered where it hit the wall. Josh closed his eyes for a minute then looked at everyone with a greedy face. Although he didn't say anything, it was obvious that something had happened.

"Josh, what happened?" Adam asked him, and he thought for a minute.

"Medlocks Academy is on Medlocks Island," Josh recited to his triplet, and Wyatt ran up to him and pushed him. He flew back and fell to the ground, stuck to the ground by the grass wrapping around his body.

"That was our only way of finding Sam, Neva, and Morgan! What's your problem?" I shouted at them, but Forrest tapped me on the shoulder.

"Why don't you try looking to your left?" Forrest smiled, and I turned to see what he was talking about. There were three people walking toward us from the airport. Even from here I could tell that one was a lot taller than the other, and had long blond hair. The two boys had short, cut hair and were waving to us.

"How 'bout that, only when we try to get something to find them, we happen to find them," Forrest laughed and waved back. We ran over to the three people, wondering how they ever could have gotten back. It was a long run compared to what we had expected. They were farther away than they looked. In the end, we reached them and questioned them about their journeys.

"How did you guys even get back?" I asked them instantly, but then we heard a shouting coming from the school. Five people were running toward us from the school, and we laughed as we watched them slowly tire out and stop running. Then they walked for a while, and then sped up for the last couple yards.

"Neva, we can't believe you came back! We missed you so much," Kamille was the first to hug him, then she hugged Sam, and then the other younger kids smiled at the three and skipped their hugs. There was a couple seconds where we all just smiled at each other and waited for someone to bring the question back up.

"So, how did you get back anyway?" Craig had to ask, and they were silent for a second. Sam, Neva, and Morgan smiled at Cobalt and gave us half an answer.

"Let's just say we have our ways," Morgan kept it a secret.

Cobalt told us that he made Morgan invisible with one of the gadgets he had kept from earlier. So even though she was still in the cell, they thought she had escaped. And since they thought there was still one curer out there they just gave up and quit their plan. Then after they quit all the curers were released and Sam and Neva snuck out with Morgan, who decided to come visit us to tell us the good news.

The holidays finally passed, January ending anticlimactically. It was February in the blink of an eye, and most of that went by just as fast. Valentine's Day was approaching faster than we could expect. Before we knew it, the week of Valentine's Day was on our hands. Everyone in the school was begging the teachers for a dance on Friday, since everyone wanted another shot since the one in the beginning of the year was "interrupted." It was our turn to ask, and we weren't too excited about it. The thought of having another dance made me nervous, because even if I didn't want a date, I either had to ask someone or be the part of the group who couldn't get one.

So on Monday, three days before Valentine's Day and four days before the desired dance date, we went to Miss Monohan's office to see if she was in a good mood.

"Okay, who wants to be the one to ask her?" Rhochelle asked the group and everyone turned to face someone else. But then people kept changing their opinions when they saw most of the people looking at Gabby.

"Why me?" she wondered, then thought for a second. "Well it's not like I can make myself look all sunny and cheery because of my power, I'm not doing it." We stared at her for a whole minute and then she sighed. "Okay, so maybe I can make myself seem sunny and radiant, but still, I don't want to—" Gabby stopped talking when I knocked on Miss Monohan's door. There was a moment of silence as everyone stared at the window on the door.

"Come in," the voice rang and Wyatt opened the door then pushed Gabby in with his mind. We all put our ears to the door to hear what was happening.

"Miss Monohan, I know that you've said no a lot to having a dance this Friday. But I mean Valentine's Day is a romantic time of the year, and . . . people like . . . dancing. You can have students set up the entire thing; all you would need to do is supervise. So I was just wondering, if you could change your mind about saying no," Gabby smiled nicely to the principal, and she returned the gesture. I think her skin was actually shining.

"Gabby, if you promise that the students will do all the work in this, then I can't say no," she answered and Gabby thanked her. Then she walked out, and we pretending as if we didn't eavesdrop.

"So what did she say?" Neva asked sarcastically, and Gabby rolled her eyes, not answering. We all jumped in the air and cheered as if we had just heard her reply, then everyone went back to the tree house to call a meeting of the whole school. We had given a watch to the oldest person in each family, so if we needed to spread the word without letting a teacher hear we could just call them.

When every student in the school had assembled in the larger meeting room that Forrest made a while ago each of us stood on a small stage.

"We just asked Miss Monohan about the dance, and she agreed to it!" Sam's voice boomed and then the whole school cheered.

"I know, it's great! But . . . there's a catch," I added, and everyone quieted.

"The only way for us to have the dance is if we set it up completely by ourselves. We can't have any help from teachers, unless they want to.

Plus Miss Monohan isn't going to do anything," I told everyone, and they didn't seem to care.

"So are you guys ready to do this?" Forrest shouted and the room was filled with noise. Every family was assigned something to do, and then the only inhabitants in our room other than us were the animals. We were supposed to be in charge of food, one of the main things involved in the dance. It was our job to have all the food because we were the only ones that could get it for free.

"Isn't this like the third time we had to make a ton of food for everyone?" Selene thought, and we all looked back.

"Well, there was our end of the year party last year, but I can't think of another time," Aura replied, and everyone tried to remember themselves.

"We've had to make food for ourselves a couple other times, but never for the whole school," Forrest knew better than any of us, he was the one who made it.

"Yeah, so what are we gonna make?" I wondered, and Forrest pulled a handful of crumpled slips of paper out of his pocket and put them on the table in front of us, since we were in the kitchen.

"Those are all the recipes for all the things we've made," Forrest explained, and we stared at him.

"Were you carrying these around?" Neva asked him nervously.

"Yeah, 'cause I carry around all the recipes we've ever written in my pocket. Of course not, I just went to my room in the secret base and got them," he rolled his eyes, and we got to work.

The next day while I was sitting on a beanbag chair supervising Forrest's farming process, Daven walked up to me with a shy look on his face.

"Don't tell me you're asking me to the dance or I will get Mom and Dad to have a very stern talk with you," I shuddered at the thought and then he turned bright red. Such an awkward one, Daven was.

"Can you come with me to ask Nicole to the dance? You're friends with her, right? Maybe it would just comfort her a little to have her friend there . . . in case it gets weird." He stared at me and I made a disgusted face, then a blank one.

"Fine, but I'm standing behind you so I could make gestures to Nicole if she needs to say no." I lied, but then considered taking back my mean remark . . . I didn't.

Daven and I were walking to the thirteenth floor, Daven seemed confident that he could ask Nicole to the dance again. I opened her door and pushed Daven into the room, and then I walked into the room that was like walking through New York City. There were different areas of the room that each showed completely diverse places. And each wall had wallpaper that was a different type of map. We went over to her room, and knocked on her door.

"Nicole?" Daven called her name and waited a couple seconds.

"Yes?" the voice answered, but it was not coming from her room. We turned around, and Daven immediately turned red. She knew he was going to ask her for sure, or else Daven wouldn't be here. There was no point in bothering with some conversation, so he just came out and said it.

"Will you go to the dance with me?" he asked her. She didn't make any notion that he had said something weird, but I could tell that Daven was close to passing out. His face was red, he was slightly shivering in his stance, and he leaned his head forward so much that I wanted to say no for Nicole. But, being the greatest big sister in the world that I am, I stopped myself. But while I watch him it was like his ears had just closed up and his tongue was stuck to the bottom of his mouth.

"Okay . . . yeah," she answered and smiled.

"Really, cool. Okay, so I'll uh . . . come meet you here before the dance," he told her, knowing that he had made a mistake last time when he said he would meet her at the dance. She nodded, and he had a loss for words, so he just waved and walked out. I rolled my eyes to Nicole and followed him. As soon as he was out of her sight he danced through the hallway and skipped down the stairs to our room. I burst into the room laughing and told everyone that he had asked her, and that she said yes.

"Good job, Daven. You got the same date to the dance that you did in the beginning of the year—she must really like you," Gabby smiled since she was also a close friend of Nicole's. He grinned, feeling like he had just asked the most popular girl in school to the dance and she said yes.

"Did you guys ask anyone yet?" Daven wondered just to keep the conversation going, even though he didn't care about anything except Nicole and him dancing on Friday. There was no point in asking anyway, we all lied about our dates to the welcome back dance in September. They shook their heads, but the younger kids were quick to answer.

"Yeah, I asked Dave," Kamille looked around, noticing that Cobalt was staring at her in shock.

"Actually I broke up with Brian, I decided that I don't need a man to complete me. But now there's a dance, maybe I should just ask him . . ." Aura thought, but no one helped her out. Then we looked at Cobalt, Selene, and Ion to see if they were going to say anything.

"Are you serious, Connor broke up with *me*!" Selene glared at Aura, who was trying not to laugh.

"I asked Kaitlyn, she said yes," Forrest randomly brought up, and we smiled at him, wanting to taunt him but decided not to.

"What about you guys?" I asked the Venturas, now a little bit more interested in who was going with whom. None of them answered, it was still a little early since the dance was just scheduled yesterday.

"Then who do you want to ask?" Neva changed the question when he realized that none of them had asked anyone.

"There aren't really that many cute guys in this school," Gabby nodded. Lianna was silent, she never thought about dating or boys. We turned to Sam and Craig, who had been silent all this time.

"Come on, Craig, there's gotta be someone you want to ask," I joked around, and everyone smiled at him.

"No," he shook his head and everyone sighed.

"What about the Tecco girl in our class. Isn't her power . . . amoebas or something?" Cobalt asked and all the older kids stared at them.

"What can you do with amoeba as a power?" Rhochelle thought, a little disgusted.

"A lot of cool stuff, you know how amoebas stick together to get bigger. She can make people do that, it helps when you want to get through a crowd. She can also turn into an amoeba, so she can slip through stuff too small for any of us to get through . . . except me," Ion explained and we rolled our eyes. Some of the powers of people in our school were a little upsetting, as if we were the only ones that got powers good for combat. But I held my tongue and waited for someone to talk again.

"You know if you get dates, you'll have to get them Valentine's Day presents," I told them, and they all rolled their eyes, but then stopped and realized that I was right. It wasn't very important, but it was traditional.

"Then let's go to The Mall," Kamille found an excuse to go to the solar system's biggest mall.

"That's . . . actually a good idea," Forrest realized and Kamille grinned at her ability. "We should go tomorrow," Forrest suggested, causing Kamille to slouch down and sigh heavily.

"Well, we can't go today; we have class," Lianna told Kamille and she rolled her eyes, not caring about class.

"Speaking of class, we missed like three weeks of it this semester," Wyatt told all of us and we groaned.

"Do we have to make all of that up?" Sam questioned in amazement. There was another moan from the group, but we went to our class and listened carefully for our piles of make up work.

That night I thought about the dance. Why did everyone have someone they liked, but the one person I've ever really liked acted like he hated my guts? Was that his way? Or should I not even dare try to bring up the idea of us dating in front of him again? Ugh, life is so unfair when you put on the façade of being a rough, dangerous girl.

Saturday morning arrived, and we got ready to the go The Mall. It was closer than some of the other places that we go to. I had gathered up some of the money I had saved from the allowance I had gotten from my parents. Without the store contest we had last year, all of us were broke and had to wait for companies to ask us to give them supplies for their stock. Cobalt still was rich from the time he made all that silverware for the Japanese restaurant. But I only got the money that we split whenever we did one of those big jobs.

"Is everyone ready? Come on," Sam asked each person but there was no answer, nor was there anyone that sped up what they were doing. Finally we were all assembled, and even though half of us didn't have dates, there were still a ton of other fun things to do at The Mall.

"If anyone falls behind, we'll just meet at the entrance," Forrest told everyone, and we all took off by jumping off the front step of the school. But everyone hit the ground, and got up groaning.

"Great! We're having a blackout—that's fantastic!" Wyatt complained and got up. I laughed at Forrest because while failing to turn into a bird he did a face plant in the dirt. We started walking and then jogged a little because it was taking forever. When we got there, we paused to let a couple of the younger kids catch up. Then we stepped toward the doors and watched them slide open, revealing the hundreds of stores that made up the four story high mall.

"Okay, everyone has their watches?" I asked and each person held up their wrist. Then without another word we split up, and I first went to the holiday store to look at cards, which didn't turn out to be good at all. They were all cards that involved telling someone they loved them, not right for people just going to a dance. Then I found a gadget store, and I thought I could find something in there.

It was probably the coolest store I've seen in my life. There were so many things invented by people with their powers. I saw a Worlds, which was priced at more than a medium sized house. There was also the power enhancing ring that cost more than an engagement ring.

"I'm not going to find anything in here that I can afford," I told myself and left the store. Then a store caught my eye right across the hall. It was a gift store, and it was filled with cool things that looked like cheap gadgets. Smiling to myself, I walked into the store and looked around. There were miniaturized pets, like lockmeds and other things I couldn't identify. I saw perfumes and cards and chocolates, but I didn't want any of those.

After walking around a bit, I noticed an entire shelf covered with the same thing—probably because it was on sale. I walked over it, and grinned, nodding in agreement with myself. It was called a "love note," but it wasn't a real love note. When I first looked at it I thought it was a blank piece of paper until I saw the directions. The person giving it as a gift would write their name and their powers on it. Under that they would write the powers and name of the person they were giving it to. Then whenever they would open it, it would show the feelings of the first person of the second person, and something different every time.

I paid for it and left the store, anxious to see if it really knew how I felt about Jerod. As soon as I was sitting on the bench outside the store, I opened the pen that came with it and unfolded the paper.

"Ember Barker, Fire and Flexibility, Jerod Anderson, Weights," I wrote and the words faded away. Then I folded it up and unfolded it again. I didn't want to let anyone hear me reading, but I just felt like reading out loud so that I could take in what I was reading. Speaking as quietly as I could, I read the paper, nodding in accordance with each line as I went on.

"Jerod, I think about you when the sun sets, rises, is in the sky, and is on the other side of the planet. You are the stars that I look up at every night. When you are apart from me, I wonder what you're doing. When you're not talking to me, I wonder what you are thinking. When I wish upon a star, my wish is to be with you. If you were going to the dance with someone else I would have them beheaded in the hour. My thoughts, my dreams, and my desires are about you. Thank goodness you go to the same school as me, I'd destroy myself if I weren't. I must be the luckiest girl in the universe to have a guy as cool as you that I can see everyday. I'm thankful everyday that you were born, and want to freeze time so that our time will last forever. Sincerely, Ember." I finished reading and read it once more to make sure it was for real. Then I gagged and threw it out in the nearest trashcan. Stupid love letter.

Eventually it was the night of the dance, and Daven forced me to go up to the thirteenth floor to get Nicole with him. She had been combing her hair when I walked it, which made Daven sweat even more noticeably. The school decided on making it a semi-formal dance because of the small amount of dances that we have. She was wearing a silk, pink dress that went down to about two inches above her knees.

"You look . . . fantastic," Daven told her, which made me want to choke on a fork. She smiled, and Daven took her by the hand so that he could lead her down to the cafeteria that had been transformed into the dance hall again.

"Thanks, you look nice, too," she said to Daven just because she knew it was polite. I walked ten feet behind them and tried to block out their disgusting talk. It wasn't that I hated the idea of dates, but it just wasn't something for me anymore. Maybe one day I could be a super cool widow, like a Wiccan or something. We pushed open the doors of the ballroom, and watched a hundred or so eyes turn to us, if only for a second. Then I noticed a couple that wasn't a couple before the dance. Jerod was with Becca, the two most popular people in school, and I wanted to strangle them both with dental floss.

After that I walked over to the only two people in my family that had dates, Kamille and Forrest. Forrest was wearing a green shirt with a darker green jacket and dark blue pants. Next to him stood Kaitlyn Bradley, Alaina and Caroline's sister who has swimming for a power. She had a short, green dress covered in sparkles.

"Aw, that's so cute! You guys match," Nicole pointed to them and they rolled their eyes. "How come we didn't wear matching outfits?" she asked Dave and he turned red. Quickly making up a lie I pointed to her dress.

"I don't think you'd want to see him in pink." I told her and she ended the conversation. Kamille stood with Dave, who really didn't look like they were having any fun. Dave couldn't stop thinking about Kamille being with Cobalt, and Kamille couldn't stop thinking about Cobalt altogether.

"Oh my gosh, I love this song! Do you want to dance?" Nicole asked Daven on the first song we heard, and he smiled, walking to the center of the group with her. They started to dance, and I finally felt like I could leave them to be gross alone.

The hours passed, and the dance slowly came to an end. Everyone was extremely surprised. They all thought that it would take a miracle for the dance to go uninterrupted. I basically did nothing but eat all night, there were hot wings and energy drinks on the table, my two favorite things. I noticed Daven was slow dancing with Nicole, with her head on his shoulder and his arms around her waist. I laughed, and then looked over at Jerod. For my whole life, I pictured how that moment should be, but my imagination was clearly not good enough. It felt as if I had just jumped into a pool of needles, and now I wanted to use them to acupuncture Becca a little too deeply.

"Okay, it's been a great night everyone, but we've gotta pack up and go home. Everyone bid each other farewell and get the heck out of here," the annoying DJ who thought he was so cool told us. I watched as Daven stepped back from Nicole and looked her in the eye, and I hoped that eventually he would be able to think of something to say.

"So, did you have a good time?" he asked her and she nodded. I smacked myself in the forehead and sighed.

"Yeah, thanks for dancing with me," she smiled, and they slowly started walking out the door. He didn't even acknowledge his family as he glided past us. We were all watching him, he could tell, but he wasn't about to ruin this moment.

"Here, I'll walk you to your room," he suggested, and she was silent. I walked out of the cafeteria and walked a few feet behind them. For being so disgusting, I kind of wanted to find out what happened.

"Okay, thanks," she thanked him again and he grinned. They walked up all the stairs, me following about two floors behind wishing that they had something to say.

"I had a really fun time too," he told her and she nodded, having to stop herself from repeating that she had a good time. They came to the door on the right level and Daven opened the door for her then led her all the way to the door to her family's room.

"Oh, wait, I have a present for you," Daven remembered and dug through his pocket until he found a note. It was folded up sort of like an envelope. The same love letter I bought today at the mall! But it also had a red ribbon going around it as if it was a present. "It's called a love note, it never says the same thing every time . . . and it never lies." She opened it and read it silently to herself.

I wished that I could've read it over her shoulder, just in case it said something too awkward, but I soon figured out that it was just as disgusting as I had assumed. She bent down a little, since she was taller than Daven on her high heels, and kissed him on the lips. I turned away at the gross sight, I've never felt so protective for anyone in my family and I wanted to set her hair on fire. Why did I even come to see this disturbing image? I opened my eyes for just a second, and noticed her foot kicked up just a little bit. Smiling, I closed my eyes and told myself that I would not stop their kiss. Then finally they backed off, at the same time actually, and she opened her eyes. Staring at Nicole, I noticed her eyes flash a little, but thought it was just the lighting.

"I just realized, I got you something," she told Daven and ran into her room. I waited, so excited that Daven wasn't the only one that got a present for their date. She came back out with a wrapped box, the shape gave no indication as to what it was.

"Should I open it now?" Daven actually bothered to ask, even though he started opening it just before she nodded. The box was Medlocks colors, a dark red and a light blue. Then he slipped his hands up the side of the box, pushing the lid off and catching it in one hand and holding the open box with the other. My smile immediately dropped, my brother's date to the Valentine's Day dance had just given him the Metronome.

CHAPTER SIXTEEN: THE GOOD, THE BAD, AND THE GREEDY

RHOCHELLE

Daven came to us with the news just that night, but we decided to wait until morning to go to Miss Monohan with it. Now we were on our way there, with Daven holding the cursed thing with his hands. It was just the six of us older Barkers, we had no time to get the Venturas or wake up the younger kids. Oddly enough we found Lianna on her way to the library.

"Do you think she was possessed?" Forrest asked Daven specifically, and stopped walking. He opened his mouth, as if he was gagging, and shook his head.

"I hope not 'cause then I kissed Glacthia," he held out his tongue, making it look like he was about to wash it with soap.

"You kissed her? Oh my gosh—does that mean I'm the only one out of us six that hasn't had their first kiss yet?" I realized, and Wyatt put his hand up.

"I haven't kissed anyone yet," Wyatt told me and I started smiling, laughing a little bit even. He ignored the insult and we got back to the more important issue.

"Why can't we just destroy it?" Neva wondered, and we were reluctant to answer it for the fifth time because we were so annoyed.

"Well, what if it destroys the universe or something and causes the big blackout that ends all powers forever? Then we'd really have a problem," Ember told him, and he nodded, still thinking it was a good idea. We knocked on the door for the hundredth time this year it seemed like, and we waited for the usual call that invited us in.

"Oh, Barkers," she said then figured out that she needed a nicer way to greet us, despite how she felt about our visiting her. "What's on your mind?"

"This is," Daven started off the explanation by putting the Metronome on her desk. She gasped, pushing her chair back so that she was against the wall. Then when it didn't cause something horrifying to happen, she scooted forward and stared at it.

"Where in the universe did you get it?" she asked, causing my siblings and I just to giggle a little. But then we turned serious again and started to fill her in.

"Nicole Magerr gave it to Daven last night. We have three theories on how she got it," Neva looked at one of us to continue for her.

"Well what are they?" Miss Monohan questioned furiously when no one told her.

"One, Glacthia possessed her and gave it to Daven. Two, Glacthia wore a disguise and convinced her that it was a good gift for Daven. Three, Glacthia forced her to give it to Daven. Four . . . she is working for Glacthia and gave it to Daven," I thought, making up the fourth one. Daven glared at me for even suggesting it.

"That makes no sense. Why would Glacthia want us to have it? Then he knows that we could just destroy it. Someone *not* evil must've given it to Nicole," Neva thought of his own theory and we agreed that it made some sense.

"Here, I have a book on the Metronome. It can tell you how to stop it and everything," Miss Monohan went digging through her desk and pulled out a yellow manual with a title in Glacthian. She handed it to Wyatt, who looked through the table of contents.

"Okay, page 78, stopping the Metronome from causing the ultimate blackout," Wyatt flipped through the pages and waited for someone to read out loud while he read it to himself. Eventually, Neva ripped it out of his hands and read it to everyone.

"In order to dismantle the Metronome and stop it from taking the universe's powers forever, you must smash it within sixty seconds of the final blackout. If this is not done correctly, certain parts of the universe may get their powers back while others do not. Finding the exact minute of the ultimate blackout is impossible, so keeping the

Metronome until the final blackout will be necessary." We all stared at the book for as long as possible and then looked up at each other.

"Keeping the Metronome until the final blackout will be necessary? Does that mean that we have to guard it until the blackout happens, then smash it within sixty seconds?" Ember made sure, and when everyone nodded she moaned.

"Well the Peractio Blackout is June 15, 7:47 p.m.," Lianna recited, and everyone stared at her in amazement.

"I thought you couldn't tell the future?" Wyatt asked her.

"It's a simple math equation, using the number of people alive and the different times each person has a blackout, I can figure out when everyone will have a blackout at the same time.

"That's amazing, now we just need to guard it until June," Ember sighed, and we stared at the Metronome, our eyes filled with hatred for it.

"We could make a schedule telling each of us when to guard it. That way we have a watch on it 24-7," Forrest suggested, but didn't like the idea himself.

"Yeah, if there are fifteen of us then we each have to watch it for about an hour and a half," Wyatt figured and we all stared at him curiously.

"How did you know that?" I asked him to enlighten us.

"Fifteen plus 7.5 is the same as saying fifteen times one and a half, and that equals 22.5, which is close enough to a day," Wyatt told us, and we nodded.

"Yeah but if we each watched it for an hour and thirty six minutes then it would be exactly twenty four hours," Forrest explained and then looked at the ground, not wanting us to ask him how he knew that.

"Anyway, thanks for your help, Miss Monohan. Just in case, would you mind if we borrowed this book?" Daven asked her and she nodded, handing him the book.

"Sure, sure, but do be careful. The Metronome is the single most important thing that keeps our powers intact," she looked at us for a long time, then back at the Metronome. Finally she put her hand up, waving her finger at us and looking at the desk. "Actually, I think it would be better if I took it off your hands altogether," she reached and grabbed the Metronome before we could react. "We have better ways to keep it safe. Now all of you, out of my office, I have to take this to someone who can keep it locked up until June." We left her office, and she watched us until the door was completely closed. We headed back for our room, suspicious of Miss Monohan's behavior.

"That was strange, how come she just took it from us?" I wondered, and everyone shrugged. We were almost at our floor, so we all sped up a little toward the end.

"She said she thought she could find someone to protect it better," Wyatt quoted, and I nodded, knowing that part.

"Well who could protect it better than us, I mean, our powers are . . ." Ember looked around to see if anyone was listening, then dropped the sentence.

"Phenomenal I know, but there's something they have that we don't. Power proof rooms and stuff," Wyatt told us and we decided that he was right.

"We could get some of that . . . is it anyone's power?" Daven thought the same thing we were all thinking.

"It's probably one of the Ancestors," Forrest assumed and everyone nodded.

"How come we never learn about their powers? We always learn about people in our school's powers. Where will that ever get us?" Neva wondered.

"They're preparing us for the ultimate goal, becoming an Immortal. We learn about things that will get us jobs on Earth, trying to convince us to move there so that we can do something amazing and become Immortal. We learn math in numbers class, literature in letters class, geography in . . . geography class. It's like this big plan of theirs to get Earth to find out about us, but not all at once," Forrest finally explained, and everything started to make sense.

"I guess 'superhero' isn't really an occupation here," I sighed, staring at the ground. Eventually we reached our floor, and everyone walked to the door but Daven.

"I'm going to go talk to Nicole," he told us and walked off.

"Hold on!" I called to him and he turned around, thinking that I was going to stop him. "You might need some backup just in case." He smiled and we began walking to the unlucky floor, the thirteenth.

"What are you going to ask her, exactly?" I questioned him and he shrugged.

"I'm not sure. Probably if she was possessed," he told me calmly and I gasped.

"No, bad idea. What if she still is? Glacthia would kill you . . . he would kill us," I realized and ran in front of him, putting my hand out so that he could not move anymore.

"I won't literally ask her if she was possessed, I'll disguise it to make Glacthia think that I'm not suspicious and to make her tell me if she's not possessed," he explained and I stepped aside. We reached her room inside her family's room and knocked on her door.

"She's not there," George told us and we swerved around to face him.

"Where is she?" Daven asked, worried and suspicious at the same time.

"None of us know, she's been gone for a while," George informed us and Daven threw her door open. "Nicole!" he shouted, but knew she was not here. Thinking of all the possible things that could've happened to her, he barely noticed the note on her dresser. I grabbed it and everyone read it to themselves instead of me reading it aloud.

> *Daven, if you ever want to see your precious Nicole again, you must listen carefully. Come to The Aquarium as soon as possible. Past noon is too late and Nicole will not be there to ▮ ɛat you.*

"What does it say right there?" George pointed to the ink splotch.

"I think it said meet, but that isn't spelled with an 'a,'" Daven explained, and then we looked up.

"We better go fast, no time to tell the others," I ran to their window, and hoped that I was right. Quickly I dove out the window, and made a rock appear under me. Then I turned it around and started laughing. "Good thing there wasn't a blackout. Then Tower of Terror would be an attraction on Earth and Medlocks."

"Come on, I have a better idea," Daven grabbed George's hand and used Ion's copied powers to make the window bigger. Then just for the heck of it, he dove out the bigger window, holding George in one hand and grabbing for me with the other. Once he was touching both of us we disappeared and appeared at the entrance of The Aquarium. I looked at my watch then stared at Daven.

"11:49, we don't have a lot of time," the three of us ran in. The Aquarium was spooky when it was empty, which was strange because it was open right now.

"All the workers, you don't think . . ." George didn't finish when he heard a creaking coming from the ceiling. All of us looked up, wanting to scream but not truly that worried. A fake swordfish swung from the ceiling on one of the cords holding it up, the other dangling behind it, the end of it on fire.

"Watch out!" I pushed George down and put my hands out to stop it with a rock. But nothing appeared, and I soon realized that I was in trouble. It swung past us; I didn't feel it at first. But when I saw the nose dig into the wall behind us and stop it from swinging back I fell to the ground in pain. There was a cut down my left arm. Not a serious one, but it was bleeding heavily.

"Rhochelle, you have to get out of here, it's too dangerous," Daven forced me up and pushed me toward the door. I moved to the side, allowing him to fall forward and then get back up.

"And leave you two to die at Glacthia's feet?" I asked them, but gave neither of them a chance to answer. "Not a chance; I'm staying. Besides . . . I barely feel it," I lied, and we continued our walk to find Nicole. We had eight minutes left, and the lights were starting to flicker.

"Guys, come to The Aquarium as fast as possible," I said into my watch and then turned it off so that I didn't have to answer their questions. This way they'll really come running here knowing it was something important.

"Ah, there are three of you this time. Where's your little gang, Barkers?" the voice croaked from the room that we weren't even headed for. We turned to our right, and walked into the big room shaped like an auditorium. It had stone steps all the way to the ceiling where people could sit. On the stage was a giant tank, and in it now, the biggest, most deadly looking underwater creature I've ever seen. At first it looked like a shark, but it had tentacles coming out of its sides. And instead of having just suction cups on its tentacles, it had spikes.

"This is a thalassinus, creature of the ocean depths," Glacthia reported, and I noticed a rope coming from the ceiling and dangling over the tank with a loop on the end. "I said if you came after noon, Nicole will not be here to *eat* you. But you're on time, so here goes." Glacthia waved his hands and we disappeared from the floor, and became tied in the loop on the rope.

"Don't worry, I got this," I nodded to them, and attempted to cut the rope with a rock then catch us on a slate. But no rock appeared, we were still in the blackout. "Okay I don't got this." The three of us suddenly started to panic, and we looked down at the tank. It was about fifty feet under us, but the rope was being lowered towards it and the thalassinus that was actually Nicole was attempting to jump out of the water. It made it pretty high up, but we were safe . . . for now.

"Nicole, come on, you know it's us, just try to remember," George told his sister, who was reaching up with its tentacles to wrap them around us and pull us into her mouth. If this was how it was going to end, I would rather it not be Nicole trying to eat us. A regular thalassinus wouldn't be as bad since we weren't friends with it.

"That rope moves way too slowly, and why are these ceilings so high anyway?" Glacthia was asking himself.

"Shut up, Glacthia. You're a terrible person," I randomly shouted, maybe thinking it would make a difference. He started to smile at me, I could tell . . . but then again we could never see his face. All of the lights were off; it always got dark when Glacthia was around. If we saw him in the light then maybe we could actually *see* him, but that wasn't going to happen.

The rope was getting lower, and we were coming closer and closer to the monster. Nicole probably didn't know what she was, or that she was about to end our lives. I thought about my life—if I was ready to die or not. There were so many things that I wished I could do, kiss my first guy, get married, be a parent. I would never be able to do any of that if my life ended right now.

"Nicole, come on! We know that if you try hard enough, you'll remember us," Daven was talking to her still, trying to make her remember, but she flung her tentacle into the wall and it stuck. When she realized that it was sticking, she pulled herself out of the tank and stuck another tentacle into the wall. I looked at her sides, there were no gills, a thalassinus must have lungs.

"Oh, wow, this is bad," I stared at the creature scaling the wall. It looked sort of like a spider, but it still moved its tail from side to side and snapped its mouth shut and opened it again.

"It must be really hungry," Daven recalled, it was almost level with us. The wall was pretty far away, so it would have to jump to be able to get us.

"I have an idea," George suddenly whispered to us when it was figuring out how to jump to us. "If we could untie ourselves we'll fall into the tank, and we could get out just as it jumps in. Maybe if we're lucky we can outrun it," he nodded, wondering if his plan sounded good to us.

"It looks really fast with its spiky tentacles. Maybe if we found something for them to get stuck onto, like a log, then it would slow it down," I suggested, and they nodded. The creature leapt at us before I could count to three, so I slipped through the rope. A moment later, Daven and George fell through the rope after me when the loop had the extra slack, and we headed for the tank. Although it was ten feet off the ground, it stretched under ground for at least a hundred yards.

We hit the water with a loud crack. As soon as I hit the water I started swimming for the edge so that I could get out. Daven and George came out after me and a second later Nicole hit the water. We were already sprinting for the wax exhibit, so we had a pretty good head start. But I looked back and noticed it dive out of the water and start running for us. It moved slowly, but took such big steps that we didn't have much time.

A few seconds later we made it into the wax exhibit. It had tons of underwater creatures made of wax, just sitting on the floor. We ran through it, and the best thing happened when we got to the other side of the room. Nicole came in, reaching her tentacles out to grab anything that could pull her closer to us.

"Watch, it'll get its spikes stuck in the wax and will stop chasing us," I told Daven and George, who were still watching to see if I was right. But of course I wasn't, the thalassinus was too smart for that. When it came in, it breathed fire on every wax creature it passed. It was a horrible sight, we had just stopped running and let it catch up to us, knowing we would never regain our lead and we were done for.

"Look, maybe it will slip in the wax," Daven noticed all the melted wax all over the room, covering the floor and drying in places where it was cold.

"Heads up!" a voice shouted and I felt it start to get really cold. I put my arms around myself and watched the creature run toward me. It was slowing down—it felt the cold as well. Finally, it just stopped, and I looked at the wax under its tentacles. It had completely frozen to the ground with one of its tentacles reached out to grab me. I turned with a guess of who it was.

"Neva . . . but how did you . . ." I asked and he shrugged, letting the ring glimmer on one finger. I smiled, so happy that he came in third place that day on the plane.

"Sometimes I just sit around storing power in it. It tires me out, but then I can have extra power when I do use my powers," he explained, and I nodded. The rest of the group came behind him, and I hugged them all, suddenly happy to be alive.

"That took you guys long enough. Two minutes ago would've been great too, you know," I hit Wyatt on the shoulder girlishly. He smiled, and I walked back to Daven and George, who were staring at Nicole.

"There's still one order of business to take care of," Daven lowered his eyebrows to Forrest, who was happy to oblige. He waved his hand and the giant thalassinus, frozen in place, became the ordinary girl it was before.

"You guys saved me," she went to hug George, but tripped in the still unfrozen wax in front of her and fell on her face. Everyone laughed as she slowly wiped her face from the melted wax. Then she walked over to Daven, who was smiling, hoping for a kiss or something. She smiled, silently laughing, then gave him one just because. Then her smile was gone, and she looked down.

"I'm sorry I got you the Metronome. I found it on the desk in my room, with a note saying that it was a really good present for you, from someone who called themselves the Secret Assistant. I seriously didn't know that it was bad, is there anything I can do to make it up to you?" she asked, and Daven looked around then smiled.

"I can think of one thing, but I wouldn't do it in front of my siblings," he told her and she laughed, along with the rest of us. After that, Wyatt held up the Metronome to me, all of its horrors filling the inside like souls.

"It just appeared in our room, someone must want us to have it and not Monohan," he explained and I rolled my eyes, half wanting it and half not.

Everyone went back to Medlocks, and we decided to play a game of manhunt with the Magerr's that night. It was remarkably fun, Forrest made it really dark and then in the end we all roasted marshmallows over a fire. They left late in the night to go back to their rooms, which took them a while to find because all of the lights in the hallways were off.

I had the night shift guarding the Metronome. Forrest put together a schedule so that the shifts were an hour and a half during the day and one hour at night. Mine started at midnight and went on for an hour. I had coffee and soda and candy to keep me awake, but the only real way I could stay awake was by standing.

When we lived in Wisconsin, we had our Eight Perils guarding our secret base. There was something like that here, but there were fifteen. It was like a labyrinth behind me, there were hedges shaped like a maze and every couple feet was a different one of the perils. None of us could get in by ourselves; it took every single person to get inside. Then in the middle, the Metronome sat with a forcefield around it. The entire labyrinth has a powerproof forcefield around it, which Wyatt finally remembered he could create. I had a few gadgets with me while I guarded it. The first one was important—a flashlight strong enough to light the entire room. Another one of them was a teleporter that could teleport me anywhere but inside the perils themselves. I also had a ray that could freeze, melt, teleport, and even kill things. There was even a ray that could check to see if people were being possessed or had anything to do with Glacthia in the last 24 hours. The last gadget was the most important and the simplest. All I had to do was point it at the hedges, and it would tell me if the Metronome was still there. I did this every minute or so, just to give me something to do.

So there I sat, waiting to go call Forrest on his watch so that I could sleep. I only had about fifteen minutes left, and as sure as I was that nothing was going to happen, I was nervous as well. Here I was, over a mile away from the tree house near the mountains, standing with my back to the hedges, hoping that nothing bad would happen.

"This isn't that bad. I even have something to do. Look," I talked to myself so that I wasn't bored. I started replacing my hands and feet with rocks so that I could make it look like I was doing backflips randomly on the ground. I did a cartwheel, a round-off, then turned it into a back handspring. When I finished the four backflips I added on the end, I turned to go back to the spot and screamed. It wasn't loud, but I fell to the ground, not able to breathe. Finally I regained my strength and stood up, with the arm outstretched to help me up.

"Um . . . I'm sorry that I scared you, but I need to talk to you about something," Mr. Williams said with a completely sane and serious voice, and I couldn't help but smile a little.

"Sure, would you mind talking over here?" I asked. "Here, just let me turn some lights on." I smiled, grabbing the possession detector. I pointed it at him and pressed 'detect.' It showed the reading a second later, and I turned my head to the side, not sure it was right. It read, "No contact with Glacthia in the last 24 hours." Then what would Mr. Williams be doing two miles from the door? I noticed that he was staring at me, and started to laugh.

"Oh I'm sorry, all of these gadgets look the same. Ah, here, this one is the light," I pressed the light button and a small light post came out of the ground and lit itself over our heads. Another one also grew out of the ground where the Metronome rested on the ground in the middle of the Fifteen Perils. A scary picture appeared as I watched the Metronome glow under the light from the lamp from about a hundred feet away. The swirls of color inside it represented the people who were having a blackout right now; they flew around like souls trapped in a glass sphere. The lamp was freaky too, it was made of a dark, antique looking metal and had big spirals coming off of it at random places. Turning back to Mr. Williams I crossed my legs, nervous about what he was going to say, and smiled.

"So what did you want to ask me about?" I wondered, and he lifted his head briefly to show that he was about to start.

"Right, I need to talk to you about your grade in power practice," he said, and I didn't like where this was going. "It's not that you're failing . . . exactly. But it's steadily dropping, and I came to ask you if there was something . . . someone . . . that was causing you to lose your interest in power practice. Because I do know students, and if they aren't doing well, they clearly don't like the class." He looked at me for a minute, but I didn't really have anything to say. Last time I checked,

I had a perfect grade in that class. It was the only class that I really did like.

"Do you have a copy of my last couple test grades or something? I'm sure I can't be doing that bad," I wondered, and then I realized how stupid of a question that was, considering he came empty-handed.

"Well I didn't bring a paper, but for your last four tests you had a Basic, Failed, Unbearable, and another Basic," he recited, and my mouth dropped. There were seven grades in Medlocks, and those were three of the lowest four.

"But I don't remember ever getting those grades, did you hand those tests back?" I wondered, pressing the Metronome detector on the perils. It was still there, and then I turned back to Mr. Williams.

"You weren't at any of the classes I handed the tests back," he told me and I rolled my eyes nodding that at least it made sense. We had missed so many classes ever since the episode at the Ancestor Day parade. It's like we hadn't gotten a break from fighting Glacthia and the Iron brothers since then.

"Well I see you don't want to talk about this right now. Come to my office and we can chat . . . if you want to of course. But unless you want to be in classes with the younger kids next year, you need to pass my class," were his last words, and then he walked off. I sat down on the chair, only having five minutes left of my turn. The thought that I was failing my favorite class was just terrible, especially this late into the night. What had he come here at this hour for anyway? No one walks two miles just to tell someone they're close to failing, especially since I had that class tomorrow. The more I was thinking about it the more suspicious I got, and finally I pointed the Metronome Detector at the hedges to check one last time. As soon as I saw the results I shouted loudly and made the light brighter, since Mr. Williams would still be in sight right now since he only walked away a minute ago and the place was pretty clear. The Metronome was gone and it was all my fault.

CHAPTER SEVENTEEN: METRONOME MADNESS

FORREST

I had just come back from hiding the Metronome in the woods. Several minutes before, while I was walking to go meet Rhochelle for my turn I saw a dark figure running through the woods. The person was holding the glowing Metronome, so I tripped him or her and made the Metronome come to me. But just when I was about to figure out who it was, the person disappeared on me and I was left with the Metronome. I was going to put it back in the Fifteen Perils, but then the idea came to me. If less people knew where it was, the less chance it would have of getting stolen. So I found the perfect hiding spot and put it there, swearing that I wouldn't tell a soul where it was no matter what.

Just when I got back into my bed Rhochelle ran into my room to wake me up. She shook me, thinking that I was asleep, and I pretended to wake up.

"Forrest, Forrest, the Metronome is gone! I think Mr. Williams took it, I don't know. I found him in the woods, he wasn't being possessed, but when he left the Metronome was gone. I don't know what to do, should we try to catch him or something? I'll wake everyone up and meet you in the meeting room," she ran out and I was left to think about how I was going to tell them this. I know they would be mad if I just said I didn't trust them enough to know where it was. The fewer people that knew the better, and I knew that what I was doing was right, that's all I had to say.

I walked into the meeting room to find everyone there, arguing about what to do. Some people were suggesting that we go to Mr. Williams and ask him if he was being possessed, and believed that the detector wasn't working. The other party argued that if the detector wasn't working, then Glacthia could still be possessing Mr. Williams, so we should go to Miss Monohan.

"Guys!" I finally shouted and they silenced immediately. "I found the Metronome and I hid it," I told them, about to get to the part where I wasn't going to tell them where it was.

"Did you see who took it?" Wyatt asked, and I stared at him for a minute.

"No. It was too dark and they disappeared before I could get to see them. It was most likely Glacthia in a holographic disguise," I assumed, but wasn't telling them some other theories.

"So, everyone can get back to bed, and . . . since Forrest saved it, someone else can take your spot for guarding it," Rhochelle told me generously and Aura stood up.

"I'll do it," she volunteered, "I haven't gotten to do it at night yet. So I'll just go down to the perils and you left the gadgets there, right Rhochelle?" Aura wondered and Rhochelle nodded to her. She turned to leave and I had no choice but to tell everyone now. I wanted to wait until morning, but I didn't want Aura to go all the way there and wake everyone up again when she saw that it was gone.

"Aura . . . guys," I said and everyone turned around. They were waiting for me to say something, but I couldn't bring myself to tell them. So I just took a deep breath and tried to say it as lightly as possible. "I thought it would be a good idea to only have one person who knows where it is. That way it would have less chance of getting stolen. So I . . . hid it somewhere where you guys can't find it," I looked at the ground and turned around to walk away, but someone told me to stop.

"Wait, so you're just not going to tell us where it is?" Neva asked me and I stopped dead in my tracks. Without even turning around I answered the question and walked off without another word.

"Yes," I murmured quietly and went to bed feeling more alone than I ever had in my whole life.

The following morning I woke up to find that I didn't need to walk down nine flights of stairs to get breakfast. A huge table lay at the foot of my bed, covered in food that would take at least twenty people to eat. Then everyone walked in, commenting on how amazing the breakfast was.

"Wow, that looks so delicious, doesn't it?" Lianna asked me and I nodded, thinking it looked delicious as well. But then I looked away, starting to feel bad again.

"I'm sorry guys, I just don't deserve this," I replied, and all of them looked at me like I was stupid to pass up breakfast in bed.

"Of course you deserve it—you're just such an amazing brother and cousin, why wouldn't you deserve it?" Selene crammed into one whole sentence and I smiled.

"Because I'm not going to tell you where I hid the Metronome," I told her with a warm smile on my face and all of them started glaring at me. Slowly they took back their plates and walked away.

"Oh, so you guys didn't even cook it, you just took it from our table and gave it to me instead of eating it yourselves?" I called to them, but they didn't reply. Although I didn't mean it, I felt as if I shouldn't have said it.

I spent almost the entire day ignoring their questions, which later turned into insults when they were sure that I wasn't going to tell them. I walked proudly, but I walked alone. It probably wouldn't be that bad if I told them, it's not like they would tell Glacthia himself. But he could get it out of them; they could be possessed right now for all I know. Maybe that's why they wanted to know so badly—because Glacthia was possessing them. The only person I could trust right now was myself, and so far it had been working. I checked on the Metronome twice a day and it was always there. In fact, I was on my way to check on it right now.

Like usual I went as a different creature, this time a panther. I pretended I was hunting, so I walked slowly and constantly looked around. It felt so much better to walk this long distance on four legs than it did with two. Four legged creatures can stand so much easier than us, it's like trying to balance a two-legged chair verses a four legged one. The two legged one can stand, but you have to keep checking on it. And the weight is divided up better so your legs don't get tired.

As I passed the rock where the lions lived, I smelled someone near me. Turning, I saw Aura, staring at me in fear and curiosity. She didn't know it was me, but she was thinking it and becoming more suspicious with every second that I continued to stare at her. I looked away, and she came down toward me on an air vent.

"Forrest," she told me, not asked me, but I still decided to see how long I could make this go on. I started to walk away, pretending I was afraid of her, but she came after me.

"Forrest, come on I know it's you," she told me and I had to give her credit, no one's ever discovered me in a forest of animals before.

"What gave it away?" I decided to ask, and she jumped.

"Aw, thank goodness it's you, I was just guessing," she told me and I rolled my eyes. Then I looked at up at her, ready to give her a speech Dad would give her.

"You shouldn't do that; it would've been bad if I was a real panther," I told her and she looked at the ground, feeling bad. Then she looked back up and spoke in a happier voice.

"Yeah, for the panther," she joked and I couldn't help but turning back into myself so that I could laugh.

"How do you spell cool?" she finally asked, and I looked at her with a suspicious and worried face.

"C-O-O—" just as I spoke the second "o" she threw a test tube of some liquid at me. I instantly reacted and turned into a mouse. Then I made a ton of leaves on a nearby tree wrap around each other to make a small bowl and catch the liquid. Aura was making it so that it flew in a straight line, like it was still inside the test tube that had become invisible. I caught the liquid in the bowl and threw it back at her. It felt weird being a mouse but standing on two legs and using my hands to direct the bowl. But it splashed back into her face and she swallowed some of it. Then she stepped back in horror, and then sat against the stone wall.

"What was that?" I demanded when I had turned back, and then I noticed her eyes. They were wide, like she was in a trance, and she had her head tilted slightly to the side. Her arms were perfectly straight against her sides with her legs straight out in front of her. She sat with faultless posture, despite the slanted rocks.

"Truth potion," she recited in a nasally voice.

"How did you get it and whose idea was this?" I asked two questions at once to get faster answers.

"We borrowed it from Mrs. Morse in chemistry—everyone's," she said without putting a word between the two answers.

"How could you?" I asked, but then realized that I wouldn't get the right answer from someone on a truth potion. But Aura stood up, and walked toward me as if she couldn't believe I had just asked that.

"How could I . . . how could I? Forrest, you hid the Metronome and don't even want us to know where it is. How could you?" she didn't let me answer, she walked away and then turned into wind, making herself look all mysterious.

"Urg!" I yelled and turned into a fly to check on the Metronome.

That night I was walking back from sports—alone of course—when I decided that I needed to see someone. Not Mr. Williams or Miss Monohan—they weren't on my side right now; they thought the Metronome was being kept safe with someone who has more powerful guards. It had to be someone I knew, could trust, and had not already talked to my family. They practically told the whole school that I was a selfish know-it-all who didn't share. Someone who I felt comfortable talking to, that was my friend. The more I thought about it, the more I realized that our only friends were each other. We were a group of friends and more, a family.

Then I bumped into my answer while I was going down the stairs. She hit me in the shoulder, paying attention to the books she was holding. Both of us dropped our books, and when I bent down to pick them up I blushed and smiled.

"Hey," I said to Kaitlyn, hoping that she wasn't in a rush to go anywhere.

"Hey, Forrest; what's up?" she asked, and I felt as if I should've asked her that first. I never do the right thing when I'm around Kaitlyn. Once we went on a date and the whole time we were walking toward the taxi I felt as if I should open the door for her. But once we got there, she was standing in front of me, so it would be awkward for me to walk in front of her, open the door, and let her walk around me to go in. And I never ask her how she's doing or what she thought of the movie until after she had asked me first.

Either way, I said that nothing was up and asked her what was up, just to get the same reply. I don't even know why we bothered, it's like all of our conversations were, "Hey; hey, what's up; nothing much, you; same," then an awkward silence.

"What are you doing tonight?" I asked as if I were about to ask her on a date, just as nervous as if I were.

"Nothing," she said like she always did—no one did anything around here.

"Do you wanna go to dinner with me?" I asked, having a good idea.

"Sure," she smiled, and I started walking up the stairs. "Forrest—" she started, and I turned around. "The door out of Medlocks is this way . . . and I can't fly," she explained to me, thinking that I was about to feel really embarrassed. But I shook my head and filled her in.

"I know, trust me," I grabbed her hand and started running up the stairs. I wanted to see if I could make a restaurant on the roof. When we got there, I was so relieved to see the sign that it will be closed tomorrow for reconstruction, since everyone else told me that it was already closed. Quickly, I set everything up for a romantic dinner and found that they actually had saved restaurants for it. Randomly I pressed one and led Kaitlyn into the portal. She grabbed my hand while it started shaking, and I smiled and turned red. When we got out I frowned in disgust. It was a table, a red and white checkered tablecloth, candles, a violinist, and two plates of spaghetti. Although people told me that I was not human for this, I hated spaghetti. It just had a horrible plain taste to it, I only ate it with tons of sauce on it.

"Forrest, how did you know I loved spaghetti?" she hugged me tightly and walked over to the table. Although it was extremely embarrassing and clichéd, I was happy if she was happy.

For the next five minutes, I filled her in on the whole story: starting with how we got the Metronome from Nicole and ending with how losing the Metronome to Glacthia will be an end to super powers and probably all life in the universe as we know it.

"Well I think that you should just trust your siblings and tell them where it is," she told me her true opinion after I had explained everything to her. I didn't like her words, but I guess she was right.

"Well, thanks for that, and the dinner," I said, and she got up to leave. When she opened it she looked back at me smiling.

"By the way, you got the dinner—you shouldn't be thanking me," I stood up and walked over to her. She kissed me, but only for a second, and closed the door behind her. I sat down, smiling. Then I angrily banged my fist on the table.

"But Daven gets to kiss for like half an hour!" I exaggerated to the violinist. He continued to play the violin, but shrugged.

"Daven took Nicole to the welcome back dance. They've liked each other for longer," he told me and I stood up, completely freaked out. I pressed the "clear" button on the machine and everything shimmered away as if they had all been holograms.

When I got back to the room, I opened the door and looked at the night sky I had recently seen outside. Then a giant body bag fell over my head and was zippered up when it got to my feet. I started kicking and yelling while I floated toward the tree house. Finally the bag opened and over ten people grabbed me. They chained my hands and feet to the chair I had been laying on; it felt like I was at a really mean dentist's office.

"What the heck are you guys doing?" I shouted to them, but I knew the answer.

"We want to know where the Metronome is," Neva answered simply, and I thought of all the torture methods they had. But Wyatt pulled a small test tube of blue essence from his pocket and took off the cork covering it.

"Mrs. Morse must have a lot of that stuff for her to not notice that you took it," I smiled at them, hoping that they didn't think about that.

"Yeah . . . but I cloned over a dozen bottles of it so it doesn't matter," Daven told me and I raised my eyebrows, feeling like I was surrounded by super villains and I was still the good guy.

"Just pour the whole bottle in his mouth, that way he'll have to swallow some of it," Sam thought as Daven leaned the bottle over my mouth and Wyatt opened my mouth telekinetically. It was forced into my mouth, but I spit out as much as I could, so it got all over my shirt and face.

"He only got enough for one question," Wyatt shook his head, and Ember waved her hand at him.

"It doesn't matter that's all we need . . . where is the Metronome?" she asked me sternly. I only drank enough to be forced to tell part of the truth, but I was able to bend it a little at my own will.

"In our room," I told them, then couldn't help but smiling. They all looked at me angrily, some of them banging their fists on the wall and complaining.

"Why won't you just tell us?" Neva finally yelled and I stared at him.

"Do you really wanna know why?" I shouted back and they all got nervous. "I'll tell you why! Because . . . the person that stole it the first time was one of us!" I finally blurt out and Daven dropped the caliga onto the floor, causing it to break. Wyatt let all the chains off of me and I got up, cursing under my breath. I walked off, knowing that I couldn't put it off anymore. I went to Miss Monohan's office and knocked on the door reluctantly. She actually came to the door and opened it this time, she must've been standing when I knocked.

"Oh, Forrest, how are you?" she asked, and I didn't bother filling her in on that part. But I sat her down and explained everything that happened from when we left her office and found the Metronome again to when I told my siblings that I wouldn't tell them where it was.

"Well I think you should hand the Metronome over to me, I will protect it better," she told me, and I stared at her. She hadn't been herself lately, and now it was becoming more obvious and suspicious.

"But last time we gave it to you we just got it back for some weird reason. Don't you think that whatever did that wants us to have it?" I asked her then realized the extent of my words. Maybe whatever gave us the Metronome isn't a good person? It could even be Glacthia.

"I think that if you're not going to give it to me then you're endangering you and your siblings. So if you want that to be your fate then leave my room!" she shouted and I stepped back, scared a little. She had never yelled, Miss Monohan had always been kind to us. Just as I walked out I looked at the corner of her room where the door would usually block if it were open. It was a small metal box, with curved corners. From a far off distance it could be mistaken for a weighing scale. But the top of it was a red screen with a small hole in the center that a toothpick could only fit through. I walked out, nervous about the machine. As soon as I left I went straight to my room and went to bed.

A few weeks passed, and March pulled in. My days were lonely and my nights felt like I was the last person in the universe. No one talked to me, no one said anything to me. If this traitor was one of my siblings they were really good about hiding it. All of them stuck together and stayed in their conspiracy group against me. I constantly found truth potions in my drinks, and once even in my food. It was hidden in a sandwich, and I had eaten it when none of them were looking so they didn't know to ask me any questions.

One night I was walking alone in the woods, as I usually did when I went to check on the Metronome. I was a misquito this time, since I knew no one would bother to come up to me to see if it was me. I was thinking about every piece of evidence to the puzzle that I had come across in the past couple weeks. Nicole receives the Metronome from some mysterious person, gives it to Daven, and then Miss Monohan takes it from us. Then we get the Metronome back because someone took it from Monohan and gave it back to us. Someone later tries to steal it from us, but I foil their plan and hide it for myself, not telling anyone. Later Miss Monohan yells at me to give it to her. For some reason Miss Monohan wants it, and someone mysterious wants us to have it. The person who stole it was on Miss Monohan's side clearly, or else she wouldn't have been so furious when I told her I stopped them. But the mysterious person who gave it to Nicole and took it from Miss Monohan can't be on our side either, because the Metronome is too hard to protect. On top of it all, we have no leads as to who this mysterious person is.

At that time, I suddenly saw something so surprising that I turned back into myself. I was right, it was definitely the thing I saw in Miss Monohan's office a few weeks back. Just as I was staring at it, a leopard walked up to it, sniffing it as if it were food.

"No don't—" I tried to say, but it was too late. The leopard, whose name I remembered as Kanora, stepped on it and froze. The red screen lit up and a metal wire appeared out of the hole in the center, wrapping up her paw and strapping it to the trap.

"It's okay, here I'll get you out," I walked nervously over to the trap, and pressed the off button nervously. Then a different wire came out, pointed at me, and shot a black mist at me. Before I realized it my molecules were turning black, and splitting apart from each other. Within seconds I had completely fallen apart and disappeared.

CHAPTER EIGHTEEN: THE NEW HEIR

NEVA

We searched for Forrest for hours. He wasn't anywhere in the school, and nowhere outside either. It was as if he had disappeared completely from existence, or he was on a different planet. Although we didn't want to admit it, we couldn't blame him for not telling us where he hid the Metronome. If he said that one of us stole it, then we should be the ones turning against each other, not us against him. But right now we didn't need that. We just needed to find him so that we could start interrogating each other to see who stole it the first time. I know it wasn't me, unless I was possessed by Glacthia while I was asleep. So for now we just decided to stick together and figure this out.

All of us were sitting at the table eating lunch on Tuesday, about a week and a half before the girls' birthday. They were planning to bake a giant cake bigger than a wedding cake, and have a Hawaiian party in the poolroom. But we couldn't afford the cake mix, since we had planned on Forrest helping us make it. Now we were eating our sandwiches discussing how we would get him back.

"Did you get the ingredients for the red caliga?" Rhochelle asked, and Selene pulled the post it out of her pocket.

"Hair of a capillus, teardrop of a flere, hoof of a ditus, and grass from the planet of Gramen," she read of the list and we stared at her. We had never heard of any of those creatures, and we weren't planning on it. But Wyatt had a book open and flipped through some of the pictures of the creatures.

"No wonder a red caliga is the most valuable, look at this," he showed us. It read "ditus" at the top and had a picture with a small illustration. The creature looked half human and half horse, but different than a centaur. It had only two legs, and the body of a human, with a head all its own. The head was purely unique, it had an almost human face, but the lips were in the shape of an upside down fat tear, and the nose was small and sharp. It had two blue eyes like crystals, hypnotic even. Then the hair was like watching a rainbow appear, blond with silver as if it had glitter in it. The two legs were definitely horse legs, with fur and two hooves. The hooves were as shiny as diamonds, and perfectly cut as well.

"The ditus is a rare creature, only about a hundred in existence. The hoof of a ditus is worth more than an entire planet of gems, it has the power to revisit the dead without having to die. One of the reasons it is endangered is because its hooves are not removable, and they were used a lot in making red caliga. The only way to extract a ditus hoof is to kill it and cut it off by severing the leg just above the hoof. This is now illegal of course unless there is a document allowing it, which only can be granted by the Ancestors." Wyatt stared at us for a while then shook his head.

"We could never get that document from the Ancestors, we'll have to find him the old fashion way . . . by waiting," Ember explained, and I randomly had an outburst.

"How could you say that? He's our brother; how stupid are you?" I shouted and then sat back, not wanting to catch her glance. She stared at me for a while then looked away. There was a long silence, until people eventually picked up the conversation.

"Oh, Ember, could I have a mint?" Gabby asked quietly, who was sitting next to her. But then everyone turned to Ember, and she lowered her eyebrows. She started passing each person one, and finally when she got to me she smiled, skipping to the next person, Wyatt, who awkwardly refused. I gasped silently, and then stood up and walked off.

I walked the halls for a while, bored with her attitude. Although I realized that I probably shouldn't have shouted at her, I couldn't help but think that I was right. Forrest was the only one who knew where the Metronome was, and now he was gone.

Just as I was leaving to go back up to our room to apologize, I noticed the small hole in the wall where the crayhorn named Crepe lived—the one Forrest and I had met last year and learned about the store contest.

"What's this?" I asked myself and pulled the rolled up slip of paper out of the crack in the wall. Opening it, I slowly dropped my mouth then looked around to see if anyone was there. It was a diagram, with pictures and everything. It only had a few words, so I read them out loud because I was too shocked to read them in my mind. "Part A: Check to make sure Monohan was possessed," there was a picture of Monohan holding up three fingers. "Part B: Steal Metronome from bottom drawer, give to Nicole," there was a picture of the Metronome. "Part C: Make sure Monohan doesn't take Metronome, steal it if she does," this time the picture was Miss Monohan holding the Metronome. "Part D: Protect Metronome until blackout date," the picture just had the words "June 15, 7:47 p.m." scribbled in. I stared at the diagram for a while, not understanding it. If the person had a way of figuring out if Monohan was possessed, then why would they take the Metronome from her? It would only make sense if the person had teamed up with Glacthia, then quit and decided to side with us. But if that happened then Glacthia had taken Forrest, hoping to figure out where the Metronome was. If that's true then Forrest is in real danger.

"Guys, guys!" I shouted when I ran into our room, and they gathered around the triangle of grass where the rivers joined at the front of the room.

"What do you want?" Ember asked, crossing her arms.

"Ember, I'm sorry I called you stupid, but look what I found," I told her and just when I pulled out the diagram, she leaned over against Lianna and tried very hard to keep her eyes open.

"I'm so tired," she told me and closed her eyes completely. Then Lianna was the next to go, causing both of them to fall to the ground. As I watched, everyone closed their eyes droopily and fell asleep on the ground. I even had to pull Ion out of the river so that he didn't drown. Looking at the thirteen sleeping bodies I thought I should take them to the nurse, it wasn't normal to just drop sleeping randomly. As I went to the tree house to get teleporters for each of them to go the nurse's, I thought about what could cause them to fall asleep but not me. I wondered what they had been doing here while I was gone, but I would not know until they woke up. When I placed all the teleporters on their chests I typed in the nurse's office, which was luckily one of the saved places. They all turned white and blue and then disappeared into the air.

I walked down to the nurse's office to check on them, but they were all still asleep and the nurse had her hands full. If they had thirteen different cases she wouldn't allow them in here, but since it was the same for all of them she agreed to let them stay. I watched as she ran around the room, pulling out potions and pouring them into some of their mouths. Sometimes puffs of smoke came out of their mouths, other times their entire bodies lit up the color of the potion.

"How bad is it?" I finally decided to ask, she hadn't noticed me walk in.

"Well, they've been dosed with a powerful sleeping potion. They took it in such a small quantity that I was surprised it had this great of an effect. But however they got it; I'm not going to be able to wake them up until it wears off. You're welcome to sit on the bed if you'd like," she pointed to one of the few extra beds and I nodded. I sat down, thinking of what could have happened. Then I remembered the mints, how I hadn't gotten one and everyone else had. But then I remembered Wyatt didn't get one either, and I looked over at the bed he was in. He was sound asleep, I could see his head sticking out from the sheets with his eyes closed, and his chest slowly rising and falling.

"Would you mind if I stayed here until they woke up? I don't feel comfortable going back to our room alone," I lied, and she smiled.

"Sure, but as long as there aren't any more patients who need those beds," she pointed to the three beds next to me and also the one I was sitting on.

"Ugh, what am I going to do here all night?" I asked myself, and she turned around from her work smiling at me, admiring my loyalty to my family.

"Here, you can have some of this gum, it's really good," she opened her purse and handed me a piece. I thanked her and threw out the wrapper, sticking the gum into my mouth.

A few hours passed as I sat on the bed and thought. If the person who made the diagram was the same person who stole the Metronome, then that means that they're working for Glacthia again. Unless it was Glacthia who stole the Metronome, and the diagram writer is still on our side. The whole affair confused me, and when the nurse left to get some more ingredients for potions, I felt nervous being in the dark room by myself, except for my sleeping family. The wind howled against the windows, and leaves and sticks hit the walls. Then it began to rain, and lightning struck the building over and over again. I thought about the storm last year, the Procella—it couldn't possibly happen again, could it? And if Miss Monohan were still possessed, then would Glacthia turn on the forcefield that protects us from it?

All of these thoughts ran through my head, and I started to back up so that I was sitting against the wall—that way, no one could come up behind me. But that didn't matter, the door creaked open, and I gasped, covering my mouth. If it wasn't the nurse, then I am in real danger right now. It opened all the way, and I got a good look at the person in the doorway. They were dressed in all black, but the mask was what caught my eye. It was red, with black teardrops on the eyes. There was a black mouth, with small parallel slits so that the person could breathe. The eyes had holes so that the person's real eyes showed. I didn't get a good look at the eyes, but they had a familiarity to them.

The person turned its head to me, and I froze. Quickly reacting, I twisted my hands in a circle, and ice formed in a spiral around the person's feet. I felt proud of myself, getting up to walk over to him. But suddenly my whole mind was fogged, and I couldn't keep my balance anymore. I fell against the bed and closed my eyes.

A few days passed, I had told my siblings and cousins about the person in the room, and even showed them the diagram. Everyone was avoiding the food in front of us. We were supposed to be eating lunch. No one wanted to eat because anything could have the sleeping potion in it. I stared at my distressed, hungry family and regretted putting all of this on their shoulders. One day we would have normal lives, even if it meant defeating Glacthia or losing our powers.

"Well, were any of us missing from our beds when you saw the person?" Rhochelle asked me.

"I didn't even check," I told her and she sighed.

"Well, it could be Jerod," Kamille suggested, but Ember elbowed her.

"No it's not," was all Ember said.

"It has to be someone; it was too short to be Glacthia or Monohan," I started calling her Monohan now because for the moment she wasn't a Miss anymore.

"Shouldn't we turn Monohan in for being possessed?" Gabby wondered, but we thought about it for a minute.

"When have adults helped us in the past?" Wyatt asked, and everyone silently agreed.

"We've been arrested, accused, and ignored by them on every occasion," Daven explained to her, and we all thought about our pasts. He was right, adults have never been a big help to us before.

"Guys, there has to be something we could do," Aura insisted, banging her fists on the table. We all looked at her, and some people shook their heads.

"We're out of ideas," Sam told her and she sighed. There was a long silence, and then I noticed Ion look up from the other side of the conjoined table.

"What's the worse that could happen if Glacthia takes over the universe?" he asked, and we stared at him in shock.

"We'd probably be wiped out or be his personal slaves," Wyatt thought, and everyone looked away, not wanting to continue the conversation. We went back to our rooms and did nothing, just worked on some of our missed work and sat in the study room. It was quiet for a while, and eventually we went to our next class.

That night we sat in the study room and waited, hoping he would come. Wyatt had made a sensor that could tell us if the Metronome was stolen, even if we didn't know where it was. It helped, but still all we could do was sit and wait until the alarm would go off. But nothing happened the entire night, and the next morning when all of us wanted to sleep, we had to go to class. The entire day was torture, everyone was trying to stay awake and fight the exhaustion.

"We're going to die if we don't sleep," Ember told me in sports, which all of us were doing horribly in now. It was as if this was his plan, to make us all tired and then just leave us to wither away to nothing. I hesitated when I was holding the football, which only got me tackled. Then in chemistry, I spilled a potion that melted through the floor and fell all the way to the grass several floors below. I had never thought about there being nothing under me when I stood in the classroom, but now I realized that all of the classrooms had nothing holding them up except the pole that was the staircase on the inside. Afraid to fall down eighteen stories to the ground, I backed away from the hole and waited for Mrs. Morse to deal with it.

We slept through every study hall, but set an alarm so that we wouldn't miss our classes. The entire day went by so slowly, like at night when you want to fall asleep but you can't, each minute feels like ten. Finally, at the end of the day, all of us zombies trudged to the ninth floor and went to the tree house by means of teleportation. When we had piled into the study room all of us found the comfortable chairs and slowly lowered our eyelids until we could no longer keep them open. It was Friday night, so we could sleep all the next day if we wanted to.

"Wait, we have to stay awake, what if he comes?" Lianna asked, we were all set on the fact that the apprentice of Glacthia was a boy, but it was just a stereotype. We couldn't picture any of the girls being the one following Glacthia's orders and eating his horrible meals. But then again, we could barely manage to think of any of us doing that. Presently we could only assume that it was Forrest, but hated the idea of it. It made sense, he was the one to catch the guy stealing it, so maybe he stole it, gave it to Glacthia, and said that he caught someone else stealing it and hid it himself, not telling us where it was. But it was horrible to think, so we just kept telling each other that we were jumping to conclusions.

"How 'bout we watch for him in shifts, and then we can all sleep most of the night. We can't go on much longer without sleep, we'll slowly turn into mutant bald cats," Daven explained vividly, and all of us shook our heads to get the mental picture to go away. But he was right, we couldn't all stay up.

"Well with fourteen of us we could do groups of seven, but then we wouldn't get as much sleep as having three or four groups," Wyatt explained, and we all thought about it.

"How bout fourteen groups," I waved my hand, laying back on the computer chair and closing my eyes.

"No I think two is perfect," Lianna decided, just because she was the oldest out of all of us. "Who wants to be in the first group?" she asked and the room got silent. We could hear the crickets chirping and the bats clicking, along with the river dolphins surfacing.

"Everyone with a name from N-Z is going to have to stay up for an hour then wake everyone else up," Ember decided just because she wasn't in it. No one was in the mood to argue, so minutes later we heard the snoring of the beginning of the alphabet people. It wasn't even groups.

We only had Sam, Wyatt, Rhochelle, Selene, and me. There were a lot of people with names in the first half of the alphabet. I watched the window after I switched from the computer chair for internet related homework to the beanbag chair for written homework.

When we only had half an hour left, I noticed that half of us were asleep anyway. I only noticed Rhochelle and Sam, everyone else had their eyes closed and their mouths open. We watched the window and the balcony fixatedly, but then sleep went through our bodies. It felt like weights had been tied to our eyelashes, and the room kept getting darker until we realized that we were just closing our eyes. I noticed Sam lay down just to rest his eyes and then he started snoring. Rhochelle went off as well just a minute later and I promised myself that I would stay awake for the rest of the hour. Now that I only had twenty minutes left I was fixed on waking the others up at the next hour. The digital clock on the other side of the room was bright, so I could read it from here, but my eyes were playing tricks on me so it got harder to look at each time.

About ten minutes later I was still awake, completely set on my goal to stay awake until the next hour. It wasn't that dark out because we had just gotten back from dinner so in ten minutes it would be eight. I thought about staying awake, which just led me to thinking about sleep. I closed my eyes then forced them open again. I continued this routine until I only had five minutes left, and then excitement filled me. There was a chance that I would actually make it if I tried hard enough. I thought about soda, sugar, and candy. But it only made me more tired, and just before eight o'clock, I closed my eyes and didn't open them again.

The sound woke the entire room up; it seemed loud enough to knock over the entire tree house with vibrations. But the tree house was still standing and we stayed laying on our couches and beanbags. We first thought it was an alarm someone set to wake us up. But then everyone jumped up in horror, and we stared at each other, looking around at the giant speakers placed on separate parts of the tree house. The alarm had gone off, and the apprentice was probably lightyears away with Glacthia and the Metronome by now.

CHAPTER NINETEEN: THE WEEKDAYS

AURA

Just a few days after the Metronome was stolen, Selene, Kamille, and I started planning my birthday. It was an onerous task, since we had to gather together the change from everyone, it was just enough for a couple boxes of cake mix. Cobalt said he could make the tiki torches out of metal, then we just needed to put some sticks in them to burn. I woke up on Monday and walked around the tree house, looking to see if anyone knew where the food was. Then as I passed from the dining room to the theater, I heard a small, moaning cry. It was faint, so I knew I was close enough to hear it but not close enough to find it.

I jumped off the balcony to start flying, but then started to scream when I realized that we were in a blackout. I looked down, to see that I was about five feet from the roof of Ember's room. Hitting the ceiling with a thud, I waited for the pain to come. Then I crawled to the edge of the roof and looked in through the balcony. Ember had just looked up to see what had fallen onto her room, and then she put her face back into her hands to cry. I looked down and noticed that if I didn't land on her balcony, then it was a straight drop to the ground. Slowly turning around I let my feet hang and lowered myself with my arms until I was only about a foot from her balcony. Letting go I fell to the ground and then dropped to the floor because my legs still hurt.

"Ember, what's the matter?" I asked her and she looked up, just now noticing me. She turned around, wanting to ignore me, but I walked over to her and she was forced to answer my question.

"So now you're playing stupid just to get me to talk about it," she cried, her face wet with tears. "I told you yesterday, so I'm not going to tell you again."

"Ember, yesterday we went to The Zoo, is that where it happened?" I asked her, and she turned to face me, shaking her head and giving me her worried face.

"We went to the zoo on Sunday, this . . . this that happened to me . . . happened on Monday," she nodded, and then turned away again.

"Ember, I think I should take you to a hospital, today is Monday," I explained to her, thinking she was the one with the problem. Ember looked at me with a concerned face and let me know the truth in the calmest voice she had.

"Aura . . . today is Tuesday." I stared at her with wide eyes, thinking either there was something strange going on with me, or Ember had just lost track of time. Without another word I ran out of her room and went across the escalator to Rhochelle's room. Each of us having our separate rooms that didn't involve our powers was a new addition, since none of us wanted to sleep on the ground or in the secret base anymore. But I went to Rhochelle and asked her the quick question.

"Rhochelle, what's today?" I asked her and she looked at me.

"The eleventh," she answered and I nodded, then shook my head.

"No is it Monday or Tuesday?" I asked and she gave me the same worried expression that I received from Ember.

"Tuesday?" she asked me as if it were a trick question. I went to the meeting room where everyone was gathered, just as we usually do before we go down to breakfast, and noticed everyone talking about Ember.

"I feel so bad, she found them making out in the tunnel of love ride at the zoo," Cobalt explained to Ion, but he made a confused face.

"Since when is there a tunnel of love at the zoo?" Ion questioned him.

"There is . . . one time my brothers and I set this trap that would switch the boys in the boats with one of my brothers. But Mac accidentally took the girl and ended up sitting next to the guy," Cobalt snickered and Ion laughed as well.

"She spent some of our money on chocolate and ice cream," Kamille and Selene were talking to each other and I ran over to them.

"Guys I think I skipped Monday," I started off by grabbing their attention and they started at me, forcing me to go deeper in my explanation. "Last night . . . for me . . . was Sunday, I'm a million percent positive. I think my powers made me jump ahead and skip from Monday straight to Tuesday. When I think back, I have no idea what happened on Monday, and last night I remember falling asleep and it was Sunday," I told them and they stared at me, doubting the chance my mind took me forward in time overnight.

"That's impossible," Selene told me and I shook my head.

"How, maybe my powers just sent me forward in time, it's possible that in my dreams I wanted to travel forward twenty four hours and my mind did it for real," I told them and they shook their heads.

"It's impossible because we've been in a blackout since Sunday night, all Monday and this morning none of us have had powers," Selene told me, and the appalling truth finally hit me.

"Then someone is doing it for me," I stared at them and their eyes widened.

We didn't speak of this to any of our siblings, and I tried to live out the day normally. My day wasn't very eventful. I went to my classes, did my homework, and ate my meals. But it wasn't until later in the day that I learned why my puppet master wanted me to see this first. I was walking through the hallway when I heard two people talking. Their voices were so soft that they were inaudible, and the desire to hear what they were discussing was consuming. I crept over to the door and put my ear against it, trying to think of what floor I was on now.

"Ember . . ." the voice started, and I recognized it the moment I heard it. "Would you like to go out with me sometime?" The voice paused and stuttered a little, it made me doubt that it was Jerod at all.

"Yeah, that'd be great," Ember said with her voice filled with revenge and anger. I instantly ran off when I heard Ember walk toward the door and I was an entire floor above her when she stepped out so she thought nothing of it.

"Hey Aura," Ember waved to me in a jittery voice. She began to skip up the stairs and I continued to walk upstairs as I let her pass me. Once I was behind her I ran straight to my triplets and told them the gossip.

The following morning I sped straight to Selene's room and asked her the date.

"Today's Friday of course, our birthday!" Selene jumped off her bed and started to run around in a hyperactive way.

"Oh my gosh I skipped three days this time," I put my hands to face and weaved my fingers through my hair. She stopped running and stared at me with unbelieving eyes.

"Last night was Tuesday for you, you mean you have no idea what happened on Wednesday and Thursday?" she asked in amazement and I shook my head. "Oh boy, this is a problem." I stared at her for a long time as she was thinking to herself.

"Why is it a problem?" I dared to ask and she looked at me, getting ready to drop some bad news on me or something.

"Well Kamille's not speaking to you because she's still mad about the whole . . . you know . . . well actually you don't know," Selene realized and I threw my arms up.

"Well why's she mad at me?" I realized that I was bugging Selene with the questions and I had to stop, but she answered the last one.

"You stole her spotlight yesterday, that's all I'm going to tell you," Selene waved her hand and then jumped in the air. "We're fourteen!" she shouted and I smiled a little.

"I just figured out how I could stop this," I smiled, and Selene froze, throwing all of her attention at me. "We can't stop the Peractio Blackout unless we get to Glacthia, and we can't get to Glacthia unless we stop his apprentice. If I figure out who that is, we can defeat him and this will stop. And I know just the person to talk to. If Ember and Jerod have been going out for three days, maybe she knows some personal stuff about him." I smiled a wicked smile and ran out of the room to find Ember. Selene stopped me by stopping gravity on me, and I rose into the air. I turned around and she put me down.

"You'd have to do it during our party, it's the only time everyone will be too occupied and you can go to Jerod's room to look through his stuff," Selene explained and I nodded, thinking it was a decent plan.

"What time is the party?" I asked her just to make sure.

"Four," she answered and I thought of what to do until then.

That night I ran to Ember's room to find her just after everyone but Ember and Jerod had arrived at the party. Her room was dark and desolate, and I learned why when I first walked in. There was a gaping hole in the ceiling, and ashes all around it. On the floor below it I saw a mask. It was red and black, just as Neva had described it to us. But the entire thing was burnt, as if someone had a flamethrower put on it. Then on Ember's desk I opened a folded up a piece of paper. It had the plan that Glacthia's apprentice had, just as Neva showed us. I was absolutely positive, Jerod was the apprentice of Glacthia.

When I awoke I went to Kamille, giving Selene her sleep. She told me that it was Wednesday, and I got confused.

"The Wednesday after our birthday?" I wondered and she shook her head.

"No the Wednesday before our birthday," she told me then sighed. "Oh you're still going through time, what day was it yesterday?" This was my first time travelling back in time. The person toying with my time obviously wants me to see every day, just in a different order.

"Our birthday," was my last reply before I ran out. This meant that Jerod had just asked Ember out. I ran to her room and noticed that the fire and mask weren't there, so Ember didn't know yet. Maybe I am supposed to be the one to tell her, that's how she finds out. But I wasn't ready to tell her yet, so I went to my room to think about this. I had lived Sunday, then Tuesday, Friday, and now it was Wednesday. I still had Monday, Thursday, and Saturday if that was part of it. After a while I ran to the meeting room and noticed a clutter of people around Selene and Kamille. The person enjoying the attention the most was definitely Kamille.

"So what do you guys want for your birthday?" Wyatt asked them and they smiled, listing the things.

"Fourteen's such a great age," Lianna told my triplets.

"I have something important to tell you guys," I spoke up and the group turned to me. Ember and Jerod weren't there, they were spending way too much time alone together, and I was worried for Ember. "Jerod is Glacthia's apprentice." The whole group was silent for a second then everyone ran over to me in shock.

"How could you say that . . . what proof do you have?" Neva agreed with the thought of Jerod being Glacthia's apprentice, but didn't think that I should just accuse him like that.

"Well . . . it's hard to explain, but I'm living my days in the wrong order. Yesterday was Friday, and the day before was Tuesday . . . for me of course. And yesterday . . . on Friday . . . I found out," I told them and all of them stared at me in horror.

"Oh, now I know something else I want for my birthday," Kamille remembered, but no one looked at her.

"Not now Kamille, this is more important," Sam waved his hand at her and she gaped at him. Then she glared at me and walked out of the room. Now I understood why Kamille wouldn't talk to me on Friday, because I "stole her spotlight." Although I felt bad for my sister, I thought that was a really long time for her to hold a grudge.

"What are we going to do?" Gabby wondered and everyone turned to me. I shrugged, not having a clue, but told them what they shouldn't do instead.

"We can't tell Ember without any proof; she'll just defend him," I explained, and we split up, looking for the proof I was talking about. We checked the entire tree house, along with Jerod's room, even when we were unwelcome. The entire day Ember and Jerod were gone, and when they returned that night we learned that they had been on a date the entire day. I slept that night knowing that my sister was dating the follower of a horrible monster.

I opened my eyes and didn't even want to know what day it was, but asked Kamille anyway; happy she was talking to me.

"It's Monday, what other day would it be?" she told me and I gasped. I told Selene and Kamille about me living in different days on Tuesday, so they didn't know yet. I didn't bother to tell them, I would do it tomorrow . . . well . . . their tomorrow. But instead I ran off, knowing that today was the day Ember would find Chris cheating on her. We were at the breakfast table and I was thinking of ways I could follow Ember to find out how she found him. It wasn't that important, but if I had a way of figuring out how it happened it could lead me to figure out if she knew about Jerod being the apprentice or not. As soon as I finished eating I learned where we had been when it happened.

"Does anyone want to go to The Theme Park today?" Craig suggested, and we looked at the vacant space on the bench. Forrest was always the one who had asked us to go to The Theme Park. We turned back to Craig and nodded, today we had no class because of a holiday that we didn't know about that well. It was called Creo Day, but we weren't sure if it was the day Medlocks the planet was created or the day people started going to school here. It wasn't the day that the Ancestors first brought people to Medlocks, because that was already a holiday, Ancestor Day.

"We can go after lunch, that way we have the most time," Daven assured us. We always went from lunch to dinner because from breakfast to lunch was shorter and we were usually tired.

"Okay, but we don't really have any money," Rhochelle told the group, who suddenly became irate and distressed.

"But I thought we did that job for the department store?" Lianna remembered, and shouldn't have bothered to make it a question.

"We spent that money on the birthday supplies," Neva whispered quietly and everyone sighed, turning to Selene, Kamille, and me. We turned red, feeling guilty and embarrassed. After another silence Ember spoke.

"Well good thing your amazing sister's boyfriend got fired from the department store." Ember grinned brightly as the group stared at her and waited for her to continue. Finally she rolled her eyes and said, "He got a job at The Theme Park." We all nodded, smiling, and waited for lunch to come.

At the moment the last person had finished their lunch a few hours later, we ran to the front door and stepped out. All of us tested their powers, this time not daring to jump off the front steps. No one's worked, and we sighed once more.

"This is crazy! We've had constant blackouts. I think the only time our powers are working is when we're not using them," Craig complained and started to walk, even though he couldn't fly anyway. We walked the entire way, over two miles, and when we finally got there, we didn't want to take another step. But Ember glided over to one of the farther away ticket booths and smiled at the man there.

"Hey, Ember, how's it going? Would you guys like some *free* bracelets?" Chris smiled, holding up an entire sheet of them. As he passed them out we took them from him reluctantly.

"Are you sure you won't get in trouble for this?" I asked him curiously, and he smiled at me, telling me that he didn't really care.

"Well I told my boss that I had to give some free bracelets to a couple of friends, and he said it was fine. And then when I told him that I had to give out fourteen, I had to explain that it was their birthday present from me. He said he'd only take out a little bit from my pay this week," he smiled as if it were the nicest thing his boss had ever done. We rolled our eyes as Ember put her chin in her hands and her elbows on the counter.

"But what if you can't pay for our date on Friday?" she asked him through the glass, wishing it were gone so that she could kiss him.

"Oh, don't worry, I've been saving up for that, putting aside a little bit from all my paychecks," he smiled, and then put his hand through the small hole in the bottom of the glass to hold hers. It was easy to make money on Medlocks. All of the workers lived in The Inn, and rent cost so little there that most of the money they made was for them. Hence a lot of young kids work on Medlocks in random jobs to save up money quickly.

"Have fun guys," Chris couldn't keep his eyes off Ember, and all of us wanted to push them apart as soon as possible. "I'll be on my break soon, meet me at the swan ride at two," he waved to her as we dragged her through the gate and looked for insane rides that we didn't ride too many times already. Then we all just split into groups, and I went with both of my triplets. We went on some of the little rides since none of us were really daredevils. After going on the swings and a small roller coaster, I checked my watch and found that it was five minutes till two.

"I have to go to the bathroom," I told them and started walking to my right. Selene called to me and I stopped, wondering what it could possibly be.

"Aura, the bathroom's over there," she pointed to a small blue building with a flat, metal roof. I waved at it and started to blush.

"That bathroom is disgusting, have you ever been in it? The last person in there had just eaten three plates of cheese fries then went on the standing roller coaster," I lied, making both of them make aghast faces and look at the bathroom in horror. I walked off and went to the nearest map to find the tunnel of love. It was close by, so I headed there while I fished something out of my pocket. It was a gadget I had taken from Wyatt's room after breakfast. He had made gadgets that gave anyone the ability to use his powers. This one was invisibility. Studying it, I pressed the button and looked down at my hands. I was a little noticeable when I moved, because it made whatever was behind me appear on me, different for each person looking at me. I moved slowly and stealthily toward the ride, and found Ember waiting there.

I sat on the bench for a long time, fifteen minutes at least. When Ember had given up all hope that Chris was coming, she went into the line to ride it once and then come out to check if he had arrived yet. I got in line behind her, and was very thankful that the line was short enough for me to get into an empty swan without anyone wanting to get in it.

"How does Ember see Chris cheating on her if he isn't even here?" I whispered to myself, causing Ember to turn around. She watched me for a while, studying the swan as if she knew I was here. I waited, just staring at her, for her to turn away. Finally she turned back, and I sighed, thankful that she didn't say anything. If she knew that I was here than it was okay, but as long as she let me stay here disguised. The ride went on, there was nothing to look at, just music and dark water. We went through, and I hesitated, expecting something extraordinary to happen. Well, in the end, I got my wish. Just before the ride ended Ember stood up, looking into the swan in front of her. All that I saw was the top of two heads over the back of the swan.

"Chris?" Ember finally shouted and he stood up, the blonde girl he was with did as well. Ember stared at her with so much hate that I was glad we were in a blackout.

"How could you . . . I thought . . . you weren't even in . . . you came from . . ." Ember couldn't put together any of the words that she was feeling, but I understood what she meant. The girl was alone in the line in front of us, which means Chris must've hopped on from one of the sidewalks on the side of the river. This was bad; it meant that he had been hiding from Ember.

"Ember, I wasn't even on this swan, someone put me under the water and placed me here," he told her, and deep down it looked like he was telling the truth.

"But you're dry, how could you lie to me like that?" Ember wanted to know and when the ride was over she exited and stepped off, running toward the girl to strangle her.

"He's telling the truth, he just appeared next to me, I don't even know him," the girl explained, but Ember didn't believe either of them. Her face was trickled with tears, and they were also filling up in her eyes. She ran off, and I took off the invisibility when I was out of sight. There was something wrong about this, Chris would never cheat on Ember, and if he had, he wouldn't have told her where he'd be when he did it. And if someone had meddled, it had to be none other than the apprentice, Jerod.

Although I cared about what day it was the following morning, I didn't bother to ask anyone until I found out for myself. I decided to go to the library instead. Even though it made the most sense that the apprentice was the one making me travel through time, I doubted that

Jerod had the ability to do that. The first book I found about blackouts explained that a long time ago some villain stole the Metronome and attempted to make a blackout. His name was Malum and he stole it just soon after people started getting powers. The only reason they stopped him in the end was because an Insumo was born. Although it didn't matter I found a book on names for people with certain powers. I noticed Otium was one of them, and thought of Kamille. Then I found Insumo, and looked at the definition.

"A person who has the power to grant wishes, one is only born every 200 years," I read out loud, and closed the book. "Well that won't help us now; Malum probably existed barely a hundred years ago." I found another book on blackouts, this one explaining symptoms of people with certain powers during blackouts. Thinking scientifically, I turned to "s" for space time continuum warping, but it wasn't there. Then, feeling ashamed for this author, I went to time. After reading it I learned that people with time travel as a power sometimes experience a rare symptom called degero. It causes the person to wake up on different days of the week, but Sunday and Saturday will always be first and last. It can only happen once, but its events can cause a person to change the course of the future. Also, when a person is experiencing a degero, it is helpful to stay out of major events or trying to stop something that they saw happen in the future.

This meant that Jerod had nothing to do with me traveling through time in my sleep, and neither did Glacthia. Thinking of the last sentence, I ran to Ember, knowing exactly what I had to do. I ran back to the room and found her at the tree house in Wyatt's room. She jumped when I came in, and I stopped to stare at her for a minute, wondering if I was doing the right thing.

"Aura, what are you doing here?" she asked, and I raised my eyebrows.

"I could ask you the same thing . . . but I won't. There's something important I have to tell you, and I don't know how you're going to take it," I stared at the floor and she took a seat on the bed.

"It's okay, you can tell me," she comforted me when I couldn't find the words to tell her that her boyfriend was working for the universe's most wanted.

"Jerod is Glacthia's apprentice, the one who wore the mask and the one who stole the Metronome," I explained to her, and she shook her head.

"No, that's not true," she said, more sure of herself than I had expected.

"But, Ember, think about it, the Metronome is missing, none of us know where it is, Forrest is missing," I tried to explain to her, but the sweat on her face was turning to steam. I stepped back, afraid now.

"Jerod isn't the apprentice, now get out!" she shouted in a voice that was definitely not hers. I left the room in a hurry, and lay in bed all day thinking until I finally fell asleep.

The following morning was the only day of the week that I was sure that it was, Saturday. Skipping to breakfast, happy that the degero was over, I recalled Friday's events, my birthday. I had found the blueprints and the burnt mask in Ember's room, and Kamille was still ignoring me. When I got to the breakfast table there was a group of people around Ember, begging her for something.

"Come on Ember, please just tell us," Neva was saying, but Ember had her chin in her palms and her elbows on the table.

"Tell you what?" I asked and the group turned to me. Our family looked different with Forrest missing, and I was just noticing this now.

"Ember knows who the apprentice is, and she says it's not Jerod," Daven told me.

CHAPTER TWENTY:
ILLEGAL POTIONS 101

KAMILLE

All of us bribed Ember to tell them, but it was all in vain. She began avoiding us and was by herself a lot. Aura told us about her being in her degero, and I forgot all about being mad at her. We became a trio again, and we put our heads together to figure this out.

One day in chemicals in the beginning of April, I was busy working on my sleeping potion, but suddenly I became distracted by something. Staring at the shelf across the table from me, I saw a book with the title written on its spine, *Caliga and Their Ingredients*. As soon as the class ended I opened the book and found the page on the blue caliga. I stared at the page for a while with intrigue and disgust.

> The horn of a lockmed.
> The leg of a puffrat.
> The suction cup of the Kraken.
> One cup of mud from Azmarith.

For a while I stared at the four ingredients, all of the caliga were made up of four completely different things, but since blue was so rare it had some of the least common ingredients. Knowing that there was only one Kraken, one lockmed, and one planet called Asmarith probably lightyears away, I figured that I should probably get some help on this. I ran to my triplets and told them about my idea for our next adventure.

"That's a lot of work for just one answer. Are you sure we can't just use one of the ones we have?" Selene wondered as we headed for the kitchen.

"No, the book said they only work for seven days after you make them, so they can't work now," I explained to them as we stepped into the kitchen.

"Then Glacthia's apprentice must not know that," Aura said, gaping at the cabinet where we kept a quart of the blue caliga. It was spilt all over the floor, its blue radiance leaking out onto the balcony and dripping down onto the leaves.

"The apprentice must really not want anyone to get Ember to tell them," I said as we walked back out, Aura and Selene would definitely want to come with me now.

"I say one of us goes to get the Kraken suction cup, one gets the Azmarith mud, and the other gets the puffrat leg and the lockmed horn, since they both live here," Selene suggested, and Aura and I stopped.

"Are you kidding me? We're definitely getting all of them together," Aura said in a scared voice. I nodded, seconding her judgment, and Selene was overruled. We ran straight to the library to figure out how we would go about this.

Each of us was given an ingredient to look up, but we all looked for a book on Azmarith. I had to find out if there was a way to safely remove a Kraken's suction cup. The first book I found was called *Alien Water Creatures*, and I found Kraken in the index. Quickly flipping through the pages I found the page that it was on.

"Here, listen to this," I said to my sisters and they stopped what they were doing. "The Kraken, created in 1793 by a scientist named Fidero Montoya gave it to his nephew, Malum, as a gift. He used it as his pet to try to take over the universe. With its power he became known as one of the greatest villains to ever live. The Kraken is a creature with the body of a giant crocodile but with 27 tentacles over 50 feet long. It has horns down its spine, and on its sides and nose. This creature is the only one of its species, and there are no known whereabouts of this deadly creature." I made a horrified face at the picture. It was attacking a spaceship flying over the water with some of its tentacles wrapped around people, pulling them into the water.

"Well we should get that last then, here I found out how to remove the horn of a lockmed and a book about puffrats, sorry Aura," Selene apologized for stealing her topic.

"It's fine, I found a book on Azmarith, it has a map to the mud that we need, there's only about 100 gallons of it in the universe and it's all on this planet," Aura explained and Selene continued.

"Well this says that puffrats sometimes detach their legs when they are touched by water, so we just need to get one wet. For lockmeds it's a little more complicated. You have to throw a potion at them and then their horn will fall off. The name of the potion is familiar; I think Mrs. Morse might have some. So . . . which should we do first?" she asked and the tutorial became an open discussion.

"We should get the mud first? The ride could takes weeks and we should just get it out of the way now," I suggested but neither of them backed me up.

"But if we got the lockmed horn and the puffrat leg now, we won't have to come all the way back from Azmarith just to find out that the Kraken was like an hour away," Aura figured and I rolled my eyes.

"Let's find out where the Kraken is first," I told her and Selene and I grabbed Aura's hands. She looked confused for a minute then jumped up and smiled. We warped through space-time and then appeared outside an old fashioned looking bar.

"Look . . . The Food Court," Selene smiled at the sign above the small saloon.

"This must be Medlocks in 1793, a few years after kids started attending Medlocks," I realized, and walked into the saloon. Usually when Aura was looking for something in the past, her mind teleported her right to it.

"Fidero Montoya?" Aura called into the bar and a couple angry looking men turned around from their drinks.

"Who's askin'?" said the meanest looking of them all. His arms looked like he had steel balloons inserted into his skin where his muscles would be. His face was long with a neatly cut, black beard. He reminded me of a pro wrestler.

"Could we talk to you in private?" Selene asked, shaking. He led us to a back room with just one table and the four of us sat down. I wasn't as afraid of him as I should've been. The book about the Kraken had a small caption next to pictures saying that he was the first person to ever have the power of underwater aliens. Plus if I attempted to shake his hand he might rip mine off.

"Do you know anything about the Kraken?" Aura started off with a simple question, just in case we had the wrong person.

"Yeah, my nephew jus' got 'imself blown up wit' it," Fidero explained without a hint of emotion.

"But is it still . . . alive?" I wondered, knowing that it had to be true if the blue caliga still existed.

"O' course it's still alive!" he yelled, standing up. I noticed that a vein in his neck stuck out so much that a doctor could probably use a thumbtack to draw blood from him.

"We're sorry; um . . . do you know where it is now?" Selene finally said, and he looked for a second like he was about to eat her in rage.

"Well where else would 'e be, me nephew jus' got beat yesterday on Medlocks Island by that stup'd Calypso," he banged his fist on the table, leaving a dent along with a crack that could've caused the table to collapse if my knees weren't holding it up.

"Okay, thank you, we'll be going now," I stood up nervously and we walked out. As we were leaving one of the guys at the bar whistled to us, and I realized that we were in our future clothes.

"Hey, why don't one of y'all come over here and give me a little sugar?" he smiled, and we turned around with disgusted faces.

"What are you, like forty?" Aura retorted, and his face dropped. He picked up his knife and threw it at her. Quickly I pushed Aura and Selene onto the floor, but I applied so much force that I was falling into the knife's path. Instantly I stopped my fall, causing me to be leaning a lot more than any normal person could.

"It's an Otium. There's a Otium!" the bartender yelled, and rang a very loud bell, sort of like a siren.

"Uh oh," Selene grabbed my hand and Aura's hand and we started glowing silver until the scene finally flashed out of sight. We landed back in the library and stared at the books on the floor.

"Do you think if we time travel too much and keep arriving the second we left, then we'll grow up faster than everyone else?" I asked Aura and she shrugged.

"I guess, but if we went back in time for an hour I usually arrive an hour after we left, or else after a couple years our birthday might have to moved a day back because we are getting older and no one else is,"

Aura tried to make sense, but no one continued the conversation. The three of us sat back down on the floor by the shelf of books and started picking them up and putting them back.

"So we go for the mud first, since the Kraken, lockmed, and puffrat are here?" I made sure and they nodded.

"Yeah, do you want to get on a taxi now?" Selene wondered, and Aura stared at me. I shook my head, getting ready to answer, but Aura took the words out of my mouth.

"Let's leave a note for the older kids," she suggested. I wrote the note and we left it on the meeting room's announcements table. Minutes later we were ready for our journey that could take over a month. We brought the suitcase of gadgets with us, so we could teleport home after we got the mud. That way we would only have to endure the trip once.

We assembled by the airport and went up to a taxi. The driver, Brian Mullen, had agreed to take us there for the little money we had. Taxi drivers living by themselves didn't need to make a lot of money unless they had a family or wanted to go to a college on Earth, since the taxi can create its own food.

"Are you all ready to go?" he asked. We looked at each other with hesitation; I was clutching the book with the map to the mud pit.

"Yeah," we finally replied together. The taxi slowly took off, and we looked down on the small island that was currently our home.

If there were one word that could describe the ride to Azmarith, it would be monotonous. We spent a few days trying to play games, Aura had packed over ten different card decks. But that became boring because for some reason only one person won every game. I always one Uno, I just started out with a lot of good cards every time. But Aura always won Go Fish, she just happened to run out of cards when there were only about four cards left in the deck. She would pick them all up in the middle of her turn and ask us for our last cards, usually only winning by one pair.

The first two weeks weren't as bad as the next two. We would count down the minutes until our arrival time, May fourth. After we knew how many hours left until the day it was only a matter of time before we multiplied it by sixty. Trying to sleep as much as possible, we would wake up in the middle of the day and stay in bed for the rest of the day.

But time passed unbelievably slowly, and we reached our destination in the end.

"Here we are; nice having you," Brian told us and we got out. His name reminded me of Selene's old boyfriend. It had been almost a month since we had heard anyone's voice at all. It must've been even harder for the driver. The three of us stepped off and paid him, just to watch him drive away and leave us on this deserted planet.

Azmarith is one of the natural planets, it is almost all desert, just like the planet that Glacthia's wine cellar was on until Cobalt blew it up. The only spot that's not a desert is the mud pit, and we were only a few miles from it now. I opened the book and tried to figure out how we were ever going to find our way. The map was almost all desert orange, except for three symbols, one which we had landed next to. The first one was a cactus, one of the probably dozen or so on the whole planet.

"So if we're here, then the next one is two miles northeast," I said. We flew that way for a couple minutes, but had a blackout just about a hundred feet from it.

"Is that the next symbol?" Aura pointed to a couple creatures ahead of us. There were three, and they were definitely aliens.

"It says, 'Now you will reach the carneros. These three dastardly creatures are like bulls, but have a scorpion's tail that can shoot a toxic poison. They don't need to drink water, but live off of the cacti, only eating about a pound every hundred years. The only way to reach the limus is to ride them to it. They are the only ones that can find it because it's invisible to Altrians. Good luck, be careful.'" Selene stared at us and we stared at the carneros. They had red, glowing eyes, with the tail curling up behind them.

"What are we gonna do? We can't use a tornado to blow their tails off. We can't have gravity lift them into space," Aura gave up, but I was still smiling. Our powers were returning as Aura was pessimistically listing all of the things we couldn't do.

"No, it says only carneros can see the mudpit, so if we were to turn into one . . ." I told them and they seemed perplexed for a second, and then got it.

"Get ready," I told them and started to open my mind. I assumed Forrest would be far, considering that I usually switched powers with people I was looking at. But considering that we were lightyears from our family, he was closer than I expected. I looked around; all I saw were the three carneros. They weren't looking at us but I started to walk over to one. Its eyes widened when it saw me, and I switched powers with it. That was a stupid thing to do to a bull, I might not have been able to switch back if it didn't have any powers, which no creature does.

But I suddenly felt like I was connected to someone I knew, so I pointed at the ground and concentrated. A small rose came out of the sand and I made it disappear as my mouth dropped. I turned him into a human, not picking any human in particular, and it became our brother, Forrest.

"Forrest!" Aura cried and ran up to him. She was crying and hugging him, he was holding her closely and watching Selene and me, who were watching him in amazement. The two of them had always shared a connection that none of us had.

"How did you get here?" I wondered, as I turned us all into carneros and gave Forrest his power back. We began sprinting to the mudpit, or limus as the book called it, and talking at the same time.

"Well you know how Daven in the beginning of the year got trapped into the power practice room and attacked by the scelum? Glacthia told him that he was going to try to get rid of all of us individually. He said that since I had been taken with the Metronome that it was my turn. He put me on this planet and turned me into a carnero, killing the other one and taking my first power. I started giving all of you the desire to make a blue caliga, which is hard from this far away. Then you came, and when you switched powers with me you felt how close I was. I'm lucky it was you that came, Ember or Rhochelle might've tried to feel around for the limus. Speaking of which, do you guys want some?" Forrest said as he dug his hooves into the ground.

We stopped, and stared at the crater like the meteor that gave us our powers made. The mixture in it wasn't brown like mud. It was a bright, glowing blue.

"Why is it that color?" Aura wondered, her face wet and her hair messed up.

"Its magical properties . . . and how else would the caliga be blue?" Forrest smiled at her as we began collecting it, happy to be speaking English.

"The Kraken's suction cups?" I guessed as Selene dipped the jug into the mud and then pulled out about a gallon. Forrest turned us into humans and Aura opened the suitcase and pulled out the teleporter.

She set it and grabbed our hands. We arrived at the steps of Medlocks and sighed deeply, the long part was finally over.

The lockmed horn and puffrat leg were easy, it turns out that the zookeepers bathe the puffrats once a month, there were legs all around the glass environment that they lived in. Mrs. Morse gave us a potion to take the horn off of the lockmed. It was a dangerous task, but as soon as I threw the potion at the lockmed it cowered away in fear, leaving the horn behind. We hid the items in a safe, having only the suction cup to get. The four of us were in the library, Forrest had sworn to help us in total gratitude for saving him, but told everyone else that we found him outside the building.

"We have to find a way to call the Kraken, or a way to track it," he explained, flipping through pages of Earth books. Usually fantasies on Earth were real here, they were just secrets passed from Altrians to their most trusted friends, which eventually slipped to the humans, which nobody believed. Also, someone asked Mr. Williams one day if the Altrians were ever discovered by humans. He explained that the Egyptian and Roman gods were actually the Altrians. Humans caught each one while they were using their powers and began worshipping them for protection.

We read old fiction stories from Earth, which were similar to the ones in the nonfiction section here. Finally I looked up caligas on the internet and found how to get each of the ingredients for one. For the Kraken it explained how you had to create a potion to get the suction cup to fall off, and there was a poem to call upon it.

"Okay, here it is," I didn't want to read it just in case it worked, but then I saw that you had to stand on the beach holding the other three ingredients, and you had to have four people saying it. We were ready in less than five minutes, gathered on the beach at the edge of Medlocks Island. Forrest and Aura were at my right holding the leg and horn, and Selene on my left carrying the mud. I held the potion in one hand and the poem in the other.

> *Here the four of us stand*
> *Now gathering hand in hand*
> *To my far right is the horn*
> *From the lockmed it was torn*
> *On my right, the leg off a puffrat*
> *Short, furry, and pink is that*

Next but not last comes my left
Azmarith mud was their theft
Finally it comes down to me
So here I call upon thee

There was no noise; I was holding my breath to keep the silence. The four of us stared at the open sea, going on for thousands of miles until it reached Medlocks Plains. The sun was setting and the clouds were flying over our heads, time was moving faster than normal. In the quiet we watched it turn the sky a beautiful red and orange. Finally it was dark and a rumbling interrupted our awe. I looked behind me; nothing was there but the back of The Movie Theater.

"Put the stuff in the bag, I'm not sure how this is gonna work," Forrest stepped in front of us, pushing us back. The water started to ripple against the cliff wall that we were on, and I looked out at the horizon. A huge tentacle had just crawled out of the water, about a hundred feet in front of us.

"I'll handle this," Forrest put the potion on the sand and put his foot over it, getting ready to turn into a bird. But I pushed him a little and picked up the potion.

"No, I have to throw it, I read the poem," I explained how it was supposed to be done, and gripped it tightly. Finally a huge tail whipped out of the water and slithered back in. It was green and scaly, definitely like an alligator's. But when I pictured the Kraken I pictured a normal sized alligator with normal sized octopus tentacles, despite the description. This thing from head to tail was about fifty feet, and the tentacles longer. It could swallow the four of us like I could swallow a mint.

When it saw us it reared from the direction it was headed in, and came straight for us. I expected it; if it was Malum's companion it probably had a killing instinct. But what I had not expected was for it to leap out of the water at us. When I saw it's whole body out of the water I quickly threw the vile, breaking it on its nose. The green fog blocked its eyesight, but that wasn't what saved us. When the potion hit it the Kraken flew back as if it had just been hit by a meteor.

All four of us watched a suction cup the size of a dinner plate fall into the water, but no one acted as instinctively as Selene. She dove down twenty feet off the cliff and into the water that was probably even deeper than the drop.

"Selene!" Aura screamed so loudly that the Kraken got into a furious rage. It dove down into the water after Selene, grabbing Aura with a tentacle on its way down.

"Oh, wow, hold on I got this," Forrest dove into the water, and I knew what he wanted to do. He wanted to turn into the Kraken, but he flipped over in midair and gave me a confused look as he hit the water. I figured that since the Kraken is one of kind, and Fidero made it so that Forrest couldn't turn into it.

"That's definitely not good," I said, then realized that I was by myself. I jumped in at last, having a plan. When I hit the water it hurt, not like I had expected it to. But I looked around even though I hated opening my eyes under water unless it was absolutely necessary. There was a fight going on, between a huge shark and the Kraken. Blood was everywhere, and I noticed two girls chained to the ocean floor trying to swim up. I switched powers with Wyatt, broke the chains, and then went over to the fight. The Kraken noticed me and began swimming straight for its target. I put both my hands out, feeling stupider than a person standing in the middle of the road trying to stop a truck. The Kraken smashed into me, and the whole ocean seemed to glow white. I flew back, and closed my eyes for maybe the last time.

I woke up with a smile on my face, glad that I could see the ceiling of the nurse's office. Selene and Aura were around me, smiling as well.

"How did you?" I wondered, and looked at the bed next to me. There was a boy, bleeding in every spot I could see, and asleep.

"We didn't do it at all, you did," Aura told me, and I smiled, but was confused.

"You did it, you calmed the Kraken with your balance power," Selene explained, causing me to smile so much that it hurt.

"Well I don't want to know who Glacthia's apprentice is anymore anyway," I told them, but they laughed.

"But that would be a really big waste," Selene pulled a vile out of her pocket. When I saw that it was filled with a blue liquid, I laughed quietly but it still hurt my lungs. The nurse told me that I only sprained my arm and my ankle, but she healed it and I was free to go.

"Forrest, are you sure you want us to find out without you?" I asked the boy, not recognizing him.

"Go, I don't want to know anything about it," he spoke in a broken voice, and the three of us left. We walked up the stairs cheerfully while I was thinking about the nurse. I wonder if people who have the power to heal other people are stuck with being a nurse or a doctor even if they don't want to be.

We reached Ember's room quickly, it was pretty low down and we felt like using the teleporters. As soon as we walked in we saw her lying in her bed, awake and looking at newspaper cutouts and other things. She saw us and threw them under her bed and glared at us for interrupting her.

"Ember . . . what's that?" Selene shouted and Ember turned around. Aura pulled the cork off and threw the potion at her, guiding it with air and letting it slip into her mouth like it was going through a straw. She sat up straight and her pupils became very small. I hated everyone's nasally voice that they used when they were under the potion's spell, but braced myself to be ready for it.

"Who is Glacthia's apprentice?" I asked her in a serious voice.

"Wyatt," she answered without hesitation and Aura dropped the vile, causing it to break on the floor.

CHAPTER TWENTY ONE:
GLACTHIA'S OBSTACLE

SELENE

We ran out of the room, I had picked up the remains of the potion with my mind. When we stopped we were in the room next to Wyatt's room, the study room.

"How could he do that, that jerk-headed loser face . . ." Kamille didn't know what else to add to it, her face was covered in tears. I held up the liquid floating in front of us, we only had to use a couple drops of it on Ember because it was one question. The rest could've supplied about five or six questions.

"Let's just go ask him," Aura walked into his room and I followed, slipping the liquid around like it was jelly on a plate.

"Wyatt!" Aura pointed over to the window and Wyatt turned around. Then she guided the potion into his mouth while I anticipated his answers to our questions. The three of us stared at him as if he were Glacthia himself, but tried not to speak. But the blue liquid suddenly stopped inches in front of his face.

"That was pretty sad, did you go all the way to Azmarith for that?" he stared at us, and I gasped.

"No . . . we got it for Ember so we could figure out what you are," Aura glared at him, and he stared at the floor in shame.

"Guys, you're too young to understand," he whispered, thinking that the whole family was standing on the other side of the door.

"But why, what purpose could you possibly have to work for him?" I cried, tears filling up in my eyes.

256

"I . . . it's just better than death," he looked away, and he seemed as if he was about to teleport. I quickly pulled to the caliga off the floor with my mind and threw it at his mouth. He got the dazed look Ember got, and I stared at my sisters.

"Where is Glacthia keeping the Metronome?" I asked quickly, thinking I only had one question.

"On Earth," he disappeared and left our mouths gaping wide open.

Forrest's cuts didn't heal as quickly as we planned, it turns out that bites from a Kraken are impervious to healers. They had to heal on their own, which took weeks. It wasn't until one week before the final blackout that we were okay to go, and even then the marks were clear. We never told anyone how he got them, just as the way he got back was still a secret to everyone but Ember. It was the five of us that knew everything, and we swore to tell no one until they found out on their own.

Wyatt came and went as he pleased, acting as if he never worked for Glacthia. We yelled at him to leave sometimes, and he would when he was in the right mood. But he tried to tell us that he was doing the right thing, and we would only get madder. We were in the tree house when Forrest finally got back from the nurse's. Everyone was working on their end of the year papers.

"What are we gonna do, none of us . . . but Ember . . . knows who the apprentice is and none of us at all know where Glacthia's keeping the Metronome. The Peractio Blackout is next week. It's over . . . we lost," Lianna sat in the comfortable chair and moaned.

"Ember, maybe if we knew who the apprentice was, we could figure out how to make a blue caliga and ask them where Glacthia kept the Metronome," Sam suggested and suddenly people started agreeing with him. I rolled my eyes and glared at Wyatt, he was sitting in the corner on a beanbag chair, just watching the conversation with fixed eyes. But then I looked at Ember, Forrest, and my triplets. They nodded, and I turned back to the group.

"Guys, we're going to be completely honest with you, since families aren't supposed to keep secrets from each other!" I yelled in Wyatt's direction and everyone made confused face. Wyatt sank into the beanbag chair and turned around.

"They found out who the apprentice is, and we used the blue caliga to figure out where the Metronome is. It's on Earth, but we have to go fast because it's a week's trip," Ember butt in, and the group gasped.

"They found out, but not us, why can't we know?" Ion shouted, and I sighed.

"You're just . . . not ready, none of us were," Aura stared at the floor in disappointment.

Minutes later we went to Mr. Williams' room to find the gadgets we would need for the mission. We took plenty of teleporters, in case Wyatt decided to turn on us. Mr. Williams helped us as well when we couldn't figure out what each gadget did. There weren't any new ones, but some we had never used before. When we were finally done he stared at us and slowly opened a drawer.

"This one was made for the police a couple months ago. It can track the Metronome, but only if you're on the same planet as it. And since you know which planet it's on you can take it there and it will show you which way to go." The drawer had red, foam padding on the bottom with something that looked like a game spinner resting on it. I put it on the palm of my hand and studied it. The bottom was a rubber circle, and there was a gold arrow on top of it. The arrow blinked red; probably meaning that it was not on this planet.

"Thanks Mr. Williams, that'll help," I put it in the bag and we started to leave.

"Good luck, Barkers," Mr. Williams smiled to us as we walked out. Most of us headed for the stairs, but I noticed Wyatt step a few feet away from everyone and get on his watch.

"They're coming," Wyatt spoke into the watch and I made a confused face. Wyatt can mind speak, so why would he need the watch? But then I tried to lift off the ground and I couldn't, this meant that Miss Monohan was right. She told us that the week before the Peractio Blackout there are blackouts more often than we can actually use our powers. The time there aren't blackouts the week before the Peractio Blackout is usually about two minutes a day.

As soon as we got into the taxi we started annoying the driver so that he would leave the car to us.

"What were you thinking about during breakfast this morning?" I asked him the question that made him go completely crazy.

"Oh my gosh, just drive there yourself!" he yelled and got out of the taxi.

"That's awesome, now we have the whole taxi to ourselves," Gabby instantly sat in front of the wheel and turned on the car. We were in space in a few minutes, and everyone sat in the back area, wondering what we could do for a week in a car this small.

"I still don't know why we can't just teleport to Earth, it would take seconds," Cobalt questioned us and we rolled our eyes.

"Two reasons. First, we're in like constant blackouts for the next seven days. We might never find a time to teleport there. Second, if we found a time to use our powers, Wyatt would only teleport us to Wisconsin. Not only would we have no money for planes, but also we wouldn't have our powers. Then if the Metronome was on the South Pole it could be too late before we got there," Ember explained to him.

One day on the trip, all of the kids went to the driver's room with the door shut. The only people that didn't bother to go were Wyatt, Forrest, Ember, Kamille, Aura, and I. We glared at Wyatt, but then made confused faces.

"How do you live with yourself?" I had to know, but he didn't want to answer.

"You wouldn't understand," he looked away, but we only got more aggravated.

"We're your family; how could you say that? If we wouldn't understand, how are we sure that you even understand?" Forrest explained to him.

"I just . . . can't tell you," he left it at that and we didn't want to continue the conversation any further.

The last day came eventually, and all of us anticipated us entering the atmosphere so we could figure out where the Metronome was. We were starting to place bets as Earth came into view. I guessed Australia or something, just because I thought Glacthia would pick some place remote.

We were slowly coming toward Earth, but suddenly the scanner picked up a nearby ship. All of us were in the driver's room, and we looked out the window to see a stone hurtling toward us.

"Could that crack this window?" Daven asked anyone who would give him the answer he wanted.

"No, this glass is stronger than the glass they use in the tanks at the aquarium," Lianna explained to him and he sighed.

"Yeah, but that rock's beeping," Aura pointed to the little red light flashing on it, and all of us had no time to react. The rocket exploded, but somehow a forcefield formed around all of us when the fire tried to consume us. The fire dissolved instantly because there was no oxygen in space.

"You little cheater, you still have your powers, I hope you—"

"This wasn't me," Wyatt was staring at me, as well as everyone who didn't know about him and Glacthia.

"Then who was it?" I asked, and then noticed the ship behind us. It wasn't a small ship, but it resembled a needle with a ring around the tip. Although I wasn't there, it sounded like the thing Ion described that left the permanent mark on him that shows that Cobalt's brothers owned him. Then, typically, the forcefield started to be pulled in by the ship, and we went into a room that suddenly filled with air. The forcefield dropped.

"Is this . . ." Craig started, and Cobalt nodded.

"They were talking about it when I was with them. They were saying they would get this amazing ship if they made a deal with Glacthia," he told us, and we looked at the room that we were probably locked in. Then the doors slid open, revealing to us four boys that smiled and showed us their crooked teeth.

"We've caught 'em boys. What were Glacthia's orders again?" Mac asked, rubbing his hands together in thought. We cowered before them as they plotted to probably kill us.

"Keep them here until tonight at 7:47 and then drop them off on some desolate planet with no airport," Reggie smiled and I glared at them.

"Put them in those cages," Mac pointed to some cells that were built into the walls. Reggie, Johnny, and Ashton forced us into the cells. They sat on some stools and stared at us, expecting us to break out or something. Finally they got bored and left Johnny to watch us alone. Hours passed, and then in the end he dozed off on the floor. As soon as he was out we started discussing.

"So if we found a way to break out we could probably take them," Cobalt told us and we nodded, fifteen on four wasn't very fair, but we didn't need to be fair right now.

"But Reggie has powers and we don't," Ion reminded us and we realized that he was right; Reggie could probably take us when we were powerless.

"Then how are we gonna get out of here if we don't get out and stop Glacthia? No one will have powers again," Lianna reminded us. Wyatt was starting to sweat, and I took advantage of the moment.

"What do you think the world will be like when no one has powers? I mean, we won't even have a reason to come to Medlocks anymore. All those good times we had . . . we might as well just give ourselves up to Glacthia now. A universe without super powered people is like—"

"Oh my gosh, you guys are driving me insane," Wyatt finally yelled and stood up. "I don't know how, but I've had my powers this whole time. I'll get you out of here." I was thankful that Wyatt gave in since I was running out of things to say.

"How do you still have powers?" Gabby was asking as he was levitating the lock out of the door. We opened the door slowly, but Ember stopped him.

"No, I can't do this anymore. We can't trust him, he's working for Glacthia," Ember pointed to him and the whole cell gasped.

"Ember, don't say that, how do you know?" Ion questioned her and I stood up.

"She's right, I don't like where this is going. Wyatt could be taking us straight into Glacthia's clutches for all we know. I used the blue caliga on him, he's definitely Glacthia's apprentice," I explained, and everyone gasped again.

"That's not possible, why would Wyatt do that?" Lianna had to know; everyone was still hooked on him being innocent.

"Who knows? He won't tell us," Forrest told them as Wyatt was still standing with his hand clutching the barred door.

"I'm going to take you to Glacthia and prove that I'm good," Wyatt finally stated and opened the door. He lifted Johnny off the ground while he was sleeping and hung him on a bolt coming out of the ceiling by the belt loop in his pants. The doors into the other room opened when Wyatt threw his arm in the air and Reggie and Ashton were standing there.

"Didn't Johnny tell you?" Ashton stepped back into a fighting stance. "We got our powers," he threw a blinking metal ball at Wyatt and us and he leaned back. It flew inches over his face and hit the ground under Johnny. An explosion took up the room, sending us flying out the door and Johnny soaring through the room. He woke up in midair and turned into a bouncy ball just before he hit the wall. Then he started to ricochet off all the walls and finally turned back into himself right in front of us.

"You're not going anywhere," he told us, blocking us from going through the threshold. We got ready to battle him, but three on fifteen was starting to sound a lot fairer.

"I can take 'em," Wyatt threw Johnny and Reggie in separate directions. They both hit the walls and got knocked out. But Johnny shot rubber spikes at us, which were very dense even when they weren't sharp. All of them went for Wyatt, who guided them around his back and shot them straight for Ashton. He reacted, shooting bombs at each of them so they would explode. But the last one hit him square in the forehead. He fell back, also unconscious.

"That was scary," Sam told him. We were all worried for Wyatt, his powers were progressing far more than anyone could've expected.

"Now, Mac," Wyatt opened the door into the driver's room. Mac stood up, surprised that we got out without our powers. Wyatt smiled at him, and then threw him out of the driver's seat. But unlike Reggie or Johnny, he didn't fall unconscious. He turned into a black liquid on the wall, and then slid down the wall until he was back on the floor. Then the liquid started standing up on its own, shaping Mac's figure. It was very viscous for a liquid, like syrup or molasses. Then finally when it enveloped Wyatt and started to drown him, I knew what it was.

"Mac got tar as a power!" I shouted, and we watched as the tar slowly devoured our traitor brother.

"We should help him," Gabby stared as the boy covered in tar gasped for air.

"We don't have our powers, and he can handle himself," Ember watched as a forcefield suddenly expanded and tar flew everywhere. Some got on us, but then it flopped off like a fresh fish. Wyatt put forcefields around each piece and then grabbed all of our hands. All of us appeared on Earth, and I recognized the place immediately.

"Glacthia used our old secret base as his lair?" Ion shouted as we stood at the backdoor to the house that most of my family grew up in.

"He said we'd never check here," Wyatt walked inside, and gasped. Dr. Dryden sat against a wall, his hand pierced by a white cone. His skin was gray with his veins green and bulging out of his body. His hair had turned white and he looked frail and sickly.

"Dr. Dryden!" Rhochelle ran over to him and inspected the horn. "It's unicorn poison."

"I'll get it out," Wyatt told us and walked over to him. With a flow of Wyatt's hands a gross looking liquid slipped out of the wound in Dr. Dryden, and landed on the wall behind Wyatt. Dr. Dryden suddenly jumped in the air and backed away.

"No, you're working for him; stay away from me!" he yelled, tears streaming down his eyes. Wyatt ignored him and walked up the wall that was the empty space under Rhochelle's room. Wyatt knocked on the wall in a rhythmic pattern and the wall slid away.

"Stay away from him. You don't know what he's capable of," Dr. Dryden watched Wyatt with eyes that made him look drunk. He was slumped against the wall clutching his wound, he had an unshaved beard and long, gray hair. All of us slowly walked into the room and Wyatt placed his hand on a scanner that wasn't there before. The handprint was accepted and the dirt wall formed into a set of stairs, the ones Rhochelle had built two summers ago.

Wyatt led us down the stairs, and then there was a door with a ton of locks on it. Wyatt put in the combination to all of them and the door that looked more like a vault suddenly opened. All of us gasped when we stepped inside and saw Death Row.

CHAPTER TWENTY TWO: THE APPRENTICE'S DECISION

WYATT

The obstacles seemed familiar, but they were not the ones we created that summer we got our powers. We were on the conveyor belt, but it still had our perils that we made for every secret base. As it started to move, all of us watched the wall of vines come closer. As easy as it seemed to climb over a wall of vines, the vines had mouths at the end that were snapping in every direction.

"How does he expect us to survive this?" I wondered as we were feet away from the snapping vines.

"You tell us," Forrest stared at me. Everyone was mad at me, and I couldn't stand it. A vine finally pounced at me, and I grabbed its neck with my hand. The vine started flipping out of control, lifting me off the ground. I let go when it was on top of the wall and flew over to the other side.

"Grab its neck and try to let go when it flips you over," I told them. One by one they started flying over the wall, which I noticed wasn't very safe. The width of the vine wall was the same as the conveyor belt, so if they didn't let go perfectly at the right time they could fall into the endless darkness on either side of the belt. We heard Selene scream as she let go of the vine, and all of us ran to where she was landing. I dove off the conveyor belt to catch her and felt someone grab my feet. Looking behind me I saw Neva, Forrest, and Ember in a human chain stopping me from falling. When they pulled the two of us up I smiled, thinking that they really cared.

"Thanks for saving me," I told them, thinking that we could just put everything else in the past and move on.

"We saved Kamille, you have your powers anyway," Neva told me off, and I sighed, knowing that I could never tell them why I was working for Glacthia.

"If Glacthia catches me using my powers he'll kill me for trying to save you guys," I explained, but they didn't seem to care.

"What's next?" Craig looked at the small room sitting on top of the conveyor belt. For some reason when the path moved all of the obstacles stayed in place.

"It's either Selene's antigravity room or my airless room," Aura walked toward it. She stepped inside and then instantly stepped back out. "It's mine; do we still know the code?" All of us looked at each other.

"Wasn't it your birthday backwards?" Rhochelle remembered. There were only eight perils, because that's how many there were when we first built this place.

"I'll go in," I stared at the floor, since if they had to choose one person to not make it I would be the one. But when none of them were looking, I made an invisible forcefield around my head. When I was inside I started to think of the code. I put in "413" but it didn't work. I started to struggle; my air was beginning to feel used. Then I remembered that Glacthia changed all of the codes to involve him. When I tried "912" it didn't work either, so I tried it backwards. Just before I entered it the door flew open, revealing Forrest and Neva. They were holding their breaths unlike me, so I had to put it in fast. The door flew open and we stepped out thankfully, along with everyone else.

"You actually came in to see if I was okay?" I asked them, smiling. They instantly frowned at me, and I rolled my eyes.

"Well if you died we'd have to think of the password with a dead body on the floor and no air," Neva told me, but then looked at the floor. "If you tell us why you did it, we'll forgive you." I stared at them in amazement; they had offered to forgive me.

"I'm sorry . . . I don't have a choice in that," I stared at them as the next room started to come up. We knew it had to be Selene's, because she and Aura were the only ones that had rooms for their perils.

"Who's gonna do this one, if you're in there for like five seconds the ceiling of spikes will drop," Selene told us and we got closer to it. I could tell that she was talking to me, so I stepped inside and quickly put an invisible forcefield under the spikes so they couldn't fall.

I thought about everything I ever knew about Glacthia. This code was a five letter word, which brought me to the right guess instantly. It took me a while to type it in since I had to scroll through the whole alphabet on the lock instead of 0 to 9. When I typed it in the door clicked open, I knew it had been over five seconds. Staring at the word "Malum," I held the door open and dropped the forcefield. This time Ember threw open the door to see if I was okay. I smiled as the ceiling fell between us. Everyone stepped through the door staring at me.

"That was a little more than five seconds," Ember told me, she had clearly been worried. I smiled at her and she nudged me with her elbow.

"Selene said '*like* five seconds,'" I told her and she rolled her eyes. We turned to Neva's obstacle, the spiked ice wall. This one was just a block of ice, with no sides that could keep you from falling off the path into oblivion. Every second or two spikes would shoot out of the wall and stay there before slowly retreating. They came in handy when climbing the wall, but when they disappeared and you were halfway up they were a pain.

"How are we supposed to do this?" Cobalt stared nervously at the wall that was coming closer by the second.

"If we could make it to the top while the spikes are out and retreating, there's that one spot on the top where no spikes shoot out," Lianna waited for her hypothesis to be true, but even she jumped when the icicles shot out of the wall. I went first; as soon as the spikes were out, I started climbing to the top. They retreated pretty slowly; I made it easily. I had my hands on the top of the wall that was probably only ten feet high when they spikes were gone. I pulled myself up and stood on the spot, hoping Lianna was right. When the spikes shot out, all of them missed me, so I started climbing down. Slowly everyone started to climb over, Aura waited to be last because she was nervous. She was trying to climb onto the top when the spikes were gone.

"They're about to shoot out!" Neva shouted and I panicked. I lifted her leg with my mind and swung it onto the top. She stood up just when the spikes shot out, one of them barely ripping her jeans.

"These are my favorite jeans," she growled and started climbing down. She was halfway down when the spikes were gone so she fell to the belt and stepped back.

We instantly turned to the next obstacle, we were halfway done now. Ember's jet streams of fire were next. There were several flamethrowers placed in a circle so that it seemed to form a wall of fire. They only stopped every five seconds for about half a second. I stepped forward to go first, but Ember stopped me.

"I got this one," she actually smiled; she knew I had been using my powers to help us get through. She walked forward, timing it exactly so that when the fire turned off she dove through. She made it, but that wasn't who I was worried about. After all the older kids had gone we told the younger kids to start going. Ion made it, as well as Cobalt, Selene, and Kamille. Aura barely made it even though her shoe looked a little melted when she was on the other side. Finally it was Craig's turn; it probably wasn't a smart idea to make him go last because he was by himself on the other side.

"I'm going now," he said nervously, and we saw him running just as the fire turned off. He ran too late, he was supposed to be in the air by the time it turned off. He dove through and the fire turned on. He came out screaming and his pants were on fire. We put them out, but he had a burn on his leg.

"Craig! Are you alright?" Gabby asked her little brother.

"I'm fine, let's just get to the end of this thing," Craig said calmly, but his stance was greatly weakened by the burn on his ankle. We slowly walked to the next one, there were only three more. Rhochelle's avalanche was something that I didn't have any ideas for. I could've made a forcefield over the rocks so they wouldn't fall, but then Glacthia would know that I'd been using my powers to help them.

"We can't cross that, we'll surely get crushed by the rocks," Gabby quit and walked back toward the fire wall, but she was going really slowly since she was walking in the opposite direction the conveyor belt was moving.

"Look, every couple seconds the avalanche is only made up of tiny rocks, they don't hurt that much, they're practically sand," Rhochelle pointed to the fact that for about half a second it would randomly shoot out dirt rocks. Rhochelle ran through when this happened, covering her head with her hands, and she made it. Then larger rocks started falling when she was on the other side.

"Fine," Gabby ran through when the rocks were small again. All of us made it, but when it was Neva's turn I noticed a rather large rock fall. It was going to land on his head, so I quickly guided it in the air so that it wouldn't land on him. But since the archway that was shooting rocks out was only about the height of the fire archway, ice wall, and vine wall, the rock hit Neva on the arm. But he fell down, just making it out. We ran over to him. He clutched his arm to hold it up and let his hand hang limp. His wrist was bleeding excessively and it looked broken.

"It's gonna hurt a lot, but you can move on," I was forced to tell him, if I teleported him anywhere Glacthia would realize it and punish me. We walked onto the second to last obstacle, Ion's electrocuting wall.

"We're never going to get past that; its shock must be stronger than lightning," Cobalt explained, knowing a lot about Ion's inventions.

"But remember when I made it, how it only shocks . . ." Ion smiled to us, and everyone who grew up with Dr. Dryden smiled as well.

"Clothes," I laughed and took off my shirt. I held onto my pants, and stared at everyone, hoping they would realize. "Would you mind closing your eyes? But make sure you walk toward the avalanche, if you stay still the conveyor belt will take you into the electric wall." I took off the rest of my clothes and threw them over. Thankfully all of them landed on the conveyor belt. The wall basically looked like a door with metal all around it. I nervously turned the doorknob and walked through. Nothing happened, so I told my family to open their eyes because they couldn't see me getting dressed on the other side of the door. One by one they all went through, I had to walk toward the door or else I would be pulled to the last obstacle by the conveyor belt. But the last person, Selene, threw her clothes clumsily over the door. Her shirt went in the wrong direction and flew off the belt. I would've caught it with my mind, but Glacthia would notice.

When she came over I took off my shirt and handed it to her. It went down to her knees, but she thanked me for it. Everyone turned around slowly to face the final obstacle, and I bit my lip. A small floating forcefield sat just above the path. It was filled with water, and

I remember filling it myself two summers ago so that the water was so dense that stepping into it could kill a person.

"How are we going to do this?" I asked my family and they stared at me.

"Aren't you . . . Glacthia's . . . Apprentice, don't you still have your powers?" Neva asked me, finally realizing how resourceful it was for me to be his apprentice.

"No, I only have my second power; he said if I help him get the Peractio Blackout to happen then he'll give me all the powers I want," I explained to them, and they began to think that I became his apprentice for this reason.

"Is that why you did it? To get all the powers you want?" Ion asked me angrily.

"No . . . I mean . . . I don't know," I told them, hating everything about Glacthia.

"Here, we don't need your help, we got this on our own," Forrest walked over the forcefield. He didn't understand the properties of water.

"Don't do it!" I yelled as Forrest put his hand through the forcefield. He immediately pulled it out, screaming in pain. Now there were three injured people in our group, Neva's wrist was broken, Craig's leg was burnt, and now Forrest's arm is broken. His arm looked somewhat smaller; like the water condensed it then crushed the bone.

"We're never going to get through there," Forrest glared at me, like it was my fault for getting everyone into it. Thinking about it, I realized that he was right, it was all my fault. I wiped the tears from my eyes and started walking backwards because I wasn't ready to face this. With my teeth clenched I slipped my hand into the water, putting an invisible forcefield around it. I looked at the lock, it was different then the other ones. The top said "Following in my footprints" and I looked at the letters of the word. It was five letters, and I got even madder. The forcefield was getting hard to control. I could feel the water trying to crush it into nothing. I spun the letter wheels until the lock read my name. It clicked open and then the forcefield that took up the entire path suddenly disappeared.

We stood still as the path moved us toward the door; this was the moment we had been waiting for. It was unlocked, so we stepped inside to reveal total darkness. All we could see was a lamppost, shining down on an object that we knew well and recognized. We watched the Metronome sit under the light, and a voice echoed the room.

"Peractio Blackout . . . it means final darkness. Final darkness . . . final blackout . . . last blackout . . . the end of all Altrian's powers as we know it." A glove was now visible under the lamppost, and it pulled a string that turned the light off. Now we were in absolute darkness; if there were any light at all, our eyes would've picked it out by now.

Then finally the entire room lit up, there were huge spotlights on the ceiling, one shining on each of us as we stood in a sideways line, much like the way we stood on the cliff last year on Medlocks' moon, Caelum. The room was a completely empty dirt room with only a few objects in it. On one side of the room all fifteen of us stood, and on the other was the Metronome with the lamp over it. On our left sat a small stage, with a gold throne sitting in the middle, with Glacthia on it. Then on the right wall there was a small circular stage, only big enough for one person.

"Five minutes," Glacthia pointed to a timer that I had just noticed on a table next to the Metronome. It looked like it had spaces for years, months, weeks, days, hours, minutes, and seconds. I also noticed Glacthia holding a remote, probably the one he explained to me, it could take any power from the Metronome and put it into a person. Glacthia pressed a couple buttons and a green, swirling substance came out of the Metronome. It flew into his chest and he felt a surge of power.

"Wyatt stand over there," he pointed to the stage that I was forced to walk over to. It suddenly rose out of the ground until I was near the ceiling of the tall room.

"We'll start with you, Forrest," Glacthia made three animals appear around Forrest, a cheetah, a raptor, and a scelum. He started wrestling all three, even without his powers he knows where the animals' weak spots are. But there were too many for him, the scelum cut him in the chest and then all three were attacking him. Then the animals disappeared and a bloody Forrest was left on the ground.

Now Glacthia started taking everyone's powers from the Metronome and using them against my family. Lianna was unconscious from too much knowledge, and Gabby was having molten hot suns being shot at her. Sam was getting hailed on, and Craig's ears started bleeding from all of the voices he was hearing.

I also was forced to watch my own family being attacked by their powers. Neva was frozen on the ground, Rhochelle was buried in rocks, Daven was being attacked by his clones, and Forrest had almost bled to death already. Aura couldn't breathe, Selene was being pushed into the ground by gravity, and Kamille looked the worse. She couldn't get up because she had no balance, and her eyes couldn't stay in the way they were supposed to be, they rolled around her head but usually stayed under her eyelids. Ion was being electrocuted and Cobalt was having spikes going through his arms and legs. I watched in horror as I saw my family start to die in front of me. The puddle of blood under Forrest was getting bigger, and Cobalt was being hung onto the walls by spikes and needles.

"You can make it end, Wyatt, choose them and call the deal off," Glacthia smiled hideously at me, even though I couldn't see his face. Tears were falling down my face like a waterfall, but I had to stay with him.

"You can't kill them," I told him with some pride, but he only laughed.

"That's true, but I can torture them until they kill themselves," he explained to me, and he was right. Ember was the only one that was all right and she was begging me. "Choose us, Wyatt, we're all going to die!" she yelled, and Glacthia set her legs on fire. She fell to the ground, screaming in pain and crawling toward me. "Choose us!"

"Oh, and I forgot about our guests of honor," he pressed a button on the remote and the left wall disappeared. It revealed an extra room, which four hooded figures stood, covered in chains. A huge metal block appeared above the Ancestors, probably weighing over a hundred tons.

"Ten, nine, eight," Glacthia counted down the time until the Peractio Blackout, watching the Metronome exploding with color. I watched in horror as the seconds to decide were slim. "At one I will drop the block and let your family go. Five, four—"

"Three, two, one!" I gathered up all the energy and rage I felt. I swung the metal block like a bat, almost dropping it because it was so heavy. All of the tortures that my family was feeling disappeared, the Peractio Blackout had started. I only had a few seconds to do this. The metal block swung into Glacthia's throne. Although he teleported as soon as it hit him, the throne flew into the table holding the

Metronome. It only hit the legs of the table, but that was what I was expecting to happen. The table tipped sideways as the throne flew into the wall and smashed into a million pieces. The Metronome slid off the table and smashed onto the stage. All of the powers swirled and faded into nothing. Gathering all my siblings together, I nodded my head to the Ancestors, and teleported everyone to the nurse's office.

The last few days of the school year passed, and my family healed quickly. They all refused to forgive me for siding with Glacthia, and I basically got the silent treatment from all of them. Everyone got their powers back, and Miss Monohan told us that the Ancestors permanently destroyed the Metronome, which would've been even greater if they did that last year. Yet I didn't complain, I knew that they weren't expecting for Glacthia to try the same type of plan twice.

Everyone did well on their exams. They were rather easy considering it was Miss Monohan's first time organizing the end of the year exams. Now we were sitting at our tables in the cafeteria when Miss Monohan walked up to her podium and began her usual end of the year speech.

"This year, unlike the last, has included all of our students in various activities. We would like to give a special thanks to the Barkers for their courageous efforts in saving the school once again." Everyone applauded for us, except the oldest three Andersons. "Now, I would like to make a few announcements about next year. You will be receiving your sign up schedules for next year this summer. You will be allowed to drop some of your classes and take more of others." The applause was even louder this time, I could think of fifteen classes that I would drop in a heartbeat. "Lastly, we will be having a team of ten students going to Voliturus for the Venatus tournament. Tryouts will be in early September and Coach Tustin will be in charge of those until a captain is selected. All of you have a great . . . and safe . . . summer."

The plane arrived to take us home, and we all decided that it was tradition to take it. Thankfully it was the same plane we took home last year, so we had the circle of the chairs that came in handy when having a conversation.

"So Wyatt, are you ever going to tell us why you did it?" Neva joked with me, no one seemed to care that I had teamed up against them with the most evil thing to ever happen in the universe.

"Nope," I told them in a joking matter, but they made sad faces. "I can't tell you," I explained, and they rolled their eyes like I didn't have a reason. A few more hours into the day we started talking to the girls from the Slomowitz family. The triplets, Becca, Whitney, and Melanie, were crowded around our circle as we described the story to them.

"And then I took the metal block and swung it into Glacthia. His throne broke the table and the Metronome crashed to the floor," I smiled, feeling proud for being the hero.

"Wow, Wyatt, you're so brave," Melanie congratulated me with a hug, and I blushed. I felt even worse now, I didn't deserve this.

"Really, I remember the story a little differently," Ember looked at me, causing me to stare at the ground with a sad face.

"Hey, let's play what's your favorite," I smiled, and started off with a question. "What was your favorite part of this year?" I asked them, and we started off going clockwise, with Neva.

"When it ended," he stared at me; I knew they were never going to let this go.

"When Kamille found me," Forrest smiled to Kamille, he forgave easier than most.

"When we defeated Glacthia," Ember emphasized her answer while looking at me. Melanie stared at me with a confused face. The rounds when on, and everyone started giving more and more rude answers.

"Come on guys, we're staying in a penthouse this summer, how cool is that?" I tried to cheer them up. We were hooked on the idea of switching guardians this summer; we were going to stay with the Venturas next summer. They were on our plane but they had their own conversation because their circle wasn't near ours.

"But we just want to know why!" Forrest finally blurt out, keeping his opinions to himself the whole night.

"Why what?" Melanie asked, more interested than I had expected.

"Why Wyatt didn't trust us enough to tell us?" Ember set her straight, she never liked her ever since she got Forrest and Neva those dates on the first week of school.

"Okay, I'm sorry, I really . . . really . . . am. I was pretending to be something I wasn't and I'll never go back there, I absolutely promise . . . that I'll never do it again, just please forgive me," I begged them. It was quiet for so long that I thought they hadn't heard me, and when I was about to say it again Forrest began to finally speak.

"It wasn't that you did it in the first place, Wyatt. We don't care if you side with Glacthia if you think that it's the right thing to do. But when a person pretends to be something they're not for too long, they might lose who they used to be in the process," Forrest said deeply, and I was speechless.

When everyone had fallen asleep I was talking to Melanie on a small bench in the back of the plane about what they had been talking about.

"Did you really side with Glacthia?" she asked, and I nodded, but then explained why I answered the way I did. I stared at the floor and told the truth for the first time in a long time.

"I sacrificed my freedom . . . to save my family."